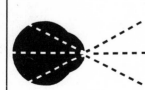

This Large Print Book carries the
Seal of Approval of N.A.V.H.

TOO GOOD TO BE TRUE

Too Good to Be True

Trish Perry

THORNDIKE PRESS

An imprint of Thomson Gale, a part of The Thomson Corporation

Detroit • New York • San Francisco • New Haven, Conn. • Waterville, Maine • London

LIBRARY OF CONGRESS CATALOGING-IN-PUBLICATION DATA

Perry, Trish, 1954–
  Too good to be true / By Trish Perry.
    p. cm. — (Thorndike Press large print Christian fiction)
  ISBN-13: 978-0-7862-9909-6 (hardcover : alk. paper)
  ISBN-10: 0-7862-9909-6 (hardcover : alk. paper)
    1. Divorced women — Fiction. 2. Male nurses — Fiction. 3. Large type books. I. Title.
  PS3616.E7947T66 2007b
  813'.6—dc22   2007027434

Published in 2007 by arrangement with Harvest House Publishers.

Printed in the United States of America on permanent paper
10 9 8 7 6 5 4 3 2 1

to my husband

Hugh Perry,
from God's answer to
your prayer for patience.

ACKNOWLEDGMENTS

Writing may seem a solitary profession, but many people contribute to a finished novel. I'd like to thank some of the people who helped me.

Tamela Hancock Murray. Always in my corner, always accessible, and *apparently* always working — I don't know how she does it!

Kim Moore, for her keen eye, savvy know-how, and diplomacy in making things right.

The terrific people at Harvest House. What a blessed house to work with.

The generous authors who spent precious time to read and endorse this book.

Betsy Dill, Mike Calkin, Gwen Hancock, and **Vie Herlocker** — the most kind, constructive, and funny critique partners any writer could have.

My friends at Cornerstone Chapel in Leesburg, Virginia, and **my fellow writers at Capital Christian Writers,** for keeping me grounded in the Lord during this project. And **my friends** and **avid supporters at American Christian Fiction Writers.**

The remarkable prayer patrol: Linda Wallace, Betty Shifflett, Cindy Williams, and **Gerry Stowers.** I still owe you ladies a hot fudge sundae!

The fine women of the Open Book Club, with whom I've shared many books and much laughter. And dessert. Ah, heaven.

Michelle Ochoa, for walking me through an emergency birthing process. I will never travel again without a packet of clean dental floss in my purse.

Bob and Lyn Krivanek, for their expert advice about miniature horses.

Betsy Wymer, for providing cardiology-nurse information when I needed it.

Wendy Driscoll, for *so* much: love, prayers, laughs, *and* my book title! You're the best.

My parents, Chuck and **Lilian Hawley,** my sibs, **John, Donna,** and **Chris Hawley,** and my excellent extended family — **the Johnstons, the Rabideaus (especially Bryce),** and **the Perrys.** Thanks for your support and encouragement over the years.

My husband, Hugh, and my superhero kids: **Tucker the Genius, Stevie the Radiant, Kevin the Ultra-Cool,** and grandson, **Bronx the Hilarious.**

My awesome Lord Jesus, from whom all good things come. Praise Him!

ONE

Seconds before Ren passed out, she considered what her mother would say: "In a *Wal-Mart?* You couldn't collapse at a Nordstrom's, at least?"

Ren struggled back to consciousness. The air buzzed like a room full of katydids. The smell of popcorn, heavy in the air, filled her head. She felt wrenching pain as strong hands lifted her. "That hurts," she mumbled, her tongue thick.

"Good," a clipped female voice said. "That means you're coming to. Set her down here, Bruce."

Ren was lowered, not quite to the ground, but not exactly to a chair, either. She opened her eyes and brushed her dark hair out of her face. All the dots before her quickly joined together. She appeared to have become part of a fall fashion display and was resting on a platform against two strapping young mannequins in hiking gear.

11

People had gathered to look at her — clerks, shoppers, a gawking child. The child brought Ren's memory back. She thought of little Casey and started crying.

A heavy hand rested on her shoulder. She looked at the hand — large and rough skinned. She turned around to see whom it belonged to. She'd often seen him here and walking around town, this man-mountain. One of the store's "challenged" employees. Such a dear, concerned look he gave her.

"Okay, Bruce," the curt woman's voice said. Ren looked at her. Another familiar face. Like magma that had hardened mid-melt. "Go on back to work now," she told Bruce.

Ren tried to thank him as he left, but her voice cracked like a twelve-year-old boy's. Bruce smiled and nodded — not too challenged to give or appreciate kindness. And, of course, that made her cry too. She thought of her husband, Greg — her ex-husband, actually — and remembered how little kindness had passed between them during the past year. Or rather, how little kindness he had shown. Ren hadn't behaved so badly, really, considering what he had done.

She considered the Bible verse her best friend, Kara, quoted the morning Greg walked out: "If the unbeliever leaves, let him do so. A believing man or woman is not bound in such circumstances." True. Ren wasn't bound. She wasn't trapped. She wasn't much of anything. Not cherished, certainly. Not loved.

She looked around for her shopping bag and purse. She desperately needed a tissue. As if her actions were that obvious, someone handed her a well-pressed handkerchief over her shoulder. He spoke behind her, his voice like dark rich coffee. "Will this help?"

Ren whispered, "Yes, thanks." She took the handkerchief and buried her face in it. Maybe no one else would see her. She would just keep her face covered and feel her way out of the store, like in blindman's bluff.

Then she felt her wrist lightly pressed by warm fingertips. She hesitated, and then she peeked out and saw him — her handkerchief hero. He was checking her pulse! Even in her distraught state, Ren found that just a bit cheeky. With amazing eloquence, she said, "Uh . . ."

"Shhh." He spoke so gently, so sweetly, that Ren wanted to fire her family practitioner instantly and ask this man if he took Blue Cross/Blue Shield. He squatted down to her level and smiled at her. "I'm counting your heartbeats."

Ren couldn't take her eyes off him. Maybe she shouldn't have studied his face while he counted, but what else was she to do? She couldn't exactly flip through clothing racks with her free hand. Besides, a full year had passed since Greg divorced her. She certainly wasn't betraying him. And the crowd had dispersed at the command of the magma lady. Ren had no one else to look at.

So she observed Dr. Heartbeat the moment he looked down at his watch. His lashes were thick and dark, like his hair. Great skin. Tanned, or maybe you'd call that olive. So maybe Mediterranean background? Maybe South American? He smelled like his handkerchief — crisp and clean.

He released her wrist. "Your pulse is racing."

Yes, indeed. Ren looked into his eyes. Like a movie star's, and darker than chocolate. Coming from a long line of blue-eyed Anglos, she'd always been drawn to dark eyes. Even Greg's eyes were dark. But brooding dark. This man had kind eyes. Beautiful. Ren was in mourning for her marriage, truly. But she had to admit — this guy's looks temporarily took the edge off.

14

"Are you a doctor?"

"A nurse," he said. Again with the smile.

"A nurse? I mean, I know there are men nurses these days, *regular* men, of course, who are nurses, but . . ."

Ugh. The epitome of charm.

He said, "You should see me in my white dress and orthopedic shoes."

She laughed, but only for a couple of seconds. Something about laughing while her real life broke to pieces . . . well, she was teetering. And she felt oddly guilty. So, like a character in a bad soap opera, she crumbled into tears. And sobbed. Actually sobbed. Her mother's specter flashed through her mind again. ("Honestly, Ren! A little self-control!") She struggled to push her mother out of her mind and get a hold of herself.

He helped, this wonderful nurse-man. "Look, I'd be happy to get you a cup of coffee at the snack counter. Would you like me to call someone for you?"

"Thanks. I'll be all right. I just want to splash some water on my face in the ladies' room. Do you know where it is?"

He chuckled.

"Oh! Not that you've ever used the ladies' room. I mean, just because you're a nurse and all, it's not that I think . . ." She paused

15

and then took a big breath, in and out. "Just shoot me now."

And he laughed. *What* a laugh. So appreciative. She hadn't heard that from a man for so long. She swore he could have made her smile before a firing squad.

"You're funny."

"But, honestly, I don't always blubber and fall all over myself like this. Today's been kind of rough —" She stopped, a tight ball suddenly in her throat. And, of course, she started to cry again. She was head majorette in her own pity parade today.

He said nothing. He picked up her purse and shopping bag. He softly cupped his hand under her elbow, helped her stand, and guided her to the snack bar. Ren sat down in a cold, vinyl-covered booth, and he went to get coffee.

She had almost regained control by the time she heard Kara's voice behind her.

"Rennie? You *are* still here!"

Ren turned around, knowing her expression was as pitiful as Kara had ever seen.

Kara made a face — the one you'd make if your child were the last to be picked for either team. "Aw, doggone it." She scooted into the booth next to Ren and put her arm around her. "Come on, now." She gave Ren's shoulder a squeeze. "I thought you

16

just came here for a T-shirt. What happened? I got worried when you didn't answer either your home phone or your cell."

"The T-shirt," Ren muttered. She wanted to stop crying. Her contact lenses were killing her. Yet she couldn't seem to stop. Couldn't seem to be strong. Especially now that Kara had arrived. Kara was her best friend, and she seemed to be able to see right through her. And she didn't let Ren get away with pretending. Sometimes that drove Ren crazy, but right now Kara was a godsend.

"What happened?" Kara asked again, running her hand through her pale, cropped hair.

Before Ren could answer, someone cleared his throat, and both women looked up at Ren's nurse. She hadn't noticed his build before. But he was casual perfection in jeans and a V-necked sweater of the softest blue cotton. He held two cups of coffee and looked at Kara, expectantly.

"Yes?" Kara asked. "Can we help you?" Her tone was an odd mix of haughtiness and flirtation.

"Kara," Ren said, "this —" She did a double take at Kara, who was now looking at the man with what Ren would call ex-

treme approval. Ren tried again. "This is
—"

"Truman Sayers," he said. Ren looked at him, and she confessed feeling a quick thrill that he was looking at her, telling her his name.

"Truman." Ren said his name, just like that, and for some reason she suddenly felt embarrassed. Naturally, more verbal stumbling ensued. "And we're . . . I mean, she's . . . this is my friend, Kara Richardson." Ren looked at Kara as she finished her name, and now Kara was looking at Ren.

Kara's expression — one eyebrow raised, one corner of her mouth forming a wry smile — horrified Ren in its frank understanding. This was one of those moments when Ren dreaded Kara's ability to see right through her. She hoped Kara could read the look she shot back at her, her eyes flashing open, glaring, and warning her to keep her observations to herself.

Ren looked back at Truman. "And I'm Rennie Hurd. I mean, Rennie Young. Thanks so much for your help, Truman."

"Call me Tru." He handed her a cup of coffee. "May I get you a cup?" he asked Kara.

"No, but thanks, *Tru.*" She looked at Ren

as she said his name, that eyebrow raised again.

"Yes, well," Tru said. He looked at Ren and smiled. "You seem to be in good hands here, Rennie. Nice meeting you."

"Yes, thanks. Thank you so much."

He gave her a friendly wink just before he turned away. Ren watched him go, and before she looked back at her friend, said, "You're going to pull a muscle if you don't relax that eyebrow, Kara."

"My, my, my. I'm slipping. I could have sworn you were in trouble when I dashed in here, desperately worried you were obsessing about the divorce's anniversary. How'd you meet up with Mr. Dish there?"

"It was awful. I fainted."

"I might have too. He's gorgeous!"

Ren gave her shoulder a shove. "Not over him. It wasn't like that. He just came along and helped me afterward."

Kara nodded, looking back in the direction Tru had gone. "Nice." Then she looked back at Ren. "Any idea why you fainted? Have you eaten anything today?"

"Plenty, as usual. If only Greg's leaving had killed my appetite. At least something good would have come from it. It's been a year, Kara. I've been such a fool, hoping he'd come back to me."

Kara reached around and patted her back. "Not foolish. Just faithful. God's going to work out something good for you in this, Ren. At least you've survived well materially. That's worth considering. Greg's deciding to let you keep the house was a huge blessing, don't you think?"

Ren shrugged but nodded. That was good news when she and Greg finally settled. But she couldn't help wondering why Greg had suddenly become so gracious in the settlement. And she wasn't sure she wanted to find out why.

Kara picked up Ren's coffee and took a sip. "Tell me what happened here."

Ren knew she'd start crying again, so she clutched Tru's handkerchief. "It's not just the anniversary of the divorce. Greg called the adoption agency and told them we were through. That they should have stopped the adoption process a year ago."

Ren heard Kara gasp. "That lousy —"

"I would have had to tell them sooner or later, anyway. The adoption depended on our happy home being intact." She shrugged. "I just kept hoping."

"Rennie, I'm so sorry."

Ren looked at her. The tears in Kara's eyes were all it took. Ren had to yank several small folded napkins out of the dispenser for her — she wasn't about to share Tru's hanky. They sat there in the Wal-Mart snack bar, sniffling and sharing sips of lukewarm coffee. Ren spoke between wavering breaths.

"So I came here to get Casey a gift. A cool T-shirt or something. You know, to maybe soften the blow when I tell him."

"Oh, Ren."

"And you know how he loves that Mighty Man character? I wanted to get him a Mighty Man T-shirt. They sell them here, but they were all too big." She sighed. "Too big. They had lots of small sizes, but he's . . . he's . . . so small."

Kara reached past her to grab more napkins.

"He's too small for more disappointments," Ren said. "I don't know if I can stand to see him go through that. I guess it was all that at once — the anniversary of the divorce, the adoption officially falling through, and then not even finding the shirt for Casey. I felt stressed. So defeated. And the next thing I knew I was facedown on the linoleum."

Kara took her hand. "We need to pray. Right now, we need to pray."

"Yeah, okay. Will you do it?"

She nodded. They bowed their heads.

"Dear Lord," Kara said, "we're coming to

21

You on behalf of Casey. That poor little guy. He has a mommy here just waiting for him, but, well, You see what's going on here. We're asking for Your help. Please send help for Casey. Please send help for Ren. In Your precious name we pray."

"Amen," Ren said. But hers wasn't the only amen. She spun in the booth to see Tru standing behind them. He shrugged and held up Ren's shopping bag. He had accidentally left with it. Ren thought of Kara's prayer: send help for Casey; send help for Ren. She thought about Tru's having joined them in their prayer. She looked at him and smiled and could think of only one thing to say.

"Amen."

TWO

Ren hadn't expected the divorce.

"The adoption was the last straw," Greg said as he listed his reasons for leaving her. But that's what he had said about her job change too. And her attempt to curb her swearing and her friendship with Kara and, of course, "the whole God thing." At some point during their final days, Greg called everything about Ren a last straw. Apparently, she'd broken many a camel's back since becoming a Christian.

Kara had warned her that her marriage might go through some rough times after she found Jesus. "You might have seen the light, but don't count on Greg's peering out from the darkness anytime soon. We'll have to pray for that."

Before Ren came to Christ, she had interests and goals that matched Greg's. She was raised that way. Her father had been an influential lawyer and her mother had always traveled in the loftiest social circles in the Washington area. Ren craved financial success and a high-powered career. Independence. She prided herself on having succeeded without accepting financial help from her parents (if you didn't count her expensive college education). Stuff. Ren wanted to own a lot of stuff. Greg and Ren bought a brand-new home in Leesburg, Virginia, a charming small town that catered to big-city tastes. They furnished their home just so. They drove his-and-hers Beamers; red for Greg, silver for Ren.

And her idea of a good time often involved alcohol and other forms of numbing self-gratification. It was all about gratifying herself. Greg was comfortable around that kind of behavior. He considered the old Ren more "fun."

As a Christian wife Ren cared about different things, but she still loved her husband. And she prayed he would join her one day at church and start to understand the joy Christ could give him. She listened to the advice of her women's Bible group: *Win him to Christ through your gentle spirit.*

Well. That would be a challenge for her. A number of words came to mind when Ren considered her spirit. "Gentle" wasn't among them. She didn't do a bang-up job in the living-by-example department, she had to admit, but she gave it her best shot.

Her career change drove Greg nuts. "Why would you want to leave an awesome job, making the kind of money we deserve, to do something as stupid as teaching? Why?"

Ren struggled with her thoughts — such as, *Only a moron would call teaching "stupid."*

"I think God wants me to do this, Greg. The money isn't as important as following His will. We'll have enough money."

After she began teaching first grade, Ren met Casey. The school counselor filled her in. Casey was a foster child, living with his fifth family. His biological father was long gone, and social services took him away from his mother, a drug addict who didn't care a bit about her loss. She called Casey a mistake she just didn't get around to destroying in time. Casey survived his brief time with his mother mercifully unscathed, despite her neglect. And he was amazingly sweet, even after getting passed through the system like a cold no one wanted to catch.

Ren fell in love with Casey the day he joined her class. He was quiet and shy, but his sad, blue eyes showed such a dear quality — a promising core — that she ached to reach. At first he wouldn't look directly at her.

"You know, there's a poem about a baseball player named Casey," Ren told him. She didn't remember until later that "Casey at the Bat" described an arrogant baseball player, humbled by striking out. Praise God, Casey didn't know that, either. Instead, he looked up at her and almost braved a smile. She saw a child starved for love, attention, and reassurance.

She worked with the school counselor to help Casey feel accepted. In short time the class welcomed him as one of the gang. One afternoon Ren heard the most delightful giggling behind her on the playground. She recognized Casey's small, husky voice and turned to see him with a classmate, Teddy. They each had planted a foot in the empty bucket they used for sidewalk chalk. Arm-in-arm, they strutted around, a three-legged mass of fun.

Another teacher, lips puckered as though with lemon juice, strutted toward them. No doubt she meant to Save the Day on behalf of the chalk bucket. Ren cut her off at the pass and grabbed the two boys in a big, awkward hug. She hugged Teddy for warming up so well to Casey. And she hugged Casey because . . . well, just because he was Casey. And he had such a cute giggle, and Ren loved the way he crinkled his eyes when his blond curls fell into them. She glanced up at the pill-faced teacher, who actually cracked a smile, albeit a strained one.

Later, when the school counselor told her that Casey's foster family planned to move out of the Leesburg area and couldn't afford to adopt him, Ren panicked. She wasn't sure why.

"So what's the big deal?" Greg asked her when she told him that evening. He didn't look at her but at some paperwork he brought home from the office. "You said he's survived changing families a bunch of times. He'll survive again. You act like it's happening to your kid."

Ren caught her breath. As if God had spoken through him, Greg answered her question about the panic. She had begun to think of Casey as her child. Had the Lord put that in her heart, or did her mind just go there all by itself?

She had never suggested adoption to Greg before. It was a subject guaranteed to bring conflict between them. For four years they'd been married — and childless. They both felt disappointment early on, but when Ren suggested they get medical testing, Greg refused and lost interest in their having children.

"The problem's probably mine," Ren told

him. She had undergone minor surgery for endometriosis as a teen — most likely she had scar tissue. "How about just I get tested?"

But he still refused. The old Ren would have pointed out that her body was her own to get tested or not. But by that time she had accepted Christ, and she felt she needed to honor her husband's wishes. In hindsight she thought Greg feared she'd check out all right, which would suggest what he'd consider a failing on his part.

After his comment triggered her thoughts about adopting Casey, Ren spent time in prayer. *Dear Lord, if it's Your will that Casey join our family, could You make that clear to Greg and me? And could You please open Greg's heart to the idea and give me the strength to bring up the subject gently and at the right time?*

Then she tried to be patient and let the Lord work. She lasted until dinnertime.

"Absolutely not," Greg said, scooping potatoes onto his plate. He had the TV tuned to a show about business finance.

Ren lowered the volume, prompting a frown from him.

"But why? Can't we at least discuss the idea?"

After a harsh chuckle, he said, "I can just see your mother when you tell her about this one. 'The daughter of wealthy socialite Clarissa Young adopting a little ghetto baby.' She'll croak."

"Casey's not a ghetto baby. And Mother's not as heartless as you think. She adores my brother's kids."

"They're Youngs, Ren. Family blood. Of course Clarissa accepts them."

Ren didn't respond. She was afraid he was right. Moments like this made her miss her father. He always had such a softening effect on her mother, and his death two years ago seemed to shut something down in her. She lived just a few towns away, in McLean, but Ren felt as if she were becoming more and more distant from her. More distant from the kindness Ren knew she had inside herself.

Greg cut his steak while he talked. "Look, you said yourself that the kid's parents were drug addicts. Who knows what kind of messed-up genes he's got? We could be bringing a future serial killer into the family."

"Casey? A serial killer? Give me a break, Greg. His doctor says he's in excellent physical health. And both the social services psychiatrist and the school counselor rave about how well adjusted he is. He just needs two parents who will love him, and I'm already there. If you meet him, I swear you'll love him too. He's adorable."

Greg looked up, fight in his expression. But he stopped short of talking, looked her in the eye, and then looked down at his plate. Ren shot another quick prayer up to God.

"You never got tested, right? For the fertility thing?"

"What? The . . . oh! No. I never did. You didn't want me to."

He nodded and set down his knife and fork. "Okay." He looked up at her. "You respected me enough to keep from doing that. I guess I can return the favor and come meet the kid. Casey."

She jumped up from the table and hugged him from behind, trying to suppress a tiny squeal of joy. She saw how the Lord had blessed her for honoring Greg's demand that she not get tested.

"Okay, okay." He patted her arm, as if to signal she should let him loose. "Don't get worked up too soon. No guarantees, all right?" He reached for the remote control and turned up the volume.

Ren released him and sat back down, still smiling. "No guarantees. But wait 'til you meet him, Greg. You're gonna love him."

And he did. Even though Greg held back, Ren could see it in his eyes — Casey won him over the first time they met.

"He's not like I pictured," Greg said after their first meeting. "You made him sound like such a needy little thing, but he's full of . . . spunk, I guess. A real boy."

Ren laughed, giddy with Greg's favorable impression. "Must be my mothering instinct that made him sound needy. I just want to cuddle him up all the time, and he's so open to that."

"Yeah, well, you can overdo that. He's not made of fluff, Ren."

She didn't argue with him. This felt like the typical male-female balancing act that most parents went through. As long as Greg was open to considering adoption, she wasn't about to make waves.

That became her motto with Greg from then on: Don't Make Waves. Not just with regard to his attitude toward Casey, but also with his comments about everything he found wrong with her since she "got religion." He seemed willing to continue in their marriage as long as she allowed him to vent his disappointment in her without a fight. Greg hadn't seemed a negative man before Ren found Christ, but her newfound faith seemed to change both of them. Once Casey's adoption was at stake, she tried to shrug off her husband's increasingly cynical comments and to trust the Lord for her sense of worth. Of course, she struggled with the occasional uncharitable thought about Greg: *jerk, creep, idiot.* She wasn't perfect, after all.

And now she realized that what she kept shrugging off was the disintegration of her marriage. She pinned so much hope on Casey's changing their home life that she didn't take seriously enough the fact that Greg was straying away from her. In more ways than she knew at the time.

"The adoption's not going to happen, Ren. Just face it," Greg said before he left her. "Sure, Casey will be disappointed at first, but he'll bounce back just fine. This so-called family would have been as much torture for him as it's become for me."

Torture? So-called family? Ren couldn't believe how quickly he wrote everything off — their marriage, their future, their chance to become parents.

She wasn't so quick to write it all off, even after he left her. She held out hope for his return. And she kept the adoption process going, even when they moved into the next school year. Ren reached the one-year anniversary of her divorce with her hopes weak but still hanging in there.

When she learned of Greg's call to the agency, she was amazed that her heartbreak over him was nothing compared to the hole torn through her when she realized she'd probably lose Casey.

So here she sat, in the Wal-Mart snack bar, with her broken heart, her best friend, and a handsome stranger named Tru.

THREE

"Oh, my goodness, you're kidding me," Kara said when she looked up after their prayer and saw Tru.

He stepped closer to give Ren her shopping bag. "I suppose Freud would say I kept this on purpose. That there are no accidents." He smiled at her.

Ren had always considered Freud a complete joke, but she loved Tru's insinuation. "Thanks." She stood and took the bag from him. "What a nice thing to say."

"Listen," he said, pulling out his wallet and sorting through it. "Let me leave my card with you."

She read the card that linked him with the local hospital. Her eyes widened when she saw what kind of nurse he was.

"You're a baby nurse?"

He nodded. "Labor and delivery, yes. At the Loudoun Hospital Center down the road. I live just a few blocks from there."

Ren smiled at him. "We're nearly neigh-bors."

"Mmm-mmm-mmm," Kara muttered. "Like babies, do you, Tru?" She shot the quickest glance at Ren, who felt a flush run up her neck. Ren knew Kara was already plastering Tru's face over Greg's in Ren's family album.

"I love babies," Tru said. "Love kids, period. I come from a big family. Two broth-ers and three sisters. All younger than me."

"And yet you're not married?" Kara asked, causing Ren to gasp before she could stop herself.

"You don't have to answer that!"

Tru laughed. "I don't mind, Rennie. My sisters ask me about that all the time."

She smiled. He remembered her name!

He shrugged when he looked at Kara again. "Just haven't met the woman God has in mind for me yet. But, listen," he said again to Ren, "please keep my card. I didn't hear everything when I barged back in on you, but I think I heard enough to guess you're having adoption problems?"

Ren looked down at her shopping bag, reminded of the husband she couldn't keep, the son she couldn't adopt, and the simple T-shirt she couldn't find. "Yeah. Looks as if I got my hopes too high."

"I'm so sorry. I know that's hard, losing the child you thought God planned for you. I see that too often in my work."

Tru lowered his head and looked Ren in the eyes when he spoke, as if he were soothing a child. The gentleness of the gesture almost made her cry. "When you want, please give me a call," he said. "I can't do anything for you on my own, but many of my friends are involved in the adoption process. I'd love to help you and your husband reach the best people in the system."

"Oh. My husband . . ." Ren paused, hoping that Kara would step in and say something brutal about Greg, but she didn't. So Ren just took a big breath and said, "My husband divorced me. That's the problem with the adoption."

How could she explain the expression on his face? He looked as if she had just spoken in Swahili. Complete . . . confusion? No. Disbelief. Shock.

"He divorced you?"

Ren studied his eyes — those striking eyes — as she answered. "Yes. He did. He was sick of my Christian faith and my Christian choices. The divorce was final a year ago today."

She glanced over at the booth to see why

Kara was so silent. She was gone. Not out of sight, and probably not out of hearing range, but out of Ren's conversation with Tru. Ren spotted her just beyond the coffee counter, looking at street maps she didn't need. Ren loved that girl.

"Idiot," muttered Tru, sighing softly.

"Pardon?"

"Oh, nothing. I'm sorry. I mean, I'm really sorry. I hope your husband's lousy decision doesn't destroy your chances with the adoption. It *is* possible to adopt as a single parent, you know."

"Oh, no," Ren shook her head. "I don't think I could single parent. I, um, I could probably swing it financially, if I'm careful with my money. But I think two parents are God's plan, if possible. I had . . . well, I kept the adoption process going just in case my husband . . ."

"I understand," he said.

"I have to work now," Ren said. "How fair would it be to adopt a child and not be there for him? And he'd really need a father. The whole thing, my situation, is quite different now."

The slightest smile appeared on his face. Ren absolutely loved the way he was looking at her. "You're right, of course. And sensible."

She had no idea what to say, so she just smiled and looked down at Tru's card. She held it out to him. "Thanks anyway."

He held his hands up. "No, no. Keep it. Please."

"Keep it?"

"Yes. Now I really want . . . please hang on to my card. I know you're going through a lot right now. But at some point you might want a friend to talk with. I'd like to be first in line, if you're ever interested."

"Yesss!" Kara whispered far too loudly from the map rack. Tru and Ren looked over at her. She stiffened before peeking over her shoulder at them and laughing weakly. "Uh, found a terrific map of Maryland here!"

Tru and Ren laughed. She put his card in her purse. "Thanks. I'll think about calling." *Maybe constantly.*

They said their goodbyes. Kara returned, wrapped an arm around Ren, and squeezed, her green eyes sparkling. "How's that for a quick answer to prayer?"

Ren smiled. "Maybe. But, we don't know much about each other. I don't want to jump into anything too soon."

"Doesn't sound as if he's in a rush either, Ren."

"Yeah. I'll try to remember that on those

lonely nights when I start obsessing about
—"

"Relax. God's going to work everything
out for the best."

Ren nodded. "True."

"What about him?"

"No, I mean, that's true, what you said
about God." She laughed and gave Kara a
playful shove. "Now who's obsessing? Come
on. Help me search through the T-shirts
again. I have a feeling the Lord's going to
help me find what *He* wants me to look for."

FOUR

The restaurant's friendly atmosphere cheered Ren the moment she walked in, despite the busy workday she had just finished. The natural light and flourishing green plants brightened her mood. She was surprised at how crowded the place was, so early in the evening. And everyone seemed to be talking and laughing. Soft rock played, but not too loudly. Ren headed for the nonsmoking section and looked for her friends.

"Ren, over here!" Jeremy called from the booth he and Sandy had taken, near one of the beveled-glass windows. Kara and her boyfriend, Gabe, weren't there yet. Ren waved and walked toward them, passing a few tables of early diners and revelers.

Jeremy and Sandy were coworkers at the school, and they were also her best friends, after Kara.

Sandy wasn't able to get away after work

that often. She liked to go straight home to her eleven-year-old son, Michael, and her husband (about whom she raved so consistently that her coworkers referred to him as The Marvelous Rick). But tonight Sandy's boys were at the local high school basketball game, so she was on her own. A die-hard fan of sweets and rich food, Sandy was on the heavy side and looked a little older than her thirty-five years. Did she care? The woman had more self-confidence than a runway model. The kids loved her and gathered around her like pigeons at a park bench whenever she visited the classrooms. Sandy was the school counselor. She and Ren had become close over the last two years because of Ren's interest in Casey. Sandy knew how fragile Ren felt because of her divorce and its effect on the adoption.

"We were starting to worry about you, girl," Sandy said. She cocked her head toward Jeremy, whose pale brown hair had fallen softly onto his forehead. "This boy's chewing my ear off about his latest heartbreak, Rennie. If he were a drinking man, his beer would be half full of tears by now."

"Yes, well, so's my iced tea," Jeremy said, exaggerating a gloomy face. "I really thought this was the one."

Ren sighed. Dear Jeremy. He moved to

41

Virginia from London just three years ago, eager to make big changes in his life and surroundings. He had visited the States as a teen and had fallen in love with Virginia. Like many Leesburg residents, he liked the idea of living in a cozy town that was just around the corner from the excitement of Washington, DC. So, as he put it, he left England "straight away from university" and earned his teaching certificate in time to start teaching last year. He taught the third graders, many of whom tried to imitate his "awesome" accent to hilarious effect. Jeremy was often told he resembled actor Jude Law — not a bad compliment. He was blue-eyed, adorable, and funny, and forever searching for Miss Right in the worst places.

Ren slid into the booth next to Sandy and gave Jeremy a sad smile. "Remind me, Jeremy. Was this latest heartbreaker the woman you met at the bar or the one you met at the nightclub?"

He gave her a sideways look, frowning. "No lectures from you, love. I don't want to hear about meeting girls at chapel or the Moose Lodge or Aunt Edith's garden party. There's bound to be a keeper out there who's also spicy. I won't find her by joining a bridge club."

Ren laughed. Jeremy wasn't a believer —

neither was Sandy, for that matter — and he lived his life as Ren did before she saw the Light. But both Jeremy and Sandy were wonderful, thoughtful friends with whom Ren loved to spend time. She hadn't laughed much in the last year or so — the past week had been particularly dry — so she had accepted this invitation to dinner without hesitation. Distractions were her life's blood these days.

"Are Kara and Gabe still coming?" Sandy asked.

"Pretty soon, yeah," Ren said. She ordered a diet soda and joined Sandy in munching on chips and salsa. "Kara had a four o'clock aerobics class to teach, and Gabe has an employee closing the deli for him tonight. They should be here any minute."

Jeremy perked up at the mention of Kara's name. "How are they getting on these days, anyway? Bored with each other yet?"

Confused — and suspicious — Ren frowned at him. "Why?"

He shrugged. "Just keeping abreast of things. You never know. Maybe if Gabe decides to move on, Kara'd be interested in a sensitive, heartbroken, unbearably handsome schoolteacher."

Ren smiled. "Afraid not, Jeremy. It's been almost a year. Gabe's smitten. They both are. Anyway, Kara's one of those spicy girls you won't be meeting in chapel."

He blew air through his lips like a frustrated pony. "You Christians."

"I'm telling you, you should come with us some Sunday." Ren looked at Sandy. "You both should. Could change your lives."

An awkward silence followed that comment. Ren considered how her life had changed since she first went to church with Kara a few years ago. She had the Lord now, which, of course, was too wonderful for words. But she no longer had her husband, and it looked as if she wouldn't have Casey, either. She tried to swallow the lump that formed in her throat.

"Here's to Ren." Sandy raised her glass. "A beautiful woman, made even more beautiful once that ugly growth was removed from her back last year."

Ren frowned and laughed at the same time. "What?"

Jeremy clinked his glass against Sandy's. "To Ren, and to whatever it took to get Greg off her back. Hear, hear!"

Ren looked up to see that Kara had arrived. Her blond hair was cute and tousled. She smelled fresh, as if she had just stepped out of the shower.

"Well, I will drink to that. Move over,

handsome," she said to Jeremy, who obliged, puppylike.

"Where's Gabe?" Ren asked.

Kara shook her head. "He can't come. His employee got sick."

Their waitress approached.

Kara said, "Did you guys order food yet?" She smiled at the waitress. "I'd love a humongous glass of water with lemon slices, please."

"We haven't ordered," Jeremy said. "We were waiting for you, you dazzling creature."

Ren rolled her eyes.

Kara looked at Jeremy for a split second before sighing. "Oh, Jeremy. You didn't get dumped again?"

Sandy snorted. "You poor boy. You'd better stick with the barflies. These church ladies are on to your games."

Ren laughed. "Sandy, stop. Jeremy, they'd eat you up at church, really. You're a doll, and you'd find plenty of dazzling creatures there if you'd come with us."

"You, Ren, have renewed my faith in the fairer sex," Jeremy said. He arched his brow and looked from Sandy to Kara. "Not all women are heartless and vile."

Sandy picked up a menu. "Well, this vile woman is hungry. What's everyone getting?"

They ordered way too much food, as they

usually did. When the waitress left their table, Sandy looked at Ren. "By the way, Jeremy and I are treating you tonight. Happy birthday."

Ren gasped, smiling. "How sweet are *you?* Thanks! I didn't think anyone remembered." She looked quickly at Kara. "I mean, I didn't think you forgot, Kara. And it's not as if I expected you to remember. That's not why I said that —"

"Stop yer babblin,' woman," Kara said, pulling an envelope from her gym bag. "Don't you know how much we love you? If anyone forgets your birthday this year, of all years, I say ditch 'em."

"Why this year? I don't turn thirty 'til next year."

"Thirty, schmirty," Kara said. "You've had one of the stinkin-est years ever, topped only by the year before. You need something special." She placed the envelope in front of Ren.

Ren opened it to find two tickets to a show she'd wanted to see for years.

"Riverdance!" Her voice was as high and squeaky as a teenybopper's. "You angel!"

Kara grinned, pointing to the tickets. "And look. It's at Wolf Trap!"

The Wolf Trap concert center was located within a lovely national park not far from

Leesburg. It was one of Ren's favorite spots in the whole area. The lush natural surroundings were part of the enjoyment of any performance there.

"And you'll go with me?" Ren asked Kara.

"You betcha. I'm even having my roots touched up for the occasion."

Jeremy mocked a gasp. "You mean you're a bottle blonde, Kara?" He shook his head and waved her off. "No, no, no, it would never have worked out between us. It's truly for the best, my darling, that you stay with Gabe and try to get over me."

"I'll try."

"You know," Ren said, "I've been thinking about doing something different with my color too. I actually found a couple gray hairs the other day."

"Hmm," said Sandy. "Can't imagine who put those there."

"Ren, your hair is great," said Kara. "So long and thick, and your color's nice and warm. Like cocoa."

Ren pulled some of her hair forward to look at it. "I guess I was thinking of darker cocoa."

"I'd like that," said Sandy. "You'd look more exotic."

Ren saw Jeremy studying her. "Right," he said. "Exotic, yes. Say, Ren, is this about that swarthy male nurse you gushed about the other day? You do realize he fell for you as is, don't you, and not all dyed up to look like a darker chocolate truffle?"

Ren threw a French fry at him. "I didn't gush. I only shared. If you don't want me to share with you anymore —"

"Besides," Kara said. "Since when did you become anti-hair color, Jeremy? There's nothing wrong with Ren wanting to cover the gray —"

"Well, yikes, Kara," Ren said, looking around at the other tables. "I only found two gray hairs. Let's not broadcast that too loudly."

"I'm not anti-hair color," Jeremy said. "I just keep thinking about that ex of yours, Ren. I'd gladly sock that twit on the jaw with a half brick." He looked at Kara, who was laughing. "I just don't want to see Ren get hurt again by some brute she tries too hard to please."

Sandy laughed. "Yeah, Ren. You tell that brute of a male nurse to stop forcing you to change. So what if you *are* riddled with gray hair. And stop gushing, for pity's sake. You're making a mess."

They all made her laugh. Ren loved her friends so much. And how kind of Jeremy to say that Tru had fallen for her.

"Okay, I'll admit it." Ren held up her thumb and index finger in a "little bit" gesture. "I gushed a smidgen."

"Gushed a smidgen?" Kara repeated. "Personally, I'm thrilled if you're thrilled about Tru. I think you should call him. Get to know him."

"Same here," said Sandy. "Time to start over. I want you to end up with someone like —"

"The Marvelous Rick," the rest of them finished in unison.

"Exactly," Sandy said, unfazed. "And you said Tru's the same religion as you, right? So you won't have the same problems you had with Greg."

"Just mind that you don't simply end up with a whole new set of problems," said Jeremy.

"Well, I think he's a Christian," Ren said to Sandy. "We haven't talked enough for me to know much more than that."

"Too right," said Jeremy. "His being 'a Christian' doesn't tell you much. You be careful, love."

"Good grief, Jeremy," said Sandy. "The way you worry, I'm going to start calling you Old Lady."

"He's all right," Ren told Sandy. She turned to Jeremy. "You're just being chivalrous, aren't you? And reacting to being hurt by that last girlfriend." She looked back at Sandy. "It's scary to start over. Right, Jeremy? Jeremy?"

But he didn't respond. An attractive young woman had just walked into the restaurant. He seemed mesmerized and actually surprised when they all laughed at his next comment.

"Blimey. I think I'm in love."

FIVE

"Let's see if we can get just a little closer to the stage," Kara said, trudging ahead of Ren on the Wolf Trap lawn. "The acoustics are better up close, and I want to be able to hear every single clippity-clop of their tap shoes."

She carried a wicker picnic basket with one hand and a lawn chair with the other. Ren dutifully followed her, clutching her own chair and a comfortable quilt.

One of the charms of the Wolf Trap center was its design. The concert stage sat before a backdrop of natural forest. Half of the seating was under cover, but the sides of the center were open, giving concertgoers a glorious view of God's handiwork during the shows. The other half of the seating was sprawled across the center's sloping lawns. Many patrons brought picnic dinners to enjoy under the open sky — under the stars — before and during the concerts.

Kara and Ren had reserved seats in the covered, open-air section of the center. But they wanted to find a good spot among the lawn seats to enjoy the gourmet picnic Kara had brought, courtesy of her boyfriend, Gabe. His deli was one of the most popular in the area, with good cause.

They probably weren't going to make any friends when they packed up their leftovers and tramped through the lawn seats to the reserved seating, especially if *Riverdance* was in full swing. But they didn't know what else to do, since Ren had thrown them off schedule.

They had allowed enough time for a leisurely meal well before the show started. And Ren started getting ready far in advance of Kara's picking her up at home. She laid out her jeans, a pale pink top, and a light sweater to bring, in case the May evening grew cool, as it often did. And she left plenty of time to dye her hair.

Ah, yes. Her hair.

She swore she followed the directions to a T. And the hair color in the picture was exactly what she was going for. It was called Espresso, and Ren couldn't wait to look like the woman on the box.

Maybe her hair just dyed faster than the average hair. Ren didn't know. But even after she finished drying it, she was shocked by its darkness. It would have to be several shades lighter just to be black. She looked as if she should be wearing black lipstick and leather. By comparison, her eyebrows — which were actually quite dark — didn't even seem to exist on her face. She darkened them with an eyebrow pencil to catch up to the shade of her hair. She stepped back and looked in the mirror. For a brief, too-horrible moment, the image of Groucho Marx flashed through her mind.

Just as tears threatened to flood her eyes, the doorbell rang.

Ren threw the door open to face Kara, who looked fresh and perky as always in a pale green velour jogging suit. But Kara actually looked frightened for a moment when she saw Ren's hair.

"My goodness. You've been busy today, haven't you?"

Ren dropped onto the couch and put her face in her hands. "What am I going to do, Kara? I'm the bride of Frankenstein!"

"Now, it's not that bad. But, you know you're not supposed to put the dye on your eyebrows, right?"

Ren moaned. "I know. That's eyebrow pencil." She looked up at Kara. "Please tell me you didn't think of Groucho Marx when you saw me."

"To tell you the truth, I thought of that Mexican painter lady they made the movie about a few years ago. Frida something."

"The one with the unibrow?"

Kara pointed her finger at Ren. "Yeah! That's the one."

Ren groaned into her hands. "I'm doomed."

"Come on now. Cheer up." Kara sat next to her and wrapped an arm around her. "Maybe I can help. Did you use dye or rinse?"

Ren plodded into the bathroom to dig the box out of the trash can. She wanted to spit when she saw how lovely that woman looked in the picture. "It's a rinse," she called out to Kara.

She heard Kara rummaging in the kitchen before she walked back to join Ren. She had thrown Ren's chef apron over her clothes and was rolling up her sleeves.

"All righty, then. Let's get your head under that faucet and give it another washing."

"But the instructions say not to wash it for another day or so."

Kara didn't even look at her as she walked over to the tub and turned on the water. "Yep, I know that. That's so the color won't wash out. So it'll just settle into those follicles *real* good." She looked into Ren's horrified eyes, one hand on her hip. "What do you say, Frida?"

By the time they washed Ren's hair twice, it was still dark but not as harsh. Ren could smell the chemicals from the dye, but they were at war with the scented conditioner she had used to keep her hair from frying to a frazzle.

"Wear your deep blue top," Kara said. "You can't wear that pale pink. It'll show off the dark too much. Too much contrast."

Ren sighed. "I'm so sorry I cut into our picnic time, Kara. Little did you know you'd have to add personal beauty care to your birthday present."

She shrugged. "Hey, no big deal. We needed to get you a little less Gothic, didn't we? We'll still have our picnic as planned. Maybe we won't lounge quite as long as I expected, but we'll just go to our seats whenever we finish. What better dinner music than Celtic ballads and Irish pipes, right?"

They were blessed with a cool but comfortable May evening. This time of year, the rich green surroundings provided as much pleasure as the show did.

"Aw, nuts," Kara said, searching through the basket. "I can't believe I didn't pack the water."

They both looked up at the long lines at the concession stands. "We still have time before the show starts," Ren said. "Let's go together. We can people-watch while we wait in line."

And that's why they were where they were, and saw what they saw, and did what they did. Ren would have given just about anything for things to be different. But they weren't.

They stood in line, joking about themselves, their jobs, their coworkers, their families. They were having fun and getting a little giddy. They started playing their people-watching game. You choose a person far off in the crowd who looks interesting. You give that person a name. You create a persona for him or her, which could include family history, profession, special talents, quirks, and so on. Kara and Ren had become quite imaginative at the game, always trying to surpass one another in creativity.

After Ren chose Lenny — the opera-singing lumberjack and father of twelve, married to the long-suffering and ever-fertile Edna — Kara chose a beautiful woman with hair like the model on Ren's hair-color box.

"Carmella Desdemona Prunella Jones is a prima ballerina," Kara said. "Observe the perfect posture and proudly held head. And see how she points her toes outward as she walks, consistently practicing first position —"

"I think that would be second position, if I remember correctly."

Kara raised her brow at her. "Did *I* point out the unlikelihood of a lumberjack hanging out in suburban Virginia? Did I?"

Ren bowed her head, humbly. "Forgive me. You were saying?"

"Carmen is —"

"Carmella," Ren said.

"*Carmella* is constantly followed by adoring fans and the paparazzi, which she secretly enjoys. She pretends to want her privacy, but tonight she wants to be seen. You see, she is attending this show with that famous hero of stage and screen —"

Kara abruptly gasped.

"What?" Ren asked, following her frozen stare. Ren found Carmella, just as she gracefully sat down in a lawn chair. Then Ren gasped too.

She spoke softly. "Carmella's attending this show with the famous labor-and-delivery nurse, Truman Sayers." Even though Ren had no claims on the man, it hurt that he looked so happy to see Carmella.

"That dog."

Ren sighed. "No, he's not a dog, Kara. He's not doing anything wrong. I never even called him. He's got a life to live too."

"But he was openly flirting with you at Wal-Mart! And look how familiar he is with Carmella."

Kara was right. Tru was laughing at something Carmella said, and he put his arm around her and squeezed. You could tell he cared for her. That couldn't have happened overnight.

"He looks so . . . taken."

Kara sighed with exasperation. "Blasted Carmella. You know, the ballet director's about to fire her. She's a total donut hound — just can't get enough of 'em. And Tru doesn't know it yet, but she's merely toying with him. There are others —"

"But none of that's true!" said the young woman in front of them in line. Apparently, she had been listening to them, and she frowned at them as she spoke. "None of that's true about either of them."

Kara and Ren stood there, mute, staring at this younger version of the woman Kara had just called a donut hound.

Ren said, "We didn't really —"

"And her name's not Carmella. It's Anna."

"Anna," they both repeated, like moronic robots.

She turned and paid for her drinks before speaking again. Kara and Ren shot dismayed glances at each other.

As the girl walked away, she glanced at them. "And she's not dating Tru. She's his sister." She turned and walked two steps before addressing them again. "And so am I."

She headed toward Tru and Anna just as the young man inside the concession booth said, "What can I get for you?" Both Kara and Ren continued to stare after the girl, appalled at what was about to happen.

"Ladies?" the young man said. "Can I take your order?"

"Water!" Kara said, without looking away from the girl. "Two bottles of water . . . she's going to tell him what we said!"

Frozen on the spot, Ren watched the young woman take her seat on the other side of Tru.

"There you go," the fellow in the booth said. "Four dollars, please."

Ren heard Kara's hand slam money on the counter.

"Don't do it, little sister," Kara muttered.

The girl started talking, very animatedly, and both Tru and Anna were clearly enthralled with what she was saying.

Ren was vaguely aware of a voice from the concession stand. "Miss? You want your change? Miss?"

"What do we do?" Ren said in panic. "She's going to point —" And no sooner had Ren said it than the girl was doing it. She saw them, the two pillars of salt at the concession stand, and her eyes grew wide. Ren could see her lips saying, "There!" as she pointed.

In the same instant, Kara's hand closed quickly around Ren's forearm, and she yanked her away. "Run!" Kara said.

Ren blindly ran with her a short distance, and then she stopped abruptly. "Run? What are we, ten years old?"

Kara stopped running too. "Sorry." She grimaced. "I freaked out a little there."

Ren looked behind them. They were out of Tru's line of vision. "Kara, we have to go talk to them."

"What? After what we said?" She shook her head. "Look, let's take the back way around to our blanket. Pretty soon it'll be dark and they'll never spot us."

"They're going to see us! This isn't downtown Manhattan, Kara! We can't just blend.

Tru will recognize us as soon as he sees us."

"Maybe not! He probably won't remember me, and you look like Harpo Marx."

"Groucho!" That turned a few heads.

"Whatever! I'm telling you, Ren, if we lay low 'til dark, he doesn't have to know it was us saying that stuff."

"Great plan, Agent 86. But remember? You mentioned the Wal-Mart thing."

Kara smacked her palm against her forehead. "Sorry about that, Chief."

"Besides," Ren said, "what if I finally get the nerve to call him after this? As soon as his little sister sees me, I'm busted."

Kara opened her mouth to argue but then changed her mind. She sighed, resigned. "You're right. Should we just crawl over, or do you want to wait 'til we're closer before we grovel?"

They waited until they were closer, and grovel they did.

"I'm so sorry," Ren said to the back of Tru's head, after they maneuvered their way between picnic blankets and lawn chairs to reach him. And, oh goodness, Ren was distracted by the subtle wave in his hair at the base of his neck.

He had been chatting with his sister, Anna. As he turned to look at Ren, his

61

younger sister looked at them and gasped. "That's them! They're the ones I told you about!"

"We *tried* to tell you," Kara said. "We didn't mean any harm to Anna. We were just —"

"Do we know each other?" Anna asked.

"Rennie!" Tru said. Ren was sure she saw him do a double take on her hair. "Anna, Michelle, this is the woman I mentioned. From Wal-Mart. And this is her friend, Kara."

Anna said to Ren, "You're the one who fainted?"

Ren felt the heat run up her cheeks. "That's me, yes."

Young Michelle still seemed stunned. She pointed at Ren. "You're the one he thought was so nice?"

Ren wasn't sure if anyone heard her groan. "I'm just so sorry. We were joking around back there. I really *am* nice. I mean, I'm not nice a hundred percent of the time, of course. I'm not perfect, but —"

"So, how do you two know me?" Anna asked them.

Kara shook her head. "We don't. Michelle told us your name."

Anna looked at her sister. "Michelle, you didn't tell us you knew them."

Michelle, Kara, Tru, and Ren all said various versions of "she doesn't!"

"Look, I apologize, Anna," Kara said. "This was my fault. Ren and I were playing a stupid game in the snack line —"

"She called you a donut dog," Michelle told Anna.

"Donut *hound*," Kara and Ren both said without thinking.

Tru laughed. So did Anna, and Ren knew at once that she and Anna would be just fine.

"But Kara wasn't really talking about you," Ren told her. "She was making up a story, a life story about you —"

"I just picked a stranger out of the crowd, ya see," Kara said.

"And she just happened to choose you," Ren said.

"Ah," Anna said. "Well, did you say anything nice about me?"

"Oh, sure!" Kara said. "You were a famous ballerina! It was all pretty good stuff, until we thought you were dating Tru."

An excruciating silence fell between that sentence and the *Riverdance* MC's voice over the PA system. The show was about to start. Ren dropped her head, feeling shyer than a schoolgirl. She remembered her creepy hair color and just wanted to run and hide. "We'd better get back to our spot."

As they stood, Ren looked at Anna. "I'm really sorry, Anna. Please forgive us."

She smiled. "No problem, Ren."

Ren stole a glance at Tru. Not only was he smiling a gorgeous smile at her, but he was standing up too. "I'll walk you to your seats."

"No, really — ouch!" Kara had pinched her the moment she tried to protest. Kara and Ren said their goodbyes. Even Michelle managed a smile for them.

The three of them wove through people, blankets, and coolers. The music had begun, and the crowd was cheering. Once they reached their chairs, Tru tried unsuccessfully to say something to Ren. He put his mouth closer to her ear. He felt warm, and he smelled like soap. Admittedly, Ren enjoyed letting him try to communicate for a while before signaling that she couldn't hear him. He reached into the back pocket of his jeans, retrieved his wallet, and pulled out another business card. He signaled his request for a pen, a need Kara already saw coming. She handed him one from her purse before kneeling to make herself busy retrieving food from the picnic basket.

Tru jotted a few things down and handed Ren the card, grinning. She looked down and saw he had circled his telephone number several times and put a couple of exclamation points next to it. He had also drawn an arrow so that Ren would flip the card over. He had written two words that, at first, made her cringe. "Your hair . . ."

Good grief. Here Ren was so busy noticing his clean soapy smell that she had let him linger around her chemical-stinking, horror-show freak hair. She looked up at him, awaiting maybe a look of puzzlement, like *What happened?* or *What were you thinking?*

But the moment he caught her eye, he brought his fingers to his lips and did that wonderful thing French chefs do when they taste something delicious. He kissed his fingertips lightly and sent the kiss airborne in the direction of her dreadful hair. Ren knew her hair didn't merit the gesture. She had a pretty good idea he was being gracious because he could tell she was self-conscious.

It was all she could do not to give him a big hug and kiss. Instead, she grinned right back at him, pretended she had a telephone to her ear, and then pointed at him. He nodded, and they both mouthed goodbyes.

If Kara hadn't eventually tugged on the cuff of Ren's jeans, Ren might have stood

there watching him leave until the show
came to an end.

Six

"Okay, so what happened to you yesterday?" Kara asked when Ren walked into her gym two days later. "Did you call Tru?" She handed Ren a towel from behind the counter. "Did you guys get together?"

"Whoa. Slow down there, little missy." Ren draped the towel over her shoulder. "I never said I was going to call him yesterday."

Kara walked with her to the dressing room. "No, but you did say you were going to come in to work out. And you never showed. I just figured, you know . . ."

"That I jumped right on the phone and asked him on a date?" Ren laughed and put her hand out, as if she wanted to shake Kara's. "Hello, there. You don't seem to know me. Ren Hurd's the name."

"Nuh-uh." Kara tilted her head and gave her a look of pity.

After a gasp of realization, Ren said, "I mean, Ren Young." She stomped lightly on the floor. She couldn't believe she still used her married name so naturally. "Ren Young," she repeated. She found an open locker and started to change into workout clothes. "Anyway, I haven't called him." She breathed deeply and then looked at Kara. "And if you'd check your answering machine once in a while, young lady, you'd have gotten my message yesterday, saying I had papers to grade so I wasn't coming in until this evening."

"Ah, sorry. I'm getting better with checking messages, really. Half the time I do remember. But the other half . . ." Kara lifted a shoulder. "So. Are you going to call him tonight?"

Ren laughed. "What is your rush? I'll call him when it feels right to call him, okay?"

Kara lifted her eyebrows and acted as if she were walking out of the changing room. "Fine. I just want to make sure you get things rolling so you'll have a date to bring."

Ren looked down to tie her shoe as Kara spoke, and it took her a moment to hear what Kara had said. Then she shot her head upright and saw that Kara had stopped at the entrance, smiling at her. She looked ready to burst.

"What did you say?" Ren asked. "Bring a date to what?" She was still holding her other shoe in her hand when she stood upright and gave Kara her full attention. "Kara? Are you —"

Kara reached her left arm forward as if she were a crossing guard, halting traffic. Then she dropped her hand down to show off the brilliant engagement ring she was wearing.

Considering the route Kara and Gabe had taken — choosing to avoid dating, to become very good, platonic friends, and then to court each other for nearly a year, with marriage in mind — you'd think an engagement would be anticlimactic.

Tell that to the crowd of people outside that dressing room, who heard Ren screaming wild-woman style as she jumped all over the place like her second graders on an after-lunch sugar buzz.

Kara and Ren were still hugging and laughing in childlike joy when Kara's co-worker, Tiffany, rushed into the changing room.

She tsked in disappointment and looked at them as if they were wearing sweatpants at an inaugural ball. They didn't let her sour attitude stop them from enjoying the moment.

"Let me guess," Tiffany said. "They've extended the all-you-can-eat hours at the

Ponderosa."

Ren looked at Tiffany. What could you say about her? She was as physically perfect as she was emotionally vacant. Beautiful and selfish, gorgeous and calculating. In the two years Ren had known her, she'd found herself alternately feeling sorry for her and steeling herself for her inevitable verbal attacks.

Such as the Ponderosa comment. Neither Kara nor Ren were heavy, but Tiffany had a way of striking at that universal female *thing*. For a moment Ren actually felt her hips spread like Jell-O on a hot plate.

She fought against the urge to strike back. This particular piece of news carried a bit of weight with Tiffany.

"Tiffany!" Ren deliberately kept her voice light. "Congratulate Kara! She and Gabe are engaged!"

Although Tiffany looked poised to deliver another barb, she was suddenly silent, save a tiny intake of breath. She had always had a crush on Gabe, despite his efforts at discouraging her.

Kara shot a glance at Tiffany and gave her the friendliest smile Ren had ever seen. Ren loved Kara — the girl never liked hurting people if she could help it.

Finally, Tiffany lifted her eyebrows and

shrugged a shoulder. "Oh. Well. Congratulations, I guess." She blew out a quick breath of air. "Took him long enough to make up his mind, didn't it?"

Kara's smile didn't waiver a jot. She just gave Tiffany a quick nod and spoke gently. "It's an important decision."

"So tell us about the proposal," Ren said. She didn't like the idea of Kara having to defend anything about the event. She deserved this happiness. "How did he ask you?"

Tiffany put her hand up as she turned to leave. "I'll have to hear about it later. I have an aerobics class to teach."

Ren looked at her watch after Tiffany left. The class didn't start for another half hour.

"Never mind," Kara said, putting her hand over Ren's watch. "Thanks for giving her a reason to leave." She grasped Ren's other wrist and they both giggled again.

"He asked this morning," Kara said, releasing Ren and looking at the ring. "I went into the deli to grab a quick breakfast with him, and he totally ticked me off by insisting I have eggs."

Ren frowned. "So to make it up to you, he proposed?"

Kara rolled her eyes at Ren. "He had cooked it into the eggs."

"Ick! The ring?"

She nodded. "Fried. Sunny side up. It was just under the white part. You know, that part near the center." She smiled at Ren. "He didn't even break the yokes."

Ren nodded. "Boy can cook some eggs. Very important in a fiancé."

Kara's grin spread, and she did a little hop. "I have a fiancé!"

Ren laughed and put on her other sneaker. "Yes, you do! And when will you have a husband? Have you guys set a date?"

"The week before Christmas. Gabe's worried he'll forget our anniversary every year if he doesn't have a worldwide event to remind him it's coming."

Ren shook her head. "Gotta love 'im. He does have a bit of a forgetfulness issue. At least he's doing something about it. Will that give you enough time to prepare?"

Kara waved the idea aside with a flip of her hand. "Oh, sure. It's going to be a simple wedding."

They walked out of the dressing room together.

"Yeah, simple," Ren said, smiling at her. "I thought my marriage to Greg would be simple too, but things have a way of getting complicated."

Ren stopped in her tracks when she realized the words she had used. "I-I meant my *wedding* to Greg."

Kara put her hand on Ren's back. "I knew what you meant."

Before Ren could say anything else, Kara smiled at the handsome young man walking toward them.

"Well, if it isn't himself," Kara said to him. She walked up to him and gave him a kiss on the cheek.

Ren gave him a hug. "Congratulations, Gabe!"

"Thanks, Rennie." He hugged her back before turning to Kara and draping an arm across her shoulders. "Finally talked her into it."

"Well, I guess so," Ren said. "What girl wouldn't want to marry a guy who serves eggs like you do?"

Ren was honestly happy for them. Inspired by them. But something in her stomach bothered her. As if she had once felt as they did about marriage, but . . . what?

But she had been wrong. That was it. She was feeling fear.

She was probably going to date again at some point. But when she slipped about her marriage to Greg a moment ago, she had suffered a stab of pain in her heart. Those stabs were slowly losing their strength, and

Ren knew that was a good thing. But what if she went through this whole awful process of elation, disillusion, and loss again?

How many times could she go through that before becoming bitter? Insecure? Downright angry?

The longer she put off dating, the less likely she'd have to find out.

SEVEN

"Ah, yes, Ms. Young," the elegant maître d'
said to Ren. "Your mother called just a
while ago. She thought you might arrive
before she did." He flashed a professional
smile at her. "Let me show you to your
table. Right this way, please."

With a quick glance Ren judged this a
"man's" restaurant. Rich mahogany walls,
deep hunter green carpet, and polished
brass trim everywhere. Cigars and personal
wine caches at the maître d's station. And
— despite the hearty aroma of grilled steaks
and seafood — Ren could smell those cigars
being smoked too. No nonsmoking section
here, she'd bet. She half expected moose
heads and hunting rifles to adorn the walls.

She followed the man through the darkened rooms to one of the restaurant's more
private corners. Not a window in sight.
Despite the glass-covered candles at each
table, Ren felt as if they were having lunch

in a beautifully furnished basement.

Places like this reminded her fondly of her dad, in a way, but they also depressed her for their lack of brightness. Ren thought her mother continued dining at her husband's old haunts these two years since he died because she missed him. The whole place had such a "gentleman's" air about it, as if everyone would don monocles and sniff brandy at any moment. No wonder her mother had asked her to dress conservatively.

"I'm bringing a surprise for you," her mother had said this morning, when she told Ren where to meet her. She called from the beauty salon, and Ren had to compete with the hair dryer for her attention. Her mother hung up before Ren could ask for details about what she was bringing.

Ren's mother, Clarissa Young, was raised around wealth and could be very generous, financially. But, at the risk of sounding ungrateful, Ren tended to cringe when Clarissa warned her about one of her surprises. She and Ren had significantly different taste in just about everything, especially fashion. Clarissa had never owned a pair of jeans — not even designer jeans. Ren was usually in denim within minutes after getting home from work. And, even at her most materialistic, Ren had always dressed well on the job or when going out, but never with an eye on whose label she sported, if anyone's. Nevertheless, her closet was full of expensive, but over-the-top, designer outfits and accessories, all courtesy of Clarissa. Party dresses with enough ruffles to embarrass Madame de Pompadour. Beaded handbags that weighed a ton but were too small to carry anything but a lipstick. And shoes made of some of the most bizarre, extraterrestrial-looking reptile skins Ren had ever seen.

So she had to work at suppressing her shock when Clarissa walked up to the table, perfectly coifed, dressed in an elegant off-white silk dress, and without a package for her daughter. Instead, she was linked arm in arm with an attractive older man. Clarissa hadn't dated, as far as Ren knew, since her dad died. Yet here Clarissa was, her blue eyes sparkling, smiling with admiration at this tanned, silver-haired fellow in a sharp, tailored suit. Ren had never stopped to consider whether her mother's dating would bother her. But now she found she kind of liked the idea. This would be good for Clarissa. It was time for her to find love again . . . and to stop calling Ren all the time.

But the first thing Clarissa did was to stop and look aghast at Ren's hair. Until that moment Ren had begun to think the black color was less arresting than it was at first. Apparently not.

Clarissa pursed her lips and patted at her own uniformly dyed blondish-gray hair before regaining polite control of herself. "Rennie, darling, I want you to meet Gus Kendrick. Gus, this is my daughter, Ren." Clarissa was as thrilled with Gus as Ren had ever seen her.

Gus took Ren's hand and gave it a strong shake. He had big, warm hands. "Your mother's told me wonderful things about you, Ren."

Ren smiled. "That's good to hear. Nice meeting you, Gus. I suppose you're the surprise Mother mentioned on the phone this morning."

At Clarissa's wild-eyed reaction, Ren realized she had said the wrong thing. "I mean —"

"Sit, Gus, please," Clarissa said. She sat across from Ren, and Gus sat in the chair between them. Only then did Ren see that the table had been set for three. So he *had* been the surprise her mother planned. Clarissa placed her hand on top of Gus's and was about to say something to him when the waiter stepped forward.

"Ah, good afternoon, Mr. Kendrick," he said to Gus.

"Edward," Gus said, smiling at the waiter.

Edward looked at Clarissa and nodded at her. "Nice to see you again, Mrs. Young."

Hmm. It sounded as if this twosome had been meeting for a while. Well, that was fine. Clarissa wasn't trying to replace Ren's dad. She was just trying to move on. But Ren couldn't believe her mother hadn't even hinted at this new man in her life. It might have been fun to have her confide in Ren about him. To huddle together and talk, girlfriend-like, about how they met at one of her charity functions or wherever. Clarissa and Ren hadn't been that way with each other since . . . well, ever, really. But it would have been nice just this once.

Edward, the waiter who knew more about Clarissa's social life than Ren did, left menus with them and went to fill their drink order. Both Clarissa and Gus ordered cocktails. Ren's request for iced tea resulted in a subtle scowl from her mother, as if Ren had just stood on a soapbox and delivered a Carrie Nation speech verbatim.

They looked over their menus. Ren hadn't yet decided between the almond-encrusted salmon and the rack of lamb when Gus said,

"So, Ren. What can you tell me about yourself?"

Ren put her finger on her place on the menu, as if interrupted from a novel. Gus was smiling at her expectantly, as was Clarissa. Except Clarissa's smile looked pasted on, just a little. As if it hurt.

"I teach second grade. I live in Leesburg."

"Yes, I know Leesburg well," said Gus. "Excellent place to invest your real estate dollar these last few years."

"Gus is in real estate," Clarissa said to Ren. With a smile of pride, she told Gus, "Ren's in the Berkingham development."

He nodded with approval. "Good development, Berkingham."

Ren smiled. "Yeah. Nice neighbors, pretty yards. My husband and I bought the house about five years ago, when we first married. I certainly couldn't afford to buy there now. I'm . . . not sure if Mother's mentioned that I'm divorced."

Clarissa smiled at Gus. "It's been over a year now."

"Yes," Gus said to Ren. "Yes, of course Clarissa mentioned it. I'm divorced as well."

That was kind, Ren thought, his mentioning that he, too, was divorced. It made her feel that he wasn't judging her. Not that his judgment of her mattered that much. But if he were seeing her mother, Ren would hope he wasn't some snob who would consider her a loser because her husband had dumped her.

Edward came and took their lunch orders, after which Gus looked at Ren again. "So. What else can you tell me that Clarissa hasn't yet?" He smiled at Clarissa.

Ren was starting to feel as if she were on a job interview. These wide-open questions weren't easy for her to handle. When she tried to think of something to say about herself, she seemed to come up short. Was her life that boring?

"I'm . . . oh! I'm a Christian. Maybe Mother mentioned that?"

Clarissa suddenly jumped in like a trial attorney. "Yes, yes, aren't we all, dear," she said with a dismissive chuckle and a cautious glance at Gus.

His cell phone rang, and he pulled it out of his jacket pocket. After glancing at the incoming number, he said, "Excuse me, ladies. I have to take this. Be right back."

Clarissa smiled graciously at him as he rose and walked away. The moment he was out of earshot, she turned on Ren as if they were conspirators in some fraudulent caper.

"What in heaven's name are you doing, Ren?" She spoke under her breath. "Are you deliberately trying to drive him away?"

"What?" Ren was shocked. "What did I say?"

"And your hair! Have you gone hippy on me or something?"

"Hippy? Mother, hippies are, you know, from forty years ago." Wow, where was *she* during the sixties?

"You know what I mean," Clarissa said. "You're all black-haired like those teenagers who wear the ripped clothes and tattoo their tongues —"

"I think you mean pierce their tongues —"

"Don't change the subject," Clarissa snapped. She gestured toward Ren's hair. "What is this? Some lifestyle change now that Greg's gone?"

Ren had to laugh. She didn't mean any disrespect, but you'd think she'd shown up dressed as the Cat Woman or something. "Stop worrying, Mother. I just messed up on a hair rinse I did at home. It'll fade soon enough."

That seemed to calm Clarissa a bit. "Well," she sniffed, frowning at Ren's hair. "I only hope you've learned your lesson."

"What lesson would that be?"

Clarissa blinked slowly to emphasize her edict. "You do things on the cheap, you get what you pay for."

Ren would have argued, of course, if Clarissa hadn't been right in this case. But Ren made a mental note to color her hair at home again next time and prove Clarissa wrong. In the meantime, she tried to change the subject. "Gus seems nice."

Clarissa altered her expression at once, arching one eyebrow. "Very nice. A real catch."

Ren smiled. She didn't know Clarissa was after a catch. "Well, well. I'm happy for you, Mother."

Clarissa nodded. "Yes, as you should be —" Abruptly she stopped talking and looked at Ren, frowning. "What do you mean, you're happy for me?"

Now what had Ren done wrong? "It's just, I'm pleased to see you dating. I think it's healthy for you to —"

Clarissa's jaw dropped, and she raised her hand to stop Ren. "Darling, you misunderstand. I have absolutely no interest in dating anyone. Your father was the only man for me. Those days are over."

"But . . ." Ren looked in the direction Gus had gone. "What are you doing with Gus, then? I don't —" And it finally hit her. She looked at Clarissa, horror in her eyes. "You don't mean to tell me he's here —"

"Yes, Ren." Clarissa spoke to her as if she were a child who had just figured out the whole Santa/Tooth Fairy/Easter Bunny thing. "Gus is here to meet you." She sat back and chuckled at Ren's misunderstanding. "Me. Dating. That really is *so* humorous."

Ren was speechless. And trapped. He'd be back any minute.

Eww. He'd be back to scrutinize her some more. To size her up. Maybe even to ask her out. In front of her mother! Her mother, who had switched from surprising her with designer frou-frou to surprising her with lecherous old men on the hunt for young divorcees.

"I-I've got to go." Ren started to stand.

Clarissa sat up straight. "What? But you can't just leave, Ren. The man's bought us lunch. What are you thinking?"

Ren sat down and whisper-yelled at her. "Me? What am *I* thinking? Mother, why did you just spring him on me like this?"

Clarissa leaned forward and kept her voice low. "Now, Ren, you and I both know you'd never have shown up here if I had told you beforehand."

Ren's eyes and mouth popped open. She held her hands, palms up, as if Clarissa had just uttered something worth getting a hold of. "And does that not tell you how wrong this was?"

Clarissa glanced quickly over her shoulder. "Enough, now. Here he comes. I expect you to behave."

Ren looked over at Gus as he approached. With her newfound knowledge, Ren had gained insight. Rather than the tanned, well-dressed, silver-haired older gent who walked in with Clarissa on his arm, he was an oily dandy. A gray-haired, dirty old man. Ren saw him glance quickly at her legs before he reached the table.

Lord, please help me, Ren prayed. *Please get me out of this mess. I don't want to be rude or to lie or anything like that. But please, please, please, Lord, keep him from asking me out. Strike him dumb if You have to. Strike me dumb, if it will help. I'm fully open to suggestions. Amen.*

Gus sat down looking pleased, either with the results of his phone call or with the lunch the waiter placed before them. Or maybe in anticipation of his first date with Ren.

She couldn't help the shudder that ran through her, and she saw a flicker of warning in Clarissa's eyes.

"Well, this looks great," Gus said, sounding a bit like Tony the Tiger. Then he looked directly at Ren. "Where were we?"

Her mouth was so dry. How had she not seen it? He wasn't trying to charm his date's daughter. He was flirting with her! Ren took a sip of her iced tea and stalled.

As she often did when nervous or just thinking something through, Ren reached up and fiddled with the tiny golden cross she wore on a necklace. And the blessing happened right then and there.

"You wanted to know more about me, I think, Gus. I mentioned that I was a Christian. That's pretty important to know about me. Really strong Christian. How about you?"

"Now, Ren —" Clarissa said.

"I mean, we could talk about careers and hobbies and real estate," Ren said. "But there are certainly more important things in life, don't you think?"

He actually perked up at that. So he wasn't just a geriatric babe hound. He had the look of someone who enjoyed a philosophical talk as much as the next person did. "Certainly! And faith is important, yes."

Ah, good. This didn't have to be a total washout. Although, nothing, not even a shared love for the Lord, would make Ren go out with this old dude.

"But," he said, with a hint of admonishment in his voice, "religion is one of those things that shouldn't be discussed in mixed company, as far as I'm concerned."

Clarissa sighed, embarrassed by her daughter.

Ren sighed too, but for a different reason. She just wished she always felt as bold as she did at that moment. "Oh, but I'm not talking about religion. I'm talking about a relationship. I mean, I know I'm going to heaven when I die, Gus, because Jesus paid for my sins when He died on the cross."

Despite Clarissa's groan, Ren asked him again, "How 'bout you?"

Gus choked, literally, either on his food or on his words. He suddenly had a rousing hack attack, prompting their waiter's attention and the turned heads of nearby diners. With his napkin Gus wiped his watering eyes and struggled to slow the coughing down. He brushed his hand through his hair, strands of which now flopped, disheveled, on his forehead. He downed his cocktail and looked as uncomfortable as a middle schooler at his first dance. Then he attempted to resume some normalcy, but Ren had to say she'd never seen a man eat filet mignon that fast. He was polite, finished his lunch like a good boy, paid the check, and left.

It was amazing. Despite Clarissa's appalled expression, Ren felt as if she had witnessed a miracle in Gus.

It was almost as if he had been struck dumb.

EIGHT

Monday morning, back at school, Ren stood before Sandy's office door and read the sign: Guidance Counselor. The very person she needed to see. Sandy had served as Ren's guidance counselor more than once before. Ren knocked and then noticed her hand was trembling. She didn't have to dig deep to figure out why she was shaky.

For starters, her mother had called that morning and attempted one of her control-freak numbers on Ren, this time with regard to one of her charity events.

"You can't just throw away perfectly eligible men like Gus Kendrick and hope to ever find a suitable husband, Ren. You've done absolutely nothing constructive for your social life since Greg left. I really must insist that you come with me to the upcoming High Blood Pressure Ball."

The *what?* Ren snorted and said, "High Blood Pressure Ball. Sounds like some kind of physical rehab tool or something."

Clarissa didn't laugh.

No doubt, Clarissa's typical crowd would attend the event. Snooty old women who had outlasted their wealthy husbands. Men like Gus, who hoped to feel virile by dating women younger than their daughters. And bored trust funders with allowances as large as their egos. But Clarissa was certain Ren would find Husband Number Two among the attendees.

"And this time he'll be from money," she said.

"Yeah, and he'll be Dad's age, Mother. I never wanted a rich husband. Just one who would accept me for who I am."

"Well, darling, right now you have neither. Is that how you want it, really?"

Ren let that one go. She was certain that sometimes her mother's sharp comments were the result of her loneliness since her dad died. And he was no longer around to chide Clarissa gently when she found fault with Ren.

She didn't seem to find fault with Ren's older brother, Matt. He and Ren hadn't yet figured out why. He also had made the "mistake" of marrying for love, not money. His wife, Sybil, adored him and was a terrific stay-at-home mom to their two daughters. Matt's veterinary practice was successful but not something that ever landed him on the society page of the local newspaper. Yet his situation was, apparently, satisfactory to Clarissa, while Ren's never had been.

With Ren, Clarissa let zingers fly at random, but Ren seldom bothered to address them, especially since becoming a Christian and trying to control her tongue. For that matter, even Ren's accepting Christ and changing some of her priorities — about her profession and lifestyle choices — seemed to have hurt Clarissa's assessment of her. Ren appeared to be getting farther and farther from Clarissa's concept of the ideal daughter.

In the end Ren struck a plea bargain with her mother about the Heart Attack Ball, or whatever it was called. They would shop together for dresses (ball gowns, Clarissa corrected her), as long as she understood Ren wasn't committed to going.

But they both knew Clarissa was probably going to get her way.

And on top of the call from her mother, Ren had to talk with Casey this morning about the change in adoption plans. That was why Ren was at Sandy's office door. She just didn't know how she was going to do this and still wear a happy face for Casey.

But when Sandy opened the door, her upbeat expression made Ren feel hopeful, for some reason. "Ah, great!" Sandy said, wiping donut crumbs from her face. "Come on in, Ren. Change in plans for our talk with Casey." She looked at Ren's hair. "Wow."

Ren waved it off. "I know. It was even worse before I put the lighter color on it. It'll fade, eventually. I put in a prayer request at church."

Sandy looked at her blankly. "Huh?"

Ren shook her head. "Never mind. Stupid joke." She walked into Sandy's small, cheery office. Soft morning sunlight filtered in through the peach-colored blinds. Ren didn't remember offices like Sandy's from her school days. In what Ren would call organized chaos, Sandy had toys, stuffed animals, dolls, and games everywhere. She certainly knew how to make a trip to the counselor's office as inviting as possible.

Ren sat in one of the little-people chairs in the play area. "So, what do you mean, a change in plans? It's only eight in the morning. What's happened?"

"Two things, believe it or not." Sandy grabbed some papers from her desk. "I had messages waiting for me when I got in." With the grace of a swan, she settled onto another tiny chair, facing Ren.

Ren had to hand it to her — Sandy might be a plus-sized gal, but the woman looked ten times more comfy than Ren did on munchkin furniture.

"First, the easy one," Sandy said. "The Hallstons — Casey's foster family? They finally got word. The job change didn't go through. They're staying here."

Ren gasped and broke into a smile. "And they want to keep Casey under their care?"

"Yep," Sandy said. "Not terrific news for them, apparently, since it was going to be a promotion, but good news for Casey. And maybe for you too, Ren."

"Well, I'm thrilled he isn't going to have to change families again anytime soon. But this really just means I might be able to put off the inevitable for a while longer. Let's face it. At some point I'm going to have to tell him that Greg and I aren't going to adopt him after all."

"Not Greg and you, no. But single-parent adoptions *are* possible, remember."

Ren sighed, looking Sandy in the eye. "I don't think that's God's will for me, Sandy. I still feel strongly that Casey needs two parents."

Sandy patted her hand and nodded. "Okay, I understand. But you let me know if God tells you otherwise, and I'll see what I can do." She sat back and cocked her head at Ren. "How're things going with the handsome nurse?"

Ren laughed at her obvious train of thought. "We haven't even had a full conversation yet. I don't think we'll be picking out china patterns anytime soon."

Sandy smiled. "Can't blame a romantic for hoping."

Ren nodded. "I hear ya, sister. I never said anything about not hoping." She pointed to the papers Sandy held in her lap. "So what was the second message about this morning?"

"Oh. Yeah. Kind of strange, really." Sandy grimaced and picked up a sheet she had taken notes on. "Britney Michaels," she read before looking up at Ren. "Sound familiar?"

Ren shook her head. "Hmm. Vaguely. Who is she?"

"She's Casey's mom."

Despite Casey's haphazard origins, he went by his father's surname, so his mother's name was foreign to Ren.

"His mom? She called you? Isn't she still in jail?"

"Prison, yeah," Sandy said. "And she

didn't call. Social services called on her behalf."

Ren felt acid churn in her stomach. "Why do I have a bad feeling about this, Sandy? What's going on?"

"Ever hear about the MILK program?"

"Milk? Like what we drink?"

"Mothers Inside Loving Kids," Sandy said. "MILK. It's a program that allows kids to visit their moms for several hours at a time. And under less scrutiny than usual. Britney wants Casey to come visit her in prison."

Ren put her hand to her stomach. "You're kidding me. They're not going to make him go, are they?"

Sandy sighed. "I think it's probably her right to see him, Ren, and Casey's not of an age to refuse."

Ren stood up and paced the small office, dodging bins of Legos and hand puppets. "This is ridiculous. She's a drug addict, Sandy. And isn't she in there for theft or something?"

"Grand larceny."

"Grand larceny! How can this be in Casey's best interest? What's this going to do to him? He's so *okay* right now, despite how she neglected him when she had him."

"This doesn't necessarily mean she'll get

him back, Ren, even if she decides she wants him when she finishes her prison time. She lost custody of him, so he's still available for adoption."

Ren wanted to fill out the papers right then and there.

"If it makes it any easier for you to handle," Sandy said quietly, "women don't qualify for the MILK program without becoming model prisoners. They also have to take a parenting class. And pass an interview to judge their efforts at rehab. It sounds as if she's trying to reform."

Ren brought her hands to her temples and rubbed. "It does, you're right. But, Sandy, just listen to what you're saying. Grand larceny. Prison. Rehab. Trying to reform." She looked at Sandy. "Not exactly a *Leave It to Beaver* kind of mom, is she? I don't mean to judge her, but Casey deserves more than that, doesn't he?"

Just then they heard a muted knock at the door from a small, balled-up fist. Sandy got up and opened the door to Casey, escorted by Mrs. Hallston, his foster mother. Mrs. Hallston was already walking away, but she turned and waved to Sandy, calling, "Thanks, Sandy, I'm late for work! Bye-bye, Casey!"

"Bye," Casey said, waving. As soon as he

saw Ren, he ran into Sandy's office toward her.

Ren squatted down to his level. He threw his warm little arms around her. She hugged him back and just wanted to grab him and run away.

"Hi, buddy." She tousled his blond curls. "Did you have a good weekend?"

He pulled back to look her in the eye, and Ren thought he had a few more freckles on his nose than she remembered.

"Yeah, cool weekend!" His husky little voice bowled her over every time he spoke. "Mr. and Mrs. Hallston took us to the movies. A pirate movie! I got my own bag of popcorn!"

"Ar, matey!" Ren said in a deep voice. "Ye had a treasure, did ye?"

Casey laughed. "Mr. Hallston did a voice like that too. Arrr!"

Sandy had closed her office door and walked back in to join them. She sat in one of the kiddy chairs and pulled up a third. "You like the Hallstons, don't you, Casey?"

He nodded and released his grip on Ren. He bent down to pick up a stuffed animal, a puppy. "They're nice. Nicer than the last ones, the Thurgoods? They didn't like me much."

Sandy patted the chair beside her. "Come

sit, Casey. You can bring the puppy."

He took Ren's hand. "You come, too, Ms. Young."

They formed a small circle, all facing each other. Casey's feet barely touched the floor.

"Casey," Sandy said, "you remember that the Hallstons were going to be moving?"

He nodded, still examining the puppy. "Yeah, but they're not going to anymore. I heard 'em talking. So I can stay with 'em longer." He looked at Ren. " 'Til I can go live with you."

Ren tried not to wince. Sandy cleared her throat. When Ren looked at her, she subtly shook her head. Ren gathered that Sandy didn't want to throw too much at Casey in one sitting.

"Okay," Sandy said to Casey. "That's good. That was one of the things I wanted to tell you, but you already know. So you'll be with the Hallstons for a while longer." She hesitated and looked at Ren before speaking again. Casey looked up at Sandy, expectation in his blue eyes.

Sandy said, "Now, I want to talk with you about another thing, Casey. I know you and Mrs. Glen, the lady from the social services office, have talked before about your mommy, right?"

Casey frowned. "My real mommy, you mean?"

"Yes."

He looked down. "She's too sick for me to be with her." He appeared to be explaining to the puppy. He began rubbing his thumbs over the hard, plastic eyes on the toy. "That's why she forgot about me, 'cause she was so sick."

Ren reached and put her hand on his tiny shoulder. "Honey, she hasn't forgotten about you at all. Even though she was sick, she never, ever forgot about you."

"Casey," Sandy said, leaning forward and gently placing her hand on top of his. "Your mommy has asked if you'd go visit her."

He looked up at Sandy. "At the hospital?" He gave Ren a pleading look. "Do I have to? Will you come too, Ms. Young?"

"I . . ."

Sandy said, "Casey, I'll be going with you, if that's all right with you. Or if you'd rather have Mrs. Glen take you, we can do that."

"I want Ms. Young to take me," Casey said, swinging his legs forward and back.

"See," Sandy said, "only Mrs. Glen or I would be allowed to take you this time. Maybe Ms. Young could go next time. But we'd have to get permission. Okay?"

He continued swinging his legs. Frowning, he studied his puppy. "Why does she want me to visit her? What's she gonna do?"

"Well, Casey," Sandy said, "I'm not sure, to tell you the truth, but I'll be with you when we go. You'll be okay. She's probably going to hug you and tell you she loves you. And she'll probably want to play some games or even shoot baskets with you for a while. There's a gym there where you can play. Could you handle that?"

He looked at Sandy, still frowning. "Yeah, I guess. But, I mean, what's she gonna do after I visit her?"

Ren wondered if Casey was sharp enough to understand that his mother might try to get him back. Ren hated the idea. She said, "After you visit with her, Casey, after you come back here . . ." She glanced at Sandy, who looked worried about what Ren might say. "She's going to miss you all over again and be so happy she got to see you."

Casey looked at her closely. Ren knew he was probably watching her in order to gauge the seriousness of his mother's request. She smiled and raised her brows, willing her eyes to stay dry. She prayed he wouldn't ask her if he was going to have to live with his mother again.

Ren saw his frown relax. He smiled back at her. His trust in her made her heart ache.

So it was arranged.

The morning left Ren with conflicted emotions. She was relieved about the short reprieve from change for both Casey and her, thanks to the Hallstons. But when she thought about that Britney woman possibly getting Casey back and then lapsing back into her old lifestyle . . . well.

Ren felt that she should have a husband before having children, adopted or otherwise. But she couldn't believe that God's will included Casey's living with a single mother who was a drug addict and a felon, versus a single mother like Ren.

The first chance Ren had, she went to the ladies' room to find a private place to pray.

Lord God, sometimes it's just not so clear. I want to do what's right. Please help me recognize the open doors and the shut ones with regard to Casey and me. Help me to see the difference between Your will and mine, Lord. Sometimes it's just not so clear.

NINE

Ren called Kara during her lunch break.

"They'd actually send that poor kid back to a woman who cared more about heroin than her own child?" Kara asked.

Ren ran her hand through her hair. "Insane, huh? But . . . well, to be fair, it sounds as if she's worked pretty hard at rehab." She bit into a carrot stick. "But, you know, you always hear about all those movie stars and sports figures who go to rehab and end right back in the druggie lifestyle a few months later. Imagine little Casey living with that uncertainty."

"Hang on, Ren," Kara said, before responding to someone off to the side: "Yeah, okay. Could you tell her I'll call her right back?"

"I'm sorry. I shouldn't bother you at work."

"No problem," Kara said. "That's just a travel agent calling. I can call her back later."

"Travel agent?"

Ren could hear Kara's grin right through the phone. "Gabe and I are looking into honeymoon packages."

Ren smiled back at her, even though Kara couldn't see her. "Oh, Kara, this is so exciting!"

"Yeah," Kara whispered, as if she were floating. "But, hey, I didn't mean to ignore what you were saying about Casey. Listen, Ren, I know how you feel about single-parent adoption. And you know I agree with you about that — if there's a way for Casey to have a two-parent family, that's the best. But . . ."

Ren sighed. "I know. I'm struggling with the same thoughts. If Britney ends up deciding she wants to play mommy for a while, Casey's not going to be in a two-parent home, anyway. At least with me he wouldn't have to worry about his mother going back to drugs. Or neglecting him while she knocks over a Seven-Eleven."

Kara said, "And he's been thinking all this time that he was going to be with you. Well, you and Greg."

Ren rolled her eyes and rested her forehead in her hand. "Yeah. Frankly, I wish Casey had never heard about the idea. Now there's just one more expectation to be yanked away from him. Greg told him about it, even though Sandy said not to."

Jeremy walked into the lunchroom just then and gave Ren a smile before switching to a look of concern. "You all right, love?"

Kara asked her, "Is that Jeremy?"

"Yeah." Ren nodded at Jeremy. "I'm okay, Jeremy. Just some Casey issues."

"Hey," Kara said, "can you tell him I have to reschedule his training session to six tonight?"

Ren pointed at Jeremy with a carrot stick. "Kara says can you switch your time at the gym to six?"

He shook his head, so Ren just handed him her phone.

"Can't do it, Kara," he said. "Got a hot date. But no matter. I'll ring you tomorrow and we can reschedule. Right. Ta." He gave Ren back her phone and dumped the contents of his lunch bag onto the table.

"Listen," Ren said to Kara, "I should go. But I wouldn't mind a few prayers if you think of it."

"You've got 'em. And try not to worry too much. The Lord's going to look out for Casey. Maybe that will include his being with you. You never know."

Ren nodded. "Yeah. I'll talk with you later."

Jeremy leaned back in his chair as Ren closed her phone. "What's the issue with Casey?"

But she had to give him a shake of the head for an answer as three more teachers walked in with their lunches. Ren knew better than to blab Casey's story all over the school. Jeremy glanced at the other teachers and gave her a quick nod.

He patted the seat next to him, so Ren pulled her lunch over and sat down.

"So who's the hot date?" she asked.

"Katerina, of course," he said, a hint of surprise at her ignorance.

Ren frowned. "Katerina? Isn't she the one you spotted at the restaurant last week?"

He dipped his head. "The very same."

"But I thought you found out she had a boyfriend."

He winked at me. "*Had* is the operative word, Rennie. Had a boyfriend."

"But he showed up at the restaurant while we were all there."

"That was ages ago!" He waved his hand in the air. "Ancient history."

Ren smiled at him. "How ancient are we talking?"

His confident expression wavered just a tad. He glanced in his empty lunch bag and said, "They broke up last night."

Ren snorted. "So you're giving her a whole day to grieve the loss, huh?" She gave him a gentle poke in the ribs. "Please tell me you didn't have anything to do with the breakup?"

Jeremy looked at her, shock in his eyes. "Rennie! You cut me to the quick. Jeremy Beckett will never stoop so low as to interfere in a relationship." He unwrapped his sandwich. "Besides, Katerina — that gorgeous vision — called *me*."

"Mm-hmm. And how did she get your number?"

He paused for a moment, right in the middle of biting into his sandwich. He chewed quickly and then said, "Ah, well, that was an instance of ignorant bliss. I handed her my name and number the moment I approached her last week. How was I to know there was a boyfriend? She hadn't spoken two words to me yet."

Ren shook her head at him. "Very convenient."

He arched an eyebrow at her. "Not all that different from what that bloke did with you at Wal-Mart, eh?"

That caught her off guard. "I wasn't involved with anyone when Tru gave me his card."

Jeremy nodded. "And how, exactly, did he

know this fact?"

"But . . . no. He was only trying to help. He heard that I wanted to adopt —"

"Minor details, love. You can't tell me he wasn't interested in you. How long after he handed you his card did he pull that old trick and casually mention your husband?"

Ren didn't need to review much to remember. She had replayed that scene in her head more times than she liked to admit.

"As a matter of fact, smarty pants, we talked quite a while after he gave me his card. Not a bit of flirtation. And he didn't mention my husband until he offered to help us with the adoption."

Jeremy gave her a haughty lift of his eyebrows. "All right, then. I apologize. Sounds as if you've got a bit of a dim one there, after all."

Ren laughed and punched him in the shoulder. "And I don't *have* him, either."

He gave her his winning, fond smile. "You could, Ren. No doubt you just need to say the word."

Ren couldn't help returning his smile. Good old Jeremy. Such a natural charm. No wonder Katerina was so quick on the rebound.

Jeremy had deftly taken her mind off Casey for a while. He had even redirected her attention to Tru — a much less troublesome issue, but one equally up in the air.

TEN

Ren needed to stop at the local library on the way home from school. They were holding a book she requested, and the hold was about to expire.

"You have to read this book," Kara told her a month or so ago. "I swear, it's the whole single-woman's life all over, and it's hilarious."

The book was *Helena's Search for a Soul Mate (and Other Tales of Horror).* Ren wasn't sure if she was ready to laugh at her enforced state of singlehood, but she knew it was better than crying about it. A healthy dose of chick lit would probably be a good diversion from her worries about Casey and her confusion over God's will for her, adoption-wise, romance-wise, and otherwise.

And for her there was always something therapeutic about a trip to the library. When Ren was given her first library card as a child, she sensed something magical and promising about the place. She loved the fact that there was usually only one copy of each book. Each borrowing seemed special and privileged and full of responsibility and trust. The crinkly plastic covers on the book jackets suggested the importance of protecting these valuable treasures.

She liked that no one ever rushed while at the library, either. Everyone calmly read, or slowly ambled up and down the fiction aisles, searching for the one book that would fit that moment's desires. And the enforced quietness, while annoying to many children, always brought Ren great peace.

But not today. At least not after she had been there a while.

She was fine when she walked in, making her usual beeline for the used-books-for-sale shelf. Even when she was married and earning twice as much as she was now, Ren got a special thrill when she found a good book for a dollar. She didn't know where that came from. Both of her parents were liberal when it came to spending money. But Ren received more enjoyment from unearthing a good, deep-discounted, secondhand book than most women got finding designer duds hidden on a fifty-percent-off sales rack.

After browsing the used books and finding nothing, Ren went to the checkout desk. There was no line, and the young woman behind the desk was engrossed in a thick book until Ren cleared her throat.

She wasn't your stereotypical librarian, that's for sure. She had a dark, sun-worshiper's tan. Her hair was dyed a vivid red. Not redhead red, but red like ketchup. This was clearly no dye-job mistake, as Ren had made with her hair. This was as deliberate as the leopard-print T-shirt and neon-blue rubber bracelet she wore. She looked up and flashed a brilliant, genuine smile at Ren.

"Oh! Sorry! I was so into this." She gestured at her book, which, Ren gathered from a quick, upside-down glance, was some upper-level math textbook way beyond anything Ren had studied at this girl's age.

Ren smiled at her. "No problem. I'm not in a hurry." She handed over her library card. "You have a book on hold for me."

The girl scanned Ren's card across the computer gizmo, studied the screen, and pushed away from the desk. "Yeah. Oh, that's a good one. Really funny. Be just a minute."

As the girl walked to the back room, Ren glanced in the direction of the conference rooms near the library lobby. A crowd of people was emerging from a meeting. Just as Ren was about to look away, she saw him.

Tru was in the thick of the crowd, explaining something to several other people. Her stomach fluttered. He was absolutely mesmerizing to look at. A few wavy strands of his dark hair had dropped down onto his forehead, and he had a faint five o'clock shadow. He had achieved, during a hard day's work, a casually rumpled look, which Ren found utterly appealing. He seemed passionately interested in whatever he was describing, using his hands to enhance his words. Then the man next to him spoke. Tru nodded agreement and listened intently to what the man contributed to the conversation.

His crowd stopped near the library exit. Ren had a sudden urge to get his attention as soon as he seemed detached enough from his group to look in her direction.

Surely God's hand was in this coincidence, wasn't it? Leesburg was a small town, but Ren could have picked up this book anytime over the past week. Why today? Why this moment today, if not because the Lord wanted her to come across Tru yet again?

Ren cocked her head sideways, as if the

gesture would get his attention from afar. Where was that girl with her book? Ren cocked her body sideways, a sailboat keeling over, hoping to stand out in Tru's peripheral vision without drawing too much notice to herself from others.

Ren thought he glanced her way, but their eyes didn't meet, even though his glance prompted a little wave from her before she knew what she was doing. She felt like a groupie standing behind the satin rope beyond the red carpet.

Certainly the ketchup-red girl had found her book by now? A line was starting to form behind Ren. She felt obligated to remain where she was, rather than impose any additional waiting time on those behind her, should the girl return while Ren chased Tru down.

Goodness, he was so wonderful looking — not just handsome, but the animation in his gestures and the engaged interest in his eyes . . .

All right, Ren was going to go ahead and really wave. But the moment she did, a man stepped directly between Tru and her, blocking Tru's vision. So Ren used up her allotment of attention-demanding flapping for nothing. Where was that girl?

There! He looked in her direction. Directly at her. But . . . nothing. No recognition. Could he have forgotten her already? He had asked her to call him. Was he mad at her for not calling yet? He had to understand that this step was a hard one for her to take. She was vulnerable, after all. Was he less sensitive than Ren thought he was?

Or maybe he was just doing one of those zoned-out kind of stares while listening to someone. The kind where you look ahead without really looking ahead. Maybe he was still interested in her but hadn't really focused on her. Still, it was a little disconcerting, considering how quickly Ren had focused on him the second he came within her sight.

"Sorry," the young librarian said with a sweet laugh, forcing Ren to look away from Tru. The girl had returned to her seat at the desk and held the book up to show it to Ren. "It was totally covered up by a big pile of *National Geographic.* What a mess! Sorry to make you wait." She bent sideways in her chair and looked at the line of people behind Ren. "Sorry to make y'all wait."

"That's okay," Ren said, assuming the role of Line Spokesperson and trying to keep the edge of impatience from her voice.

Funky Girl scanned the book's label and waited for the computer printer to ploddingly cough up a due-date receipt for Ren. "I've read this one." She tapped a short, hot-pink fingernail on Ren's book. She really was a dear girl, from what Ren could tell, but Ren wanted her to sense her urgent need to go. "Made me laugh out loud. Lots." She smiled at Ren and waited for them to connect. The poor thing was dealing with a woman possessed.

The receipt had printed. It sat there, ready. Waiting. Glowing. Pulsing. Ren glanced over at the lobby and saw the back of Tru's head as he walked toward the exit with the remnants of his group. Ren gasped and grabbed the book off the counter. "I can't wait to read it!" she blurted.

The girl finally caught on, uttered a little "Oh!" of urgency, and ripped Ren's receipt away from the printer. "Your receipt!" she said, lifting out of her seat to get it to Ren as she dashed away from the desk.

"Thanks! Sorry!" Ren hoped that would keep the girl from thinking Ren was insane or rude.

As the library's automatic doors slid shut behind Tru, Ren tried to use her indoor voice to call his name. He didn't turn, but all was not lost. Ren could catch him in the parking lot.

"Ms. Young!" two little voices chimed at

her from behind.

Ren turned to see Janna and Jimmy, twins from her class. They were with their mother, who was carrying their baby sister or brother — the gender wasn't clear at the moment, and Ren really didn't care, to be honest. But, with a quick sideways glance at the library exit, Ren knew she had to take a moment to at least excuse herself.

"Hi, guys!" she said to the twins. "Wow, don't you have a lot of reading to do!" They were each carrying a pile of books to check out. Ren looked at their mother, who extended one hand to her as she held the baby in her other arm. "Hi, Mrs. Dawes," Ren said, shaking her hand. "I'm so sorry. I'm in a huge hurry to catch someone who just left."

"Oh! Go!"

Ren knew she loved this woman. Excellent mother and fine PTO member.

"Kids, Ms. Young's in a hurry. You'll see her in class tomorrow."

They were all right with that, calling their goodbyes to Ren as she smiled, waved, and hurried away.

She nearly ran right through the sliding glass doors, waiting for them to open. By the time she got outside, Tru was gone. There weren't even any exiting cars to wave down. All was still, as calm as the library itself.

Ren had to deliberately stop herself from saying or thinking a swear word. And, as she always tried to do when that happened, she switched to a quiet prayer instead, asking God for patience and a peaceful heart.

This had to be her first bad experience at her beloved library. She heaved a big sigh. But then she remembered how she felt when she first walked in there tonight. Magical and promising, she had thought. Well, there was no such thing as magic, but there was certainly promise for her as a child of God. She knew that.

Maybe His will had been for her to run across Tru but not to talk with him, necessarily. Maybe just to consider him. Maybe the Lord just wanted her to notice how interested she really was in getting to know Truman Sayers better.

She smiled and reviewed her desperation while waiting in line, inside. Somehow she knew that, despite looking right at her, Tru hadn't seen her. This encounter wasn't for Tru. It was for her. Just for her.

ELEVEN

"Honestly," Clarissa said, walking briskly beside Ren, her shopping bags rustling against her linen suit. "Did you give any thought to your choice of undergarments this morning? That was so embarrassing!"

A cute teenaged boy walked out of the mall's bookstore as they passed. Obviously he heard Clarissa's comment, and he glanced Ren's way before looking down and smirking. Ren waited until he was out of range before she muttered a response.

"Mother, could you save that for later? I didn't realize you and the saleswoman would hang out with me in the dressing room."

"Of course we needed to be in there with you," Clarissa said. "The High Blood Pressure Ball is on Friday. You're in extreme need of emergency fashion guidance."

Ren looked around them. "Well, I'm not eager to discuss the quality of my underwear in front of total strangers."

"Quality!" Clarissa scoffed and pointed toward Ren's chest. "That has nothing to do with quality, believe me."

"But —"

"Is that the kind of thing you buy at Wal-Mart while having your nervous break-downs?"

"It wasn't a nervous breakdown! I told you I was just under a lot of stress that day. I simply fainted, just for a second or two —"

"Is that the kind of thing you used to wear in front of Greg? I mean, did you care at all how he saw you?"

Ren released some of her exasperation in a big, groaning sigh. "Mother, please. Greg saw me as a religious nut. As a boring, no-fun, pain in the neck. It's been a long time since he's cared about my underwear."

Of course, the teenager from the bookstore passed right in front of them again as Ren spoke. This time he chuckled. Ren smacked the palm of her hand against her forehead and hurried on.

She supposed she brought this on herself by dressing so carelessly this morning. She had stayed up the night before reading *Helena's Search for a Soul Mate*. Hilarious novel. This shopping trip with Clarissa loomed in the distance, but Ren needed the laughs she got from the book. As a result, she overslept and had to dash to get dressed and meet Clarissa on time.

Really, the only thing wrong was that the bra Ren grabbed from the drawer was a lacy one. At one point, anyway. The lace had seen better days, Ren would admit, but nothing that a handy pair of scissors couldn't fix. She said as much to Clarissa, who looked at Ren as if she had asked her mother to eat bad cheese.

"When you have to trim your bra, Ren, it's time to throw it away."

She has a point. Ren sighed and gave Clarissa a smile. "Were there any other places you wanted to check for dresses? I mean, ball gowns?"

Clarissa gave her a pert nod and pointed her well-manicured finger straight ahead. "Two, yes. Gucci and Dolce Gabbana."

"Isn't that three?"

Her mother looked at her in dismay. "Ren. Gucci is one." She raised her eyebrows, a look of pity on her face. "D and G is the other." She shook her head. "However do you get along on your own?"

Before Ren could answer her, Clarissa held up an index finger, signaling for her to wait. She pulled her cell phone from her purse and pushed buttons with the skill of a Gen X techie, retrieving telephone directories and who knows what else. Within seconds she had someone on the line. "Yes, Margot, this is Clarissa Young. I'd like a table for two in an hour, near the window." She nodded at the woman's answer. "Wonderful. See you then." She closed her phone and looked at Ren. "We'll have lunch after we shop."

At that precise moment, Ren's attention wandered away from her mother as, just beyond her, Ren locked eyes with none other than her ex-husband.

He broke his stride when he saw her, snide confidence oozing from him like oil. And he was not alone. A woman trailed him slightly, pushing a stroller.

"Well, well, well," he said, lazy humor in his voice. He reeked of strong cologne and cigarettes. He looked at Ren as if he had caught her doing something embarrassing, and despite the nature of her shopping trip, she felt embarrassed.

"Hi, Greg."

He nodded at her. "Ren." He looked at Clarissa, who was the picture of disdain. Ren couldn't remember the last time she saw her mother's nostrils flared like that, but it wasn't when she was happy.

Greg said, "Clarissa, you look as charming as ever."

Clarissa broke into one of the iciest smiles Ren had ever seen, not unlike Cruella De-Vil's. "Gregory. Don't be a pig. Introduce us to your little friend."

Gregory put his arm around his little friend, a woman about Ren's age, with bleached blond hair and very black eye makeup. "Of course!" he said. "Where are my manners?"

"I wouldn't know," Clarissa said, her eyelids slightly lowered.

Greg paused for a second before continuing. "This beautiful woman is Glenna."

The woman smiled, hesitantly, and she instantly appeared more attractive. She looked at Greg, who was studying Ren, before glancing at the baby in the stroller.

"And this is Greg Junior," Glenna said.

Clarissa gasped, and explosions went off in Ren's head. She didn't know what her face looked like at that moment — she was trying to calm everything else down. She was vaguely aware of smiling and reaching out her hand. "Nice to meet you, Glenna. You have a lovely son."

"Greggie's told me about you," she said, shaking her hand. Her palm was wet. "I'm . . . I'm sorry."

Ren realized her face probably broadcasted shock at this development and confusion at Glenna's apology. This was it. This was why he gave Ren the house.

Greg pointed to the nearby food court. He said to Glenna, "Baby, why don't you go grab us a couple pretzels and a soda. I'll be right there."

Glenna looked at him uncertainly, as if every move she made was subject to his authorization. "Oh. Yeah, okay." She smiled at Ren again. "Nice meeting you." She glanced at Clarissa and quickly turned away from the chill.

"Take *him* with you," Greg said.

"Nice meeting you too," Ren called to her as she left with the baby. Before Ren even looked back, Greg practically hissed his next comment.

"That's right. He's almost a year old." He looked directly into her eyes. "And he's mine."

A year? But, how long ago did he leave her? *Don't cry. Don't.*

Ren prayed quickly. *Lord, help me to be gracious.*

Clarissa said to him, "Yours. Yes, well, I'm sure that's a relief. You seem quite proud of yourself."

But not terribly proud of his child.

Greg jutted his chin forward and smiled at Clarissa.

"I suppose someone has to be proud of you," she said. "And I'm sure there's a good explanation for why your child's mother isn't wearing a wedding band."

Greg glared at Clarissa, who glared right back. "Had to get divorced first, didn't I?" he said.

Clarissa laughed at him as if he had said something pitifully stupid. "Please! You've been divorced for a year now. And you walked out on your wife just six months before that. It doesn't take a genius to do the math, *Greggie.* Don't even try to pretend you weren't dealing with that . . . that blonde while you were still married to Ren."

Greg's angry glance shot over to Ren. She couldn't speak, but she was able to look right back at him. Mother was right. That's why Glenna had apologized to her. But the Lord answered her prayer, and she managed to sound at peace when she said, "Congratulations on the baby, Greg. We've got to go now."

Something flashed through Greg's eyes. A brief moment of kindness. It happened so quickly Ren couldn't tell if he felt regret, nostalgia, or pity toward her. But she couldn't stand any of those options right now. She was able to keep from crying until they were well out of the area. Then she sobbed outright.

Clarissa pulled a tissue from her purse and handed it to her. "That lousy so-and-so. Had we known, *you* could have sued *him* for divorce. For adultery! Oh, you could have made him pay."

Ren shook her head. "Mother, don't you get it? I could have sued him for divorce anyway, if I had wanted a divorce. But he's the one who wanted out. He's the one who messed around with someone else. He's the one who . . . who's able to have a baby."

At that, her mother put her arms around her. Clarissa wasn't a terribly affectionate woman, but she came through in these extreme moments. She patted Ren's back. "Come on, now, Rennie. Just because Greg managed to get that Glenna person pregnant doesn't mean you definitely can't have children. Endometriosis doesn't always lead to infertility, you know that."

Ren nodded, her forehead against Clarissa's shoulder. "I know. I just feel as if I should have known about her. How long was he lying to me? Am I that stupid? Do you think everyone knew? Did you know?"

"Oh, Ren, no." She sighed. "This is just confirmation that you're well rid of him.

And you can be sure that anyone who's worth their salt would have told you if they knew. You aren't stupid for not suspecting him. You're trusting. Maybe to a fault. But Greg was just never terribly gifted in the character department. Think about it."

Ren didn't want to think about it. She didn't want to think about Greg, period. Not anymore.

She worked at controlling her tears. "I guess that was just too much stuff to learn in one sitting. No wonder he lost interest in Casey near the end. He was going to have his own son soon."

Clarissa pulled back to look at her. "I want to tell you something, Ren. I'm proud of how you handled that entire situation back there. Well done. Very classy."

Ren thought that was the nicest thing her mother had ever said to her. She smiled through her tears. "Well, it was easy to be classy with you tearing him to shreds like that."

Clarissa cupped Ren's face in her hands. "My darling, that's what mothers are for."

Ren laughed, and so did Clarissa. Ren opened her purse to get another tissue.

Clarissa looked ahead of them. "Now, let's try to have a stiff upper lip, darling. Get your mind on better things. I think we should see what gowns Gucci has to offer. Maybe that brush with Greg will at least serve the purpose of driving you forward. It's time to move on with your life."

As Clarissa talked about ball gowns, charity events, and eligible men, Ren only half listened. She found a tissue in her purse, but she also found something else. She pulled out the business card she had read so many times, and she did feel a fresh breath of encouragement, like a gentle whisper from the Lord. Suddenly it seemed so right.

It was time. Ren was going to call Tru.

Twelve

"I don't know what I was thinking," Ren said to Kara the next day. She wiped her hands on her apron. "There's no way I'm calling Tru."

Kara, who stood beside her at her kitchen counter, dropped her jaw. "What?" She stopped slicing scallions and turned to face Ren, hand on hip. "You were dead certain yesterday that God wanted you to make that call. You said so. And I heard it in your voice."

Ren looked away from her and focused on the wok. She added a plateful of sliced chicken and crushed garlic to the hot oil, sending smoke and fragrant steam heavenward. "I'm going to need those scallions in two minutes. And it's too soon."

"Too soon for the scallions or too soon for Tru?"

Ren sighed. "For Tru." She pointed at the scallions. "Chop, chop."

Kara scowled at her but went back to work. "But why? What about how you felt after you saw him at the library? And after running into Greg? I mean, the divorce was a year ago, and Greg left, what, six months before that? Obviously, he's moved on." She snorted, chopping the scallions more vigorously. "Jerk moved on before he even left you, from the sound of it. You're not waiting for him to come back to you, mistress and child in tow, are you?"

"Of course not." Ren sprinkled cornstarch over the chicken and nodded her head toward a bowl of Chinese mushrooms. "Hand me those wood ears, will you? I've finally accepted that Greg's a lost cause. Someone else's lost cause now. Well, the Lord's lost cause, I guess. But I can't help feeling burned. I'd rather be alone than have my heart broken again. Plus, it just feels too forward, calling Tru. I've never been the one to make the first phone call. It feels so —"

"Okay, I give up." Kara scanned Ren's counter. "What in the world are wood ears and why are we going to eat them?"

Ren pointed at the small bowl farthest from her. "Those. Mushrooms. See? The ones that looks like skinny slices of wet leather."

"Ooo, yummy!" Kara picked up the bowl.

Lip curled, she looked closely at the mushrooms and gave them a sniff. "You sure these things were in the recipe when you made it for me before?"

"Yep." She took the bowl and added the mushrooms to the wok. "Trust me. And pay attention. You said you wanted to learn how to make this."

"Forget the stir-frying lesson." Kara shoved the bowl of chopped scallions toward her. "Let's work on your calling Tru."

Ren looked her in the eye and pouted. "I don't wanna."

Kara's exasperated growl made her laugh. Kara took Ren by the shoulders and held her firmly. "Woman! You can do this! You gonna make-a me crazy!"

Ren laughed again and shrugged out of her grip. "You gonna make-a me ruin dinner. Toss it all in there now."

They added the rest of the cut-up veggies to the wok. While Ren stirred it all together, Kara dished steamed rice into a serving bowl.

"Smells sooo good, Ren. I'm starved." She put the rice on the table.

Ren loved these times with Kara. The two of them had become fast friends when Ren joined the gym several years ago. But they had grown even closer after Greg left because of the evenings Ren now had free. She never had a sister, and she had lost touch with most high school friends when she left for college and got involved with Greg. So she treasured the friendship that had developed between Kara and her, especially since she accepted Christ. Now Kara was her eternal sister. Ren loved the fact that she'd always be in her life.

And Ren knew Kara was pushing her on the Tru thing only because she wanted the best for her. So did Ren, of course. She wanted what God wanted for her. And Kara was right. Ren felt His urging pretty strongly with regard to calling Tru. And Tru had even encouraged her to call. But Ren couldn't get over her fear. She was scared of rejection after what happened with Greg.

As they sat down Ren noticed a mischievous twinkle in Kara's eye.

"What?"

Kara looked as though she had eaten the last chocolate in the box. "Oh, nothing." She took Ren's hand. "Let's pray."

They bowed their heads and Kara began. "Lord God, we love You so much. We thank You for this food and for all of our blessings. We thank You for Your guidance, and we want to obey You always. Lord, You know what Ren's been thinking lately, feeling she should call Tru. If that's guidance from You, please help Ren to follow Your leading. Please help her to obey. We pray in Your gracious name."

"Amen." Ren looked at Kara and smiled. "You think you're clever, don't you?"

Kara did a silly victory dance in her chair. In a singsong voice, she said, "He's gonna make you dooo it. God's gonna make you call him."

Ren shook her head at Kara, laughing. "Good thing I put so much time into this dinner or we'd be in a serious food fight right now." But she loved the way Kara believed in prayer. And she could already feel the fear of rejection melting away.

Ren picked up the phone before Kara left. As Kara closed the door behind herself, she gave Ren a thumbs-up sign and whispered, "Call me after."

The number Tru circled on his card was his cell phone, so Ren didn't know where she'd be catching him. Even before his phone rang, she envisioned disturbing him in the middle of delivering a baby. But, no, he wouldn't bring his cell phone to a delivery.

First ring. What if he was on a date? What if she was calling him while he was sitting across the table from some fascinating new woman? How awkward would *that* be?

Second ring. Or what if he was asleep, working the hospital's night shift and catching up on sleep and she —

"Hello?"

That smooth, amazing voice, then absolute, stark silence. Ren was frozen. Mute. *Speak, idiot, speak!*

"Hello?" he said again. He sounded a little breathless.

Like a dog with hiccups, Ren barked, "Uh! Tru! Is this Tru?"

"Ren?"

Ren swore she could hear a smile in that one word.

"Do you have caller ID?" she asked. Oh, good grief, she sounded as if she were trying to sell him a phone service plan. She collapsed on the couch. She used to be good at this. What happened to her?

"Caller ID? No, why? Because I knew it was you? It *is* you, right?"

Why was he breathing heavily? This sounded like an obscene phone call in reverse. "Uh, yes."

"Yeah, it's just your voice," he said. "You have a great voice."

Warmth spread all over her. She had a great voice? "Did I catch you in the middle of alligator wrestling or something?"

He laughed. "I just got home from running with Sammy."

"Sammy?"

"My pooch. My running buddy — keeps me in line."

"What kind of dog is he?"

"Golden retriever. He's terrific. You'll love him."

Ren heard so much promise in that last line that she couldn't speak for a moment.

"Whoa," Tru said. "I just realized what time it is. Hey, have you had dinner? Want to grab a bite to eat?"

This was way easier than Ren expected. For a moment she considered eating a second dinner. She could change into those pants with the elastic waistband. But, no, they made her look chunky. "Actually, I already had dinner. With Kara. She just left."

"Ah, okay. You two spend a lot of time together, don't you?"

"Yeah. Best friends."

"Hang on a second, okay?" He left the phone briefly, and then he came back sounding more at ease, his breathing normal. "Better. Had to get that sweatshirt off. Not a pretty sight — Sammy was a taskmaster tonight."

Unbidden, an image flashed through her mind. Perfect, hairless, bronze chest, skin glistening like a male model's, wind blowing through his long, wavy hair, swashbuckling music soaring in the background. Ren rattled it all out of her head with a shake.

"I have a friend like your Kara. Guy at work."

"What's his name?"

"Guy."

They both laughed.

"He's an OB/GYN. Really helped me fit in when I first started at the hospital."

"How long ago was that?" Ren relaxed on the couch.

"Let me think. I started there straight from school, which was . . . wow. This summer it will be ten years. Can't believe it's been that long already."

"You must like it, then, if you lost track of the time."

Ren could hear the smile in his voice again. "Yeah, I love it. I really do. Every day's a blessing there, you know? Birth! It's life at its most intense. Its most innocent. Who wouldn't love that?"

Ren felt such an urge to see his face while he was saying that.

Before she could speak again, he said, "So I take it you work?"

She chuckled. "Yeah, a little. I teach. Second graders this year."

He whistled softly. "Boy, I'll say you work! I'm surprised you've looked so full of energy when I've seen you."

That made her laugh. "You mean like when I was passed out?"

"Hey, don't knock passing out. I probably wouldn't have met you if you'd been conscious."

"Well, no guarantees, but I'll probably be conscious next time we meet."

"And when will that be, Ren?"

Something about the way he asked that, with such a gentle but serious tone in his voice, made her feel sought after. It was downright exciting.

She almost made a comment about having seen him at the library but decided against it. She might sound as if she had avoided an opportunity to talk with him. Unless she told him she had practically done cartwheels trying to get his attention. Or, worse, she might sound a bit like a stalker, hiding behind library patrons and eyeballing his every move. *Keep it simple, Ren.*

"I'm free Saturday," she said. "Is that good for you?" As soon as she said it, she felt panic. Saturday seemed so near.

"Saturday's perfect for me — oh, wait. This Saturday's not the twelfth, is it?"

"I don't —"

"Ah, no, it's the fifth. Good," he said. "I have my mother's birthday party on the twelfth. Command performance, you know."

Ren chuckled. "Sounds as if we have something in common."

There was a comfortable silence on his end of the phone for the briefest of moments before he said, "I have a feeling we have a lot in common."

Oh, my. She definitely liked this man. He had such a gift for putting her at ease, even while giving her goose bumps. "So let me give you my address," she said, picturing him standing at her front door. The image made her happy. "And what time should I expect you?"

Tru said, "Are you . . . are you smiling, by any chance, Ren?"

His question threw her. "Uh, pardon?"

"I know this sounds funny, but sometimes I can hear a smile in your voice. You ever hear that? Makes me feel good."

Her heart pounded a bit harder. "Yeah," Ren said softly. "I hear that. Your . . . your voice sounds even better when you smile."

He said, "Hmm," the way people do when you say something they like hearing.

And suddenly Saturday seemed too far away.

THIRTEEN

Saturday approached slowly. But Friday night — and Clarissa's High Blood Pressure Ball — came at Ren with all the immediacy of a society matron whose bouffant hairdo was on fire. Which could almost describe Clarissa herself. The irony of her manic supervision of this particular event was not lost on Ren. Ren's own blood pressure was starting to feel a bit edgy by the time she left work and dashed home to throw herself together for the evening.

Clarissa had called her at the school three times before morning recess, driving poor Peggy in the office to an uncharacteristic point of annoyance.

"I'm so sorry, Peggy," Ren said after the third time. "I've asked her to call my cell number if she has any more instructions today."

Peggy gave her an understanding smile. "This must be an important dance."

Ren snorted. "It is for my mother. I'm afraid she's putting a lot of store in my finding Mr. Right tonight."

Peggy shook her head and jotted something down on a pad of paper. "I've got to make note of the pressure your mom puts on you. My daughter's only eighteen, but I could probably take some pointers from you on how *not* to drive her insane once she's out on her own."

Ren rolled her eyes. "Honey, we'll have to do lunch."

She turned her cell phone to vibrate and snapped it onto a belt loop of her slacks. The phone hummed against her when she got to the playground, but she let the call pass to voice mail.

"Your class has been a virtual band of angels," Jeremy said, when Ren joined him near the jungle gym.

"Thanks for watching them."

Jeremy glanced at her waist. "Are you buzzing?"

Ren sighed. "It's Mother. You'd think she had enough to focus on for this fancy, schmancy ball. She's making me nuts, Jeremy."

"I didn't realize you were helping her run the show," Jeremy said, supporting one of his students as she crawled down from the cross bars.

"Run the show? I *am* the show!"

To his confused frown, she said, "She's husband shopping for me."

Ren called for her students to line up and return to class, and then she looked back at Jeremy.

"I mean, she's very devoted to her charity projects, but I think I'm quickly becoming one of them. She's turning this ball into my own personal Sadie Hawkins dance."

Jeremy called to his class. "Right ho, then, let's line up." He looked at Ren. "And who's this Sadie woman?"

Ren smiled. "I think she was a cartoon character. Man hungry. They don't really do Sadie Hawkins dances much anymore. But back when women were more, um, old-fashioned, they used to have these dances. The women invited the guys instead of the other way around."

He grinned. "What a smashing idea!"

Ren laughed as she led her class away. "I knew you'd like that concept." She waved at him and slipped back into her formal teacher mode, for the kids' sake. "Thanks again, Mr. Beckett."

He waved back. "Happy hunting, Sadie! Er, Ms. Young!"

■ ■ ■ ■

For all her phoning and dictating and general harassing during the day, Clarissa was the picture of poise when Ren showed up at the ball. With big band music as her soundtrack, Clarissa glided from couple to couple, granting each an elegant smile as if she were especially pleased with their having chosen to attend.

When she saw Ren, she actually gave her the same pleased smile. Despite having watched her work the crowd, Ren was inexplicably flattered.

"Darling, you look beautiful," Clarissa said, even as she reached up and adjusted Ren's shoulder strap.

Ren had to admit, the gown was perfect. Sleek, black, and softly flared away below the waist in just about the best example of camouflage she'd ever seen. You'd never know Ren lived in a constant struggle with her curvy hips.

Clarissa glanced up and down at her and sighed. "Lovely. Anyone can see you have excellent taste in ball gowns."

"But you picked it out, Mother."

Clarissa lifted her eyelids and parted her lips in innocent surprise. "Oh! That's right, isn't it?" Her light laugh almost sounded humble.

Ren glanced around the room. Couples danced. Groups gathered, smiled, and nodded polite agreement with one another. Waiters silently tended to guests, offering champagne and trays of mysterious hors d'oeuvres.

"Are Matt and Sybil here yet?"

Clarissa pursed her lips for just a second before sighing with resignation. "Your brother's coming alone. Sybil has to stay home with the girls."

Ren's heart sank. Her one bright expectation for the evening had been to hang out with Matt and Sybil, poking fun at the more snooty, prideful attendees. Even the few people from their generation tended to be old and stodgy at these things.

"Sybil told me they had a sitter. What happened?"

"Don't grimace like that, Ren. Not attractive. Tina and Mary both came down with the flu or some such thing this afternoon. Sybil wasn't comfortable leaving them with anyone."

Ren fought the urge to look at her watch. She wanted to gauge how soon she could leave and still remain in Clarissa's good graces.

"But Matt's coming?"

"Yes. He considered staying home too, but I talked him into making an appearance."

Ren smiled before she could stop herself. She'd been on the other end of that conversation with Clarissa before. At least Matt and Ren could mingle together.

"But I don't want you two clinging together once he arrives," Clarissa said, apparently reading Ren's mind. "There are a number of men you need to meet, and I don't want Matt scaring them off."

Ren suddenly had an image of herself, belly down on a platter, with an apple wedged in her mouth. "Mother, I know you're trying to help, but —"

"No shrinking violet talk." Clarissa's eyes flashed briefly with a determination Ren knew too well. "I want you to remember what we saw in the mall. That snake Greg and his chippy and their little —"

Ren put her hand up. "Please, let's not do this. I don't want to think about that right now, okay?"

"Do you realize how far gone the man is, Ren? Do you understand how much more living he's done than you have? You've always wanted a family. Children. He's already —"

"Good grief, Mother, it's not a contest,"

Ren said, as gently as possible. "I'm not trying to one-up Greg."

"No, you certainly are not."

Matt's welcome voice interrupted their conversation. "Something tells me you stunning women are discussing something more intense than the Gulf shrimp canapés. Should I come back later?"

Ren grabbed his arm to keep him there. He happened to be holding a Gulf shrimp canapé at the moment, so her action caused his shrimp to jettison over Clarissa's shoulder, missing her chandelier earring by a hair.

Clarissa gasped while Matt and Ren stifled their laughter.

"Sorry, Mom," Matt said. He walked behind her and retrieved the shrimp, gracefully placing it on a passing waiter's empty tray. Ren's big brother was Clarissa's golden boy. And Ren loved him dearly. He looked like James Bond in his tux, but Ren knew the fun-loving kid barely hiding behind that dashing smile.

"You two behave," Clarissa said. "I've put a lot of effort into this evening, and I want everything to be perfect."

Perfection, of course, was Clarissa's plan for Ren this evening too. She had gone to great lengths — generous lengths, considering the cost of Ren's gorgeous ball gown —

in preparing her for the event, and she wanted Ren and her future to be flawless.

Ren knew her mother meant well, but she sighed at the tons of hope Clarissa rested on her shoulders. She knew Clarissa already felt horribly let down by Ren's failed marriage to Greg, her change of profession, and even her adjusted priorities since finding Christ. Ren hated disappointing her, but she seemed gifted at it.

"Don't worry about a thing, Mom," Matt said. "Ren and I are going to have a dance together, and then we're going to turn on the Young charm and mingle with the best of them. We'll have a raging conga line going before you can say 'geriatric intensive care.'"

Clarissa arched her eyebrow at him before spotting another couple in need of a greeting. She flashed her elegant smile again and floated away.

"We're not really going to get a conga line together, are we?" Ren asked. She wouldn't put anything past Matt. He could be terribly embarrassing, but he created the best memories.

"I don't even know what a conga is."

"How're the girls?"

He snorted. "They're fine. Sybil pounced on that excuse the second the girls complained of tummy aches. Frankly, I think she gave them extra helpings of ice cream when they got home from school today. Imagine. Sacrificing the comfort of her poor defenseless girls so she could avoid this fine evening of tight shoes and mind-numbing small talk."

"Clever girl." Across the room Ren saw her mother walking in their general direction. She had her arm laced through that of an amazingly thin young man, his nose stuck so high in the air Ren could see his nostrils better than his eyes.

Matt must have seen them coming too. "Time to dance, sis."

Ren needed no coaxing.

And she didn't need to tell Matt how much she loved him for saving her more than once during the evening. He knew full well (as Ren thought Clarissa did) that none of the prospects Clarissa had for her were her cup of tea. Ren even saw her surprise lunch date, Gus Kendrick, the mute real estate developer Clarissa tried to foist upon her last week. Even he knew Clarissa and Ren had different ideas of what was attractive in a man — Ren could see it in his eyes, just before he about-faced and acted as if he hadn't seen her.

Matt and Ren kept the promise he made

to Clarissa. They mingled in classic Young fashion. But they supported one another through the entire event. Ren felt as if they were kids again, annoying each other at every opportunity, but sticking together like two lovable dunces at a Mensa convention, them against the world.

By evening's end Ren had managed to thwart all romantic advances by Clarissa's lineup of usual suspects. She was primed and eager for a real date with a man of her very own choosing.

FOURTEEN

Every time Ren found her pulse speeding up, she stopped to pray. *Please, Lord, help me to be calm. Help me to trust You in this.*

It was, after all, just a date. It wasn't as if she were about to perform surgery or fight a war or even take the SATs. She should be giddy, not sweaty. A date. Her first in six years. With a gorgeous, apparently perfect, golden-voiced Christian man who had yet to see her when she wasn't either out cold, blubbering like a child, insulting his family, or trussed up to look like Groucho Marx.

Please, Lord! Help me to be calm! Help me to trust You in this!

Ren took a deep breath and looked in the mirror. She could do this. Tru was a wonderful man. He had a sense of humor, clearly, or he wouldn't have encouraged her to call him. Twice. But she wanted to be more than an amusement. Who wanted to be Lucy Ricardo? Ren wanted to be more like . . .

well, like herself, but not so goofy.

She had received advice on what to wear from Kara. And from Sandy and Jeremy at work.

"Casual feminine," Kara said. "Wear that pale pink top you couldn't wear when your hair was so dark. Very Audrey Hepburn. With a black skirt."

Sandy said, "You want to look striking — make him remember you. Wear that hot red number you wore to my Christmas party a few years ago. Rick still raves about that one."

"Nonsense, love," Jeremy told her. "Don't try too hard. Something simple and elegant, like that black, high-necked thing you wear to school sometimes."

"The prison warden dress?" Sandy said. "Come on!"

In the end, Ren went with Kara's pink-and-black advice, and she was happy with the look. Now, if only she could keep from babbling like an idiot or stepping into a mud puddle or —

The doorbell rang. She prayed one last time. Grabbed the deodorant for a final go at it — she had to stop being so nervous! Opened the door and —

Wow. Ren couldn't believe it — she had seen Tru at his worst before, apparently.

How could he look even better? Had his eyelashes gotten thicker? He wore a light-weight charcoal gray suit with a crisp white shirt and royal blue tie. He looked sleek in the dark jacket, and the blue complemented his warm skin color beautifully.

"Hi," he said, almost shyly. His smile absolutely drove away every fear Ren had. Well, his smile and the Holy Spirit, she was sure.

"You look beautiful," he said.

Ren shook her head in appreciation. "Oh, man, so do you." And she gasped right on the heels of that comment. Why did it sound so much more forward the way she said it?

He laughed lightly, as he would if Lucy Ricardo had just said something cute. "Ready to go?"

He took her to dinner at L'Auberge Chez François, a charming little restaurant in Great Falls. He talked comfortably as he drove them through the gently sloping Virginia countryside. Ren was able to enjoy looking at him, the cloud-wisped sky and rolling Blue Ridge Mountains framing his handsome profile.

"Years ago," he said, "my father worked in Washington, not too far from the White House. François had a restaurant right across the street back then, so my father went there a lot. Whenever my mother visited him at work, he'd take her there for lunch. François made this plum tart that my mother really loved. When I was born — I was my mother's first — my mother got really sick, and François found out. He sent a huge plum tart to her at the hospital."

"How sweet."

"Yeah. That's how he is. So when he moved his restaurant out here, to Great Falls, we often went as a family." He fell silent then, looking nostalgic, almost sad.

"But no more?"

He looked at her as if he had pulled back from a memory. "Hmm?"

"Your family doesn't go there anymore?"

"Oh. Well, not the whole family together. My oldest sister's married and has two sons. She's busy with her own family. And my father . . . well, he's not home much anymore."

"Are your parents separated?"

They pulled into the restaurant's gravel parking lot.

"Not exactly." He came around to meet Ren as she got out of the car, taking her hand to help her out. She didn't let go of his hand when they started to walk, and he didn't appear to have any plans to let go of hers.

Ren could have just sighed right out loud.

Chez François was nestled among private estates, green gardens, and thickets of woods. With its rough-textured white walls and deep brown crossbeams, it looked like an authentic French Alsatian country inn. Ren felt as if they were deep in the heart of Europe.

When they walked in, an elderly gentleman met them at the door. He laughed his welcome, opening his arms as soon as he saw Tru. "Ah, Tru! *Bonsoir! Bonsoir!*"

"François! *Bonsoir,*" Tru said, returning the laugh. They hugged and patted one another on the back. Tru turned to Ren and placed his hand on her shoulder, to beckon her forward.

"And who is this lovely woman you bring?" François asked.

"This is Ren. She is lovely, no?" Tru was almost speaking with an accent.

Ren smiled. How cute.

The restaurant was cozy, decorated in the vivid yellows, reds, and blues of a French country cottage. Whatever was being prepared in the kitchen smelled rich and heavenly. As they were shown to their table, several of the red-vested waiters greeted Tru by name and made a great fuss over Ren. Goodbye, Lucy Ricardo! Ren was Audrey

Hepburn — delicate, flowing, graceful. Someone would take her picture at any moment.

After glancing at the menu, Ren said, "Why don't you order for me, Tru? I'm pretty easy to please, and you probably know what's best here."

"Sure," he said. "But I'll assume you don't want *le terrine du lapin* or the *cerveau de veau.*"

Ren arched one eyebrow at him.

He smiled. "Bunny pâté or calf brains."

Ren grimaced. "You know me so well already."

"They may not have those on the menu anymore," he said, picking his up. "We learned what that meant when we were kids and joked about it with every new person we brought here."

"Have you brought many people here?" Ren asked. She meant dates, and as soon as she said it, it sounded as if she had said "dates." She felt herself blush.

"Only family and family friends. Never anyone special before today."

He wasn't even joking. Ren wanted to grab his face and plant a big kiss on it. But she remained Audrey. She smiled and looked him right in the eye.

"So what's the story with your dad?"

Tru sighed. "I grew up knowing that my father had to work a lot, often staying in town if he had to be especially late. We grew used to his schedule, which seemed to keep him away from home more and more."

"What does he do?"

"He's an engineer. But he has mostly international clients, so his hours tend to conform to theirs. And he travels quite a bit."

"And that's why he's seldom home?"

He shook his head. "Maybe at first. But . . . once, when I was fifteen, I was skipping school with some buddies —"

Ren tsked. "Bad boy."

He raised his eyebrows and nodded. "Yeah, at that age I was pretty bad. This was before I became a Christian, and before I, uh, found my father."

"Found him?"

"My friends and I went down to DC. It was right in the middle of the weekday. We went to pick up the brother of one of my friends. The guy worked at a restaurant downtown. Almost as soon as I walked into the restaurant, I saw my father. He was at one of the tables. With another woman."

Ren closed her eyes and sighed. "That's what I was afraid you were going to say. Are you sure it wasn't a business thing?"

He shook his head. "It wasn't business. He was all over her."

"Oh, Tru, how awful. I can't imagine seeing my father like that, especially as a teenager."

"I was so angry. Disgusted. And hurt. I hurt for my mother."

"Did he see you?"

"No. I left as fast as I could. I didn't know what to do. I wanted my mother to know, but I didn't want her to know, either. When he got home that night, I confronted him while he was alone in his room. We started yelling at each other." His eyes darkened. "My mother ended up in the middle of it."

A waiter approached. Tru's features softened, and he seemed to mentally step back from the memory.

He told the waiter, "Jean-Paul, we'll have the *venison terrine* and the crabmeat in puff pastry first, then the saffron seafood and the lamb with fennel." He smiled softly at Ren. "I want you to try several, to see what you like, okay?"

"Sure." Ren spoke quietly. She couldn't help thinking about the fact that Greg had been unfaithful, just like Tru's father. At least she didn't have a child for him to hurt too. Although, Casey wasn't entirely unscathed by the experience.

"Well, I'm sure livening up the evening, aren't I?" Tru chuckled at himself.

"No, don't do that," Ren said. "Don't get polite. Or, you know, distant." She couldn't believe she was being so frank with him, but she didn't want to start their relationship with secrets. "How did your mother react?"

"As you'd expect. She was a mess. My father tried to blame me for hurting her."

"Amazing. And they didn't divorce?"

"No. My mother was pregnant at the time with my youngest brother, Devon. He was the sixth. The last. My mother wanted to try to keep the family together. And I guess my father didn't want to leave, not completely."

"So they just kind of coexist?"

He nodded. "Yeah, that's pretty much how it was. Is. Devon's the last of the sibs still living at home — he's seventeen. My father's not home much and lives his life, his *social* life, apart from the rest of us. I don't know what will happen between my parents when Devon graduates and heads to college."

"So your dad still supports the family financially, with college and everything else?"

"Yeah. Money was never the problem. That may be the main reason my mother stayed. But for everything else she pretty much leans on me, as the oldest."

The tiniest little red flag popped up in the back of Ren's mind, but at that moment the waiter brought their food, distracting them from their conversation.

"Gorgeous!" Ren said, looking at everything appreciatively.

"Yes," Tru said, smiling at her. He gently took one of her hands, just at the fingertips. Ren thought he was getting romantic until he said, "Are you comfortable with a quick prayer?"

"Oh! Sure!" Ren bowed her head, saying her own silent prayer of thanks for this man who was at ease praying in public.

After Tru prayed they savored their scrumptious meal. Ren "mmm'd" and "yum'd" over each new taste. She could tell Tru felt pleased. As if he, himself, had served as chef.

Finally, he said, "Okay, now your turn."

"For what?"

"When I said I was expected at my mother's birthday party next week, you hinted that your mother demanded a lot of your time too."

Ren laughed. "Not so much my time as control of my life. She feels I should be living 'better.' Mother doesn't lean on me, as in *depending* on me. Her leaning is a bit more like a stage mother leaning on a child actor who never quite gets the part."

"Yow."

Ren laughed. "I guess I'm exaggerating a little. It's just that . . . well, no one could ever accuse Mother of harboring secret opinions, especially when it comes to me. She's a firm believer in setting her thoughts free."

"And her thoughts are usually contrary to yours?"

"Usually." Ren thought about her nailing Greg at the mall. "But I have to say, she's a good one to have in your corner during the rough moments."

He sat back, smiling. He sighed. "Mothers. Powerful people. And yet so fragile." He studied her face for a moment. "What kind of a mother do you think you'll be, Ren?"

Ren suddenly felt as if she had dropped a huge sheaf of papers that she had to gather and organize — her thoughts scattered everywhere. She filled the time with "Um . . ." and "I . . ." and variations on that theme.

What kind of mother? Ren didn't even know if she could *be* a mother. Should she tell Tru that she might be infertile? Too much information so soon? He knew Ren had almost adopted, but how would he feel about adoption if it involved his own marriage? And what was Ren thinking? This was their first date, and she was thinking about marriage! Then she remembered Tru's comments about loving kids. And his caring so much about babies that he surrounded himself with them professionally —

"Ren? Are you okay? Did I say something wrong?"

"Oh!" She must have looked so ditzy. "No. Nothing wrong." Here she had all but demanded he not keep secrets, and she was trying to figure out which ones to keep herself. "I guess I'm not sure what kind of mother I'd make. I mean, I love the kids at school. And I've always wanted children of my own . . ."

"I suppose we don't know what kind of parents we'll be until we're there," Tru said.

Ah, relief. He said that on a more general tone. Although, it did sound a little as if he was talking about their being parents together, and goose bumps ran down her arms.

"But I think you'd make a great mother."

Oh, he could make her smile, this man. "Do you? Why?" *Just flatter me, Tru. Go right on ahead — I'll just have compliments for des-*

sert, thank you.

"One, you're kind. I saw how you treated that guy at Wal-Mart, the mentally challenged one who helped you when you fainted. And you were so kind to me. And my sister."

"The one I called a donut hound?"

He laughed. "I thought Kara was the one who called her that."

"Well, yes, that's true."

"And you're funny. Kids love funny, don't you think?"

Ren thought of her father. "Yes, I think that's right. My dad had a terrific sense of humor. Laughing felt like love with him."

"Is your father —"

"Yeah. He died two years ago."

"I didn't realize. I'm sorry."

"Me too. I miss him."

Tru motioned for the check. "Will you tell me about him while we drive downtown?"

"Downtown?" she said. "DC, downtown?"

He grinned. "I want to take you someplace special. Come on, it's early."

He took her to the Jefferson Memorial. He couldn't have known, but the Jefferson was her favorite monument spot in Washington. The sun had just begun to set, and the sky was rose tinted, the clouds reflecting light

161

and color everywhere. A quartet was playing at the Sylvan Theater, an outdoor stage not far away. The sweet notes of a soprano sax softly filled the air.

Tru had removed his tie and loosened the collar of his shirt. For a moment Ren imagined him with his shirtsleeves rolled halfway up his forearms, the way men often do. He had such lovely dark skin. She couldn't help smiling as she thought about how handsome he'd look.

He smiled back, unaware that Ren longed for his forearms to be part of the scenery. "I'm sorry the cherry blossoms have already fallen," he said. "But this is still my favorite place in town."

"Mine too! I mean it. But I haven't been here in years. I forgot how pretty it was."

They walked all the way around the Tidal Basin, sometimes not talking at all. As exciting as this evening felt, Ren couldn't remember feeling so comfortable with a man before. Ever.

At one point while they walked, Tru gently took her hand and held it with both of his, causing them to slow down so they barely moved. He studied her hand — it was her left hand. The indentation from her wedding ring had long since disappeared.

He spoke quietly. "What are you looking

for, Ren?"

"You mean, in a relationship?"

"Mm-hmm. Is it too soon after your divorce for you to think that way? Are you just having fun? Or —"

"I never date for fun, Tru," Ren said, her voice serious. Then she thought about how that sounded. "I mean, not that I don't have fun on dates. *This* date. This date was fun. *Is* fun. I want to have fun on a date, and be fun, but —"

He was laughing.

"You know what I mean," she said. "I see dating as a step. Not as a separate event."

"Yes." He dropped one of his hands so they could walk side by side again. "That's what I hoped. Good." And moments after they resumed walking, he began to sing quietly with the music being played in the Sylvan. It was an old love song Ren had heard before. Maybe Stevie Wonder? Tru knew the words, and Ren felt something soften in her chest, listening to that rich voice of his.

A light, warm rain started to fall. At first they both held out their free hands, testing that it really was raining. Eventually Tru took off his jacket to put around her shoulders. He rolled up his shirtsleeves, and Ren nearly gasped. Even better than she had imagined. He faced her and brushed her hair, damp now, away from her face. His own hair had fallen onto his forehead, curled a bit from the rain. In one movement, he put his arms around her and rested his forehead against hers. All he said was, "Ren." Like a sigh.

They stood together while the tender music blessed them. For a second Ren pictured how they looked to others, standing near that beautiful pool of water at dusk, the soft rain smoothing all the rough edges, like the most romantic perfume commercial ever.

Thank You, Lord!

Then she was back in the moment with Tru. This date was a step, they had agreed. And here she'd feared she'd step into a mud puddle.

Silly girl.

FIFTEEN

"All right, love." Jeremy placed his lunch on the table in the teachers' lounge and plopped down in a chair across from Ren.

She studied him. His sandy hair was less styled than it had been in the morning. He looked cute — like a little boy who'd had a very busy play day.

"Give us the details from your date," he said. "Inspire me. I've had a rough go of it this morning, with two of my little charges tossing their cookies —"

"Two?" Ren grimaced. "Oh, poor babies."

He looked forlornly at her.

"I meant you too, of course. Poor baby," Ren said. "Seems so weird to have a flu bug in the middle of spring, if that's what it is. Hasn't hit my class yet."

She noticed a beige *something* globbed on the cuff of Jeremy's shirtsleeve and pointed hesitantly at it. "Uh-oh. Jeremy? Is that . . ."

He frowned and inspected his sleeve. "No.

Glue." He wiped at it with his napkin, leaving a trace of glue and paper stuck to his shirt. "We're doing three-dimensional flowers for science. Pistils, stamens, the whole lot." He gave her a weak smile and raised the other cuff to reveal a bright green splotch. "We're painting them too."

Ren laughed. "You *are* having a tough day. Here." She scooted her dessert across the table to him. "Want a brownie to make it all better?"

"Ugh. Thanks, but no thanks. I think I'm a bit off food just now." He pushed his lunch bag aside and leaned back in his chair. "Distract me, Ren. Tell me how it went with your new bloke this weekend."

"Don't you dare!" Sandy ordered, rushing into the lounge. "Not one word without me." She dashed back to the refrigerator and retrieved a container, which she opened and put in the microwave. She bustled back to sit beside Ren, eagerly leaning forward in her chair. "Okay. Now. Is it love? Was it great? Are you going to see him again? Is he perfect? Oh, of course he's not perfect. No one is, except, of course —"

Jeremy groaned and dropped his head to the table. Ren laughed, and they both answered, "The Marvelous Rick." Ren found Sandy's attitude about her husband adorable, considering his bumbling nature and squishy physique.

"You know," Jeremy said, "I'm starting to wonder about The Marvelous Rick."

"As well you should," Sandy said. "He's quite a wonder."

"Yes, well. I've known you, Sandy, for what, almost two years now, eh?"

"Mm-hmm."

"And our dear friend Kara has known you at least as long." He raised one eyebrow and wagged his index finger in the air. "Yet neither of us has ever met this elusive Rick."

He narrowed his eyes and looked at Ren conspiratorially. "Tell me, Ren. Have you ever seen The Marvelous Rick and Superman in the same room together at the same time?"

Ren laughed. "I've never seen Superman in any room, Jeremy. But I can attest to the reality that is Rick."

They smiled at each other and looked at Sandy, who wasn't joining in their joke. She had a far-off look in her eyes.

Ren waved her hand in Sandy's range of vision. "Sandy?"

The microwave chimed, and Sandy's focus returned to them. "Sorry. I was just picturing Rick in a Superman costume."

They all laughed.

"The cape would be fetching," Sandy said. "But I don't know about the big red underwear." She stood and went to get her food. "As I said, Ren, you mustn't hold out hope to find someone as perfect as my man."

"I'm really not expecting perfection, Sandy. But . . ." Ren couldn't suppress a grin.

"But Tru comes pretty close, eh?" Sandy said, eyebrows raised.

Ren sighed. "He does. And I am going to see him again. He asked me to go with him to his mother's birthday celebration next Saturday."

"Wow, meeting the family already!" Sandy said. "Very good sign. Our girl works fast!" she said to Jeremy, who smiled at her and looked tired. Or was it sad?

Sandy sat and opened her container of ravioli. At the sharp smell of Parmesan, Ren glanced at Jeremy, but he was mercifully unfazed.

He said, "So tell me what he's doing right, Ren, besides looking like a Latin movie star. I really need some pointers on chatting up American girls. My boyish charm doesn't seem to be getting me anywhere beyond a date or two."

"But you really are charming, Jeremy."

Sandy pointed her fork at him. "Yep. The

problem has a lot more to do with where you're meeting women than anything about you."

He reached across the table and gently squeezed Ren's hand, doing the same to Sandy. "Better chums a man never had."

Ren smiled at him and squeezed his hand back. "You know, Tru asked me the other night what I was looking for in a relationship. Are you sure you're 'chatting up' girls who want the same things you want?"

"Of course I'm not sure. I'm not even sure *I* know what *I* want." He opened his lunch bag and rooted around. "I know I'd like to have a girlfriend. Maybe get married someday. Have a kid or two."

"Oh! That reminds me," Sandy said to him. "Another one of your kids got sick. In the cafeteria. Sean Morris."

Ren said, "Good grief!"

"My classroom's the Bermuda-blasted-Triangle, I'm telling you!" Jeremy said. He stood and closed his lunch bag.

"Relax, Jeremy," Sandy said. "The nurse took care of the little guy. You don't have to leave."

"I can't just leave him sitting alone in the clinic, waiting for Mum." He walked over and gave Ren a kiss on top of the head. "I want to hear about the date, Rennie, honestly. Give me a call tonight?"

"Sure. But eat some lunch, Jeremy. Ask for a teacher's aide to relieve you or something. Won't do you any good not taking care of yourself with sick kids breathing all over you."

He nodded gamely and left.

Sandy stabbed her fork into a square of ravioli. "That boy's going to make a good dad someday."

"He's such a sweetie."

"Oh, hey," Sandy said. "Speaking of parenting. I'm glad we're alone. I need to talk with you about Casey."

Ren looked at her, puzzled.

Sandy set her lunch aside, wiping her face with her napkin. "I took him for that visit with his mom this weekend. At the prison."

Ren knew it was coming, of course, but suddenly she felt as if *she* were going to toss her cookies as Jeremy's students had. "Oh. How did it go?"

Sandy raised her eyebrows. "Honestly? It went better than I expected. They got along pretty well. She seems to be taking her rehab seriously."

Ren's stomach knotted with dread. Jealousy. Shame. What did she want to hear, that it was awful and Casey was miserable with his mom?

A voice squawked out from the PA system. "Mrs. Warner? Are you in the teachers' lounge?"

"Not in here," Sandy called back. She looked at Ren and patted her hand. "It's not the end of the world, Rennie. You look as if you've just been ordered to clean my house."

"Do I? Oh, Sandy, I feel so bewildered. I guess I only want Casey to be happy with me. And I can't even adopt him. How selfish is that?"

Sandy leaned back and nodded. "Pretty selfish, yeah. And pretty natural too."

"You think?"

"I do. I mean, I gather you're still holding out some hope that things will work out so you can go through with the adoption. Maybe deep down? Maybe if things with Tru were to hurry along?"

They stared at each other while Ren considered that. For about two seconds. Who was she kidding? That's exactly what was going on in her head. She and Tru would fall madly in love, throw together a romantic, tasteful, and swift wedding, and become the ideal family for Casey's adoption. Ren closed her eyes, slouched in resignation, and leaned her head back. "Busted. Yes, that's it. I'm in pathetic denial about Casey." She looked at Sandy. "Time is not my friend in this situation, is it?"

"I don't know about that. We're only talking a first meeting between Casey and his mom. He's spent most of his life away from her, and she's not necessarily the best person for him to end up with. Not yet, anyway. She has a lot to prove in order to get back custody. If that's what she wants. There might be time for you and Tru —"

"But, Sandy, that thinking is all backward! I still barely know Tru. Granted, he's —"

"Amazing?"

Ren nodded. "Amazing. Yeah, that word fits. But we're really at the infatuation stage, wouldn't you say?"

"Absolutely. It's way too soon for you to call it anything else. But just because you're infatuated doesn't mean you aren't falling in love. It could happen."

That made Ren smile. "Yes, it could. But I need to be careful about my motives with Tru. I don't want to be so focused on getting a father for Casey that I overlook anything that could lead to problems between Tru and me later on."

"That's my girl."

Ren opened a plastic bag of celery sticks, and she and Sandy each took one to munch on.

"But you're human," Sandy said. "You've already decided you won't pursue Casey's adoption unless you have a daddy for him. Along comes this gorgeous, kind man who loves kids. Of course those two things are going to play with your perception."

Ren nodded. "You think I should just go with that? Think marriage and kids, even while I'm just on my second date with Tru?"

Sandy snorted. "Hate to break it to you, Ren, but your average woman doesn't need an adoptive child waiting in the wings to think that way. Unless you're just dating to have a good time, you will weigh everything about Tru on the husband-daddy scale."

Ren remembered Tru's question about whether she was just dating for fun. "I think he might be using a similar scale with me, Sandy."

Sandy walked her hand, spiderlike, across the table toward Ren's brownie. "You leaving that thing to fend for itself?" she asked.

"It's yours." Ren bit into another celery stick.

Sandy said, "If Tru's considering the same things you are, at least you're on the same path." She popped a piece of brownie into her mouth. "Whether you end up together or not, at least you'll know you didn't miscommunicate about the important stuff."

"Yeah."

Sandy grinned. "So what did he say that sounds as though he's thinking marriage and kids?"

Ren got a dreamy, schoolgirl look on her face as she thought about things Tru had said. "Well —"

"Oh! Wait a second," Sandy said. "I'm going to forget. I need to get your permission before I put in the paperwork."

"For what?"

"Casey's still asking for you to come with us the next time we visit Britney at the prison. I need to get that cleared with social services. You all right with the idea?"

Ren frowned. "Eww. I don't know. I'm not sure if I want to meet her. Do I have to decide today?"

"You should. You can always decide not to go once the time comes, but the clearance takes quite a while. We should get it in motion."

"Oh." Ren's face colored. What kind of self-centered wimp was she? She was a grown woman, afraid of a little emotional pain. After all the pain Casey had been through. If she couldn't do this much for him, how could she ever be strong enough for motherhood to any child? "I'll stop by your office and sign the papers. Just give me a little warning before the next visit, okay?"

"No prob," Sandy said. She shifted in her chair, looking at Ren eagerly. "Okay. So fill me in on your date with Tru." She ate the last piece of brownie. "I'll let you know if he comes even remotely close to Rick's fabulous charm on our first date."

Sixteen

Ren headed straight for the gym when she left school that day. She liked to think of herself as a self-starting type of woman. But she had to admit that, since her date with Tru, she felt new motivation for whipping herself into shape. Maybe she wouldn't be totally bulge free by Saturday, but she could at least be a step closer if she was a good girl about exercise. And maybe about skipping chocolate.

Of course, just the thought of chocolate made her crave one of those extra dark chocolate Godiva truffles she had at home. So decadent you had to eat them slowly, just a few molecules at a time. Heaven.

When she really thought about it, though, Ren decided she didn't know Tru well enough to make a decision about skipping chocolate yet. No point in going overboard. But exercise was always a good thing, so she kept her course steady and arrived at

American Gym before her resolve had a chance to falter.

She saw no sign of Kara when she walked in, which was a disappointment. Even if she didn't have a training appointment with Kara, they usually had a chance to chat when they were both there at the same time. That always made the workout easier.

Kara's coworker Mickey was behind the front desk, big and beefy as usual.

"Hey, Ren, how's it goin'?" He handed her a towel as she scanned her membership card. Ren thought he seemed more low-key than usual. He was usually boisterous and full of energy, almost to the point of embarrassment.

"Hi, Mickey. You okay?"

He briefly tipped his head to the side. "Yeah, I guess." He glanced over his shoulder in the direction of the ladies' locker room, but he offered no explanation. "I'm fine."

Ren gave him a parting smile and headed back to put her bag in a locker. When she entered the changing area, disorientation flooded her senses at what she saw. Kara and Tiffany sat together on one of the benches, their backs to Ren. Neither said anything, but Tiffany was obviously distraught, and Kara was gently rubbing her shoulder as if she were Tiffany's mother.

Of course, Ren would have fainted again had the roles been reversed — had Ren seen Tiffany offering comfort to Kara. To anyone. Still, this was an unusual sight, just seeing Tiffany let Kara act kindly toward her.

Ren didn't know what to do, so she cleared her throat. They both looked around at her. Tiffany looked drained and self-conscious, and Kara gave Ren a sad smile.

"I'm sorry," Ren said. "I didn't mean to interrupt."

Tiffany stood up. "No, you're not. I've got an aerobics class to teach in ten minutes."

"You want me to teach it for you, Tiffany?" Kara asked. She stood and looked at her watch. "My next client isn't scheduled until six."

Tiffany shrugged. "I need the distraction."

She'd clearly been crying.

Ren still stood there, not sure whether she should ask for details or not. Then her curiosity won out over her sense of decorum. "What's wrong, Tiffany?"

Tiffany took a deep breath and released it before answering. "It's my mom."

That's all she got out before a tremble washed over her chin and lips.

Kara put her hand on Tiffany's shoulder and then looked at Ren. "Her mom's been diagnosed with cancer."

Ren immediately pictured Tiffany's mom, whom they met last summer during a group drive down to Florida. Ren never saw the woman without a cigarette dangling between her lips. "Lung cancer?"

Both Tiffany and Kara nodded, and Ren didn't give a moment's thought to awkwardness. Before she knew what she was doing, she had her arms around Tiffany, who stood there so stiff yet so broken. Ren noticed she smelled like tense perspiration and felt as if she had a fever.

"I'm sorry, Tiffany. I'll pray for her. And for you and your dad."

"Oh, my poor dad," Tiffany said, pulling herself away from Ren. "He's always loved her more than she loved him. He'll —" She stopped herself abruptly, seemingly aware that she had said more than she planned to. She breathed deeply again and bent toward the mirror to look closely at her face. "I'm a fright."

She looked back and forth from Kara to Ren. She wiped her fingers quickly beneath her eyes. "Anyway. I want to freshen up before my class."

"Are you sure?" Kara asked. "I can take the class for you if you want."

Tiffany nodded and opened her locker.

She pulled out a cosmetics bag. "I can handle this better if I don't think about it. I don't want to talk about it anymore." She headed toward the sinks, but she stopped just before she was around the corner. Suddenly awkward again, she looked at the floor in front of Kara and Ren. "Thanks."

After they left the dressing room, Kara said, "She laid into Mickey almost as soon as she got here."

Ren's eyes sought out Mickey, who was helping a client with the free weights. He looked like his regular jovial self again.

"Ah, that must be why he seemed a little upset when I came in. Why was she mad at him?"

Kara shook her head. "She wasn't, really. He was just the first safe person she came across after she got the news. Then she nearly took my head off for leaving a CD in the player she uses for her aerobics classes."

"Wow, I'm glad I didn't get here any earlier than I did."

"Yeah. One of my clients took offense at how she was talking to me, and the two of them got into it, and she finally blurted it all out and kind of melted down right in front of Sarah's afternoon Pilates class. Quite a contrast, Tiffany's angry wailing and Sarah's serene New Age music."

"Yikes. It's sounding more like a Tiffany scene every moment. But how sad about her mom."

"Horrible," Kara said. "I can't imagine."

"Did Tiffany say how far gone she is? Whether there's any hope for recovery?"

Kara shook her head. "We really didn't get a chance to talk that much."

"And what she said about her dad," Ren said. "You know, about his being the more loving one."

"Yeah, that was strange," Kara said. "I certainly don't see that imbalance with my parents."

Ren ran her hand through her hair. "I think I know what she meant. I'd have to say my dad was always the more loving of my parents too. It seems as if Mother was more equipped to handle the loss of a spouse than Dad would have been if she had been the one to die."

"But?"

"But just because she handled it differently doesn't mean it was easier for her. Something definitely changed about Mother after Dad's death."

At that moment Tiffany came out of the locker room, looking for all purposes as though she hadn't a care in the world. The coward in Ren wanted to believe that she didn't, but the Holy Spirit wouldn't let her get away with that. Ren felt she had no choice about the matter.

"Hey, Tiffany," Ren said softly as she got nearer.

"Can't talk now!" Tiffany said brightly, with an almost crazed threat in her eyes. "Got a class to teach!"

Ren figured Tiffany was afraid she'd start crying again if they talked about her mom.

"No big thing," Ren promised her. "I just wanted to invite you to come to church with Kara and me this Sunday."

Tiffany stopped in her tracks and looked at Ren as if she had just beamed down from Planet Nutjob.

"Or any Sunday." Ren spoke with less conviction.

"Yeah, that's a good idea," Kara piped in, finally getting her own cue from the Holy Spirit. "I'll give you the info when you finish your class, Tiffany."

Tiffany looked at both of them, expressionless, before stating two words in clearly separate sentences, as if they would never be joined in one harmonious thought. "Church. Me?"

Then, before walking into her class, she gave them both a look that hinted at flying pigs, fat chances, and the stuff of their wildest dreams.

Kara and Ren looked at each other. "We'll work on her," Kara said.

Ren nodded. "But for now, could we work on me a little? I've got five days to fit into my new BCBG pants for Tru's mom's birthday party." She lowered her voice melodramatically. "Your job, should you choose to accept it, will be to shave off enough space for me to actually eat something without popping my zipper."

Kara gave her an evil look and spoke in a terrible Slavic accent. "Grab your towel, Miss Young. Believe me. Vee have vays of making you shrink."

SEVENTEEN

Mariachi music bounced out to Ren the moment she stepped out of Tru's car and looked at his family home. It looked cozy. It sounded happy. But, despite the rich warmth of the sun that afternoon, a shiver ran through her. Tru's smile helped a little, but Ren couldn't shake the feeling that she was being presented at court to a powerful queen.

"I'm a little nervous." She retrieved her meager birthday gift — a box of gourmet chocolates — from the car seat just as she heard a man's comfortable, boisterous laugh and a child calling out something in Spanish.

"Don't worry about a thing," Tru said. "My mother seldom goes on the attack without her telltale tribal scream just beforehand. And my youngest brother's the only one who throws things at strangers."

Ren widened her eyes in horror for a split

second before catching herself. She gave his arm a little smack. "Really! I'm going to be the only one here who doesn't know anyone."

"You'll know me!" He took her hand. "And two of my sisters."

Ren snorted. "Yeah. My fan club," she said, remembering the fiasco at *Riverdance.*

He chuckled. "Don't worry about a thing, Ren. Everyone's going to love you."

The music stopped for a moment, and the voices were easier to hear. "Wow." Ren tried to smile bravely. "Sounds like hundreds of people." Were any of them speaking English? She could see it already. She was going to glob onto Tru like a frightened chimp and whimper pathetically if he didn't translate every morsel of conversation to set her mind at ease.

Another song started up. It sounded as if the party were in the backyard.

"Some of my friends from work will be here too," Tru said. "I'm eager for them to meet you."

That was nice. He was eager for *them* to meet *her,* rather than the other way around. Ren smiled at him as they walked into the house.

Ren breathed in and said, "Mmm. Smells marvelous!" She didn't know quite what she smelled, but garlic figured prominently, and a delicious scent from the grill had wafted inside. She was right. The party was out back, so they cut through the house without Tru giving her a tour. But Ren glanced around, spotting family photographs on a baby grand piano in the living room, book collections on shelves in the den, and huge trays of food in the kitchen. She placed the chocolates with the other gifts on the kitchen counter. She heard more laughter and people talking loudly over the music as they reached the door to the patio. She said a quick prayer for calmness and felt more at ease.

But just as they were about to walk outside, one of Ren's contact lenses started bothering her. A lot. She stopped in her tracks and fussed with it.

"Are you all right?" Tru asked. He said it loudly because of the music.

"Agh," Ren shouted back, her head down. She pulled at her eyelashes. "It's my contact lens. Sometimes I get these eyelashes that just grow all stupid and irritate my lenses. I think that might be what's going on here." Was she really going to have one of these ridiculous contact lens crises here? Now? She broke out in a cold sweat. "Could I use your bathroom sink for a second?" She spoke to Tru with her head still down, and he had to lead her to the bathroom as she cautiously shuffled like an elderly dowager.

Ren popped out the lens and looked at her lashes in the mirror. Sure enough, there were two rebels hanging down, getting tangled in her bottom lashes with every blink. For some reason that insane little entanglement always gave her problems with her lenses. Her only hope was to pluck out the stray eyelashes. But without tweezers, she merely succeeded in pulling off her mascara. She put the contact back in and looked in the mirror. She looked as if she had been crying. From one eye. So she pulled off some mascara from the good eye. Now she looked a little more even and a little less attractive. But the contact wasn't bothering her as much, so she stepped out.

Tru was in the kitchen, talking with a huge man who looked as Anglo as Ren did. They both looked at her when she emerged.

"There she is," Tru said. His effort to make her feel missed couldn't have been sweeter. He came over to her, cheerful but concerned. "Everything all right now?"

Ren nodded. "I think so. Sorry."

"Ren," Tru said above the music, "this is my brother-in-law, David. Cessy's husband. You haven't met Cessy yet — she's the oldest of my sisters. David's a bear, but he's a teddy bear."

David enveloped Ren's hands in his, and they kind of disappeared for a moment. His hands really were like bear paws. He talked over the music with little effort. His voice naturally boomed. "Great to meet you, Ren! I've heard good things about you already."

"Let's go outside," Tru said. "I've got to turn down that boom box before the neighbors call the police."

"The neighbors are all out there," David said, and they laughed.

Yes, Ren thought. *This day is going to be fine.*

But as they walked out, her contact started up again. She wanted to scream. Again, she came to a quick halt. It was her natural response, the only way she could keep from walking into walls, strangers, or traffic. David had walked on ahead, but Tru, ever vigilant, saw at once what had happened. He gently placed his hand on Ren's shoulder and shouted, "Can I do anything to help you with that, Ren?"

This was too much. She shouted back, "I'd just like to go home and pluck out my eyelashes."

Of course, that last sentence was shouted into the crowd at the exact moment the song finished. A sudden hush enveloped Ren. She popped her lens into her hand and squinted up at an entire party's worth of people staring at her, the crazy lady who would rather pluck out her eyelashes than be there with them.

She looked at Tru, who was clearly suppressing laughter for her sake. The fact that she hadn't embarrassed him helped.

David the Bear stepped over to her. Just before the next song started, he said, "Don't worry about it. The first time I met the family I had just spilled half a glass of water in my lap. That was a memorable entrance." He gave her a wink.

Ren looked at Tru. "I love your brother-in-law, Tru."

"Yeah, me too," Tru said, looking at David.

The music pulled the attention away from Ren, and she said a quick prayer of thanks. A striking young woman turned the volume down before approaching them and looping her arm through David's. She extended her hand to Ren.

"You're Ren, right? I'm Cessy, Tru's sister."

Gingerly, Ren dropped her lens into her left hand before shaking hands with Cessy. "I'd like to say I usually make a better first impression, but I think I already have too much history with your family to pull that one off."

"First impressions are way overrated." Cessy pointed to Ren's left hand. "Are you having contact problems? My brother, Devon, has some cleaning stuff upstairs." She looked at Tru. "Let me take her upstairs so she can be comfortable before she meets everyone."

"Okay with you?" Tru asked Ren.

"Yeah, that'd be great."

Cessy turned her away from Tru and toward the house.

"Cessy," Tru called, "find her some tweezers too, will you?"

Ten minutes later Ren was cleaned, tweezed, and primed for action. And she could see that she and Cessy would be fast friends. Cessy was warm and considerate, just like Tru. She and David had two children. "Both of whom are downstairs," she said, "getting spoiled rotten by my mother. They're the only grandchildren so far."

Ren didn't know if she imagined it or not, but she thought Cessy's eyes twinkled at her when she said that last sentence.

They rejoined the party, and Ren spotted Tru immediately. He was surrounded by people and had just said something to make them laugh. Ren was struck again by how gorgeous he was. She felt a quiver in her stomach as she approached him. She wanted this day to go well. Tru noticed her and looked so happy to see her that she could have melted right there on the patio.

He put his hand on her back to guide her into the small group. Ren smiled at them as he introduced her, trying to play little mind tricks to remember their names. The tall, gray-haired man with the short, chubby wife — Guy and Rhonda — Gray Guy and Round Rhonda.

"Oh! Guy from work?" Ren said. "Tru's mentioned you!"

Guy laughed. "I think he might have mentioned you too."

The others laughed, at Tru's expense, and he actually turned red. Ren felt her own face flush too, but, boy was she flattered.

The other two people in the group were also Tru's coworkers, a cute young nurse named Brenda (Braces Brenda — she was that young) and another male nurse, Bill. Bill was the spitting image of Bill Cosby. He'd be easy to remember.

"Hey, we'll be right back," Tru told them. "My mother's going to kill me if we don't get over there and say hello."

Even though the distance was short, they

took forever getting to his mother. They stopped to greet, meet, and kiss the cheek of every single person between Tru's work crowd and the group surrounding his mom. Ren gave up on her little name game. Most of the people were family members, all introduced as Uncle someone, Aunt somebody, or Cousin whoever. And everybody seemed to have a name like Fabricio, Mauricio, Consuela, or Conchita. It was like high school social studies all over again, and the names of all the countries sounded exactly alike.

"Your family's gigantic!" Ren said. "How many cousins do you have?"

"They're not all cousins. We just call someone 'cousin' if they're related at all. Gets too complicated otherwise."

"And this isn't complicated?" Ren asked, overwhelmed.

He stopped in his tracks and looked her in the eye. A big grin spread across his face.

"What?" Ren asked.

He shook his head a little, as if he wasn't going to tell her. Then, "Nothing. You're just so real. It's one of my favorite things about you."

How did he do that? With a few simple words, he made it all just fine. Bring on the world! Ren could tackle anything.

Then she met Tru's mother.

Ren was surprised at how young she looked, especially considering the tough marital situation Tru had described. Ren felt that her own marital experience had aged her years. But Mrs. Sayers was simply an older version of her lovely daughters, with shorter, salt-and-peppered hair. Her expression, already happy, glowed when she saw Tru. She spoke to him in Spanish as if he were very young, taking his face in her hands and kissing him on both cheeks.

She looked at Ren politely when Tru introduced them. Not warmly. Politely. Ren might not have noticed the lack of warmth had she not just seen her gush over her son.

"So nice to meet you," Ren said.

"Yes," Mrs. Sayers said. That was it. Yes. Maybe she didn't understand much English?

"Mi hijo," she said to Tru, "go get me another lemonade, will you?"

Perfect English. Hmm.

"I'll be right back, Ren," Tru said. "You want lemonade too?"

Ren tried to will him to stay, but who was she kidding? She was a big girl, and she needed to make grown-up conversation with this lady eventually. "Sure," Ren told him. "Sounds great, thanks."

He smiled and walked off into the sunset, leaving his damsel in semi-distress. His damsel plastered on a smile of her own, squared her shoulders, and turned.

Eighteen

Those eyes of hers! Ren wouldn't call them steely, exactly. After all, they were brown — and as dark as Tru's. Brown eyes always had a certain warmth and softness, and Mrs. Sayers' eyes did have that.

Penetrating, that's what they were. But Ren was what they were penetrating. No looking away from a gaze like that, even though that's exactly what Ren felt like doing. Now the loud, cheerful music was a godsend, making constant conversation less necessary.

Be with me, Lord.

To Mrs. Sayers, Ren said, "What a wonderful party! It's so nice to have such a large family and so many friends to celebrate with."

Mrs. Sayers smiled, hesitantly. "Yes."

Again with the yes. She'd be a blast to interview. Maybe she was just shy?

"You are in love with my son?"

If Ren had been drinking that lemonade Tru was fetching, she would have sprayed it out in response. Nope. Not shy at all.

Ever articulate, Ren said, "Uh, pardon?" Yes, that was an excellent choice — get her to say it again. Ren squirmed before she could stop herself.

"You love my son? Truman." She said this last as if she thought maybe Ren had forgotten who brought her to the party.

"I . . . it's early yet. We're just getting to know each other right now."

Mrs. Sayers glanced down, considering. "Truman's father and I?" She looked up at Ren, intent. "We knew like that." She snapped her fingers.

Ren's eyes widened for a split second. *Yeah. And everyone knows how well that turned out.*

Ren froze, hoping she hadn't just said that out loud. So mean. But she felt that this woman was deliberately challenging her, and Ren had only just met her.

Then she realized the Lord's blessing in her silence. Mrs. Sayers had time with her own thoughts about her comment.

"He's not here today, Truman's father," she said. She looked into Ren's eyes. Was she trying to figure out how much Tru had told Ren?

196

Somehow Ren knew Mrs. Sayers would take offense at an offering of sympathy. But that's what she felt. Her husband had rejected her too. Ren hated to let a possible bond slip away, but good grief, this situation was sticky.

"Mamita!" said someone behind Ren.

She turned to see Tru's middle sister, Anna — the one Ren and Kara had accidentally insulted at *Riverdance.* Anna came around to kiss her mother. She said something in Spanish and then looked at Ren. With a happy intake of breath, she smiled broadly.

"Ren! Welcome!" She gave Ren a hug and kiss almost as affectionate as what she had just given her mother. "I didn't know you would be here. Haven't talked with Tru all week. You brave soul, meeting this crazy family all at once like this!" She shot a secret glance at her mother, and then she looked back at Ren with a quick raise of her eyebrows. "You okay here? I could use some help bringing food out."

Before Ren could tell Anna how very much she loved her, Tru showed up with three glasses of lemonade. He gave Anna a quick kiss on the cheek before handing a glass to his mother and one to Ren. He offered his glass to Anna, who shook her head.

He asked, "Did you bring Michelle with you?"

Anna nodded. "She was attacked by Cessy's two little hooligans as soon as she walked in."

Tru looked at Ren. "You also met Michelle at the concert, Ren. You remember? The eavesdropper?"

He and Anna both laughed, so Ren did too. But she cringed to think that either Tru's mother already knew that story or might ask to hear it now. Ren looked in her direction and saw that she had already been spirited away by some male relative, with whom she danced on the small patio with two other couples. Bless that short and stocky dancing man. Ren liked him already.

She jumped at a crashing of metal behind her. She spun around, as did everyone else, to see a jumble of people, folding chairs, and a collapsed card table. A lone chair teetered on two legs before it finally fell, and a football silently swiveled across the lawn. The laughter and giggles coming from the pile gave some assurance to onlookers that no serious injuries had occurred.

Ren felt initial relief that this scene was not her doing. But immediately after that, she rushed to help up one of the children, an adorable boy about Casey's age. When he saw the attention he had drawn, he started crying. Others rushed past them, everyone playing a part in the aftermath. They pulled another young boy and two teenagers from the wreckage.

"Oh, you poor thing," Ren said to the boy. "Where does it hurt?"

His crying slowed, and he touched his shin, looking into her eyes.

"Ooo, the shin. That stings," Ren said. "Not much meat there, huh?"

He shook his head. He suddenly smiled. "You smell pretty."

"What's the matter with you, man?" Tru said to one of the teenaged boys. "The boys could've really gotten hurt. And what are you doing, playing football here?"

The older of the two, chastened, said, "We didn't mean to get crazy, bro. We were just teasing the little guys. Got a little out of hand. Sorry."

The younger teen rubbed his elbow. "Yeah, sorry." He looked at Mrs. Sayers, who headed in their direction. "Sorry, Mami." He looked at the upset table and chairs around him. "Was this always here?"

The older one started laughing, but he stopped when Mrs. Sayers gave him a half-serious smack on the arm. She was yelling at him in Spanish, but after shielding himself from her smacks, he laughed and gathered her up in a big hug, lifting her off the ground. She kept yelling, but she was laughing too.

Ren thought her mouth may have been hanging open. So many emotions right there in front of everyone. If any of this had happened at her mother's home . . . oh, forget it, *none* of this would have happened at her mother's home. The loud music, the boisterous crowd, the casual setting, the crashing, the crying, the slapping, the laughing. For goodness' sake, even the earthy smell of garlic! That wouldn't even happen at her mother's home. Ren just loved the difference. But she was scared by it too. Could she ever fit in?

Cessy gathered up the two little boys and did a milder version of the scolding Mrs. Sayers had done with her sons. But she was the one who did the hugging, and she kissed each of them on the forehead. The boy Ren had helped whispered something in Cessy's ear, and she looked at Ren and grinned.

"Kyle, this is Uncle Tru's friend, Ms. Rennie. She's a teacher, just like your Ms. Simpson." She glanced at her older son. "And this is Johnny. These are my boys."

They both gave Ren shy nods before Cessy said, "Why don't you two go help

Aunt Anna and Aunt Michelle bring out more food. Then maybe Abuelita won't be mad at you for tearing up her party."

Cessy quickly squelched their protests by raising one eyebrow. They ran off into the house, calling for Anna and Michelle.

Tru and his brothers finished setting the table and chairs back up. Before the teens could walk away, Tru said, "Hang on, you two."

They looked at him, and Ren could see the comfortable respect they had for him. She remembered Tru's comments about his father's absence from their lives. Obviously Tru had filled his father's shoes in parenting these boys.

Tru smiled at her. "Ren, these two ruffians are my brothers."

They both held out their hands to shake hers.

"Harris," said the oldest. "Sorry for the mess." He cocked his head in the direction of the crash.

Ren laughed. "I'm glad you all survived."

"I'm Devon," the other said, grinning like the Cheshire Cat. "Want to dance?"

"Not now, Casanova," Tru said dryly. "You might want to run up and change. Mom's not going to let you sit down to eat with those grass stains all over your pants."

Devon looked down at his knees. "Right. Okay." He looked at Ren again. "Nice meeting you, Ren." And he was gone.

Tru put an arm across her shoulders as they watched his brothers enter the house. "I'm afraid Devon's taken after my father more than anyone else. Pretty strange, considering he's spent the least amount of time around Papi."

Ren looked at Tru to respond and was struck by how close his face was to hers. The realization made her suddenly flustered.

"What is it?" he asked.

Ren blushed but tried to focus on what she had meant to say. "I think that's the only time I've ever heard you call him anything other than 'my father.' "

"Truman shows his father respect," Tru's mother said behind them, making both of them jump.

How long had she been standing there? Had she seen their faces so close together? The heat of embarrassment rushed up Ren's neck.

"Mami!" Tru said. "Don't sneak up on people like that!"

"What sneak? I just came to tell you to come eat." She shrugged, as if nothing had happened, and walked away. But before she was out of earshot, she pointed her finger at Tru, like a judge. "You look guilty, mi hijo."

They watched her then, as she went from person to person, encouraging them to eat. Tru and Ren looked at each other, both of them — yes — looking guilty. Then they started laughing.

The food was delicious. Not spicy, as Ren had expected, but salty and flavorful. Tru and Ren sat with the people from his work.

"Guy and I love Tru," Round Rhonda said, between bites, "but the food at these family parties is what we really look forward to." She winked at Tru.

"You got that right," Bill said, just before shoveling a forkful of sauce-covered potatoes into his mouth.

Tru said, "Story of my life. When I moved out of my mother's home, I lost all of my friends. Had to start all over again. I got these people over here as soon as I could to get them hooked on the food. Just as I'm doing with you."

"I think it's working," Ren said.

"Hope so." Tru's smile suddenly softened as he looked at her. She didn't know if he meant it to happen, but he made the moment feel so serious that everyone fell silent.

And there was that quiver in her stomach again.

Braces Brenda put her fork down. "Well, if that isn't the most romantic look I've ever seen, I don't know romance."

Guy laughed and nudged Tru's foot with his. "You should have known better than to invite this motley crew to your second date with Ren." Then he looked at Ren. "We're all hopeless romantics, hopelessly blunt —"

"Just hopeless in general," Rhonda said. "We live for moments like this."

Bill took a bite of meat and nodded his head at someone approaching from Ren's side.

"You like my cooking, no?" Tru's mother said to Bill.

Ren had missed her in her peripheral vision. She thought about looking over her shoulder, in case her clone was behind her. She seemed to be everywhere.

"Everyone likes your cooking, Mami," Tru said, as she sat on his other side. He put his arm around her and kissed her on the cheek.

She looked content. She even gave Ren a smile, and Ren didn't see a hint of confrontation in her eyes.

"Excellent food, Mrs. Sayers," Ren said, as she reached down to retrieve the napkin she had dropped.

"Thank —" Mrs. Sayers halted right in the middle of her word, her eyes shooting a look at Ren's neck. "Thank you." She had composed herself, but she was back to that wary appraisal she had given Ren before.

Ren couldn't help herself. She reached up to her neck. The only thing there was her necklace, the one with the small gold cross. It had fallen free from her blouse when she bent to get the napkin. She looked at Mrs. Sayers again, and she knew. That was it.

Mrs. Sayers continued with her conversation, even including Ren. But that brief moment of warmth was over. Something was wrong.

NINETEEN

Ren wasn't able to talk with Tru alone until he was driving her home. He softly hummed one of the songs they had heard at the party. He had such a soothing voice. The peace in the car would have been a comfortable contrast to the party's boisterous atmosphere, but Tru must have sensed unease on her part.

"You okay?"

"I'm not sure. Tru, I almost felt as if your mother was starting to warm up to me back there."

"Yeah, she's just overprotective. She'll loosen up, I promise."

Ren shook her head. "There was a particular moment when something really shut her down toward me. And I think it was when she saw this."

Ren pulled her cross back out of her neckline, and Tru glanced over. Ren saw him wince, and her stomach pulled tight inside. Oh, no. She had assumed something about Tru — that he was a believer — and now she was going to have to detach herself from this beautiful, dear man. But . . .

"But, Tru, I thought you said . . . yes, you've said at least once that you were a Christian. Right? Did I misunderstand?"

He slowed the car and pulled into the parking lot of a drugstore. Uh-oh. This was too serious for him to discuss and drive at the same time. Ren's palms were clammy.

So, of course, he took one of her hands.

"You didn't misunderstand anything, Ren. I love the Lord with all my heart."

Ren breathed out, amazed at the relief. Now she felt as if she could handle anything else he said.

"Here's the thing," he said. "My mother used to go to church every Sunday, and she brought all of us kids with her. She used to say life would go well if we'd make sure we never missed a single Sunday."

Ren grimaced, but she didn't say anything.

"When she was pregnant with Devon and my father's infidelity came to light, she prayed constantly to God and to some saint. Saint Monica, I think. She prayed for the healing of her marriage."

"She blames God for the failure of the marriage?"

"Yeah, and she's not too happy with that saint, either."

"So my cross offended her because she's angry with God?"

He took her other hand. "There's more."

Ren took a deep breath and waited.

"Since she stopped going to church, she stopped taking us. So we didn't get any more exposure to the Lord. And no one reflected a lack of spirituality in their lifestyle more than I did." He looked down at their hands, gently stroking her fingers with his. "I hadn't planned on talking with you about this so soon, Ren. I wanted us to know each other better."

"Tru, you don't have to tell me anything until you're ready. As long as I know you love the Lord, we can take our time." Ren thought about her earlier, panicked desire to find a husband — a daddy for Casey — and was doubly convicted about the importance of waiting on God's timing.

"Well, I need to tell you this part, so you'll understand what happened at the party. About Mom. I told you today that Devon had taken after my father more than any of the kids. But when I was his age, I was a lot like him. Seeing how my father broke my mother's heart didn't stop me from getting involved with girl after girl, woman after woman. I know my mother struggled with concern about my morals, even while she was relieved that I wasn't getting seriously involved with any one woman. That way I was still the man of her house, and she could count on me when she needed help."

"Then you found Jesus?"

He looked into her eyes. "Then I found Emily."

Ren suddenly realized how his mother must have felt when he found this Emily. Ren didn't like hearing her name, and she didn't even know him then. She tried to subtly rub the goose bumps away from her arms. But that required pulling her hands away from his. That made him pause and look at her for a moment. Ren tried to give him an encouraging smile.

"Emily was a Christian woman I met at work — another nurse. She was attractive and smart. And I could tell she liked me, but she wouldn't go out with me because I wasn't a Christian. So I started going to her church just to get her to date me."

Ren couldn't believe this was *her* Tru being described. But, then again, they hadn't even started her story yet.

Tru said, "Funny thing, though, was that the Lord was able to work around my confused motives. I accepted Him as my

Savior without a further thought for Emily."

"Your mother's angry about your accepting Christ?"

"Partly. She considers my faith a kind of ignorance. But the real problem came after Emily and I started dating."

Again, Ren felt a twinge of jealousy, followed by the conviction of her own past.

"We were serious from the start — otherwise we wouldn't have started seeing each other. I fell pretty hard. We . . . got engaged. And, to tell you the truth, my mother started to support us. She saw how happy I was, so she set aside her differences with God. She embraced Emily as a future daughter-in-law."

Ren's mind raced. *Emily's gone, so what happened?*

"It wasn't until we took the premarital class at her church that Emily realized she didn't really want to marry me."

That floored Ren, which showed her how taken she was with this man. She was amazed that any woman wouldn't want to marry him. But how could she be so sure they would work out? How could he? For that matter, how could his mother? Mrs. Sayers probably saw Ren as another potential heartbreak for her son.

"I was a wreck, even though I knew it was

best that she left me before we went through with the wedding."

So he knew about that pain of rejection too.

"Your mother doesn't like my being a Christian, like Emily."

He nodded. "She doesn't like that about you. She doesn't trust the church that led — in her mind — to my pain. And she doesn't trust God, because He didn't make her husband the man she wanted him to be."

Ren sat there, concerned but not overwhelmed. She felt God's grace at that moment.

"But what I believe," Tru said, "is that Emily was a blessing in my life. If I hadn't met her, I wouldn't have been led to the Lord. He stayed when she left, and I know He'll always stay."

Yes. That was the very thing that helped Ren heal as much as she did after Greg divorced her. She was a wreck when he left. But Jesus had stayed right there, through it all. He would always stay with her.

Ren loved the belief she saw in Tru. His loss hadn't destroyed his faith. It had strengthened it. However confused his mother might be, he knew his God. Their God.

Ren almost said, "I love you." But then she realized it was her love for Jesus that she wanted to declare. So she did. "I love Jesus."

Tru put her hands together within his, as though they were praying. He planted a gentle kiss on her fingertips and spoke in a whisper. "I love Him too."

Twenty

That peck on the fingertips was the full extent of their kissing that night. But Tru seemed eager to see her again.

Before they said good night, he suggested Ren's checking out his church the next morning. "How about I pick you up so we can go together?" he said.

But Kara and Ren were scheduled for nursery duty during the first service at Christian Chapel.

"Why don't you come to my church?" Ren said. "I could meet you before the second service. You could see Kara again and meet her fiancé, Gabe."

He grinned in that stunning way of his, with a trace of the little boy in his expression. "I'd love to."

So Ren found herself taking extra care when she got ready the next morning. She went for soft and feminine, with a blue dress the color of a robin's eggs. It had a nice swing to it when she moved and was one of her more flattering outfits.

"You look amazing!" Kara said when Ren walked into the nursery.

Ren promptly put on one of the smocks the church provided for the child care volunteers and smiled. "Tru's coming to the second service today."

Kara's eyes widened, and Ren could see she was ready to ask for details about the birthday party yesterday. But two of the high school girls joined them at that moment, so they kept their conversation to more general subjects. Still, Kara pointedly interceded on Ren's behalf whenever little Danny — affectionately known as the Big Barfer — toddled in her direction.

"Gotta keep you tidy and fresh," Kara said.

Ren laughed. "What about you? Isn't Gabe coming today?"

"Oh, girl, think about it. The poor guy's seen me in flop sweats at the gym, smashing face first into walls, and covered in more wax than an exhibit at Madame Tussauds. Yet he still wants to marry me. A little baby barf isn't going to scare him away."

She had a point. Before their courtship even began, Gabe witnessed some of Kara's messiest — and least graceful — moments of all time.

Ren sighed. "I can't imagine ever feeling that secure with a man." She lowered her voice. "I didn't even experience that kind of security with Greg."

Kara glanced at the teens. They were absorbed in a make-believe kitchen scene with three of the little girls, who served them tiny plates of plastic eggs and toast. "Ren, not to speak too ill of the ex, but I don't think Greg was the kind of guy to instill a sense of security in a girl. Your lack of confidence with him just shows how savvy you were. Are."

"Hmm. Maybe. But I did wait around quite a while, thinking he might come back to me. Even after the divorce. That might not have been so savvy."

Kara shrugged and bravely lifted Danny into her arms. "So you're an optimist. You gave him the benefit of the doubt. Just another of your many good qualities."

Ren chuckled. "You really know how to put a positive spin on things, don't you? Remind me to hire you to handle my PR if I ever run for president."

"Will do." Kara looked at the Big Barfer. "In the meantime, Danny and I are going to play tractors. What do you say, Danny?"

■ ■ ■ ■

Between services Gabe came back to the nursery to get Kara and Ren — well, Kara, actually. But Ren tagged along and kept her eyes alert for Tru once they walked into the fellowship hall.

"What does he look like?" Gabe asked, scanning the crowd and waving briefly to someone he recognized.

"He's almost your height, dark hair a bit longer than yours," Ren told him. She couldn't see Tru anywhere, so she looked toward the front doors and kept up the description for Gabe. "Kind of Hispanic-looking. Warm brown eyes. Dark eyelashes. Perfect olive skin. Really handsome, kind face. Nice build."

"Likes moonlit nights and long walks on the beach," Kara said, her voice dreamy.

Ren pulled a face at her and then noticed Tru standing beyond her, near the entrance to the sanctuary. Her heart picked up its pace dramatically. Not only because he was every bit as handsome as she had just described, but because she could see that some shapely woman was talking to him.

Drat. They weren't exactly barracudas here, but competition was mighty fierce in the Northern Virginia area. There were so many attractive, single Christian women —

Her thoughts halted at the very moment Kara grasped her arm, looking in the same direction.

"That's no single Christian woman," Ren said, a hint of alarm in her voice.

Kara said, "No, that's —"

"Tiffany?" Gabe said, having followed their eyes. Ren looked at him, and he was still looking in Tiffany's direction. "Well, isn't that nice?" he said. "Looks as if she's already met someone."

Ren's mouth dropped open as she gasped at Gabe, as if he had betrayed her. He looked at Ren, and confusion crossed his face just before he glanced back at Tru and Tiffany.

"Gabe!" Kara said. "That's not someone. That's Tru."

He widened his eyes in innocent realization. "Oh, cool!" In the span of a few seconds, he smiled, looked at Tru and Tiffany again, and then looked back at Ren, a quick frown pulling his eyebrows down. "You'd better get over there."

He didn't have to tell her twice. And Kara followed right behind her, with Gabe bringing up the rear.

Tru saw Ren and broke from his polite

smile into a genuine, happy grin.

Tiffany turned around, and Ren experienced a few feelings she wasn't proud of. First, she had to struggle to keep her eyes from dropping down to the generous cleavage Tiffany's knit top displayed. How difficult must the same restraint have been for Tru? Secondly, Ren had to admit feeling relief when she saw that Tiffany was a bit worn-looking. But then she remembered why.

Her mom.

Ren felt so shameful she would have hugged Tiffany if she thought Tiffany would accept it.

"Tiffany!" Kara said. "I'm glad you decided to come, after all."

Tru looked at Ren. "We just figured out we were both here to meet the same people! Tiffany approached me to ask about the service without realizing I'm as new as she is. I'm afraid I was a disappointing guide."

Tiffany shot him a sexy glance. "Hardly."

Suddenly Ren didn't feel quite so shameful. And the urge to hug Tiffany was a distant memory.

"Uh, Tru," Ren said, "you know Kara, and you met Tiffany. This is Gabe, Kara's fiancé."

The men shook hands. Tru squinted his

eyes a bit at Gabe. "You look familiar."

"Ever get lunch or dinner from Paolino's Deli? Ashburn Town Centre?" Gabe asked.

Tru smiled. "Oh, yeah! All the time. That's your place, huh? We cater from you for a lot of our meetings at the hospital too."

Tiffany's sigh interrupted. "So what's the deal here? Do we hang out here or go in there?" She pointed to the sanctuary. "Do I have to put anything on my head? 'Cause I forgot to bring anything with me, and I'm not doing the tissue-on-the-head thing."

"No, Tiffany," Ren said, "we don't have rules about covering your head. I think you'll feel pretty relaxed here. And we could go on in, yeah. The music's about to start up."

Ren didn't know if it was female manipulation or the grace of God at work, but the way they entered their row worked out just fine. Gabe, Kara, Tiffany, Ren, and Tru. Ren was going to have a hard enough time focusing with Tru sitting next to her. Having Tiffany next to *him* would have been more than Ren could handle in her admittedly selfish flesh.

As it was, Tiffany proved quite a distraction, anyway. They needn't have worried about her feeling uncomfortable or intimidated by the surroundings. Halfway through the worship, she said, rather loudly, "Man, you guys sing enough, don't you?"

After the people in front of them turned back around, Ren whispered to her. "See, this helps us detach from the world and focus on God. We call it 'worship.' The music and singing are like prayer."

Which may have been the reason, after they prayed, that Tiffany harrumphed and said, "I thought the music was like prayer. And then you pray too?"

Honestly. Had the woman never set foot inside a church before? Seen a movie scene set inside a church?

Two things made it all right, though. First, Tru gently took Ren's hand, and when she looked at him, he gave her a brief squeeze. There was an amused twinkle in his eyes, so Ren knew he empathized with her frustration with Tiffany's loudly whispered comments.

Secondly, Tiffany's questions, complaints, and foot jiggling eventually came to a halt with Pastor Dan's sermon. As God would have it, Dan had reached the eighth chapter in Luke for his teaching that week. His sermon focused upon the healing of the woman who had bled for twelve years. If Tiffany had ever heard the story before, it didn't show. She was riveted to everything

Dan said. When, at sermon's end, he asked the congregation to pray, Ren couldn't help but notice that Tiffany bowed her head.

Kara and Gabe needed to stay after and talk with Pastor Dan about the premarital counseling class, so Tiffany walked out of the sanctuary with Tru and Ren.

She said, "If I can get my mom to do this faith thing, she's supposed to get healed of her cancer? How come everyone doesn't do that?"

Tru looked at Ren and barely lifted an eyebrow.

"Oh," Ren said. "Well, it doesn't necessarily work like that, Tiffany. The, uh, the only thing we're guaranteed by putting our faith in Jesus is a spiritual healing. I mean, I say the *only* thing, but that's really the only thing that matters."

Tiffany snorted. "Easy for you to say. You don't have cancer."

Ren bit her lip. She knew she wasn't the most eloquent evangelist. "I'm sorry. I didn't mean to sound so casual about your mom. But I just sounded kind of casual about Christ, and I . . ." Ren sighed. "Sometimes I'm just not very articulate, Tiffany."

"So what's the point?" Tiffany said. "Why'd he — Pastor Dan — why did he tell us that story if we can't expect the same healing that woman got? I understood what he said about eternal life and all that. Fine. But why bother believing, if you don't know you'll get healed?"

"Um, well, it's not like a bargaining thing, asking Jesus to take control," Ren said, "which is pretty much what that woman did — she just laid it all down when she followed Him and touched His robe. It's not even always a giving *in* thing. Sometimes faith is more like a giving *up* thing. Just throwing your hands up in the air and saying, 'Man, Jesus, I just can't do it. I give up.' Sometimes you accept things — you believe them — not because of what that belief will get you. You just accept it because you realize . . . well, you realize it's true."

Tiffany stared at her then, and Ren knew that she was at least thinking about what Ren had just said. She had this look in her eyes that was different from what Ren usually saw there. More dilated, if that makes any sense. Tiffany looked wide open for a moment.

Then Ren looked at Tru, who had remained strangely quiet during this exchange. Ren realized he had left this moment for her, Jesus, and Tiffany. Very cool.

Even more cool was the way he looked at Ren. She swore he seemed totally enamored.

Nothing like flooring a guy by witnessing. Imagine!

Of course, the very thing Tru seemed to appreciate in her was what his mother despised. Ren couldn't help wondering how that might play out, and when.

TWENTY-ONE

The following week was National Education Week at school. The chaos of activities, assemblies, and ongoing parent visits was actually a blessing. Ren was too busy to worry about Tru, his mother, Casey, *his* mother, any of it. But by Tuesday afternoon she was already in dire need of a break.

After a few calls she learned she wasn't alone. Jeremy and Sandy both jumped at the chance to go for an early dinner with friends. Even Kara wanted to go.

As Sandy locked her office door, she told Jeremy and Ren, "Rick's going to join us. Is that okay? My poor hubby. It's already been a busy week for him too."

"Super!" Jeremy said. "Glad to finally meet him."

"You guys getting a sitter for Michael?" Ren asked her.

Sandy shook her head. "He's staying with a classmate who's on his soccer team. Just going home with him after practice. Rick and I are going to a movie after dinner with y'all. Making a regular date night of it."

Ren considered calling Tru and "making a date night of it." But they were going out tomorrow night. She could wait until then, she supposed. Besides, tonight she kind of wanted to talk about Tru — or at least about his mother. She had already hinted to her friends about problems, but even with Kara she had been unable to go into detail. She needed to unload a bit, and she sure wasn't going to do that if Tru were with them.

Kara, Sandy, and Jeremy were becoming Ren's touchstones in these matters. They felt like her grip on levelheadedness. They might all have different takes on a given situation, but they seemed to balance each other out well, collectively looking at all the angles.

"Okay," Ren said to Jeremy and Sandy as they walked down the school hall together. "I'll pick up Kara in about an hour and meet you at the steak house. Five thirty-ish?"

"Perfect," Jeremy said, walking toward the school's front doors. "Cheers, then. See you at half past."

A few hours later Jeremy pulled his Mini

Cooper into the restaurant parking lot next to Kara and Ren. He wiggled his eyebrows at them, as if he were flirting with strangers. Both women laughed.

"You do my heart good, Jeremy," Ren said, when he met her at her car door.

"That's my only desire, love."

Kara walked around to them. "And what am I? I mean nothing to you, I take it?"

"My other only desire," Jeremy said, giving Kara a hug.

The three of them looped arms and walked toward the restaurant. They saw Sandy's van near the front door, soccer stickers all over the back fender.

"I finally get to meet The Marvelous Rick," Kara said. "Will I be able to behave myself, or is he just too much man to bear?"

"He's an awful lot of man," Ren said. "Brace yourself."

"Yes," Jeremy said. "I understand there's especially a lot of him right about here." He pulled an arm free and tapped his stomach.

Ren laughed. "You really are going to love him, guys. His personality . . . well, he's the perfect man for Sandy."

The moment they walked in, Ren heard Rick's laugh above the other voices and noises. Louder than anyone else there. And absolutely genuine. It made her eager to give him a hug, which she did as soon as they reached the table.

"Sandy told me you had become even more beautiful," Rick said, squishing Ren in his big, clumsy arms. "I wouldn't have believed it, but my wife is right, as always."

"I keep telling him that," Sandy said. "Rick, honey, I've told you about Jeremy, the heartthrob of the school."

Jeremy scoffed as Rick pumped his arm. "News to me. Rick, great to meet you. I imagine you know how highly praised you are in your wife's circle."

Rick and Sandy exchanged contented smiles with each other.

Jeremy sat down in the horseshoe-shaped booth, next to Sandy, and Ren scooted in next to him.

She sniffed the air. The people in the booth next to them had just received their order. She wasn't sure what it was, but it was certainly fried. She scrunched her nose and knew she'd be ordering light this evening.

"And this wonderful gal is Kara," Sandy said, just as Kara sat down.

Kara stood back up again, smiling, and shook Rick's hand while Sandy talked.

"Kara's not with the school. Ren brought her into the fold. She's a personal fitness trainer. I told her we were going to give her some business. Have her whip us into shape."

Rick patted his belly with fondness before taking his seat. "I don't know, Sandy. Do we really want to go messing with perfection?"

"Good point, hon," Sandy said. "Oh, and she's engaged to some superhot guy."

Kara laughed and then feigned a pout. "I thought you'd never get around to mentioning that."

"All right, gang," Sandy said, "we've already ordered potato skins and calamari."

"I need to lighten up this week, Sandy," Ren said. "I ate so much at Tru's mother's last weekend. I'm the one who needs Kara's personal training."

"I'll eat," Kara said, "but no dessert tonight. Gabe and I are getting together Friday night for the premarital counseling class at church."

Ren noticed Rick look at Sandy and raise his eyebrows. Sandy nodded once at him. "Told you Ren and Kara were good, church-going girls. Get used to it."

Kara beamed. "We're going out after class. I want to wear those tan slacks," she said to Ren, "and I don't want them to look too tight. Don't want the bumpers to stick out."

She looked down and poked the outside of her slim hips.

Sandy snorted. "Bumpers, schmumpers. My guess is he's a better person than that, or you wouldn't be marrying him."

A heavy sigh from Jeremy prompted everyone to look at him. Ren chuckled and put her arm around him. "No one in the picture these days, Jeremy?"

Rick said, "Or was that sigh because of all the girl talk? Maybe you ladies overwhelm him with your diets and workouts and fashion tips." He said this last in a mincing tone. The voice was so strange coming from the big man that even Jeremy laughed.

"No, mate," Jeremy said. "I love hanging with these gorgeous creatures. I enjoy everything they say. They're so wonderfully female."

Ren gave him a peck on the cheek. "You're such a doll, Jeremy."

Just for a moment, Ren sensed discomfort on his part. Then it was gone, and he continued talking to Rick. "It's just that I started seeing a girl I met last week."

"Katerina?" Ren asked.

He looked at her and then glanced down, sheepishly. "Well, no. Actually Katerina was two weeks ago. This was Denise."

They all stared at him, waiting for more.

Ren gave him a sly smile and shook her head at him.

He sighed, a helplessness in the way he held his shoulders. "Katerina had the most abominable table manners. I couldn't bear more than one meal with her. Mouth agape, noisy, wet chewing. And simultaneous talking, incessantly, about the bloke she had just broken off with."

Ren chuckled. "So . . . Denise?"

"Yes," he said. He resumed explaining to Rick. "She's quite sweet, really. A secretary in Washington. But she's . . . well, that's all she seems to be. Quite sweet."

Rick looked at his wife. "We've got to start keeping our eyes open for this boy, Sandy." He looked at Jeremy. "We have plenty of single friends. Lots of 'em are divorcees with a kid or two, but they've got something between the ears, you know?"

Jeremy gave him a smile, and Ren could just see him visualizing what women Rick might start lining up for him. He looked a tad concerned.

Rick tapped Sandy on the arm. "How about Sharon, honey? At the bowling alley? She's a bit older than Jeremy, but that might be a good thing." He looked at Jeremy. "You don't mind a smoker, do you?"

Even Sandy started snickering. "Rick,

leave the boy alone. He'll find his own girlfriend. Sharon would eat him alive, and you know it."

"Speaking of being eaten alive," Kara said to Ren, "what's the status with you and Tru's mother?"

"Why?" Jeremy asked, perking up. "I haven't heard about this."

Ren relayed most of the details about the birthday party and how Tru's mother had a number of problems with her.

"Your religion is your own business," Rick said.

That surprised Ren, since he and Sandy didn't seem to have any clear spiritual beliefs.

He said, "Even though I'd like to suggest a love match between Jeremy and our friend Sharon, I usually try to avoid the three taboos of polite conversation: love, religion, and politics."

"Well," Kara said to Ren, "it sounds as if Tru's mom didn't ask you about your politics, anyway."

"Not yet."

"Rick's right, though, Ren," Sandy said.

"I keep telling her that," Rick said, mimicking Sandy's earlier comment.

Sandy ignored him and kept talking to Ren. "You stand firm on your beliefs, and

231

don't let her drag you into some catfight over them. That's Tru's problem, not yours. He might have to step in and set some boundaries for her. Doesn't sound as though he's set *any* boundaries when it comes to what she says to his girlfriends."

Jeremy set his water glass down. "Is that what you are now, Ren? His girlfriend?"

Everyone looked at him, including Ren. For some reason his tone sounded strange, almost as if he were accusing her of something. He looked back at everyone. "What?" he said. "I'm just wondering what his intentions are toward our Ren."

"I don't know," Ren said. "I guess I'm his girlfriend. He hasn't called me that, but that's how it feels."

"Well, then," Jeremy said. "Rick's right. Your religion is none of his mother's business. And I agree with Sandy. Tru's a bit wrapped up in the old apron strings, I think."

"I didn't say *that*," Sandy said. "I was talking about boundaries."

Jeremy waved his hand at her. "Counselor-speak, Sandy. You know what I'm talking about."

Ren wasn't crazy about what Jeremy said, but she recognized the red flag she had sensed early on, when Tru had talked about

232

filling in for his father. Could Jeremy be right? Tru was wonderful and mature. And responsible. And he obviously respected his mother, with good reason. But was he letting her push him around? Ren hated to think of him that way.

A waitress brought the appetizers to the table, and Sandy changed the subject. "Speaking of mothers, Ren, I won't be bringing you with Casey and me on our next visit to his mother in prison."

Ren really didn't like the flow of their conversation this evening. "He's going again? Already?"

Sandy shook her head while she dipped a calamari ring in cocktail sauce. "Not for a few weeks. But your paperwork has been delayed — just red tape — so you won't be approved in time for the next visit."

Ren couldn't really say she minded, but she was worried about Casey. "Will Casey be all right with that?"

She nodded. "Already told him. He's fine about it. He seems to be pretty comfortable with the idea of seeing her on his own."

Ren didn't like the sound of that, either. She thought she might have sighed as Jeremy had, because now he put his arm around her. He gave her a peck on the temple. He didn't tell her she was a doll, as she had done with him. For some reason, his silence made his gesture feel more sincere.

Ren was about to tell him what a good friend he was, when Kara caught her eye.

She looked at Jeremy and then at Ren.

She looked worried.

TWENTY-TWO

Ren barely got home from school the next day before Tru arrived for their date. Fortunately, she didn't need much freshening up.

"Fairly casual" was how Tru had told her to dress. She would have loved a shower, but she knew he was coming straight from work too. Ren didn't want to make him wait for her. They'd be a grungy little couple together.

When dressing for work that morning, Ren had deliberately worn her most flattering black slacks and a light, willowy blouse in pale greens and aqua. She received several compliments on her appearance — one, close to the end of the school day. So she couldn't look too bad, despite how busy the day had been.

But, not only did Tru not arrive grungy, his hair was still damp from his shower. He looked way too handsome. Although he was dressed simply — in jeans and a pale yellow golf shirt — he managed to look as if his clothes were just back from the dry cleaners.

Merely looking at him made her want to go brush her teeth again or something.

"Oh, man! You look so clean and fresh, and I'm still nasty and sticky. How'd you manage to get a shower? I thought you were coming straight over from work."

He laughed, which certainly didn't hurt his looks any.

Ren wanted to kick him.

"We have a shower at the hospital."

She sighed and pointed at him. "That's cheating."

"You know what? You look stunning. And you smell like heaven."

Ren walked into the living room to retrieve her purse. "Well, I hope I'm not asking too much for heaven to smell a bit better than this."

He grinned and waited for her to lock up before he held her hand. Ren warmed up all over with that. Just what she needed — more sweating.

"What's up for tonight?" she asked as they reached his car.

"How about I surprise you a little?" He held her door open and gave her a sly smile. Yikes! Not only clean and fresh, but the word "fetching" popped into Ren's mind as well.

"Did you have a busy day?" he asked, as soon as they drove away.

Ren grimaced. "Do I look as if I've had a busy day?"

He laughed. "Hey, I meant it when I said you looked pretty."

"Stunning. You said 'stunning.' Don't you be backpedaling and throwing a simple little 'pretty' at me, boy."

"My apologies. Stunning, yes." He squeezed her hand. "I just remember your saying this week would be hectic, that's all."

"Yeah, it's National Education Week. We always have extra activities going on, and the parents drop in whenever they want."

"That has to be stressful."

"You bet. We can't always get the kids out of their shackles in time when the parents have carte blanche visitation rights like that."

He just smiled and shook his head at her.

They drove west toward Middleburg, a gorgeous historic town with a village atmosphere. Old stone buildings with thick glass windows, antique shops around every corner, and the definite trappings of horse-and-hound country. Wealth, history, and pristine fields and stables.

Ren sighed. "I love Middleburg."

"Good! I haven't been out here for a long time. I made dinner reservations at the Red Fox Inn —"

"Ooo, I've always wanted to go there!" Inwardly, Ren chuckled at how quickly he had given up his "surprise."

"And I thought maybe we could walk through town for a while," he said. "Window-shop."

Ren opened her eyes wide and slowly turned to look at him. "You like window-shopping?"

He chuckled. "*Like* is a strong word. I'd say I'm charmingly tolerant."

She laughed. "Is this one of those early-in-the-relationship qualities that fades over time?"

"No, it's an enduring quality, I promise." He smiled. "You haven't forgotten all those women in my family, have you? It's a wonder I played football in high school, rather than leading the cheerleading squad."

"You looked good in the skirt, did you?"

He tilted his head, an eyebrow raised. "You're not the only one who's stunning in green."

He parked the car in front of a small art gallery. "Okay, let's change that topic. I don't want you hanging on to an image of

238

me in drag all night."

Ren watched him walk around to her side of the car and noticed that the sleeves of his shirt were just a little snug on his biceps. She knew she'd have no problem losing the girly image.

The cool evening was perfect for a lazy stroll. They held hands and browsed all the shops on Washington Street, the main road through town. They saw artwork they both loved in a cozy, intimate gallery. Ren was partial to the landscapes, Tru preferred the seascapes, and they both paused in appreciation over the portrait of two Victorian-era children.

"Here, let me show you this place," Tru said, leading her into a store with wonderfully unique gifts and jewelry. They looked at some gorgeous old pieces in a glass case. "I bought a pin similar to that one for my mother for Christmas this past year," he said.

Ren oooh'd and ahhh'd about so many items in the shop, being subtly specific about those that particularly suited her taste. A girl had to do what she had to do. For all she knew, Tru might be taking mental notes.

They popped into a floral shop just before the owner locked up for the day.

"Look at that orchid!" Ren leaned forward and studied the amazing detail. "Those tiny little purple dots! It looks as if it were painted by hand."

"Let me buy one for you," Tru said.

Ren shook her head. "No, don't. I love them, but I never know what to do with single flowers like that. They give them to us at church services sometimes — carnations, not orchids, of course. You know, as a thank-you for nursery work or VBS teaching. And then you feel as if you have to carry it around until its dead and you can finally throw it away."

He smiled. "You have quite a romantic streak there, Ren."

She returned his smile. "I love the gesture. That's the important thing, right?"

Various gadgets and clever dining accessories filled the cute kitchen shop they visited.

"Look at this, Tru." Ren held up an enameled spoon rest with a thick-mustached face of a chef in a white hat. His large, flat nose was where the spoon rested.

"Mm-hmm," he said. "But look at this!" He held up a huge bone-handled knife that looked suitable for carving water buffalo. In a terrible Crocodile Dundee accent, he said, "Now *that's* a knife."

Ren chuckled as they left the store. "Everything I like here, I like even more just because of the overall boutique-type atmosphere of this town. I saw a cute little salad spinner in there and felt like Indiana Jones discovering the lost treasure of the Inca. A salad spinner!"

Tru frowned. "Why would anyone want to spin his salad? And then, what? You need a salad retriever too, right? To gather it all back together again after you've thrown it all over the place with your spinner?"

Ren gave him a crooked smile. "You don't do much cooking, do you?"

"I do when I'm home alone. But I often help out at my mother's, and she's constantly feeding me or sending food home with me."

"You don't cook at her place?"

"You haven't forgotten all those women in my family, have you?" he repeated. He laughed when Ren smacked his arm.

"I can't believe you said that! Do you really feel that way, that cooking is strictly women's work?" But she was laughing too.

"Nah. It's just that I tend to do traditional, honey-do things when I'm there. Stuff my father should be doing for her. It's a kind of group effort to make things go smoothly."

Again, Ren felt just a hint of emotional

discomfort about his relationship with his mother. She struggled to get Jeremy's apron-string image out of her mind. Dog-gone that Jeremy.

Tru glanced at his watch. "Perfect timing. My charming tolerance has just about expired, and it's time for dinner at the Red Fox." He took her hand again as they crossed the street. "You said you hadn't been there before, right?"

She hadn't. And it was so lovely she quickly relaxed and dismissed her silly concern about Tru's mother. In the short time they waited for their table, Ren read a framed article about the inn's history and told Tru the highlights.

"Built in the 1700s. No wonder the walls are so thick! And, wow, not only did George Washington sleep here, but so did John Mosby and Jeb Stuart." She ran her finger over the details. "The inn has hosted events for President Kennedy, Jackie O., and Elizabeth Taylor."

Ren looked at Tru and pulled a long, I'm-impressed face.

"And now us," Tru said.

They were seated and served a hearty meal of crab-and-asparagus casserole, lamb chops, garden salad, and strawberry-rhubarb cobbler.

Ren sighed at the meal's end. "We can't eat like this every time we go out, okay? I'm going to get fat."

"It's a promise. On Friday we won't be eating anything nearly this rich."

The idea of seeing him in just two more days brought a comfortable smile to her lips. What an ideal way to start the weekend.

"You look very satisfied." He smiled broadly at her.

"I could take a nap right here, I swear. Thanks, Tru. This was a nice surprise."

He leaned forward. "Oh, this isn't the surprise."

She perked up. "No?"

He looked for the waiter and quickly paid the check. They made their way to his car, and he played a CD for her while they drove. "Mood music," he said with a grin. It was a classical piece with mellow violins and cellos, the perfect theme for a drive through the lavish Virginia countryside. The sun had dimmed as it started to set. Every shade of green grew more rich and distinct. Ren breathed in as they passed a newly mowed pasture. What a great, fresh smell.

Before they went too far out of town, Tru pulled into a long driveway that wound back through several acres of well-tended lawn. They passed what looked like a pricey manor home — all stone and stucco — and continued to a fenced-in pasture and stables.

Now Ren was glad she hadn't worn heels. And once she smelled horse, she fully relaxed about whether or not she was squeaky clean.

Tru grabbed a bag of small apples from the trunk of his car. He smiled at her as if he were about to show her something she'd never seen before. How cute. But she'd seen plenty of horses in her day —

And then she heard it. She immediately thought of the Lord of the Rings movies, as the tiny, fairylike whinnies filled the air. They galloped to Tru and Ren from behind the stables — an unbelievable herd of miniature horses. Not Shetland ponies, which Ren already thought were too cute for words. These little fellas were even smaller. Ren had never seen anything so adorable.

They rushed up to the fence to greet them. The smallness of them — the tiny hooves beating the ground, their feathery manes flying about as they ran, their whispery whinnies. Each one was different; some were Palominos, some looked like Appaloosas, some gray. One was snow white. Ren didn't know why, but they brought tears to her eyes.

"Hey, guys!" Tru said, reaching over the fence and rubbing their foreheads. They didn't even come up as far as his waist. They were barely as high as Ren's.

"Tru, these are so sweet! I want one!"

One of the horses was the color of dried apricots, with a bright patch of white on his forehead. He stuck his nose through the fence and nudged Ren in the knee.

She laughed and bent to look into his dark, thick-lashed eyes. "I've seen dogs bigger than this!"

"Here," Tru said, handing Ren an apple. She gingerly held it toward the horse, and he snatched it and chomped it up, little pieces dropping to the ground.

Then a chocolate brown foal and its mother trotted up, and Ren couldn't help but draw her hands up to her chest. "Look at that! I swear, they look like stuffed animals!"

Tru laughed. "Now I know what to put in your Christmas stocking. I'm so happy you like them. They're really something, aren't they?"

Ren reached out to several and stroked the short, stiff hair on their heads. "They have round little bellies too, don't they? How come you can come here, though? Do you know the owners?"

"Yeah. Blaine and Linda Forrester. He's a retired surgeon. I know him from the hospital."

Ren looked around at the stables, the grounds, the manor house. "That's a lotta surgery."

Tru laughed. "I think Mrs. Forrester — Linda — came from wealth too. They've let me bring my nephews here before. You know, Cessy's kids." He pointed at a frisky Appaloosa that trotted just beyond the herd. "That's Kyle's favorite. Calls him . . . what was it? Something like Strong Wind."

"Cute. Very native American."

Tru scratched his eyebrow and gave her a grim smile. "Actually, I think he learned that name from Cessy. It's her tongue-in-cheek nickname for her husband, David. I think the big guy has some digestive issues."

They both laughed.

Tru said, "I called over here the other day, when I knew we were coming to Middleburg. Blaine said they were going to be out of town but to bring you by anytime. They're wonderful people."

Ren arched her eyebrow. "You mean we're all alone here?"

His eyes twinkled. "The groundskeeper is probably around somewhere." He grinned.

"Are you getting fresh with me, young lady?"

Ren gave him a wicked laugh. She knew he'd respond that way. "Hush your mouth, sir." She nodded toward the horses. "I'm just wondering which one of these little guys will fit in the backseat of your car."

Twenty-Three

Two days later Tru and Ren drove to his youngest sister's apartment. He reached over and squeezed Ren's hand. "You don't mind this, do you? Double-dating with Michelle and Ricky?"

"Not a bit," she said, squeezing back. "I'm glad for the chance to get to know her better."

He smiled. "I just hope she's herself tonight. She's a little obsessed about this new guy. We may have a hard time getting through to her once we pick him up."

Ren said nothing. After the week she'd had — obsessing about Tru when she wasn't obsessing about Casey — she felt in no position to talk. Just since getting in the car, she noticed her pulse quicken simply because Tru smiled at her. And every time she moved, she noticed how good he smelled.

"I think that's why my mother wanted me to do this double date."

Ren looked at him, surprised. "Oh! This was your mother's idea?"

"Not entirely, no. Actually, I asked her about Michelle the day after the birthday party. Every time I passed my sister at the party, I heard her working Ricky's name into the conversation, no matter whom she was talking with, and no matter what the original subject seemed to be."

"And?" Ren asked.

"Well, it sounded a little much. I asked my mother if she knew how serious Michelle was getting with this guy. My mom didn't even know about him."

That was a shocker to Ren, considering the eagle eye Mrs. Sayers seemed to have on *Tru's* personal business. But, then again, Tru was the one she seemed to cling to the most. Ren wondered if Michelle had been ignored growing up. Even with eyes in the back of her head, a mother could only run surveillance on just so many kids at once.

"You know," Ren said, "if you heard Michelle discussing Ricky with everyone else, but she hasn't mentioned him to your mother, maybe she just doesn't want your mother to . . ."

"Interfere?" He smiled at her.

Ren looked back at him, embarrassed. "Oops."

He laughed, the dimples in his cheeks charming her all over again. "You're probably right. But I don't like that she didn't mention him to me, either. *I've* never given her a reason to be secretive about whom she dates. So I told my mother I was going to ask Michelle if she'd mind double-dating with us so I could meet Ricky."

"And how does Michelle feel about tonight?"

He shrugged. "Seems all right with it. She just asked me not to be too hard on him."

Ren gave him a crooked smile. "Are you notoriously hard on the men in your sisters' lives?"

Chuckling, he said, "Not really. Not at all. So I'm expecting something unexpected in Ricky." They drove up in front of Michelle's apartment. "We'll see," Tru said.

Before Tru even got out of the car, Michelle stepped brightly down the steps, her dark hair bouncing on her shoulders, cute as ever. Michelle was just as lovely as her older sisters, with a dose of perky thrown in. "I didn't want you to come up," she said, leaning in to kiss Tru's cheek. "Chelsea's up there sleeping. She's been on the night shift all week."

She got in the backseat. "Hey, Ren." She reached up to give Ren a hello squeeze on the shoulder.

Tru said, "Michelle and her roommate both work at the pregnancy crisis center."

Ren turned in her seat to face Michelle. "Good for you! Is that volunteer work?"

"Not exactly," she said, the light shining in her eyes. From this angle her brown eyes looked less dark than Tru's. "Tru, go ahead and drive. Ricky lives over in Potomac Heights. You know where that is, yeah?" She looked back at Ren. "Anyway, no, not volunteer. Not Chelsea and me. We're both working there for teeny, tiny salaries to finish up our psych degree work. We're trying to qualify for the master's program and have to get a certain number of practical hours logged."

Ren thought about how hurt Michelle had been on behalf of her sister, Anna, when she thought Kara and Ren were bad-mouthing her at the *Riverdance* show. Psychology seemed a perfect field for her.

Michelle directed Tru to Ricky's apartment house, one in a long row of old, red-brick buildings devoid of front yards, landscaping, or adornment of any kind. Not the best part of town, but not the worst. Ren didn't think so, anyway.

Michelle dashed into his building and emerged with him in minutes.

"Uh-oh," Tru muttered under his breath.

Ricky looked like a complete wild man. His skin was pale next to Michelle, who had Tru's beautiful olive complexion. He was obviously dark haired, but he had bleached-blond dreadlocks down to his shoulders. His camouflage pants were huge, with enough pockets on them to store a week's worth of battle provisions. He wore a sleeveless BVD T-shirt, so the tattoo on his shoulder was visible from a distance. But Ren didn't see the ring in his eyebrow until he got to the car.

Tru had stepped out of the car, silently, as Michelle and Ricky approached. Despite being a good six inches shorter than Tru, Ricky walked with confidence toward him and thrust out his hand, smiling. He had an engaging smile. "Yo, you must be Tru. Ricky Santori. Nice to meet you."

He sounded positively normal. Except for the "yo," which sounded . . . well, it sounded normal for someone who looked like *that.*

Tru gave him a smile that conveyed acceptance, and Ren found herself breathing a relieved sigh. Ren looked at Michelle and saw she was doing the same thing. They all piled into the car.

"Ricky, this is Ren," Michelle said.

He shook her hand. "Hey, Ren."

Ren smiled at him, trying not to stare at his eyebrow. Or his dreadlocks. Or tattoo. "Hi, Ricky," she said to the general area around his nose.

He glanced at Michelle. "You're right, Michelle. They look like the perfect couple."

Michelle laughed and punched him in the arm. "Honestly, guys, I told him that and meant it just the way it sounds. Not sarcastic or anything, okay?"

Tru glanced at her in the rearview mirror. Ren could tell they had locked eyes, because he gave Michelle a mock look of disapproval before the corners of his mouth curled up.

They went to a show put on by a performance-artist friend of Ricky's. Ren had an impossible time following it because it didn't really seem to mean anything. The guy spouted free verse poetry every once in a while. Between verses he covered himself in various sheets, feather boas, and what looked like ventilation system tubing and moved around like her first grade students did when they'd spun around one too many times.

And Tru was no help. He put his arm around Ren and cuddled her up so that she was constantly distracted by his closeness. She just wanted to ignore the silly man on stage and give Tru a big kiss. And when Tru wasn't being affectionate, he was murmuring snide comments in her ear about what they were watching. Or making little snoring noises, and even whimpering a couple of times, like a trapped dog that was just dying to get outside. Ren absolutely loved this side of him, but he kept making her laugh. Thankfully, his comments and her muffled giggles distracted no one, due to the constant garbage-can banging sounds being piped into the auditorium as part of the performance.

But Ren worried about the impression they might have made on Michelle and Ricky, who seemed enthralled by the show. Here she and Tru were supposedly the chaperones. But tonight they were certainly the less mature couple of the group.

They went to a nearby diner for coffee and dessert afterward. Ricky made a trip to the men's room, and the rest of them ordered and sat down.

"So!" Michelle said, the glow of inspiration still on her lovely face. "What did you think about the show?"

Ren's heart sank when she saw that Michelle was looking at her. "Well," she said, trying to avoid looking at Tru. "It was, um, different. I don't usually go to shows like that, so I'm probably a really bad judge of them."

"Yeah, I haven't been to many performance art shows, either," Michelle said. "I think Ricky knows a lot of people who do that kind of thing."

You poor baby, Ren thought, smiling at her and nodding.

"How about you, Tru?" Michelle asked. "Did you like it?"

Ren took his hand under the table and shot him a "be kind" look. He sighed. "Hmm. I did have fun in there," he said, squeezing Ren's hand. "But —"

Just then, Ricky came back. Michelle gave him a brave smile. "We were just talking about how much we liked the show."

"Oh, it was total bunk," Ricky said, as if he were certain everyone was well aware of that fact. "Always is." He plopped down comfortably next to Michelle.

Tru, Michelle, and Ren all looked at each other before they laughed.

"Thank goodness!" Michelle said. "I was, like, totally lost."

Ricky snorted. "You and everyone else in there, including Jazzy."

"Jazzy?" Ren asked.

"The performer," Michelle said.

"So why do you go to these things?" Tru

asked, still laughing.

Ricky shrugged. "Aw, well. They're my friends, aren't they? Gotta show them some support."

He was a good guy. Ren looked at Tru and could see the same thought in his expression.

The waitress brought over their coffee and various sweets.

"Thanks," Tru said to her. He looked back at Ricky, who bit into a dry slice of pecan pie.

"Where do you work, Ricky?" Tru asked.

Ricky hooked his thumb over his shoulder and quickly swallowed. "Just a few blocks from here. The Kettering Rehab Center. I'm an OT."

"Occupational therapist?" Tru asked, sounding a little surprised.

"Yep. Just entry-level stuff so far. Working on my master's now." He looked at Michelle and tickled her under the chin. "That's how I met Michelle. At school."

Michelle laughed and pushed his hand away. "He's going to specialize in working with older people."

"Yeah, old people rock," Ricky said.

Ren studied him. This was getting stranger by the minute. But nicer too. Under all that

funkiness, Ricky seemed to be pretty terrific.

Eventually they drove him home, and then
Michelle. As they got nearer to Ren's home,
Tru said, "Whaddya say to taking a walk
through the old part of town?"

Ren smiled at the idea. "Sure." Anything
to avoid having to say good night to him.

Many of the Leesburg shops had closed
for the night, but most of them left the lights
on in their front display windows. Several
art galleries were still open, as well as
restaurants and bars. People were strolling
around town, but the evening wasn't a
crowded one. The atmosphere was intimate.

They stopped in front of a pet shop and
watched three retriever puppies sleeping in
the window.

Tru put his arm around Ren. "That's a
lot like Sammy looked when I got him."

Ren loved the affectionate tone in his
voice. "How long have you had him?" She
leaned into him and enjoyed the warmth of
him against her side.

"Let me see." He looked up, as if calculating in his head. "Only a couple of years. I
bought him —" He stopped, as if he decided
against finishing his sentence.

Ren looked up at him. "What? Something
wrong?"

He gave her a loving smile. "No. Just didn't want to be offensive. I bought Sammy just after Emily and I split up."

Ren couldn't help it. She stiffened a little. "Ah."

He pulled her back against him. "I'm sorry. I didn't really need to tell you that."

What was wrong with her? She and Emily had nothing to do with each other. She was being ridiculous. "No, that's okay. There's nothing wrong with what you said."

He pulled away to take her hand. They walked farther along the street, passing a bar with its door propped open. A mournful jukebox song floated out to them. "It's not as if I think of Emily when I look at Sammy," he said. "It's just that I went out to get Sammy right after that all happened. I was kind of lonely."

There are certainly worse ways he could have dealt with the loneliness.

But she could tell what this nasty feeling was, because whenever it hit her, its partner — guilt — hit her at the same time. She was just jealous that someone else was able to make him so lonely with her absence. And Ren felt as if she might still be competing with her. Still? Good grief, Ren had never even met the woman, yet she felt competitive with her.

Tru stopped and turned her to face him. He gently held both her shoulders and looked her in the eyes. "Have I put my foot in my mouth?" He was looking at her with such honesty, so ready to take blame if Ren wanted to throw it at him.

She moved toward him and hugged him, which made it easier to talk with him. She was too close to have to look him in the eye. "Oh, Tru, you haven't done anything wrong. I'm just being silly." She scrunched her face up against his chest, not wanting to say the next part. "And jealous."

He chuckled so softly, she couldn't hear it, but she felt it against her cheek. Then he pulled her away so he could look at her.

"You want to hear jealous? You know what I did the day I met you?"

Oh, good. He was going to make a confession to equalize them. What a guy. "What?"

"I went to my car in the Wal-Mart parking lot. My heart was just flipping, I was so excited about you. And I said a prayer of thanks right there, before I even started the car or anything."

Ren smiled. "That's so sweet." But it didn't exactly make her feel less petty for her jealousy.

He laughed, apparently at the memory. "Yeah, I thanked God for letting me meet you. Nice, right? But then I had to apologize for being secretly thankful that your stupid husband had walked out on you. I was afraid he might come back to you."

Ren gasped.

"See? I'm not such a great guy. I didn't even know if I'd ever see you again, but I was jealous of your husband." He sighed, and his shoulders drooped a little. "I think I don't like the way this evening is ending."

Ren snorted out a laugh. It was as if they were both going out of their way to make themselves feel bad. "Should I try to think of something even worse about myself?" she said. "Then you can try to top that?"

He slowly cracked a smile. Then he dropped the smile abruptly and dead-panned, "Yes. Let's hear it."

She laughed and tried to smack him, play-fully, on the arm. But he wrapped his arms around her, just as his younger brother had done with their mother when she tried to hit him.

They laughed into each other's necks, and Ren couldn't imagine a nicer place to bury her face. Warm, soft, and all Tru.

He whispered in her ear, "This is how I pictured us, that day I met you. Laughing together about ourselves."

He turned his face toward her. "This is

what I prayed for, Ren."

His lips were so close to hers, she didn't know who kissed whom first. Didn't matter. Between that kiss, the one before they got into the car, the one before they got out of the car, and the one at her doorstep, Ren would have to say they were about even.

Twenty-Four

Ren's brother, Matt, had always been her hero. Her inspiration. The very wind beneath her wings, and all that jazz. But this morning he was ticking her off.

"Just give me your hand and let go, Ren," he said. Again.

Ren had deliberately gone straight to bed the previous night, as soon as Tru dropped her off. She wanted to get a good night's sleep for an early start today. This morning she joined Matt, his wife, Sybil, and their two daughters for a Saturday hike at scenic Harpers Ferry in West Virginia. They were blessed with perfect weather — plenty of sun but no humidity yet. The plan had been a brisk, invigorating hike, followed by a picnic lunch lovingly prepared by Sybil, who honestly seemed the perfect wife and mother. Despite Sybil's fire red hair, Ren had yet to see her lose her cool, either with

Matt or the girls. Or with Ren, for that matter.

But Tina and Mary, Ren's little nieces, had tired quickly on the trail. Ren loved them dearly, but she found herself cringing with each increase in the pitch of their whining. She couldn't make out what they were saying anymore, but Syb carried on a conversation with them like a skilled UN translator.

"Why don't I take the girls back down to the park area," Sybil said to Matt and Ren. "We'll freshen up and find a picnic bench near the water. You two finish your hike and meet us when you're done."

"Sounds good to me," Matt said, finger-combing his damp, dark hair off his forehead. "You game, Ren?"

Ren took a drink from her water bottle. "Yeah. Good idea, Syb." Ren pointed at Tina, the younger, at five. "Don't you go snooping around in the basket, eating all those chocolate chip cookies before we get back."

Tina laughed. "Promise!" She ran up to hug her aunt. Ren scooped her up for a quick nuzzle, after which Tina stepped back and said, "Sweaty!"

"Tina!" Sybil said, laughing. "Ladies don't sweat, they perspire." Then she frowned in thought. "Or, wait. It's 'horses sweat, men perspire, women . . . mist?' "

Ren laughed, wiping her forehead with her shirttail. "I sweat. Nothing ladylike about me this morning." She glanced at Matt and then back at the girls. "All right, then, we're off. See you guys later."

Then Mary, a seven-year-old, ran up to Ren too. But she stopped short and held out her hand, as if we were in the middle of a business meeting. The adults laughed.

"You notice they're not coming near me," Matt said. He pulled the bottom of his T-shirt up to wipe his face dry. Ren had to smile when she saw his exposed tummy. He was still as handsome as he had been when they were teens, but his love for Sybil's cooking was starting to show, just a little.

"Okay," he said to Sybil. "We'll just go a bit farther and then we'll come meet you."

So they parted company. And that was when things went downhill. Literally.

"Let's go off the trail a bit here," Matt said. "Those rocks look great over there."

"Yeah," Ren said. "But let's not do anything too risky, all right?"

" 'Course not," Matt said, not looking back at her.

They hiked to an awesome site and stood on rocks that hung out over the Potomac and Shenandoah Rivers, where they converged. Rather than raging, forceful rapids, the two rivers flowed peacefully together, the picture of harmony. Ren thought the historic town, with shops and markets clustered around the water's edge, had probably changed little from how it must have looked in the 1800s.

"Gorgeous," she said.

"Yeah, I really wanted the girls to see this," Matt said, pulling her back from the cliff's edge. "Don't stand so close to the lip, though. I don't know how you can stand there. Makes me nervous."

"Really? I finally found something that scares you."

"Me? Lots of stuff scares me."

"Yeah?" Ren said. "Like . . . ?"

"Like my vet practice, for one thing."

"What do you mean?"

He shrugged. "People can be really weird about their animals. And it's important that I have a steady stream of sick puppies in my life. Especially now that I have a wife and kids depending on me."

Ren didn't say anything to that. No spouse, no kids. Her fears were different from Matt's. She feared experiencing infidelity again. Rejection. She feared being alone, sometimes. She feared being alone forever, sometimes.

"Want to head back down?" Matt asked. "I'm getting hungry."

"Sure. Lead the way."

But once they started down, Ren realized they weren't going down the way they came. She couldn't see the trail anywhere.

"I'm lousy with direction," she said. "Where's the trail?"

"Just on the other side of this ravine," Matt said, deftly negotiating what looked like a slippery, steep embankment.

Ren hiked across the deepening slope of ground, following in Matt's footsteps. But her footing wasn't as sure as his. The ground was covered with dusty, dead leaves left over from autumn and winter. There hadn't been rain for some time, so the leaves were powdery, and Ren had a hard time getting traction once the ground slanted below her. She got halfway across the ravine before she started sliding down. A squeal escaped before she grabbed, two-fisted, at something — a couple of roots — and held on. But her feet had nothing secure underneath them, and she was afraid to move and start sliding again. Ren froze where she was and looked up at Matt.

He reached his hand down to her. "Here. Give me one of your hands. I'll get you."

Logically, Ren knew he was probably right. But she didn't have room in her head for logic — she was up to her eyeballs in panic.

"Just give me your hand, Ren."

"I can't give you my hand. I'll have to let go to give you my hand." His insistence, coupled with her fear, was making her angry. "Why did you bring me this way?" She wasn't really asking for explanations. She just wanted to make sure he knew whose fault this was, just in case she slid to a rocky, watery death a mile below.

Suddenly, Ren felt his hand around her wrist. His grip enabled her to scramble up the embankment to where she could get a foothold and get back on the path.

"Good job," Matt said, as Ren brushed herself off.

Ren gave him an angry pout. "That was not my idea of fun."

"Mine neither." He chuckled lightly. "You weren't really in much danger, even though I know it was scary for you." He pointed to the area below the ravine. The ground came together and tapered off to a flat spot, not far from where Ren slipped. "You wouldn't have fallen any farther than right there."

Ren considered the idea of falling that far. It would have been terrifying, not knowing where the bottom was for the few seconds she slid. But, other than a scrape or two, she wouldn't really have been hurt. She felt a little foolish.

"Yeah, well, I would have gotten plenty dirty."

Matt laughed. "Come on. The rest of the trip down is painless. Let's get some lunch, Sweaty Aunt Ren."

After they'd made most of the hike down, Ren sighed. "This place reminds me of those times we went camping with Dad when we were kids."

"Hmm," Matt said, smiling. "Funny, I was just talking with Syb about that the other night. Guess I was thinking about it because we talked about doing this hike. I'd like to take the girls camping, you know? Build a few memories like those we had with Dad."

"Did you have as much fun as I remember having?"

"I loved it, yeah. But I don't know if the girls are into it." He chuckled, ruefully. "Today hasn't been exactly encouraging."

Ren chuckled too. "Well, maybe they're just too young. I was a little older, I think, when we made those trips."

"Not the one when Mom came," he said, holding a tree branch aside for her to get past. "I think you were about Mary's age then, seven or so."

Ren gasped and stopped in her tracks. "I completely forgot about Mother coming!" She searched her memory banks for a moment before walking again. "Wasn't that the trip when it rained like crazy all night?"

Matt laughed. "And the tent leaked?"

Ren started laughing at the image in her mind. "Oh, the tent floor was such a mess! You and I pretended we were on Noah's ark or something, didn't we?"

"Yeah, we didn't want to go to sleep, so we had a blast. But Mom —"

"Oh, my goodness," she said, starting to laugh so hard she couldn't walk. "Mother had even put her hair in rollers that night, camping or no camping, remember?"

"And her sleeping bag was soaked. She *didn't* pretend we were on Noah's ark."

"I think she pretended we were on *Divorce Court*," Ren said, making Matt snort.

"As if it was Dad's fault it was raining so hard."

They looked at each other, laughing, and enjoyed the mutual memory before they grew silent and walked a while without speaking.

"I know she's kind of hard on you sometimes, Ren," Matt said, out of the blue.

Now it was her turn to snort. "Ya think?

How can you tell?"

He smiled, a touch of sadness in his eyes. "I'm not sure why she's like that with you. I think she's afraid you won't do as well as she thinks you can."

"Won't do *what* as well as she thinks I can? I've already proven I can make a bundle of money if I choose to work in a high-paying field. I just don't choose to. And she was hard on me even when I was doing that."

Matt shrugged. "Maybe you need to spend a little more time with her. Just casual stuff. Going to lunch, shopping. The kind of activities she seems to enjoy these days."

"But I do that. Once in a while." Ren watched the path ahead of her as she spoke. "I always get the feeling I'm disappointing her. I don't drink cocktails with lunch. I don't gush enough over *haute couture.* It's as if she thinks I'm lacking some vital personality trait because I've scaled back on how I . . . consume."

He looked back at her, mild concern in his expression. "You having any money problems?"

Ren shook her head. "No. I just have to be a little less free with my money than I used to be. No big deal. It's just a by-product of earning a teacher's salary. And having the latest designer fashion just isn't as important to me as it used to be. I mean, I do love dressing well. And finding just the right pair of shoes for an outfit. But there are deeper things in life, ya know?"

He spoke in a nasal, Gomer Pyle voice. "I don't know, Ren. Personally, I wouldn't *think* of performing surgery on a basset hound without the latest Banolo Matlicks' on my feet."

Ren laughed. "Manolo Blahniks, dummy."

Matt waved at Sybil, who was sitting comfortably on a bench in the picnic area, watching as they emerged from the woods. "Maybe Mom worries more about your love life than your fashion sense or financial well-being. I don't know."

Ren sighed. "Maybe. I think she had Greg pegged from the start. But she's been a harsh judge of every guy I've ever dated, so she had a fifty percent chance of being right about Greg too."

Ren wasn't sure she wanted to mention Tru just yet, so she stopped talking. Matt seemed to take her silence as something that required comforting. He reached up and put his arm around her. After a nice squeeze, they pulled away from each other, wrinkling their noses at each other.

They spoke simultaneously, imitating little Tina's childish voice. "Sweaty!"

The picnic area in the park was lush and green. Warm breezes rustled through the trees, fluttering the leaves until they sounded like running water. After they ate, Mary, who was the age of Ren's students, gave a little lecture to her younger sister Tina and her Aunt Ren about what lived near the water. Ren was impressed by Mary's knowledge at such a young age. There was little actual wildlife for her to show them, but she lifted a good-sized rock and spoke to Tina with an air of serious authority.

"See, you have to take care not to disturb anything living underneath."

"That reminds me," Matt said to Ren. "Mom said you two ran into Greg and his, uh, fiancée at the mall not too long ago."

Ren sat on the bench beside him. "Yeah. With their son. You wouldn't believe how much that hurt. I had figured out that Greg was underhanded when he called the adoption agency behind my back. And I knew he could shock me just by his leaving me so abruptly. And already having the legal stuff in the works."

Matt nodded. "Yep. Greg was always one

to get his ducks in a row before striking."

"You're so well rid of him, Ren," Sybil said.

Ren sighed. "I know. But I still feel like such an idiot for not suspecting him of cheating on me. How could I have missed that? I feel like a lousy judge of character."

"Shoot," Matt said. "I'll bet more spouses are surprised than suspicious about that kind of thing. Even when the marriage goes bad, if it's not something *you're* inclined to do, you probably won't expect your spouse to do it, either."

"Well," Ren said, "it's definitely a chapter I have to close. I really hate being a divorced woman. I wouldn't have chosen that path, but I know it's time to move on."

"So who is he?" Sybil asked, eagerness in her voice.

Ren turned to her, shocked. "What? What do you mean?"

She grinned at her. "Don't give me that innocent look. Who's the new man?"

"Syb, that's not fair," Matt said. "Ren's a smart, independent, self-reliant woman. Just because she's looking forward instead of looking back doesn't mean she's found someone else. Right, Ren?"

Ren nodded at him, emphatically. "You bet."

He looked at her a moment more before rolling his eyes. "Oh, good night. All right, who is he?"

So Ren told them about Tru, and maybe she gushed a little. She told them everything. How he gallantly rescued her from the Wal-Mart sportswear display. How he helped her survive the Spanish Inquisition at his mother's party. How he turned her to putty with last night's final kiss.

"He sounds kind of dreamy," Sybil said. "Do people still say that?"

"Yeah, Gidget," Matt said to her. "He's, like, the dreamiest."

Sybil laughed and gave him a shove. Mary and Tina came back to the table, and Sybil handed each of them a cookie while she spoke. "But his mother sounds a little troublesome."

Ren nodded. "I'm afraid so." She didn't think about how this would sound before it came out of her mouth, but she asked Sybil, "How do *you* handle that?"

Sybil looked at her and got a twinkle in her eyes. "Whatever do you mean, Ren? How do I handle *what?*"

Matt pointed at his wife with both palms up, as if he were presenting her as evidence. "There you have it. That's how she handles Mom. Complete denial."

"What's denial?" asked Mary, prompting a look of caution from Sybil to Matt.

"It means pretending something isn't the way it is. But I'm just teasing Mommy. She isn't in denial. She's just really, really polite."

He winked at Sybil, who smiled back at him as if he was, like, the dreamiest.

So maybe that was what Ren needed to do with Tru's mom. Just be really, really polite.

Ren went in to use the bathroom at Matt and Sybil's house before heading home. The phone rang as she walked out of the bathroom. Within moments she could tell Matt was talking with their mother. As Ren walked into the living room, he told Clarissa, "Yeah, she was with us all day."

Ren frantically gestured, shaking her head, waving her finger at herself, anything she could think of to indicate Matt shouldn't say the very thing he said next.

"Sure, she's here. Here ya go." *Then* he paid attention to what Ren was doing as he handed the phone to her. Ren gave him the same look she had given him after she nearly fell down the ravine. She took the phone from him as he pantomimed the realization of his mistake — his eyebrows up, his eyes wide, and his hand to his mouth, which he shaped into a ridiculous "O." Ren gave him a smack on the arm, and he chuckled quietly. Brothers.

"Hello, Mother."

"Ren, listen," she ordered. "I want you to come to dinner tomorrow night, along with Matt and Sybil. They've already said they will."

"But, Mother, on such short notice —"

"Now, Ren, you owe me. You flat out refused to give Gus a chance at the restaurant, when all I wanted to do was help you make a new friend. You let me down at the High Blood Pressure Ball, and I had such hopes for you there. What are you doing tomorrow night that's more important than having dinner with your family? What?"

Ren drew a blank. She hadn't planned on lying, but she was sure she could think of something honestly more important than having dinner at Clarissa's. She just couldn't think quickly enough. She simply couldn't say, "Eating Chinese carryout and watching TV." She was cornered prey, and they both knew it.

"What time should I be there?" Ren asked.

"Five o'clock sharp." Then Clarissa followed up with a command that turned Ren's head, as she glared in horror at Matt, her bigmouthed, turncoat brother. "And bring this new fellow, Tru, with you. It's about time I met him."

TWENTY-FIVE

Ren followed her mother into her enormous kitchen under the pretense of refilling Tru's water glass.

"Mother!" she said between clenched teeth. "I cannot believe you invited someone to be my date tonight." She looked over her shoulder to make sure the kitchen door had closed behind them. "Why in the world did you ask me to bring Tru if you had already invited Mr. Fancy Pants out there?"

Clarissa pulled a tray of stuffed mushroom caps from the oven. "That Mr. Fancy Pants, as you call him, happens to be the most successful young partner in your late father's law firm."

"I don't care if he's the Prince of Wales, Mother. I *have* a date tonight. Really! After the reaction I had to your blind date thing with Gus, you'd think you would know better!"

With hardly a glance at Ren, Clarissa said,

"Don't make a scene, dear."

Ren refilled Tru's glass and got one for herself. "What do you expect me to do about, about . . ."

"Russell," Clarissa said, arranging the mushrooms on a platter with several other canapés. "Russell Freeman. The Third. Did you see the cut of that suit he's wearing? That's Givenchy, I'll wager."

Ren stared at her in the only appropriate way she could — as if she were insane.

Clarissa gave a quick shake of her head and flip of her hand. "Look, Ren, I had already invited Russell when I heard about your nurse fellow. Who knew when you'd get around to bringing him over? I didn't want to wait, and I couldn't exactly unin-vite Russell, could I? Besides, it will do your little friend good to have some healthy competition. And it will do you good to see the contrast between the two of them."

"Contrast? You want contrast, Mother?"

"Shhh." Clarissa put her finger to her lips and cut a glance toward the kitchen door. *Now* she worried about appearances.

Ren lowered her voice, but she couldn't remember the last time she spoke with such anger. "Here's your contrast, Mother. Tru is *my* date. Russell Freeman is *yours*." She grabbed the water glasses and left the kitchen before Clarissa could respond.

The acid in Ren's stomach was unbearable. She had never been so insolent with her mother before, and she was definitely outside of her comfort zone. She felt horrible. Disrespectful. And there was no way anyone would believe Russell was Clarissa's date. Ren would have to play this safe and explain everything to Tru.

More than anything, she didn't want the circumstances of this evening to hurt him in any way. He had been so kind to agree to come on such short notice. She thought part of his willingness had to do with the way his mother had acted toward Ren at her birthday party. Tru may have felt the need to make it up to her by meeting her mother at the snap of Clarissa's fingers.

Ren would probably have some making up of her own to do after tonight.

"What's with the young attorney guy?" Matt said, joining Ren outside the living room.

"I'm still mad at you," she said.

"Oh, come on, Rennie," he said. "I didn't know you hadn't told Mom about Tru yet. And you could have turned her down for dinner tonight. You didn't have to come, and you didn't have to bring Tru. Nice guy, by the way. Syb's practically drooling, but I

look beyond such things as surface appearances —"

"Oh, my goodness," Sybil broke in, rushing up to them as casually as possible. "Do
you realize who Russell Hoozit the Third is
here for?"

"What do you mean?" Matt said. "Isn't he
a friend of Mom's?"

"Keep it down, Syb," Ren said. "I need to
talk with Tru about this. Where is he?"

Sybil jerked her thumb over her shoulder
toward the living room. "They're both in
there."

Matt said, "Who's Russell the Third here
for, if not for Mom?"

"For your little sister, that's who," Sybil
said, nodding her head toward Ren.

Matt gasped, and a question was all over
his face for a moment. But Ren knew her
brother was no fool. The moment Clarissa
breezed out of the kitchen and past them,
Ren saw Matt size up the situation handily.
He suppressed a laugh, and then he frowned
at Ren.

"You have two dates? And you call yourself
a *Christian*."

"I've got to get in there before she starts
auctioning me off," Ren said. She wagged a
finger at Matt. "You helped get me into this
mess. The least you can do is keep Mother

from humiliating me. Or Tru. Or even that poor dupe from Dad's old firm."

"Probably a bit late to avoid humiliation," Matt said. "But we'll see what we can do, won't we, Syb?"

"You'd better get in there and grab Tru," Sybil said to Ren, pointing discreetly into the living room. "If I'm guessing right, Russell's just now telling him what he told me — that he's here to meet you."

Ren ran. Literally ran. She rushed in so frantically that Clarissa's cat, Frumpkins, jumped off the Steinway bench and dashed for safety.

Both Tru and Russell braced as if they thought Ren wouldn't be able to stop before she reached them. They each looked uncertain. But, where Russell's expression appeared disapproving, Tru's was amused.

"Hey!" Ren said, stopping just short of them and spilling water from the glasses she carried. "Here's that water, Tru!" She sounded like a cheerleader on caffeine.

"Well, thanks, Ren!" Tru said back, mirroring her odd enthusiasm. "I was so thirsty!" He laughed and took a long drink. But Ren thought she might have looked a little crazy around the eyes when he finished because he seemed puzzled. And concerned. "Are you all right?"

He didn't seem uncomfortable around Russell, so Ren figured she had caught them in time. She looked at Russell, whose face no longer held scorn. But he was appraising her openly. For a split second she wanted to stick her tongue out at him. Where were these bizarre thoughts and behaviors coming from? Had her mother finally tipped her over the edge?

"Um, Russell, I need to talk with Tru about something important. Would you —"

"Russell!" Matt said behind her. "Mom tells me you've dazzled them at Henley Sheering. Did you happen to work on the Bigelow embezzlement case?"

"As a matter of fact, I wrote the final arguments on Bigelow," Russell said, lifting his eyebrows.

Ren noticed he dropped his voice on "fact" the way snooty people do. After all, that's the kind of thing that makes them sound snooty.

She gave Matt her "all is forgiven" expression and pulled Tru aside.

Tru put his hand on hers. "What's going on? You seem nervous."

Ren sighed. "Tru, I'm so sorry. Please bear with me tonight. I warned you about my mother, right? About how she has this little issue with control? Of my life?"

He smiled. "Listen, Ren, don't worry about it. I don't expect your mother to like me right away. I have a mother too, remember? And she's got her own little issues, if you recall."

"Right. But your mother didn't invite a woman to her party to act as your date."

Tru laughed. "Of course not. She'd just as soon I never date again. But she wouldn't have done that, anyway. I was bringing you to the party. She knew that."

"Uh-huh. Okay, but now we have to enter *my* mother's strange little world for a moment. You are my date. You're the person *I* invited to be my date."

He looked at her in complete confusion. "Yes. And I'm . . . very happy . . . you did. Aren't I?"

"Yes, but, see . . ." Ren glanced at Russell, who stood with Matt and Sybil, staring at her. Looking very much like a man waiting for his date to join him.

When Ren looked back at Tru, he was studying Russell. His mouth dropped open half an inch, and then he looked back at Ren. "You're kidding me."

"Please don't be mad." Ren tightened her hand on his arm.

"You have two dates here tonight?"

"No! Well, yes, but I refuse to recognize

Russell as my date."

"Ren, we're not talking about Communist China versus Taiwan here. You can't just ignore him all night — he's a person. And he thinks he's on a date with you. He might start to get suspicious if he sees us kissing or something."

Despite the difficulty of the immediate circumstances, Ren got a little thrill at the thought of "kissing or something" with Tru. She shook it off.

"I've already talked with Mother about it. She will have to act as his date. She's the one who invited him."

Tru opened his mouth but closed it again. He cocked his head to the side. "I suppose there's some justice in that."

"So you'll suffer through this with me? The two of us, facing the wind together?"

He chuckled.

"And Matt and Sybil will help us smooth out the rough spots."

"They know too?" he said, looking disappointed again.

"Look, we'll get through this evening. You and I didn't do anything wrong. We're just trying to do the right thing for a dying woman."

Tru furrowed his brows. "Pardon? Your mother's ill?"

"Are you kidding?" Ren pushed up her shirtsleeves. "After this I'm going to kill her."

Ren's initial sentiment for poor Russell was exactly that: *poor Russell.* It wasn't his fault that he had been bamboozled into this awkward situation.

But as the circumstances of the evening dawned on him, Ren saw only a brief period of embarrassment in his behavior. Then he seemed to draw upon the character trait that probably served him well professionally. He appeared poised to fight. For her. Or maybe he wasn't fighting so much for her as he was fighting to prove himself better than Tru. And Clarissa joined him in his weird little battle. They reminded Ren of two characters from the movie *Camelot.* King Arthur's evil half brother, Mordred, and his equally wicked mother, whose name slipped Ren's mind. But it sure wasn't Donna Reed.

Clarissa sat at the head of the dinner table and dictated that Tru and Russell sit on either side of her. Ren quickly jockeyed into the seat next to Tru, and Sybil sat next to Russell. Ren thought Sybil still hadn't become accustomed to Tru's good looks. She tried not to stare, but Matt periodically kicked her under the table and rolled his eyes at her. Matt took the seat opposite Clarissa, at the other end of the table.

Over baby greens salad and crab bisque, they discussed professional achievements.

"As you've probably heard," Clarissa told Tru, "Russell is a partner at Henley Sheering. That was the law firm in which Ren's father was a partner."

Tru smiled at Clarissa and then at Russell. "Yes, so I understand."

Clarissa said, "He's just landed the firm's most high-profile client in recent memory. Haven't you, Russell?"

Now Russell smiled. With a quick sniff, he said, "I like to think so, anyway. Of course, I'm not at liberty to discuss our representation, but you'll all read about it. Plenty. If, of course, you read the business section of the newspaper." This last was said directly at Tru. "Certainly won't see anything about the case if you only read the comics section, I imagine." He shot a conniving grin at Clarissa.

The two of them had a cackle over that, like a couple of magpies. The rest of the dinner guests stared at them. Ren was beginning to think maybe they *should* be dating.

"And you, Tru?" Clarissa suddenly said, breaking away from her little minion. "You have a job, don't you?"

Ren could tell she deliberately called it a job instead of a career. And Clarissa knew what Tru did for a living. No doubt she just hoped it would sound bad, saying it right after Russell had puffed himself up like a goony bird in mating season.

But Tru gave Clarissa a smile that had both Sybil and Ren smiling in return. "Oh, sure. I'm a labor-and-delivery nurse at the Birthing Inn in Loudoun County."

"A nurse?" Clarissa said. "A male nurse?" She said it as if something smelled bad.

"There *are* such things as male nurses, Mother," Ren said.

"Yeah, Mom," Matt said. "You told me your plastic surgeon had a male nurse."

Little gasps erupted around the table, and then all eyes turned to Matt.

"What?" he said.

Ren wasn't sure if Matt was faking social ignorance or not, but if so, he faked it very well. He slowly developed a look of realization on his face and said to everyone, "Oh. That didn't sound good, did it? But, of course, Mom merely had a little growth removed, didn't you, Mom?"

Clarissa, for one of the few times Ren could remember, was unable to come up with a snappy response. She didn't come up with any response at all.

Finally Matt said, "I'm a veterinarian, if anyone wants to know. A male veterinarian. Won't be anything about it in the papers, business or comics section."

To Ren's relief, Matt's plastic surgeon comment appeared to have the effect of making Clarissa cautious about topics of conversation. They made it all the way to dessert before she gave it another shot.

She began with some preamble about how high income taxes were, adding a comment to Russell. "You know how it can be, I would imagine, Russell, considering how lucrative a career you've chosen."

Russell sipped his coffee and then nodded, closing his eyes for a moment. "Torturous, yes, Clarissa. I actually considered selling my boat this year."

Now Ren was the one rolling her eyes at Sybil, and it wasn't because Syb was staring at Tru.

"Tru, how about you?" Clarissa said, taking a spoonful of her crème brûlée rather than looking at Tru. "Do you find you make enough in your job to have to worry about sheltering income?"

"Mother! That's rude!" Ren found herself dangerously curious about that plastic surgeon topic again.

"No, that's okay, Rennie," Tru said.

Ren loved that he called her *Rennie* at that moment. It suggested a closeness that Clarissa and Russell couldn't have missed.

"To tell you the truth," Tru said, "my career pays well enough, but my rewards tend to be other than financial."

"Mm-hmm," Clarissa purred. "Very quaint."

"Well, not quaint, really," Tru said. "Downright exciting. Every single day. I mean, my clients actually *are* mentioned in the paper. Every day. Jennifer Lee Owens, seven pounds, eleven ounces, twenty-two inches long. Anthony Carter Smith, eight pounds, two ounces, twenty inches long."

"Oh. I see," Clarissa said. "Yes, well —"

Tru set down his spoon, so he could use both hands while talking. "And I have to tell you, when you go through something like childbirth with a person — with people — who have waited for that moment for much more than nine months — in some cases, we're talking years of waiting — there's no greater reward, no greater honor, than to be included as a part of the event. I wouldn't trade my career — my job — for any other. My job's a real blessing."

In the silence that followed, Ren smiled at Tru and sighed. Then she heard Matt's foot under the table and Sybil jumped out of what must have been another staring session. Sybil looked at Matt, and they shared a subtle chuckle, Sybil looking embarrassed with herself.

Ren stood up and gathered some plates from the table. "Well, I have to work tomorrow." She shot a look at Russell. "I'm a teacher." Not that he asked, but Ren figured she'd mention it, since they were so wrapped up in what everyone did for a living. "Tru and I have to get going. Is that all right with you, Tru?" She gave him a conspiratorial smile.

"You sure? Already?" he asked, poker-faced.

They said their goodbyes and escaped back into the real world. The drive to Ren's house was a short one, and they didn't talk much. But after he dropped her off, Ren reviewed their two family meetings — her meeting his and his meeting hers. They had, essentially, been through a form of battle together, twice. They had survived. That had to have made them stronger. Closer.

Or so one would think.

Twenty-Six

Their next date began well enough. They hadn't seen each other since Clarissa's overpopulated dinner party, and they had both worked long and hard all week.

Ren had struggled a bit at school, knowing Casey's next visit with his mother was just around the corner. The school year was winding down to an end, and Ren didn't know for certain how things would work out with Casey over the summer months. Her involvement with Tru was a lovely distraction. And she certainly had enough work at school to keep herself occupied. But those soulful blue eyes of Casey's could draw her into a state of wishing and hoping that tended to drain her of energy. Nothing so critical as what brought her down, literally, at Wal-Mart, but still.

So by Friday evening Ren was more than eager to relax and enjoy Tru's company. And he seemed to need the relaxation too. They decided they'd go to the movies.

He arrived at her door with a bouquet of vibrant wildflowers.

"Gorgeous!" Ren said. "Come on in. I'll put them in water."

He followed her into the kitchen. "Your place looks great. I like the simplicity of it. Like something from one of those architectural magazines."

Ren hadn't thought about the fact that she had never invited Tru into her home before. She hadn't had anyone there since Greg left, other than family and Kara. Tru was the only person she had dated since her divorce. She supposed it was best not to set themselves up for temptation by being so alone and so private. He was, after all, dazzlingly handsome. And those kisses last week were as far as Ren wanted to let things go.

Tru sat on a stool at the breakfast counter while she trimmed and arranged the flowers in a blue glass vase.

He sighed. "We didn't talk about which movie to see. How about something light and upbeat?"

"Sounds good. Can you tolerate romantic comedy? That one about the two musicians is supposed to be pretty funny."

"Romantic comedy it is, then." His voice

sounded resigned.

"Is something wrong, Tru?"

He took a deep breath and let it out. "No, not really. Just had a rough day today. One of my patients . . . well, the baby didn't make it. A little girl. They named her Theresa."

Ren's heart sank. She walked over to him and gave him a hug where he sat. He rested his head against her shoulder. "I'm so sorry."

"It's always hard to know what to say, especially when there haven't been any indications of trouble. It's always awful, but . . ."

Ren pulled back and looked at him. "Are you sure you want to go to a movie?"

He nodded and stood, rubbing a bit of moisture from the corner of his eye. "Definitely. Have to get away from it. If I dwell on it, it'll affect my job and how I go into future deliveries. I know I need to give it to God. It's just very sad."

So they kept their plans and went to the film. It was as entertaining as the reviews had promised, and both of them relaxed and laughed throughout. They went for coffee afterward and talked about the movie.

Ren grinned, twisting a cut of lemon rind into her espresso. "I loved the part where the woman's parents stormed the stage, you know? Arguing with the conductor about not making their daughter first chair?"

Tru nodded after taking a drink from his cup. "What characters those two were, huh?" He laughed. "Especially the mother. Watching her made me feel a little less sorry for you, in your situation."

He said a few more things, but Ren didn't hear them. She got stuck at his expression of sympathy for her because of her mother. For some reason, his saying that bothered her. She tried to shrug it off, but she couldn't. She attempted a smile. Her lips felt two sizes too small. "What do you mean?"

He was adding sugar to his coffee. "Hmm?"

"Why do you feel sorry for me?"

He looked at her, puzzled. "Did I say I felt sorry for you? You mean, about the mother in the movie? No, I think I said I felt *less* sorry for you since your mother wasn't as bad as the mother in the movie."

"But, in order to feel less sorry for me, you had to feel sorry for me in the first place. And I wouldn't say my mother is a bad mother."

"I didn't say she was." A frown marred his

perfect eyebrows. "Have I made you angry, Ren?"

Well, of course he had made her angry.

"No, of course I'm not angry."

He studied her eyes. "You seem angry."

Again, she tried to shrug it off, this time literally shrugging. "It's just . . . well, I know my mother can be controlling, but you make her sound intolerable."

"Oh, no! I didn't mean to imply that —"

"I mean, you definitely saw her at her worst, but she does have her good points too."

"Of course she does. I'm sure she does. We both have mothers who want the best for us."

"Yeah. See, you know what I mean." Ren pointed a finger in his direction. "You have your hands full with your own mother, but you know she wants your happiness, despite how meddling she is."

He almost agreed with her, but then he suddenly stopped short. "Well. I don't know if I'd say she was meddling. That seems so . . ."

"But you know what I mean," she said. "She asked me stuff that was so personal that you and I hadn't even discussed it yet. And that was, like, two seconds after I met her."

He nodded. "I know her frankness some-times offends sensitive people —"

"Tru." She looked into his eyes. "I'm no more sensitive than the average person. But she was just, well, rude, questioning me as if she were protecting a child from some predator."

Tru leaned forward. "I am her child, Ren."

She leaned forward too. "I didn't mean she was protecting her child, Tru. I meant she was acting as if *you* were a child. Not a grown man. And I'm not a predator, by any stretch of the imagination."

"I didn't say you were!"

"Well, you didn't say I wasn't, either!"

He stopped himself before he responded to that. He folded his napkin into perfect quarters and tucked it beside his coffee cup. "Maybe we should drop this subject before we say anything else we'll regret."

Ren nodded and retrieved her purse from the floor. "I should probably get home. It's been a hard week."

"Yes." He anchored money under the sugar dispenser. "We've both had hard weeks."

Their drive was silent. The air condition-ing seemed far too cold, and Ren pushed the vents closed. They were nearly to her home when Tru spoke quietly. "I didn't mean to insult your mother, Ren."

"And I didn't mean to —"

"But I have to say that, whereas you may think my mother was protective of me, I got the impression your mother was protective of herself, not you. Or protective of her money, not you. I don't know which. But at least my mother was just trying to make sure you honestly cared for me."

Ren was frankly not sure if she became angry because she disagreed with him or because she agreed with him. Either way, the dam burst. "Give me a break, Tru. Your mother was like a stealth bomber, the way she kept sneaking up on us. She wasn't looking out for you any more than my mother was looking out for me. She was looking to make sure the man of the house didn't get snatched out of her clutches."

They had reached Ren's house, which was a good thing, considering Tru was clearly too angry to drive. He jerked on the emergency break and turned to her. "Her clutches? You make her sound like some wicked crone! Yes, she leans on me too much, but your mother is crushing you with her dominance. The next time we go to dinner at her house, I'll have to bring someone for your other boyfriend to spend time with."

Ren grasped the door handle and yanked. "And the next time we go to a party at *your* mother's, I'll have to come equipped with radar!" She was out of the car and slamming the door before he had a chance to reply.

By the time she reached her door and heard his car peeling away, Ren realized she was crying. She wasn't sure when that had started. But when she walked inside and saw the wildflowers in the vase, she was certain it wouldn't end anytime soon.

Twenty-Seven

A pint of chocolate-mint ice cream later, Ren was still a weepy mess. How could she have been so wrong about him? He seemed like such a perfect guy. So cute. So warm. And he loved babies and children. Dogs, even. They didn't come much nicer than that.

Ren knew she wouldn't be able to sleep. She curled up on the couch and tried watching TV to distract herself. Almost all late-night talk shows. Who were these people? So depressing in their happiness. And the only movie playing was about some serial killer. A real picker-upper, that. Ren switched the TV off and tried to read her humorous novel, *Helena's Search for a Soul Mate.* It made her cry.

She tossed the book and walked back toward the kitchen. She caught her reflection in the hall mirror and stopped short. How could she have gotten so out of shape in the last hour? She looked completely undesirable. No wonder Tru had dumped her. The thing about her mother was all a ruse.

There were about twenty cookies left in the Pepperidge Farm Delectables box. She'd have to pace herself.

Ren plopped onto the couch and picked up the phone. She got Kara's answering machine while her mouth was full. "Kara, it's Ren. Call me. It's all over." She swallowed her cookie but still felt a lump in her throat. "Tru despises me and Mother, and I can't say I blame him. But he was mean. Tell me I'm right and he's wrong before I explode. Working on phase two of total dessert-supply consumption. Going for the salty stuff next. Bye."

After staring at a stain on the carpet for several minutes, she had an inspiration. She grabbed the phone and called Jeremy. He might be home. He was in between girlfriends, if she remembered correctly.

"Yes, hello?" came the dear, accented voice of her buddy. He sounded like the kindest chimney sweep in *Mary Poppins.*

"Oh, Jeremy," she said, before she started crying again.

"Hello? Who's that? Is that you, Ren? Ren, are you all right? Where are you?" He'd probably just keep right on asking questions until she finally got it together enough to talk.

"I'm home. I had a date with Tru tonight."

"What's wrong, love?" He spoke so gently.

She told him how the evening had gone. "So what do you think? Was I horrible to take offense at what he said about Mother?"

"No, of course not. You love your mum. A true gentleman wouldn't verbally attack a woman as he's done with her. You did right to come to her defense."

"Well, I kind of attacked his mom too."

"But surely not so harshly."

"Um . . ."

"Never mind, love. She sounded daft anyway."

Ren nodded and bit into another cookie. This was kind of making her feel better. And kind of not.

"So," Jeremy said. "You really get the sense it's over, do you?"

"I can't imagine our being able to get past the things we said to each other tonight. I mean, I accused his mother of being a stealth bomber."

She heard a quiet snort on the other end. "Look, Ren, I wouldn't be a gent if I told you I thought it was hopeless. Of course, this is *me* talking. I'm not exactly the stellar example of the successful boyfriend. But you both might have been pinpointing some problems that would only have gotten worse, whether you brought them out into the open or not."

"What are you saying?"

"You both have mothers who factor largely in your lives, yeah? You both appear to recognize how your mothers interfere. But you both love your mums and don't want to hurt them."

Hmm. She hadn't thought about her mother and herself that way. Was it because of love that Ren seldom crossed her? Jeremy's theory made her feel like a nicer person than she felt before he stated it.

"Well," she said, "I guess that's right. I do love my mother, even if she's nuts. And demanding. And manipulative. And —"

"But you love her," Jeremy interrupted, rather than allowing her to wade into a description of Joan Crawford's double.

"Yes."

"And Tru seems as devoted to his mum as you are to yours."

"More, even." She pouted and bit into another cookie.

She heard him sigh. "I suppose I can identify a bit, as I'm fiercely devoted to my dad. I grew up without a mum. Did I ever tell you that?"

"Really?" Ren was ashamed that she couldn't remember whether he had told her that or not. How self-absorbed was she? "I . . . I think you might have told me."

"She died while I was a baby. Never knew her. When I hear about how you and Tru feel for your mums, I must admit to feeling a bit envious."

He was envious of her. Her, with Clarissa. Ren tried to remember if Jeremy had ever met her mother. "I'm sorry, Jeremy. Actually, I don't think I knew that about your mom."

"Yeah. Dad never remarried. Maybe the lack of a mother figure has something to do with why I can't hold on to a girlfriend. You think?"

Now Ren sighed. "I don't know. I think any girl would be thrilled to have you for a boyfriend. You're attractive, you're smart, you're funny, and you've got that wonderful accent. I mean, the accent might not get you far in England, but in the U.S., an accent often covers a multitude of sins."

"You really think that?"

"Oh, yeah." Ren was pleased to be talking about someone other than Tru or herself. "Why do you think all the little schoolgirls have a crush on you? For your *math* skills?"

There was silence from his end of the phone.

"Jeremy?"

"What I meant was, do you really mean all those nice things you just said about me?"

"Absolutely," Ren said without hesitation.

More silence. Was she putting him to sleep?

"Ren, have you ever . . . that is, would you ever consider . . . me?"

She put her cookie down. "What do you mean?"

"I hesitate to mention this. But my hesitation has been my undoing in the past. So I'll carry on. I was wondering if you would ever consider going out with me."

The strangest sensation buzzed through her. As if everything on earth had suddenly stopped — the movement of air, the passage of time, the digestion of all she had eaten since getting home — all waiting for her to say something. At the same moment, her brain ran a rapid background search for everything she had ever said or done in front of Jeremy. All this time she had blatantly been herself, thinking he considered her a gal pal, when, in fact, he was evaluating her as a possible girlfriend.

"Rennie?"

She tried to gather her wits. "Sorry! Yes! I mean, not yes-I-would-consider-going-out, just yes, hello. Not that I wouldn't consider going out, but not that I would, either."

She heard a chuckle on the other end of the line and knew Jeremy well enough to picture him shaking his head in self-deprecation.

"But maybe I would. Wow, Jeremy. You just caught me completely off guard with that."

"Me too, love. I have to admit the thought's run through my mind some over the past month or so. But I hadn't planned on saying anything. This just seemed like a possibly opportune moment."

"I have to . . . I don't know . . . give it some thought. I wasn't thinking of you that way."

"Of course you weren't. Don't mind me, Ren. You've enough to worry about just now, haven't you?"

Before she could answer, he said, "But about that, about the row with Tru. The problem between you two isn't impossible to fix, I wouldn't imagine. I have to say, though, that were I him, I'd consider it my place to apologize first. It sounds as if he started the ruckus with that first crack about your mum and the lady in the movie. If

Tru's a gent, if there's hope, he'll call you and admit that."

"Thanks. You're a pal." Suddenly that sounded like an insult. "I mean . . ."

He laughed softly. "Not to worry, love."

She said, "I'll see you at school Monday, okay?"

"Monday. Sleep tight, Ren."

She hung up and fell back on the couch. Good grief. Jeremy? She loved Jeremy. And she really did think all those fantastic things about him. But this was a new twist. She was married when she first met him, so of course she didn't look at him that way. Then Greg divorced her so abruptly. And when she finally accepted he would never come back, Tru came into the picture, with all his overwhelming wonderfulness.

Ren remembered something Jeremy had said, something about his hesitation having been his downfall — no, his undoing — in the past. She wondered if he had been poised to talk with her about this, back when Greg first left her. Maybe Jeremy was being, as he said, "a gent," waiting a respectful amount of time before saying anything. And then Tru happened.

But when she thought about the two of them — Tru and Jeremy — even considering her fight with Tru tonight, there was no comparison in feelings. There was something so much deeper with Tru.

Then it hit her. It wasn't necessarily the difference between friendship and love. It was the difference between the present and eternity. Jeremy wasn't a believer. Tru was. Even if Ren were only friends with both of them, what she had with Tru would be more significant.

Common knowledge at church was that you needed to avoid . . . what was it called? Missionary dating? Sometimes love *didn't* conquer all. Ren saw what the unequal yoke thing did to her marriage. She couldn't allow anything similar to happen now.

But if Jeremy were to accept Christ? What then?

What if she really *had* seen the last of Tru? How much time would have to pass before she knew for sure?

She took a huge breath and moaned it out. She glanced at the kitchen and then stood up, all flumpy and Sasquatch-like. She seemed to remember half a bag of sour cream-and-onion chips in there. And an entire can of Planter's Fancy Cashews.

Something told her this was going to be a restless night.

TWENTY-EIGHT

Kara didn't return Ren's call that night, but she woke her the next morning, bright and early, with several hearty knocks on her door. She breezed in when Ren answered, and she didn't see her closely at first.

"Sorry," Kara said, "I know I'm a little early. Whoa!"

She had seen Ren.

"What'd you do last night?" Kara said.

Obviously she hadn't listened to her answering machine.

Ren had just awakened from her junk-food-induced hibernation, so she knew she was disheveled. No doubt her eyes were puffy from crying. She held up a hand, indicating that Kara should wait, and shuffled into the kitchen for a tall glass of water. And another. All that sugar and salt. She was a dehydrated, blimpy-feeling sponge.

She whispered, "Let me run back and

brush my teeth."

But as Ren ambled down the hall, she heard Kara laugh. "You're quite the ball of fire this morning. Did you forget we were going to the gym? Or are you trying to conserve your energy for a real power workout?"

Ren just said, "Hang on," and stayed on track. She washed up as quickly as possible and threw on her workout clothes.

When she came back into the living room, Kara was standing in front of the couch and coffee table, surveying various empty food containers. She looked up at Ren, alarm in her eyes. "Looks like the aftermath of a ten-girl slumber party."

"No. Just me."

"What happened?"

"I left you a message," Ren said. "On your machine. The one you never check?"

"Mercy, girl. I got home late. Then I forgot to check it this morning. You know how I do. Why didn't you just call my cell?"

"Did you have it with you?"

She paused. "Well, no. I forgot it in my car, but you could have left a message there."

"And you would have checked your messages?"

Another pause.

"Point taken," Kara said. "So what happened?"

As they walked out to Kara's car and drove to the gym, Ren explained it all. The Your-Mother's-Worse-Than-Mine argument with Tru, the I-Wanna-Be-Your-Boyfriend revelation from Jeremy, and the unbelievable list of food Ren was going to have to work off this morning.

They arrived early enough to beat the crowd. The music was mercifully low-key — smooth jazz, rather than pump-it-up rock 'n' roll. The locker room even smelled like cleanser, rather than overworked bodies. By the time they started using the machines, Kara seemed to have recovered from her shock over Ren's messed up life and body. She was into her full take-charge mode.

"First off, let's talk about that food."

Ren winced, waiting to hear her lecture.

"Don't worry about it."

Ren raised her eyebrows. "Huh?"

"Look, you're here, which is more than what most people would do after a night like yours. You'll do what you can do today. We both know there's no way to work off all those calories in one fell swoop, so why worry about it? What's eaten is eaten. Let's just focus on today. Okay?"

"Thank you, ma'am. I needed that."

"Okay." Kara shoved her toward the first machine, and Ren dutifully strapped in and started pressing the weights Kara added to the pulley.

"About Tru," Kara said. "He definitely has an issue going on with his mother. No doubt about that."

Ren nodded between grunts. "Yep."

"But . . ." She waited until Ren stopped exercising and was able to look her in the eye. "You've got a bit of an issue yourself."

Ren opened her mouth, but there really was no point in arguing with that. "You mean Mother?"

Kara nodded. "I mean how you relate to your mother."

"Well, we are related, that's for sure. That, I can pretty much guarantee, is the ball and chain that holds us so lovingly together."

"I'm serious."

"I know," Ren said, chastened. "But I don't know how to change how she acts toward me."

Kara shook her head. "Not the problem. What you need to change is how you act toward her." She pointed to the next machine, and Ren moved to it.

"You mean, get tougher with her? 'Cause I can tell you, I felt horrible when I snapped at her in her kitchen, telling her she had to be the date for that Russell Snootyman the Third. I don't know if I can do that again."

"No. You just need to respectfully allow her to face her own consequences." Kara nodded at the machine. "Do twenty reps."

"I thought that's what I was doing," Ren said. "I mean, the thing about Mother. I sat next to Tru all through dinner and left with him when it was over. She didn't succeed in getting me interested in Russell."

"Straighten your back." Kara pressed against Ren's shoulders. "Yeah, Ren, but Tru had to sit through that entire dinner, with your mother praising that jerk and belittling your date. And, because Tru's a class act, he had to be polite while Snootyman ridiculed him like some country club dandy."

Ren stopped lifting the weights. "But I had to sit through an entire dinner with that ever-present mother of Tru's hovering over me, asking everything but my panty size."

"Three more," Kara said, tapping Ren's hand to encourage her to start again. "Yes, because you're classy too. But we're talking about how you deal with your mother right now, okay? Although, Jeremy was right about Tru needing to initiate an apology." She raised one eyebrow. "Of course, as Christians, we're supposed to be turning the other cheek and all that. But Tru should apologize. I have to agree with Jeremy on this one."

"Me too." Ren sighed. "But now that you describe what Tru went through at Mother's, I'm feeling pretty apologetic myself."

Kara just smiled at her. She walked to the next machine and waited for Ren to follow. "Don't cheat on this exercise. You always hunch forward on it. See, if you and Tru had left your mother's house the moment you realized she had set you up with a second date, the problem would have been all hers to handle. You could have calmly explained what was prompting you to leave. But your mother's a smart cookie — she probably wouldn't even need the explanation. It would be best, though, for you to set some . . . barriers, I think they call it."

"It's boundaries. Remember? Sandy's talked about that before. But barriers would probably make more sense in Mother's case. Barbed wire, guard dogs, the works."

Kara rolled her eyes at Ren, smiling. "Look, you're the only daughter she has. She's probably doing the best she can, which seems really bad right now, I'll admit. But you turned out well, don't you think? And she's the one who raised you. She and your dad."

"Yes, there is that." Ren wiped the sleeve of her T-shirt across her sweaty face. "She raised the perfect lady."

"Exactly." Kara tapped the seat on the machine. "Give me twenty perfect reps."

"I'll have a talk with Mother." Ren grabbed the machine handles and curled forward, trying not to hunch. "I'll talk about the other night." She grunted with exertion as she pulled on the weights. "I'll tell her where she crossed the line." Ren sounded more confident, speaking as she forced the machine to bend for her. "And I'll respectfully stand my ground as an adult woman with clear boundaries."

"There ya go. Stand your ground as a strong, secure woman."

Ren stopped curling. "Will you go with me?"

Kara gently smacked Ren's forehead and waited for her to start again before speaking. "You need to have that talk with your mother regardless of what happens next between you and Tru."

Ren nodded. "Yeah. Mother and I were bound to reach this point eventually."

"Right." Kara glanced quickly behind herself. "Okay, so tell me. New subject. What do you think about Jeremy's interest in you? I saw that one coming, by the way."

Ren stopped again. "What? And you didn't warn me?"

Kara shrugged. "I didn't think he'd ever mention it. And I thought it might make you feel self-conscious around him. I figured it was a phase he was going through. Maybe it is."

"Maybe. I guess I encouraged him by calling him to complain about Tru."

Kara stepped to the last machine in the circuit. "Last one, Ren. Just do fifteen."

Ren obeyed as commanded. Considering what she had eaten last night, she felt pretty good about how much she had done today.

"What if it's not a phase with Jeremy?" Kara asked. "And what if Tru really is out of the picture?"

The thought of never seeing Tru again almost made Ren start crying again. She stopped exercising.

"I'm sorry," Kara said quickly. "How insensitive. I hope he calls, Ren. I think you two could work this out. But you both have to deal with your mothers."

"Yeah," Ren said quietly. She resumed the workout. "And about Jeremy. Honestly, Kara, I'm having a hard time picturing him as anything other than a friend. An adorable, funny, sweetheart of a friend. But he only planted the idea in my head last night.

And then there's the fact that he's not a believer."

"Big fact, yeah." Kara sighed. "I do love Jeremy. Such a dear."

"So how come *you* never, you know?" Ren was only half teasing.

"Me?" Kara frowned. "Go after Jeremy? For one thing, he looks too much like Jude Law."

"Who is definitely a hottie!"

"Yeah, but that wandering eye of his . . . I think I'd mistrust Jeremy no matter how faithful he was."

Ren laughed. "And here I always thought the resemblance was a bonus."

Kara said nothing. She just looked at Ren and raised her eyebrow, apparently measuring her words. Ren shrank a little under her scrutiny.

"Can I stop now?" Ren asked. She had lost count of the reps.

"Yeah. Stop." Kara rested her hand on her hip. "I would love to see Jeremy happy."

"Me too." Ren took a sip from her water bottle. "Hey, did you know he doesn't have a mother?"

"That sounds familiar. He might have told me."

Ren couldn't help the thought that flitted

through her mind. No mother-in-law. That had a nice ring to it.

TWENTY-NINE

Ren laughed out loud and poured water from Casey's cup onto a paper napkin. "Here. Hold still."

Casey sat next to her on the park bench while they ate their ice cream cones. Ren didn't notice until she turned to speak to him that he had chocolate smudges on his chin, his cheeks, the tip of his nose, and even on the wisps of hair that curled down over his eyebrows.

She winked at him. "Have you actually eaten any of that ice cream?"

He frowned as she wiped his face, but he was only grimacing to keep his eyes closed while she cleaned him up. He broke into a big grin after she finished.

" 'Course I ate some of it!" He giggled as if she were the silliest woman he knew. "Look! You can even see it on my tummy." He pointed to where his shirt covered his stomach. Little continents of melted chocolate ice cream were splotched all over the pale blue fabric.

"Oh, for Pete's sake!" she said, without thinking. "Mrs. Hallston's going to kill me!"

Ren was so clearly inexperienced in the parenting realm. Why hadn't she thought to cover him head to toe in napkins? Or a tarpaulin?

She had come home from church that morning, saddened that Tru hadn't attended, but a little relieved at not having to face him after their fight. Only one message awaited her on her machine, a frantic appeal from Casey's foster mother, Mrs. Hallston. Her husband had been called out of town unexpectedly, and this afternoon she needed to drive him all the way to BWI, the airport in Baltimore. She hated to make Casey ride all that way and back. Ren was thrilled to offer to take him for a few hours.

She looked forward to getting her mind off of her complicated love life, or her lack of a love life, and the various meddling mothers therein. The petting farm down the street from her house seemed the perfect spot for a distracting afternoon outing.

There were plenty of other groups with the same idea. The ratio of people to animals was about even. But that was fine. The squeals of childish glee, coupled with the occasional pig grunt or chicken squawk, just added to the fun.

And Ren wanted to be the good guy, buying Casey an ice-cream cone as soon as they got there and before the various animal smells became overwhelming. No boring, sensible snacks for them! Of course, grapes or carrot sticks might have been the wiser choice, given the sloppy condition in which Casey would arrive back home.

But when she looked into his earnest blue eyes, and saw him studying her so closely, she realized he thought his dirty shirt might result in chastisement from someone. Maybe he even thought Ren was reprimanding him.

So she blew her breath out through her lips and smiled at him. "Oh, well. No biggie, right? Let me grab some more napkins from the snack stand."

The girl behind the counter had apparently been watching them. "Want a few wet wipes?" she said, a grin on her face. She looked past Ren to Casey and waved at him. "Your son's such a cutie. That curly hair! He looks like an angel."

Ren looked back at Casey and saw him waving back at the girl. "Thanks. Yeah, he really is an angel." She took the wipes from the girl, sighing. "Unfortunately, he's not my son. I'm just watching him for a friend."

As Ren walked back to him, she wondered about that. The girl at the stand didn't really need to know that Casey wasn't hers, but Ren always felt as if she had to correct people when they saw them together and made that assumption. The feeling was a strange one, as if Ren would be taking credit for something she hadn't done if she let anyone think she was his mother.

"Look what I have for you," she said to him as she sat back down. She handed him a wipe and kept the others to use on him herself. "Here, you can help. We'll get the worst of that chocolate off before we go into the animal pen. I'm sure Mrs. Hallston has a super-duper way of getting this out of your clothes."

He shrugged. "I don't know. I don't think I ever got chocolate on myself before. She doesn't let me have it."

Ren gasped. "You're not allergic, are you?" Great. Here she was worried about stains, and the poor child was about to go into anaphylactic shock. But wait. Casey was her student. She'd know if he had allergies —

"Nope," Casey said. "She just has lots of white furniture and stuff. She says I spill too much."

Poor kid. As a chocoholic, Ren felt palpable pain for him in his deprived state. She decided then and there to throw caution to the wind and let him go ahead and finish that ice cream. She'd *buy* him a new shirt, if necessary! Spills too much. Honestly!

Ren ruffled his curls. "Well, there's nothing white for us to worry about right now. You go ahead and finish your cone, and then we'll go see the animals."

He smiled at her, but then he looked down at his hands and frowned. Until then Ren hadn't noticed he wasn't holding his ice cream when she handed him the wet wipe. They both looked at the bench seat next to him. Nothing.

Suddenly his eyebrows raised, as if a memory had just forced them upward. His eyes grew wide and he quickly looked at her face and then down at her seat.

It could have been worse. After Casey set his ice cream cone down on her seat, it had rolled back and onto the ground. Casey must have been intent on watching Ren and the nice, waving girl behind the snack stand.

Had an entire ice cream cone been sitting on the bench next to Casey, Ren probably would have been less likely to sit there. As it was, only a snail trail of chocolate ice cream had awaited her return.

Ren jumped up and they both looked at her backside. Within seconds Ren felt an intense bond of sisterhood with Mrs. Hallston. But she attempted to downplay the fact that her pants now matched Casey's shirt quite nicely.

"Oh, doggone it! I should have looked where I was sitting."

"I'm sorry! I'm so sorry, Ms. Young!" Casey said, his little voice full of guilt.

Ren shook her head, trying to bend around and dab at the mess with one of the wet wipes. "It's all right, Casey. This was an accident, that's all." She wiped a few more times. But, short of stripping right there in the middle of the petting farm, she wasn't about to do an effective job of cleaning up. She just straightened up, sighed, and gave Casey a smile.

The poor kid looked worried.

"Really, Casey, I'm not even that crazy about these pants. Okay?"

He studied her eyes for a moment. "Do we have to leave now?"

Ren sighed again and put her arm on his shoulder. "What, without visiting the animals? Of course not!"

He finally broke into a grin.

Ren said, "Come on. Let's get some of that animal food, okay?"

He stood behind her while she bought a couple of cones filled with food pellets. As she turned to hand one to Casey, she saw that he was staring at her pants, as she imagined many people were doing by now.

"It's like a question mark," he said.

"What?"

"Your chocolate. On your pants. It's like a question mark."

They had studied punctuation in class this week, which had likely prompted Casey's association. At least he didn't say, "It's like a *huge* question mark."

Ren wasn't sure, really, what the proper response was, so she simply smiled and nodded.

Just before they walked into the animal petting pen, Casey said, "What does it mean when an accident is a person?"

"What do you mean, sweetie?"

He frowned, thinking hard. He pointed at her pants. "Well, you said that was just an accident, right?"

"Right, that's all it was. No big deal."

"So what does it mean," he said to his pellet cone, "when a person is an accident? If someone calls you an accident."

A tight ball of tension seized Ren in the chest. She squatted down quickly to join him at eye level. "Who told you that?" She spoke as gently as she could.

He stared at the cone, looking like the loneliest person in the world.

She reached up and brushed a few curls away from his forehead. They fell right back down again. "Did Mr. or Mrs. Hallston say that to you, Casey?" *Please, Lord, not them. They seem so kind.*

He quickly shook his head. "No, no. They're nice. They're really nice to me."

Ren nodded. "Good. I'm glad. But who told you that you were an accident, honey?"

He looked up at her hesitantly, as if he felt he had done something wrong. "No one. They didn't tell me. I just heard 'em. The Thurgoods, those last people I lived with before the Hallstons. Mrs. Thurgood used to call me 'the accident' sometimes when she talked about me to people. I didn't know what she meant. But I could tell, how she said it. It isn't a good thing to be, an accident."

An overwhelming sorrow filled Ren's lungs. She struggled with that, even while fighting the rage she felt against this horrible Thurgood woman. She set down her cone of food. She took Casey's cone from him and set it down. Then she rested on her knees and pulled him to her. She hugged him — gently at first, then firmly — trying not to break into tears. When she was able to speak, Ren whispered into his ear. "You are not an accident, Casey. God knew exactly what He was doing when He created you from the most special things in heaven. You are His gift to so many people, including me."

She pulled back and looked him in the eyes. Tears glistened just above his lash line, but he reached up quickly to brush them away.

"Casey, no person is an accident," Ren said. "Even people who say mean things like Mrs. Thurgood did. Okay?"

He nodded. "Okay. But . . ." He kicked at a pebble on the ground.

"What?" Ren asked. "What is it?"

"If I'm not an accident, and God made me, and I'm a . . . gift and all, how come no one wants to be my mom or dad?"

Ren gasped. "Oh, no, Casey! Oh, my goodness." She hugged him again. What could she tell him without loading him down with his sad history? And hers? "Listen, sweetie. The only reason you're not . . . in your permanent home yet is because things got complicated. You know what that means?"

He nodded.

"It's not because of you," she said. "It's

because everyone wants you to have the best home ever. But it's going to happen, okay? Just be patient for a while longer. And trust in God." She smiled at him. "I have to tell myself that all the time: Be patient and trust in God."

He looked at her, wonder in his eyes. "Really?"

She nodded. "Really."

He frowned. "So I might have to wait 'til I'm old like you before I get a family? It could take that long?"

She softly chuckled. "No. It won't take that long."

She saw relief in his eyes. She pretended to give him a little punch on the shoulder. "And I'm not *that* old."

She handed the animal food to him and took the other cone before standing up. "Come on. Let's get in there before we run out of time, buddy. Those little goats look as if they need some snacks."

Ren had enjoyed the tiny horses in their fenced-in pasture last week. But this whole petting zoo thing wasn't something she grew up around. If they existed when Ren was a child, she had certainly never heard about them. Somehow she couldn't imagine her mother, decked out in one of her Chanel suits, strolling with Ren through animal stalls, communing with slobbery Brahma bulls and potbellied pigs. Consequently, while Ren thought the petting zoo was a terrific concept, it wasn't a scene she was all that comfy with.

So the smile she wore, when she extended her pellet-laden palm to these critters, was as false as the nonchalance she tried to show in front of Casey.

"Hold your hand flat like this, Casey. Just as the lady showed us, see?" Ren tried to keep her voice upbeat, even when some cow sort of animal left a layer of slime in her palm while licking up pellets.

Casey giggled when the same thing happened to him. Ren imagined him putting that nasty stuff to his face — in class these little guys were constantly sticking their hands in their faces. But she was out of napkins and wet wipes. She looked over her shoulder once before whispering to him. "Just wipe your hand on your shirt, sweetie. It's already dirty, anyway."

Not exactly mother-of-the-year advice, but she viewed this event as their own little *Survivor* episode, rather than a venue for teaching tea party manners.

Casey was thrilled when a herd of pigmy goats surrounded him and his measly cone of food. They were adorable, but Ren couldn't help but gasp out loud when they began jumping up on her and Casey, just as dogs do. Poorly behaved dogs, at that.

"Down!" Ren said. "*Bad* goats! Get down!" Of course, they failed to respond to her inane command. She wasn't sure if the laughter she heard came from seasoned moms laughing with her or at her.

"Hey!" Casey laughed with wonder. "He wants to eat my shirt!" And sure enough, a feisty black-and-white goat had Casey's shirt in his mouth and was attempting to eat it right off of Casey's body.

Ren grabbed the shirt and pulled it away from the goat's teeth.

"I think he likes the ice cream!" Casey said. Ren was just about to commend Casey for his logic when she remembered which portion of her body was covered with the very same stuff. And she was just about to protect her backside when she felt her slacks being attacked and tugged vigorously away from her person by two determined goats who had surely had enough to eat by now. Ren's resulting, frenzied dance to freedom no doubt rivaled what Kara and Ren had watched at the *Riverdance* show last month. Now there was no mistaking the intent of the other women's laughter. Ren had become a bit of a sideshow.

And she blew her cover completely when an inquisitive, and far too aggressive, emu headed for Casey. The bird looked like an ostrich having a really bad hair day. He may have been going for what was left of Casey's cone, but Ren couldn't help remembering an old Hitchcock film, *The Birds.* This thing had a beak big enough to take down a Cyclops, let alone a lovely little boy with two gorgeous blue eyes. Ren snatched him up in her arms and announced gaily, but maniacally, "Wasn't that fun? Time to go, buddy!"

A peacock screeched at them when they veered too close to him. He sounded like something from a B-rated movie murder scene. Ren nearly screamed back at it. It was all she could do to not kick it over the fence.

Casey giggled in her arms all the way out of the pen. It was a blessing that he was fine with their leaving. And the time had come for her to get him home.

While they walked to the car, Casey attempted mimicking the babylike bleating of the goats, and Ren tried to find something about herself that would help her feel in control. Within a four-day span, she lost her boyfriend, ate enough to feed half of New Jersey, insulted one of her best friends when he expressed a romantic interest in her, and added "confront domineering mother" to her list of things to do. She had also just guided Casey through the wilds of a petting zoo with all the effectiveness of a skittish prairie dog.

Certainly she was meant to trust her life to the Lord's control because she didn't seem to be doing a great job in the *self*-control department lately.

As she loaded Casey into his booster seat, Ren sighed. How appropriate to finish this day with a big, chocolate question mark on her backside, following her wherever she chose to go.

THIRTY

Monday morning, Ren walked briskly through the school's front doors. She peeked into the main office. The school secretary was already hard at work.

"Morning, Peggy," Ren chirped. She grabbed some papers from her mail slot and charged off toward her classroom, lively as could be. No one would ever guess her inner turmoil. No, sir, not if she kept this up. Her life was like a circus juggling act, and she was a wreck. But she could do perky for eight hours, couldn't she?

Halfway to her class she realized she was biting her lower lip. Not a good sign. *Get a grip.* But, if she actually got a grip on anything, she'd probably do it white-knuckled, unable to let go.

All right, then, loosen up. She remembered the looseness she felt just before fainting several months ago. Hmm. Maybe she'd just better stop listening to her own advice.

The weekend had ended without a single call from Tru. They'd gone days without speaking before. But considering their last conversation, this silence didn't bode well.

On the other hand, Ren's mother had called *ad nauseum.* "I want to talk with you about your nurse friend," one message reported. Later, another: "I spoke with Russell the Third yesterday. The law firm's annual party is coming up. If you play your cards right, he might ask you to go with him." That one shocked Ren to no end. Was that guy so hard up for a date that he was still interested, even after his disastrous blind date with Tru and Ren?

Ren hadn't been able to return Clarissa's calls — okay, she chickened out. She was dreading having to deal with her mother. But in putting off the confrontation, Ren had increased her anxiety to gargantuan proportions.

"Just get it over with," Kara said on the phone last night. "The sooner you explain to her that you're a grown-up, the sooner she can freak out, disown you, sulk in a corner, and then realize that you're right."

That schedule of anticipated events had not motivated Ren to answer any of Clarissa's phone calls.

So. No Tru. Lots of Clarissa. And now,

what should Ren expect today between Jeremy and herself? She didn't know about *him,* but she had developed a rock-solid plan of awkwardness and self-consciousness.

He surprised her, though, as was becoming his custom. He showed up at her classroom door just before the morning bell. He was holding Casey's hand — Casey loved Jeremy — and a cute young woman stood at his other side. They looked like the cover of a family magazine.

"Bye, Mr. B.," Casey said, entering the classroom and waving at Jeremy as if he were sailing away on a cruise.

"Right, Casey," Jeremy said. "See you at recess, eh, mate?"

Casey nodded. "Yes, sir, mate." He approached Ren, his eyes sparkling. She leaned down for their customary morning hug. Casey set his T-Rex lunch box on the floor and shrugged off his tattered backpack so that he could fully enjoy the embrace. He smelled like oranges and buttered toast. As usual, his small, warm squeeze made all other concerns fade briefly, even while reminding Ren of what she couldn't have.

Jeremy extended his hand, palm up, to encourage the young woman to enter Ren's classroom. "After you," he said to her.

She beamed, clearly taken by him, and

entered.

Jeremy smiled at Ren and addressed her by her classroom name. "Ms. Young, this is Ms. Andrea Barnes. She's substitute teaching here this week."

"Oh," Ren said, annoyed by her relief that Andrea wasn't a romantic interest for Jeremy. Yet.

Ren cringed inwardly. What was the matter with her? She didn't want to date Jeremy, did she? "Very nice to have you with us." She shook Andrea's hand.

"Thanks! I'm *so* going to love it here!" Now this girl could do perky. "The office asked me to come relieve you for a minute so you could go take a call, okay?" She tilted her head like a happy little Valley Girl.

Ren shot a look at Jeremy. His smile was subtle. It was just for her. No flirtation — Ren didn't think — just a private amusement with Andrea's animated style. He was obviously still at ease around Ren. She liked that. One less prickly facet of life to deal with today.

The morning bell rang.

"Got to run!" Jeremy said, giving Ren a blue-eyed wink before dashing away. Actually very cute. Hmm. Tru had winked at her when they first met. Ren had thought *that* cute too. What — did they all read the same book or something?

Ren handed her class roll sheet to Andrea. "If I'm not back by the time morning announcements are over, just call roll."

"Gotcha!" Andrea crinkled her nose at Ren. So much sugar so early in the morning . . .

Ren hustled quickly down the hall. This call had better not be her mother. If she was calling Ren at work about Tru, Russell, or anything less serious than a heart attack, Ren would have to add that to the list of things she would probably never discuss with her.

Peggy nodded toward the phone on the desk next to hers. "Line two. Cecilia Saunders."

"Who?"

Peggy shrugged. "She said something about her brother."

Ren was puzzled. "Her . . . Oh! Cessy!" Tru's sister. Ren grabbed the phone. "Cessy, I'm so sorry to keep you waiting."

"Don't worry about it, Ren. I'm sorry to bother you at work. I tried to reach you at your home number, but I guess I called too late."

"Is everything all right?" *Say no, Cessy. Say Tru is dying of a broken heart and has summoned me to his deathbed.*

337

"Oh, sure, everything's fine," she said, bursting Ren's little bubble. "But I'd really like to talk with you. Do you get a lunch break there?"

"Uh, yeah. Sure. You mean today?"

"Are you too busy today?"

"No. No, today's good. But I only get half an hour."

"I'll come there. We could maybe take a little walk on the school grounds?"

Ren was no longer anxious about facing Jeremy. But now, anticipation of her upcoming conversation with Cessy filled that space in her worried thoughts. Did Tru send her? Did his mother?

Ren had forgotten what a stunning woman Cessy was. She remembered her as pretty. But as they walked along the playground, Ren was struck again by her combination of exotic beauty and genuine sweetness.

Those were actually traits that described Tru too. Beautiful. Sweet. Except for that thing about his hating her mother.

"Tru doesn't know yet that I'm here," Cessy said as soon as they walked far enough from the playground to hear each other. "I'll tell him later, but . . . well, I was afraid he wouldn't let me come if he knew." She laughed softly. "A little unfair of me, I suppose."

Ren smiled. "Reminds me of my teen years. Complete honesty with my parents *after* the fact. Then, let the chips fall where they may. Got me grounded a few times, I remember."

"Tru won't be able to ground me, but I'm concerned about embarrassing him."

Hmm. Maybe he is *on his emotional death-bed after all.*

Cessy said, "I, um, overheard a conversation he had with my mother this weekend."

Ren straightened up a bit at that. She was dying to hear this. But if Cessy told her unkind stuff Tru's mother said about her, she'd have a hard time letting that go.

"I wasn't eavesdropping. They talked right in front of me. I just don't think they thought that my listening was a big deal."

"Didn't think you'd tell me, anyway, right?"

"I hadn't really planned to, but . . ." She shrugged. "I know you're important to Tru. I got the impression that you two may have quarreled over some things that happened with my mother at her birthday party."

"Yep, that would be an accurate impression. But it wasn't just about your mother, Cessy. My mother was pretty rude to Tru when they met. And I didn't do enough to protect him from an awkward situation, I'm afraid."

"Oh." Cessy was obviously surprised. "I think I heard most of their conversation, but he never said anything about your mother."

Ren caught her breath. He didn't complain about her? Or her mother? Ren suddenly pictured him, in full armor, sitting atop a white horse. What a gent, as Jeremy would say. Jeremy. Another knight in shining armor? Yikes, not now! Push that thought away or risk complete confusion and possible meltdown on the playground. Talking about *Tru* right now.

Cessy said, "I assume Tru told you about my father?"

Ren nodded. "He explained some things from the past and said your father isn't around much anymore."

"And he told you about my mother depending so much on him — on Tru, I mean?"

"Yes. But I understand that, Cessy. It sounds as if she had her hands full. Pregnant, five other children, no man around the house, really. That had to be hard."

"It was hard on Tru too," Cessy said. "He was only fifteen, Ren. That's even younger than my youngest brother, Devon. I can't

340

imagine Devon taking on that kind of responsibility. Tru had to grow up fast. And when Dad was around, he was so resentful toward Tru." She shook her head. "I don't know what Dad expected Tru to do — let Mami down the way *he* had?"

Ren was starting to feel a little guilty for fighting with Tru. Then she wondered if that's what Cessy was here for. To make her understand Tru better.

They both turned their heads when they heard an especially loud scream from one of the children on the playground. But the scream was obviously harmless, and they could also hear the child's teacher quietly chastise him.

"Actually, though," Cessy said, "Tru's problem with my mother is more his fault than anyone else's."

"Your father's fault?"

"No. Tru's fault." She chuckled when Ren looked at her, surprised to hear anything less than supportive of Tru. "He's not perfect, Ren. You knew that, right?"

"I've been having an internal debate about that ever since I met him, frankly. I know he *looks* perfect."

Cessy laughed. "Yes. Maybe it's a blessing that he's been somewhat tied to my mother's apron strings. He got into plenty of trouble when he was younger, but I think he would have had more girl trouble if Mami hadn't been so watchful."

Ren kept her mouth shut. Yes, indeed. Not one word about that one. And where had she heard that bit about Tru and his mother's apron strings? Oh. Yikes! Jeremy.

"Anyway," Cessy said, "Tru was there for my mother — for all of us, really — while we grew up. And I'm ashamed to admit this, but none of us took the reins from him when we could have."

"What do you mean?"

She took a thoughtful breath in and out. "As I said, Devon's seventeen, even older than Tru was when my father . . . when all this started. Devon doesn't help Mami the way Tru does. Harris is nineteen. Same thing. And every one of us girls has been too wrapped up in her own life to be there for our mother, knowing she would just keep leaning on Tru. And knowing he'd rise to whatever the need was."

"But you blame Tru in some way?"

She nodded. "Obviously I think the rest of us let him down. But this weekend, when I heard him talking with Mami, I realized that he allowed that to happen. I think he liked playing the man-of-the-house role, so he never encouraged the rest of us to take over. Not even when he left for college. He didn't even live at home anymore, and he was still pretty much the man of the house."

"I guess there are worse character traits to have," Ren said. "I remember the day I met him. He said he loved kids, and then he mentioned his siblings. I have to admit, I pictured much younger siblings."

"Ouch," Cessy said. "You see what I mean, then."

"I remember thinking he'd probably be a great father."

Cessy's smile was sweet and sad. "Yes. He's been a great father since he was fifteen." She looked at Ren. "That's more than half his life, which is what he pointed out to Mami. He told her it was time for him to take control of his own life and to step away from running everyone else's lives for them."

Ren raised her eyebrows. "That must have been hard for him to say. Did your mother take it well?"

"Hmm, yes. She took *that* all right. It was when he told her that she needed to stop trying to run his life that she got really upset with him."

Ren kind of whistled. "Wow. I'm inspired."
"What?"

Ren shook her head. "Just a similar problem for me, with my mother. I need to have a chat like that with her. I don't relish it."

"Well, I wish I could encourage you, but the truth is, my mother's not speaking to Tru right now. She's pretty offended."

Ren stopped strolling and heaved a big sigh. "Oh, no. Poor Tru. He loves her so much."

Cessy nodded. "Yes. He loves her enough to tell her the truth. That's hard."

Ren looked at her to see if she was trying to drop a hint about talking with Clarissa. But Cessy looked as innocent as ever.

She put her hand on Ren's arm. "Tru talked about you incessantly before bringing you to Mami's party. I've never seen him . . . well, actually, I've only seen him like this once before."

"His old fiancée?" Ren asked. "Emily?"

"Yes, Emily," Cessy said. "But I've never seen him willing to cross my mother over anyone before. Not even Emily. That's why I wanted to tell you he'd talked with her." She looked at the far end of the playground, maybe to think, maybe to avoid looking Ren in the eye. "To be honest, I'm not sure if he'll call you or not, Ren. He mentioned Mami's unfriendly behavior toward you, and I don't think he would have confronted her if not for you. But he didn't say anything to indicate whether he thought he'd see you again."

Ren spoke softly. "I see."

Cessy looked her in the eyes. "So I wanted you to know, in case he never tells you. I think you were good for him."

Ren *was* good for him, Cessy said. That past tense made Ren want to cry.

Cessy looked down and shook her head. "No. That's not it. I have to be honest with you, Ren." She closed her eyes and faced skyward. "God forgive me, I'm meddling." Then she looked at Ren. "I'm doing exactly what Tru asked my mother not to do anymore. What I meant was, I think you *are* good for him. I'd like to see you two together again."

Despite her serious expression, she made Ren smile.

Ren glanced toward the school. Her break was nearly finished. She noticed Jeremy coming outside with his class for recess. He looked over, grinned at her, and waved.

As Ren waved back, Cessy said, "I just hope Tru doesn't take too long in calling you. I'd hate to see him lose you to someone else."

THIRTY-ONE

"That was a pretty bird, your visitor," Jeremy said, when he and Ren crossed paths in the main office at the day's end.

Ren had wrinkled her nose at the stale coffeepot smell when she walked in, but now she gave Jeremy her full attention. His comment irked her, ever so little. As he pulled some papers from his mail slot, Ren forced a laugh.

"Down, boy. She's married."

Jeremy looked at her and lifted his eyebrows. "Oh, I wasn't interested. Just commenting." He frowned, as if at himself. "I'm sorry, Ren. That was rather rude of me, wasn't it? Considering our conversation the other evening."

His openness shut down Ren's irritation in a second. She even felt embarrassed for her snide comment. She lowered her eyes, as if inspecting the books she held in her arms. "Not at all, Jeremy." She looked back up at him, tilting her head. "Hey, let's not get weird around each other, okay?"

"Why would you two be weird with each other?" Sandy asked, having just escorted a student into the office. She pointed to the couch and said, "Just have a seat right there, Samantha, honey. Missing the bus is nothing to worry about. Your mom's going to be here for you any minute."

Just as she said that, the girl's mother arrived. While Sandy chatted with her, Jeremy and Ren communicated without speaking. He looked her in the eyes and cocked his head toward Sandy, his eyebrows forming a question. *Okay for me to tell Sandy?*

Ren glanced at Sandy and then at Jeremy, shrugging in resignation. *Yeah, why not?*

So by the time Sandy looked back at them, they were ready for her.

Jeremy pulled Sandy closer to himself so he could speak to her quietly. "You see, I've got a bit of a crush on our girl here."

Sandy looked at him, then at Ren, and then back at him. "And you two are just now figuring this out?"

They both looked at her, puzzled, their mouths slightly open like two ventriloquist dummies.

A teacher breezed into the office, carrying a huge cake box. "Yummy birthday cake here, folks. The mom didn't want to take it home. Lots left over." She headed toward the teachers' lounge.

"None for me, Jeanne. I had a late lunch," Sandy called to her, as the few other people in the office trailed after Jeanne and the cake. Sandy looked back at Jeremy and Ren. They had closed their mouths, and neither of them spoke. Sandy lowered her voice. "You two." She smiled and shook her head. "Too cute. So I take it the nurse fellow is out of the picture?"

"Um . . . I don't really know yet," Ren said.

Sandy gave Ren's arm a quick squeeze of support and then waved her finger between Jeremy and Ren. "This could happen." She walked away, saying, "But keep your heads, kids." She stopped at the door and looked at them. "And don't get weird with each other."

The static of an unattended walkie-talkie on the secretary's desk was the only sound left in Sandy's wake.

Ren looked at Jeremy. He had been so honest that she felt safe to do the same. She glanced around. Everyone had gone to the lounge. "I don't know how Sandy could have guessed anything. Honestly, Jeremy, I haven't been thinking of you that way. I mean, you've made me consider it, I'll admit. But I've always thought of you as my friend."

He nodded. "She must be talking about me, then. I've been *considering* it for a while." He muttered, almost to himself, "Hadn't thought I was so obvious, I must say."

Ren laughed. "You weren't obvious. Sandy's got antennae hidden in that hairdo of hers."

He smiled. "Is that what the big hair is all about? Crafty wench."

Ren sighed. "Well, I didn't have a late lunch, as Sandy did. Didn't have lunch at all, because of my 'pretty bird' visitor." They shared a smile. "I'm going to grab some of that birthday cake."

"With you, love," Jeremy said, following her to the lounge.

Most of the teachers had already gone. By the time Ren and Jeremy got to the cake, it looked as if locusts had hit.

"Wow." Ren set down her books and cut pieces for both of them from what was left. "You like lots of frosting? Want a flower?"

"No, thanks," he said. "I don't have that strong of a sweet tooth."

Ren chuckled. "I usually do, but after what I ate during my crying jag Friday night, I can't believe I can even eat sugar again."

Jeremy didn't say anything, and when Ren looked at him, he was just watching her.

Oh, man, are we going to be weird with each other after all?

"What?" Ren asked, not sure if she wanted to know.

He spoke before taking a bite of cake. "You seem to be coping fairly well now. Are you pretending? Putting on a brave front? Or are you really all right?"

Ren felt strange talking with Jeremy about this now. She felt so much different than she had Friday night, when he was just her friend. But he *was* her friend, and he was being open with her. He deserved the truth.

She sighed. "Part of it is pretense, yeah. I mean, I'm not crying every time I think about what happened, but I could. I'm that sad about it." She shrugged. "I really care about him, Jeremy."

He just nodded and looked her in the eyes.

"That was his sister, Cessy, who visited me today."

"Ah," he said, apparently considering another bite of cake before setting his fork down. "He didn't send her, did he?"

"No. She told me Tru didn't know she was coming. I believe her." Ren smiled. "She

350

said she was meddling, like her mother."

He sat back in his chair. "And how many other women are in the family?"

"There's Mrs. Sayers, Cessy, and Tru's two younger sisters, Anna and Michelle."

He smiled. "You think they're all going to be stopping by? Meddling, as you say?"

Ren widened her eyes. "What a nightmare!" But she laughed. "No, I don't think that will be a problem. Cessy just overheard a conversation that was pretty important to why Tru and I fought. She wanted me to know that Tru stood up to his mother and asked her to stay out of his personal business."

"Mmm. She didn't think Tru would tell you?"

Ren looked at Jeremy and then looked down. "She's not sure he'll ever contact me again."

"Oh."

Ren didn't hear one note of pleasure in his voice. Pure compassion.

"Listen, Ren." He casually touched her hand. "This week is barmy, with all the grading I have yet to finish. And I'm tentatively signed up for a racquetball game Friday evening with some mates. But if you decide you'd like to get out for some fun, please ring me up. I'll drop any of it: the grading, the game, anything. All right?"

To Ren that sounded like, "Let's go on a date," all wrapped up in casual words. But it was nice to hear, even from a buddy.

"Thanks, Jeremy." She looked him in the eyes. He gave her a warm grin and his blue eyes sparkled. Despite her missing Tru, despite the encouragement Cessy gave her, despite all kinds of warning bells and whistles ringing deep inside her mind, one thought jumped right up there in front.

Her buddy was an absolute doll.

Ren couldn't stop thinking about him — Jeremy — the rest of the evening. That is, she couldn't stop thinking about him when she wasn't thinking about Tru. Or Casey. Or her mother.

She began to suspect that she was using Jeremy, emotionally.

Nothing seemed to be going right with Tru. Did he even miss her? He wasn't exactly knocking himself out to patch things up with her, even though it sounded as if he took an admirable stand with his mother. And hadn't that been the sticking point between them? Then why hadn't he called yet? So Ren thought about Jeremy. Jeremy had eaten overly sweet birthday cake he didn't want just to be with her for a few more minutes. Maybe it wasn't a supreme sacrifice, but still.

Nothing was going right with regard to Casey, either. Ren still felt the Lord didn't want her to deliberately take on single parenthood, and there was clearly no daddy in the works at this rate. So she started to consider the possibility of Jeremy as a daddy. One whom Casey already knew and loved. They even looked a little like each other, with the blond hair and blue eyes. Not that that mattered, really, but, well, you put that together with the cake thing, and . . . all right, it wasn't much. But compared to Tru's complete lack of interest, it was something to hang on to.

And then there was her mother. Hmm. No emotional solution using Jeremy there. Clarissa would love his British ways, of course, but his professional ambition wasn't mercenary enough, and it didn't pay diddly. Ren could just imagine the upward tilt of Clarissa's head as she looked down at him, uttering one word: "Schoolteacher?" But Ren's thoughts dwelled on Jeremy anyway, because he represented the professional drive Ren embraced despite Clarissa's harsh judgment. As a matter of fact, Ren could see the two of them — she and Jeremy, child-loving, underpaid teachers — valiantly squaring off against Clarissa and her Russell-type prospective husbands.

Yep. Ren was definitely using Jeremy. Ugh!

Help me, please, Lord. I don't know what to do about any of these things in my life. And I want to be fair to Jeremy — I mean, I don't want to use him. But I don't want to discount him, either. And I know You don't want believers linking up with nonbelievers, but he sure is starting to look good. Maybe he'll consider You if he's considering me? Please give me guidance.

Ren didn't get any instant waves of peace or any thunderbolts of insight. But before calling it a night, she did come to the decision that Tru was going to have to come to a decision of his own. And soon. The only way Ren was able to drop off to sleep was by deciding that Tru would have to call her by the end of the week. If he wasn't ready to see her by then, she was going to give them — Jeremy and herself — a chance.

And she did drop off to sleep, but it wasn't the most restful sleep she'd ever had. She knew why too. She might have come up with a few deadlines and consequences, but she couldn't honestly say that any of them came from the Lord.

THIRTY-TWO

Ren knew she was pitiful. In the matter of waiting, that is. She would have prayed for more patience, but she was terrified of how the Lord might teach it to her.

By the end of school the next day, she was as nervous as a large cat in a small box. For goodness' sake, she had a full life — wonderful friends, the career she was designed for, and the abundant love of the Designer Himself. Yet she couldn't help obsessing.

Tru still hadn't called. Why not? It sounded as if his talk with his mother had been pro-Ren, or at least not anti-Ren. Granted, she had given him 'til the end of the week, but he didn't know that. Wasn't he aware of how heavily sought after she was?

Well, all right, maybe not heavily sought after. But if he didn't assume Ren had at least one potential suitor waiting in the wings, could he truly appreciate her as much as she *thought* he did?

Her focus had been so off all day that she still had two hours' worth of grading to finish before she could leave work. She couldn't risk taking this stuff home with her. Her housekeeping skills were deteriorating along with her mood. She'd probably end up wrapping fish or lining the veggie bin with her students' science papers and math quizzes.

So she didn't get out of school until well after five. And she wasn't about to trudge home and cook a depressing meal for one. She'd drive to that wonderful little Thai restaurant in nearby Ashburn and treat her sorry self to something ultra spicy and garlicky. What did it matter if she reeked tonight? No one was coming anywhere near her.

Honestly, it wasn't until she was near the Ashburn Road intersection that she considered the fact that, should she take a left instead of a right, she'd be a mere block away from the hospital. Tru's hospital. It would be almost rude to just turn right, wouldn't it? How Christian would *that* be? And if God hadn't wanted her to stop by the hospital, He probably would have kept her from even realizing how close she was to . . .

All right. She admitted she was pitiful, didn't she? She just couldn't take it.

Tru's car didn't seem to be in the parking lot, but she decided to visit, anyway. While riding up in the elevator she finally prayed.

From this point on, Lord, I swear I'll leave it all up to You. If I'm meant to see Tru, fine. If he isn't at work today, that's fine too.

"No, actually," said the nurse behind the desk, "he's just left for a quick bite of dinner, I think. You might want to look for him in the cafeteria. Basement level."

So. That would constitute his being at work, right, Lord? Maybe You do want me to see him.

Ren stopped for a quick comb-through and lip-gloss refresher in the ladies' room. She frowned at her reflection in the mirror. Awful. Stress wasn't pretty. But if Tru really cared about her, that shouldn't matter. He'd have to take the bad with the good.

When the elevator doors opened on the basement level, Ren followed the hall down to the clatter of the cafeteria and the smell of something like celery soup. Straightening her skirt, Ren stood at the entrance of the expansive room and searched him out. She pulled the back of her collar away from her damp neck. And then she saw him.

He wasn't alone. He wasn't even remotely alone. He had his arms around a dazzling blonde, giving her the hug Ren desperately needed from him. He looked so happy! Haggard, yes, but thrilled by this woman. And when Tru loosened his hold, Ren saw the dazzling blonde's face. There was no mistake this time. She was not a sister. Ren had met them all. And, doggone it, he hugged her again. Had he ever hugged Ren like that?

Tears burned her eyes. Should she approach him anyway? Confront him? No. She didn't want Tru to see her. She turned to leave, the question pounding in her head: *Who is she?*

Then, above all the other noise, she heard the surprised, joyful pitch in a woman's voice as she called out a name. "Emily!"

Ren spun back around to see that cute young nurse she met at the party for Tru's mother. Braces Brenda, that was it. Brenda. She gave the blonde a hug that was almost as affectionate as Tru's had been. The blonde. Emily.

Emily? Tru's Emily? The one who ditched him? Who left him at the altar, almost? For goodness' sake! The body — Tru's and Ren's relationship, that is — wasn't even cold yet, and he'd already gotten back together with Emily?

But then he started to look in Ren's direction. So she jumped — actually jumped — sideways, away from the cafeteria entrance, to avoid his seeing her. At that moment Ren flashed back to the incident with his sister at the *Riverdance* concert, when she and Kara ran away so he wouldn't see them. Why was Ren forever finding Tru with other women and then performing embarrassing physical stunts to prevent detection?

Of course, now she could no longer see him, either. But she didn't want to. She was furious. Or hurt, really. But they both felt the same, as she rushed, crying, back down to the elevator. Praise God the doors were open and quickly closed behind her. She needed to be swallowed up and taken away. She needed to think.

Why had Tru and Emily broken up in the first place? What had he told her? It was during their premarital counseling class, she remembered. In fact he didn't say why Emily left him. Maybe he was too new in the faith for her. Well, he was a more seasoned Christian now. Even Ren had to admit that. His faith seemed strong.

Ren was almost home, still in tears, when she remembered the Thai restaurant. A garbled shout of frustration accented her banging on the steering wheel with her hand. She couldn't do anything right! And now she'd lost the most gorgeous, sweetest guy she'd ever met, thanks to their insane mothers.

Of course, Tru had already set his mother straight. Wonderful. So now he was stronger in his faith and his mother was going to back off and let him live his own life. And Emily was going to get him!

Was that my role here, Lord? Was I just a catalyst for Tru to get it right about his mother so that he and Emily could live happily ever after?

Should Ren feel blessed in that? Is that how a good Christian woman should feel after getting dumped over a stupid argument about her mother?

She didn't think so. How could he move on so quickly? Just as Greg had done. Ren gasped at that thought. Maybe it was even worse than she realized. Maybe Tru had never really stopped seeing Emily. Was Ren just an oblivious idiot, doomed to keep losing her men to other women?

By the time she got home, Ren had built up a fortress of anger against that womanizing, two-timing gigolo!

Way back there, in that part of her mind where personal responsibility, logic, and common sense dwelled, she knew better. But for now she really needed that anger. She was sick of crying and had nothing but a box of fish sticks and half a loaf of raisin bread at home. If she didn't stay angry, she was going to melt into a puddle of self-pity right there in the foyer of her big, empty house.

THIRTY-THREE

Ren was in a daze that evening, and her bathtub water emptied in a loud gurgle down the drain. She didn't hear the phone or the answering machine at first. Then one or two words filtered in to her. She quickly opened the bathroom door, her towel wrapped around herself.

It was Tru.

Her heart pounded as if Publisher's Clearinghouse had just knocked on her door. She rushed to pick up the receiver but then hesitated. Did she want to talk with him?

Emily's beautiful face suddenly came to mind, and Ren's dander got all stirred up again. You betcha she wanted to talk with him! She took a deep breath and released it, hoping to dispel the sound of anger from her voice.

She brought the phone to her ear and willed a nonchalance to get past her tight lips. "Hello? I'm sorry, who was that calling, again?"

"Oh! You are there, Ren. Good! It's Tru."

Goodness, he sounded so kind. And vulnerable. Ren almost softened toward him. But then Emily and those hugs she got today flashed into her mind again.

"Ah, Tru. Yes. Hi. I'm here, yeah, but just barely. I, um, have plans." She was going to try to do this without actually lying to him. Rude but honest. Like a good Christian girl. She *did* have plans. She planned to sit around, mope, and then cry herself to sleep.

The disappointment was in his voice as soon as he spoke. "I see. I was kind of hoping to come over and talk with you. You know, about our argument the other day."

As if she was going to give him a chance to make himself comfortable about breaking up with her. So he could get back with Emily, his conscience clear. Right!

"Well, the timing's not really good for me now, Tru. Maybe another day. But I've really got to go right now."

He hesitated before speaking softly. "Ren?"

Oh, please, he wasn't going to say something dear, was he? Ren couldn't handle his pity. She put a light tone in her voice. "Yes, Tru?"

"I'm . . . I'm so sorry about —"

"No, really," Ren interrupted. He was not going to do this to her. "I'll have to talk with you some other time. Bye, now!" And she gently replaced the receiver in its cradle.

No sooner had she done so than it rang again, and she jumped so quickly she dropped her towel on the floor. Tru must have her on his speed dial! She grabbed her towel and wrapped it back around herself. Her hands were shaking.

No, she just couldn't talk with him. She let it ring. But when the answering machine kicked on, it wasn't Tru, but his sister, Cessy. Ren grabbed the receiver.

"Cessy! I'm here."

"Hey, Ren. Yeah, I knew you were there. Your phone was busy the first time I called."

Ren didn't say anything about Tru's calling.

Cessy said, "I just wanted to check in on you. You doing all right?"

"Um, I'm okay, I guess."

"Have you and Tru had a chance to discuss things yet?"

"No, not yet." Well, that wasn't a lie. They hadn't discussed anything yet.

"I'm a terrible snoop, Ren. Please forgive me. I just feel more comfortable asking you about it than asking Tru. And you're both so heavy on my heart. I guess I need to get a life, huh?"

Ren smiled. "Cessy, you're so sweet to be concerned . . ." And before she knew it, she had tears in her eyes again. A lump formed in her throat, and she couldn't speak for a moment.

"Ren? Are you okay?"

Ren nodded, even though Cessy couldn't see her. She swallowed as well as she could. "Yeah. I'm just a sucker for sympathy, Cessy. Makes me choke up."

"Oh, Ren."

Ren heard the sadness in Cessy's voice.

"I hope you two patch this up. I really do."

Not likely. Not with Emily and him riding off to happily-ever-after land, their past troubles behind them. Obviously Tru hadn't told Cessy about Emily's return.

"Um, Cessy. I need to ask you something. You go ahead and tell me if you're uncomfortable talking about this, okay?"

"All right. What is it?"

"Why was it that Tru and Emily broke up, do you know?"

There was dead silence from Cessy's end of the line.

"Never mind," Ren quickly said. "It's really none of my business."

"No, no. That's not why I . . . it's just so

weird, your asking about Emily. Today of all days."

Ren widened her eyes. Had she just given something away? Was she going to be busted about seeing them together?

But hang on there! Ren hadn't done anything wrong! She felt a wave of self-righteousness and forged on. "Why is that weird, Cessy? What do you mean?"

"Well, Emily called me this morning. I haven't talked with her since she moved. I mean, she lives on the other side of the country now. And here you asked about her on the very same day. Funny, huh?"

Yeah, hilarious. "Hmm. Funny."

"Yes. She and her husband were in town, visiting Emily's family. They wanted to swing by and see the old gang at the hospital, but she wanted to make sure Tru was working. She didn't have a current number for him —"

Ren finally got her wits about her and interrupted her. "Her husband? Did you say her husband? But I didn't see . . . I mean, I didn't know she was married!"

"Oh, didn't you? Didn't I tell you that when I mentioned her the other day?"

"Uh, no," Ren said, reviewing. She would definitely have remembered the relief inherent in news like that.

"Didn't Tru mention that she had gotten married?"

"No, he didn't!" Ren was miffed. "Cessy, if only I had known."

"I'm sorry, Ren. I guess neither of us thought it was important." She spoke so calmly, so unaware of how curt Ren had been to her brother only moments ago. "But they're expecting a baby! That was one of the reasons they wanted to visit Emily's old coworkers. She's so excited."

Ren brought her free hand to her forehead and squeezed, trying to organize all the thoughts jumping around in there. Emily was married. And pregnant. And not the slightest bit interested in Tru. And Tru wasn't the slightest bit interested in Emily.

And he had just tried to make amends with Ren, the rudest, most insecure woman in the world.

Cessy's voice broke through Ren's thoughts. "But why did you ask about her, Ren?"

Ren shook her head. "It doesn't matter anymore. Look, I think I need to just sit and think for a while. And pray. Before I say or do anything else about Tru and me. Okay?"

Cessy's voice was soothing. Or it would have soothed Ren, if she wasn't so full of self-loathing at the moment. "Sure. I'll pray too. Will you call me if you need to talk? Please?"

"Yeah. Thanks, Cessy."

Ren sank onto the couch after hanging up. Staring at the blank wall, she tried to decide what to do. She had said she would pray. That would be a good place to start.

Gracious Lord God, I've made a horrible mess of everything. I've let my temper and pride get in the way of what seemed like a wonderful, growing relationship. I've jumped to conclusions and acted on them without really leaning on Your guidance at all. I've probably destroyed any chance I might have had with Tru, and now that's all my fault. I don't deserve Your help or Tru's forgiveness. And I only have the nerve to ask for the first of those, Lord. You know what a wimp I am. I don't think I can call him, Lord. I don't know what to do. Oh, Lord, can I just give this to You? Please?

With that Ren went into her room, slipped into a nightgown, and picked up her Bible. She crawled into bed and began searching the Scriptures. She had a burning need to read as many stories as she could about people who had blundered everything and still found blessings from God. Without a doubt, Ren knew she had just joined their ranks.

THIRTY-FOUR

"You know, we can do this another day," Kara said when Ren walked out to her car the next afternoon.

Last week Ren promised to look at wedding dresses with Kara. And Ren was determined that she would not be one of those women who shut out the world and moped her life away whenever she had romantic problems. She couldn't. Based on her record so far, she'd never get out of the house again.

Kara didn't know yet about Ren's latest debacle with Tru on the phone. Ren stood at the passenger side of Kara's car and looked at her through the open window.

"Or I could just shop alone," Kara said. "I don't want you to do this if —"

Ren took a step back from the car before Kara changed gears on her.

"Oh, good grief, woman, get your backside in this car. You know I can't do this alone."

Ren gave her a weak smile and got in the car.

Kara pulled out of Ren's driveway. "Besides," she said, "we've got to look for a cheesy bridesmaid dress for you too. I'm thinking hot tangerine with big ol' poofy sleeves and tulle out to here. And hoops. Lotsa hoops."

Ren tried to laugh. The sound was like a dying woman's last hiccup.

Kara briefly looked away from the road to check her out. "Uh-oh. What's wrong? You sounded better than this on Sunday. I thought that time with Casey cheered you up a little. What happened?"

Ren shook her head. "Tru called me yesterday."

Kara immediately gasped with delight, but then her expression fell like gloom. "Not good?"

"It would have been good, yes, if I hadn't behaved as if he were trying to sell me insurance."

Kara emitted a small groan. "But why?"

"I thought he was two-timing me."

"Tru? Two-timing you? Yikes, Ren, he seems like one of those guys who really lives up to his name. What did he do to make you think there was someone else?"

"He . . . he was hugging Emily. Very affectionately. At the hospital."

"Emily? Who's she?"

"Remember? The old girlfriend? He almost married her?"

Kara opened her mouth, shocked. "Wow. I guess he didn't waste much time after you two split up, did he?"

Now Ren did the open-mouthed shock face. "We didn't split up! We had a fight! *I* didn't start dating someone else."

Kara glanced at her sideways. "But you're thinking about it, aren't you?"

Ren scratched her head. "Anyway, he wasn't two-timing me. I found out from Cessy that Emily was just visiting. With her husband."

Kara smiled.

"And they're pregnant."

Kara's grin spread. "All righty, then! That's terrific! Just a simple misunderstanding, right? But why would you be rude to Tru if Cessy told you what was up?"

"I heard from Cessy about three seconds too late. Tru called me after I got home from the hospital, and Cessy called right after I hung up on him."

"Eeesh." Kara frowned. "Hey, wait a second. Why were you at the hospital in the first place?" She looked over at Ren, one side of her mouth turning up.

Ren gave her a sheepish smile, the first she'd been able to muster all day. "I just stopped by on impulse. The hospital was almost on my way to the Thai restaurant."

"Mm-hmm. And what did you get from the Thai restaurant?"

Ren had to laugh at that. "What are you doing, having me followed or something? I forgot dinner as soon as I saw them together in the cafeteria."

Kara said, "I just figured you'd do exactly as I would have done." She shrugged. "But, hey, it's great that you did something as assertive as going to the hospital. Considering how reluctant you were to date in the first place, this is progress."

Ren blew through her lips. "And we can see how much good it did me. There's not much point in being assertive if I'm only going to get as close as a stalker would. And then I jump to conclusions and handle the case like Inspector Clouseau."

"The case? Now it's a case?"

Ren shook her head and mumbled to the window. "No. *I'm* a case. A shrink's dream case."

Kara chuckled as they pulled up to the bridal shop. "Naaah. Come on, we all make mistakes." She turned to face Ren. "Shall we review the goofy events leading up to my courtship with Gabe? Have you forgotten so soon?" She lifted her eyebrows as she opened her door. "I know I haven't. Keeps me humble."

Ren got out of the car, a whisper of hope fluttering around her. "You're right. You weren't exactly the picture of social grace, either."

"No, ma'am."

"Or maturity. Or —"

"Okay, okay. We're talking about you, missy."

"And look how well you two are doing now," Ren said.

They entered the store and stopped, overwhelmed by the vast array of white satin, lace, beads, and tulle.

"Yeah," Kara said, her voice just a whisper. "We're doing really well now."

Ren put her arm across Kara's shoulders, and they grinned at each other.

"But enough about Gabe and me," Kara said, fluttering her eyelashes. "Let's just focus on me."

And Ren honestly did appreciate focusing on Kara and her search for the perfect dress. Whenever Ren started to brood about her so-called lot in life, she was amazed at how quickly she could cheer up if she paid attention to someone else. Sometimes it was kids at the church nursery or people in situations way worse than hers. This morning relief came through her best friend, as she held a gorgeous beaded number in front of herself, swaying like Cinderella before the clock struck twelve.

"Oh, my goodness, that's *so* you," Ren said. "You have to try it on."

The store clerk seconded her motion. "That's actually a size eight, but I think that's a good place to start for you. We can easily alter it down if necessary. And the sleek style goes perfectly with your short hair."

Kara made a tiny squeal sound at Ren before she turned to follow the clerk back to the dressing room.

Ren laughed. "Call me once you have it on."

"Okay." Kara pointed at a sitting area, where catalogs were splayed across a coffee table. "Why don't you start looking at bridesmaid gowns?"

"What colors? Besides hot tangerine, I mean."

"Hmm. I don't really know yet. Just look at colors you like right now, and we'll talk about it later."

Ren walked away from Kara, deliberately mumbling aloud. "Black has always been my best color." They both glanced over their shoulders at each other, eyes twinkling.

Of course, Kara was beautiful when she walked out moments later. Ren gasped. She almost jumped up and down like a kid. "You look unbelievable! That beadwork, Kara. It's just . . ."

Kara nodded. "I know. Could I have actually found my dress so soon? I thought women searched forever. But I love this dress!"

The clerk asked, "What month is the wedding?"

"December," Kara said. "Is that okay? For alterations and everything?"

"No problem there," the clerk said. "But are you all right with wearing cap sleeves in winter? A lot of brides prefer long sleeves for winter weddings."

Ren laughed. "My wedding was in winter too, but nerves kept me plenty warm, and my gown was strapless. You could always wear long gloves. Anyway, you're not going to have a problem staying warm, not with that hot new hubby at your side." Ren looked at the clerk. "And you have pretty little wraps and things, don't you?"

So this part of Kara's bridal search was simple.

"Amazingly simple," Kara said, as they

drove to get coffee afterward. "Sometimes you expect everything to be more complicated, don't you?"

Ren nodded. "Mm-hmm." Then she looked at Kara. "You meant sometimes *people* expect complication, right? Not that I, personally, expect complication?"

Kara parked the car. "Right, I meant people in general." She tilted her head before looking at Ren. "But yeah, maybe you, personally, expect complication too."

Ren crossed her arms across her chest and arched a brow. "Meaning?"

Kara gently placed her hand on Ren's shoulder. "Call Tru. Tell him why you were short with him when he phoned yesterday. He's a sweetie. He was probably calling to apologize for the fight about your moms, don't you think? He needs a little encouragement from you. That's all."

Ren looked at her lap and nodded. She probably was letting pride masquerade as complication. Calling Tru would be simple.

Then why was she breaking out in a sweat just thinking about it?

THIRTY-FIVE

Friday. This couldn't be happening. As much as Ren prepared herself, as much as she prayed and found distractions, she was still shocked. She had gone through the motions all week. Getting up, throwing some clothes on — even maybe matching shoes and outfits together. Numbly driving to work without running a single stop sign or light. Teaching all day long, as if she were actually there. Then coming home and tending to whatever needed tending. Even herself — she'd eaten here and there. Bathed.

All the while wondering what was wrong with all the phones in her world. Why were all the wrong calls getting through, yet none from Tru?

What was wrong with him?

What was wrong with her?

She had worked up enough courage to call him Wednesday, as Kara suggested. She didn't know what she would have said, had he been home. As it was she left a wimpy "It's Ren. Please call me" on his machine. But he hadn't called.

This afternoon Ren arrived home from work. She muttered to herself, "Friday." The week had ended. Her deadline was here.

I give up, Lord. I don't know what I'm doing. I give it all to You — my deadline, Tru, Jeremy, even Casey.

She walked into her house aware of two things. Something smelled outrageously awful, and Tru's voice was talking to her answering machine. Imagine which item she attended to first.

She banged her shin against the coffee table while diving for the phone, but she barely felt it. Taking a deep breath, she tried desperately to sound as if she hadn't charged the phone, the most desperate woman in the world.

"Tru?" she said, just breathy enough to sound rather kittenish. Much better than the rude harpy she was last time he called. "Is that you?"

"Ren!"

He had the most wonderful wonderful voice in the world. Thank You, thank You, Lord, for making this voice call me today.

"Hi," she said. "I just walked in from

work." And flew across the room like a human cannonball.

"Uh-huh. Good," he said. "I have to work the night shift tonight."

"Ah."

Ah. Uh-huh. Lots of one-syllable grunting going on here. Very primal. Surely they could do better than this.

"Ren, could I stop by before I head to work? I'd still like to talk with you."

Still? What did that mean? He still wanted to talk with her, despite her rudeness? Even though he was going to break up with her? She couldn't quite tell what his tone said. But she placed hope in Cessy's encouraging words from earlier in the week.

"Sure. When did you want to come by?"

He chuckled lightly. "Well, now, actually."

"Oh! Sure." She took a quick look at herself in the hall mirror. Yeesh. Definitely the result of a busy day with second graders. Was that construction paper in her hair?

"Great. I'll be there in fifteen minutes. Bye."

"Take your time," Ren nearly yelled, but he had already hung up.

She ran back to her bedroom and changed into some jeans and a soft, white blouse. Barefoot, yes. Looked comfy-casual. She hurried into the bathroom and brushed her teeth, while pulling . . . no, that wasn't construction paper, but Styrofoam . . . from her hair. Extra troubling, in that they hadn't worked with Styrofoam today. Almost refreshed the mascara, but the lashes and contact lenses had been behaving civilly lately, and Ren didn't want to upset that applecart.

And what was that smell?

She bent over and did the upside-down, hair-combing thing. Turned upright, shook her hair into place, and looked much fresher.

She started a frantic search for whatever had died. She thought something stunk in here the last few days, but she thought it was just, you know, her life. She never had a rodent problem before, but she peeked in every nook and cranny in which she could imagine one dying. Nothing. She emptied the trashcan this morning, so it wasn't that. She opened the fridge and took a strong whiff. Nada. In fact, once she closed the fridge, the stench was magnified by comparison. If only she had a dog — one that wasn't housetrained — she'd know what to blame.

Ren pulled an apple-cinnamon scented candle from the pantry — sniffing the shelves while she was there — and lit it up.

She rushed to the balcony and opened the sliding-glass door, frantically whooshing in as much fresh air as her flapping arms could muster.

Her doorbell rang, and she realized a combination of excitement, fear, and nausea. She thought the nausea was from the smell, but it might have been from the excitement and fear.

Tru stood there for a moment when Ren opened the door. He looked a little excited and fearful himself. But he did it so gorgeously. Goodness. *Say something, Tru.*

He smiled, less confidently than he usually did. "Hi."

Before Ren could respond (she was, after all, only going to say "hi" back at him), he stepped toward her and put his arms around her. "Please forgive me, Ren," he whispered in her ear.

For the life of her, Ren couldn't remember what he had done that needed forgiving. She needed to review, but she was too busy feeling happy at the moment.

She pulled back, smiling, with a tear or two in her eyes. "Me too? Will you forgive —"

But she stopped when she saw his expression. He was frowning severely. "What?" Ren asked.

He stepped back outside her door and lifted his feet up, one at a time, to check the soles of his shoes.

"Oh. Uh . . ." Ren said. Back to primal grunting. "It's not you. It's something in here. I can't find it."

He squinted in thought and sniffed. "Smells like rotten meat and . . . cinnamon?"

"How about we go for a walk?" Ren said. She ran to her room and got her sandals.

Tru glanced at his watch. "I only have a little time. My car battery was dead when I left my apartment, so I taxied over. I need to allow extra time to get to the hospital."

"Your battery's dead?"

"Yeah. I left my lights on when I got home last night from visiting my mother —" He stopped, as if he had accidentally reopened a cut. "It was late. And I was a little distracted, I think."

So he had talked with his mother again. And yet he was here. Good sign. But, doggone it, Ren wanted to tell him that she knew he had stood up to his mother. She didn't want to pretend ignorance with him. Instead she said, "I'll drive you to work, okay?"

"Oh, thanks, yeah, that'd be great. Maybe we could talk on the way."

As they walked to her car, Ren had to ask. "Did you get my message Wednesday?"

He tilted his head. "Wednesday?" He shook his head. "I got home from work so late I forgot to check. And then yesterday my mother called me with an emergency. An overflowing toilet — you don't want to know." He shrugged. "I'm sorry. I didn't check my machine."

Ren thought about her obsessive checking and rechecking of her answering machine, cell phone service, e-mail inbox. Everything short of scanning the sky for smoke signals from the man. And here he hadn't checked for messages for two days due to a toilet on the fritz.

Men were definitely a whole different breed.

The first thing Tru told her once she started driving was, "Cessy told me she visited you this week at school."

Ren knew it was silly, but she wanted to know what happened first — his decision to call her, or Cessy telling him she had been prepped. She wanted his call to be his own decision, not influenced by any news Cessy might have given him. So she asked him. "When did you talk with her?"

"Right before coming over here. When I realized my car's battery was dead, I called to see if I could borrow her car. David has their car at work now, so she couldn't lend it to me. But when I told her I was coming to see you, she confessed."

"Did she tell you what we discussed?"

"No. She started to, but I wanted to use my time to see you. She can tell me later."

That was all just fine. Made Ren smile. He was here on his own . . . well, on his own. He had called her without feedback from Cessy and without approval from his mother. Just on his own. Very independent.

Ren glanced quickly at him as she drove. "I didn't get a chance to ask for your forgiveness, Tru. I said some mean things —"

"All forgiven, Ren. Listen, maybe Cessy told you some of this already, but I wanted to let you know that I thought about what you said. And you were right about me. About my mother. I've always been so concerned about helping her out and making sure she was happy that I've allowed her to be too involved in my personal business."

Out of the corner of her eye Ren saw him look at her, but he looked away when she glanced at him.

He said, "There's even a possibility . . . well, I know there were several reasons that Emily decided the Lord didn't want us to get married. But I think my relationship with my mother might have been one of them. I knew my mother was interfering, but I excused that because I felt sorry for her. I've been like a parent spoiling a child. It hasn't been a good thing for either of us."

"Us?" Ren asked. "You and me, us?"

"I meant, it hasn't been good for me or my mother." He laughed softly. "It's pretty obvious it wasn't good for you and me, considering our last drive together."

"Sorry." Ren winced with the memory.

"Me too. But letting my mother stick her nose in my personal life, as well as count on me for so much? It's kept her from growing. She lives vicariously through me. And there are many things she's capable of that she just doesn't give herself credit for. Instead, she asks me to take care of everything. None of that's good for her."

Ren nodded. He was right. Strangely, what he said reminded her of when she was married to Greg.

Before she found Jesus, Ren was extremely focused on being self-sufficient. Not only did she not lean on the Lord, she didn't even lean on Greg very much, maybe to the point of excluding him. Her independence helped her land on her feet when Greg left her (well, after landing on her face). But her determination to Do It All Herself also made it easier for Greg and her to become distant from each other.

Maybe Tru's mother was afraid she'd lose Tru from her life if she didn't remain fully dependent upon him.

"One thing Cessy did tell me, Tru, was that your mother wasn't speaking to you right now. I guess she doesn't agree with you on any of this?"

He chuckled. "Don't be so sure. She's a smart woman. She's coming around. And she doesn't stay mad for long." He pointed just ahead of them, as they approached the hospital. "Take this first right turn." He looked out the window. "Of course, my mother's never been this mad at me before."

"Maybe she's not as mad as she seems." Ren pulled up to the doors to let him go. "Maybe she's afraid."

He looked back around at her, some emotion strong in his eyes. Gratitude? Sadness? Happiness? He glanced down at his watch again and sighed in exasperation. "I have to go, but I . . . Want to walk me up? You can't go far into the Birthing Inn, but it'd give us a few more minutes."

"Sure." She drove away from the curb to park.

He took her hand as they walked into the

hospital.

Ren smiled. It felt like forever since he had done that.

The heavy smell of overcooked, canned vegetables told her they had arrived at the dinner hour.

"Thank you for saying that about my mother, that maybe she's more scared than mad," Tru said, as they entered the elevator and the doors closed. "I know she wasn't very warm toward you. You're so compassionate to consider her feelings like that."

Ren shrugged. "I think I can identify with some of her feelings. Don't credit me with being more kind than I am. I'll only disappoint you, I'm afraid."

He faced her and took both of her hands, like that first night at the Tidal Basin. "Don't be afraid of disappointing me. You *are* kind. And that's —"

The elevator doors opened on his floor. Ren and Tru looked away from one another and out the doors, at a quiet but chaotic scene. The first person they saw was Guy, Tru's OB friend, but he barely saw them. He darted past them, as did two nurses.

Ren and Tru stepped out of the elevator.

"Guy!" Tru called, as another nurse rushed to get around him.

Guy turned briefly and yelled, "Shoulder

dystocia, Room 303."

"Oh! I've got to go," Tru said, suddenly tense. "They might need me. Listen, can we talk later? Can I call you — oh, I won't get home 'til early tomorrow morning. Can I call you tomorrow afternoon? Will you be home?"

"Of course." Ren wanted to get out of the way and let him get to the emergency. She backed away, just as the elevator doors opened and another nurse exited in a hurry.

" 'Bye," Tru said, but he seemed torn, as if he felt needed in two places at once.

"Go!" She walked into the elevator. "We'll talk tomorrow."

But he dashed back into the elevator with her. "I can't."

"You can't? Can't what?" *Oh, no.*

He grabbed her hands and pulled her to one side so he could hold the elevator doors open. "I can't say everything I want to say right now, but I . . . I just need to know that *you* know. Ren, I love you." He gave her hands a small shake of emphasis. "I'm in love with you."

He leaned forward and gave her a kiss on the cheek before squeezing her hands once and hurrying out of the elevator. The doors closed behind him so quickly, Ren couldn't see if he turned to look at her or not.

And Ren? She stood there, open mouthed, wondering if she needed to make a stop in cardiology. Her heart felt as if it would burst.

THIRTY-SIX

Not even the overwhelming stench of Ren's home could wipe the smile from her face when she walked in the door. Came close, but no cigar. As a matter of fact, not even a cigar smelled this bad. But now Ren felt better armed for the unpleasant task of searching for the stinky culprit.

She was loved. By such a dear man.

She even felt armed well enough to take on her mother. She needed to do that before the buzz of Tru's words wore off. She grabbed her portable phone and dialed Clarissa's number. That way Ren could both search and confront at the same time. Wasn't she the multitasking wonder woman?

Clarissa's voice assaulted her almost as abruptly as her home's aroma had. Obviously her mother had checked her Caller ID before answering. No *hello,* just, "Ren, where in the world have you been? Do you check your answering machine at all? I cannot stand being forced to call you repeatedly in order to get your attention."

Because Ren didn't jump right in, she heard the words Clarissa used. "In order to get your attention," she had said. Why, she might have been Tru's mother, thinking like that. Maybe Clarissa feared the same thing Mrs. Sayers did (assuming either of them actually *did* fear losing touch with their children, as Ren suspected).

And because Ren hadn't yet joined the verbal battle with her mother, Clarissa seemed to sense that things were out of kilter. "Are you all right, Ren?" Not a great deal of affection in her tone, but the concern was kind.

Ren smiled. She began looking under the furniture in the living room while she spoke. "Yes, Mother, I'm terrific. How are you?"

"You sound funny," Clarissa said. "You sound nasal. Are you ill?"

Ren stopped looking under the bookcase and raised her head. "I had my head upside down. Does this sound better?"

"And why is your head upside down?" Ren could just see Clarissa's frown. "What's going on over there?"

Ren peeked under the sofa. "Nothing, Mother. I just — Aha! I found it! Yes! Eww."

"Ren! I insist you stop what you're doing

and talk to me. How rude, to call someone and then make yourself uncommunicative like this. What did you find?"

"A nearly empty, *way* sour-milk-smelling pint of chocolate-mint ice cream! It's been under my couch for a week. It reeks!"

"And this makes you happy?"

"Yes. Because when I got home from work today . . . You know what, Mother, could I come over? Are you doing anything right now?"

"I was just sitting down to dinner, as a matter of fact. But you could join me, if you'd like."

"You go ahead and eat. I've already planned my dinner too. But I'll come over, okay?"

"Yes, all right." She sounded suspicious. "But why can't you just talk with me now, on the phone?"

"I'll just come over. I'll be right there," Ren said. She hung up and felt better already. As simple as that was, it was a step for her, deciding that she would talk with Clarissa face-to-face, rather than what Clarissa was pressing for. And her mother didn't disown her for making a choice other than hers. Maybe their talk would lead to a sweeter relationship between them.

Yeah. That pint of ice cream seemed sweet at first too, but look at the stink it caused.

THIRTY-SEVEN

They got off to a good start, or so Ren thought. She grabbed fast food and ate it while driving, hoping to get to Clarissa's house while her courage was still strong. As she popped French fries into her mouth, she reminded herself that God would bless her efforts as long as she honored Clarissa while standing up to her. Would that be possible? What had Tru said? Like spoiling a child? She'd have to remember that too. She wasn't doing Clarissa any good caving or avoiding or whining in response to her interfering.

So be brave. Show respect. Don't spoil, cave, avoid, or whine.

Maybe Ren needed to write some of this down.

Clarissa opened her door before Ren even knocked. Had she been watching for her at the window? Clarissa gave her an air kiss on the cheek and guided her inside, all the while studying her as if she were possibly carrying a vial of anthrax.

"Hi, Mother." Ren gave her a real kiss on the cheek. "Smells great in here. Coffee? Do you have any left?"

"Of course. Help yourself," Clarissa said. But she followed Ren all the way into the kitchen. Arms folded, she rested against a counter, declining Ren's offer of a cup for herself. "What's going on, Ren? What did you so fervently need to discuss with me?"

Ren poured a little cream in her cup and smiled at her. "Not fervently, really. It's just . . ." Suddenly Ren knew she had to be point-blank honest with her mother, and it all came out. "Well, maybe I was eager to get over here while I felt brave enough. I tend to, well, I tend to be a bit intimidated by you sometimes. I wanted to talk with you while I felt strong enough to avoid intimidation."

"Are you saying I have an intimidating personality?"

Ren's knee-jerk defense almost slipped out, but she caught herself. Honesty would honor her mother, not deception. "Sometimes, yes, you do, Mother."

Clarissa gasped.

"I don't think everyone finds you intimidating," Ren said. "But that seems to be a part of our relationship, yours and mine. And I think we need to change that, or I'll never really be a grown-up. I'm almost thirty. It's time."

The frown forming on Clarissa's face reminded Ren of storm clouds.

"Let's go sit," Ren said, walking out of the kitchen, trying not to let her cup and saucer tremble. The doors swung closed behind her, and she kept walking into the living room, even though she hadn't yet heard Clarissa follow her out of the kitchen. Was that going to be their standoff? Clarissa was going to hole up in the kitchen, refusing to come sit as Ren had requested? An image flashed through her mind, of SWAT teams and hostage-release negotiators. But then Clarissa swooped out of the kitchen, lips tight and gait determined.

"Now, listen, Ren." Clarissa glanced at herself in the gilt-edged mirror directly over the couch where Ren sat. She opened her mouth and then did a double take at her reflection in the mirror.

It happened in a moment, but Ren knew what Clarissa saw. She saw an angry, aggressive woman about to launch into an argument as to how *un*intimidating she was. Ren didn't have to say a word.

Clarissa closed her mouth, pursed her lips,

and sat in the chair adjacent to the couch. Despite her perfectly coifed hair and fresh linen dress, she seemed somehow disheveled. The soft powdery smell of her perfume was mingled with a more earthy hint of . . . What was that? Did stress have a scent? Fear? Clarissa spoke with measured calm. "I've never deliberately intimidated you, Ren."

All right. Ren could accept that. Clarissa had just demonstrated that she wasn't always aware of how forceful she could seem.

"I'm part of the problem, Mother. That's really what I needed to talk with you about."

Clarissa seemed to relax a bit with that. This wasn't about her. This was about Ren. They were going to fix Ren.

Ren said, "I've failed to be frank with you when I should have been. When you and I don't agree about something — something having to do with me, anyway — I need to let you know that I disagree with you. I respect you, Mother, but I often let my respect for you get in the way of honest communication."

"And whose fault is that?" Clarissa's fingers drummed the armrest on her chair.

"Mine." Ren exhaled with a bit of comfort. Man, this felt good. "I've been a real wimp with you. Maybe I've mistaken independence for disrespect. Maybe I felt as though I were dishonoring you if I stood my ground when we disagreed about what was best for me. I mean, you and I both know, deep down, that *I* have to make decisions about my own life. The consequences will be mine, so the decisions have to be too."

"Well, of . . . course," Clarissa said, but she wasn't making a well-of-course face. She was making a don't-make-any-sudden-moves face, as if she expected Ren to pounce on her at any moment.

"So," Ren said, "I thought a good place for us to start would be with regard to Russell the Third."

"Ah, good." Clarissa went immediately into her usual shtick. "Now, I happen to know he hasn't made plans with anyone —"

"Not interested. In terms Russell would appreciate as an attorney, I'm disinterested with extreme prejudice."

Clarissa looked at Ren as if she had sprouted a full beard and mustache right before her eyes. "But surely, Ren, you must recognize what a catch he is. I'm afraid you're allowing your nurse friend to —"

"And that would be item number two. But first, let's put the Russell issue to rest. He's out. Okay, Mother?"

"Well . . ."

"Okay!" Ren got more comfortably situated on the couch. "So the other issue at hand would be Tru, the fellow you call my 'nurse friend.' And by the way, Mother, I need to say something important right here."

Clarissa's fingers no longer drummed on the armrest. They gripped, subtly. She looked tense, as if Ren were about to blast her with a fire hose. "Yes?"

"I really love you, Mother."

What an amazing series of transformations took place across Clarissa's features. Within a matter of seconds, she went from tight as a coiled spring to shocked slackness to actual softening. Especially around her eyes. She lowered them and blinked several times, as if Ren had just taken a flash photograph of her. She swallowed before looking back at Ren.

"I . . ." She breathed in. "I love you too, dear."

Ren smiled at her. "I know. And I know you want me to have a good life."

"Yes."

"But I think we have different ideas of what a good life is."

"Whatever does that mean?" A little of Clarissa's edge returned. "Just because I think you can do better than to become involved with that nurse —"

"You mean Tru."

"Yes, that one."

"Could you please call him Tru, Mother?"

She looked at Ren, her lips tight again. "Ta-rue, all right?"

"Thank you." What was the big deal with granting him a name, for goodness' sake? "Mother, let me ask you. What is it about Russell that you find attractive and missing from Tru's personality?"

Clarissa laughed uncomfortably. "Well, I don't know that one can pinpoint that sort of thing, dear."

"One could try."

Clarissa arched an eyebrow at her daughter. "Fine. I would have to say that the ambition — the focus, shall we say — that Russell has exhibited in achieving what he has at his age? That kind of ambition doesn't seem to be there — apparently hasn't been necessary — for your . . . for Tru to achieve what he has at his age."

Ren nodded. "Okay. And what kind of ambition would you call Russell's, exactly? What would you say Russell is focusing on?"

Clarissa lifted her chin. "Ren, if you're trying to get me to say that Russell only cares about money —"

"No, no." Ren shook her head. "I'm not trying to get you to say anything except what you find attractive about Russell. Wouldn't it help us both if we understood what that was?"

Clarissa sighed. "All right. Russell is on course to eventually making head partner, just as your father was at his age, God rest his soul. Obviously I considered your father's ambition admirable. I would like to see you with someone like your father." She gave Ren a polite smile. "How's that?"

"That's good!" Ren smiled back. "I understand that completely." And Ren really meant that. Her dad had been a real go-getter. A man of strong ambitions. But Ren had a hard time picturing her dad ever acting like the self-important fop Russell had seemed. "So Russell's apparent focus is making head partner, and you'd like to see me with someone as professionally successful as Dad was, right?"

"Exactly, dear." Just then Frumpkins hopped up to lie in Clarissa's lap. She rested her hand on the cat's back, but she didn't stroke him.

"Well, this is pretty good news for both of us because I think Tru and I are, well, we seem to be getting serious. And Tru's as successful in his profession as Dad ever was in his."

"But —"

"And he has another quality that I know you loved about Dad. The more I get to know him, Mother, the more I see it. Tru has what I'd call a real servant's heart. Remember how kind Dad was whenever he saw someone in need?"

Clarissa shook her head a little. She didn't appear to be discounting what Ren was saying, exactly. Just not wanting to hear it. "Well, yes, but —"

Ren smiled, recalling her dad's generosity. "That secretary at his office, remember her? The one who suddenly lost her husband to cancer? The way Dad came to the rescue, getting the firm to give her financial support until she could get back on her feet? Helping her establish college accounts for her kids —"

"Yes, Ren, I know, I know. Your father was generous to a fault. And he could afford to be, because he was not just professionally successful, as you say Tru is, but he was also financially successful. How would Tru have been able to help that secretary? On what he makes, he could be the one needing assistance."

Ren waved that off. "Oh, I'm sure Tru

earns enough to make ends meet. And I'm sure he would have been able to help that secretary in some way if he had been around. But don't you see, Mother? Tru helps women every single day of his life. He helps men too — daddies."

"Yes, yes, very nice." Clarissa rolled her eyes at Ren. "But will he be able to put food on the table? What if you wanted to quit work? To raise children, say?"

"He might not be able to put caviar on the table. But, food? Sure."

Clarissa's sigh of exasperation hinted at something beyond what they were discussing.

"What is it?" Ren asked. "There's something else about Tru that you don't like, isn't there?"

Clarissa looked down at the coffee table and then shot a quick glance at Ren.

Aha! She was right.

Clarissa stood and picked up Ren's cup, abruptly dumping Frumpkins to the carpet. "More coffee? I think I might want some myself." She headed for the kitchen.

Just as Clarissa followed her when she arrived, Ren was after Clarissa like a bloodhound.

"Tell me, Mother. Please."

Once inside the kitchen, they took up the

places they held when Ren first arrived, but in reverse. Ren even caught herself folding her arms in front of her chest as Clarissa had done. Unfolding, Ren joined her hands calmly together, but she couldn't get the tension out of her voice.

"You might as well spit it out now, because you haven't shared anything with me tonight that dissuades me from seeing Tru. You have nothing to lose."

When Clarissa turned around Ren was amazed to see unmistakable embarrassment in her expression. "I . . . I don't want you to get the wrong impression from what I'm about to ask you."

Hmm. "I'll try not to."

"Is Tru . . . are his parents . . . is he Hispanic? Latino? Whatever the correct term is?"

She could have tipped Ren right over with the slightest nudge. But Ren had to hear this one out. "Half, yes. Why?"

"You remember our running into Greg at the mall? With his little chippy?"

Ren frowned. "Yes, of course I remember."

"I don't want to see you with another unfaithful husband."

"But —"

"Do you happen to know," she asked, "if Tru's father is as faithful a husband as your father was? As Russell would probably be? No attorney — no American attorney — on the fast track to head partner is going to jeopardize that track with the scandal of infidelity. But a nurse? What's to hold him back, especially if he's . . . well, you know that, as a culture, Tru's people —"

"No!" Ren yelled. "Not one more word, Mother! I cannot believe you're thinking this stuff!"

"Now, darling, listen to me." Clarissa looked at Ren, desperation and concern in her eyes. "My cleaning lady, Berta? She's from Central America. Or maybe it's South America. No matter. What matters is that she suffers constantly with this problem with the whole macho husband thing."

"One woman? You're basing this theory on your poor cleaning lady's sad marriage?"

Clarissa lifted her chin. "And when I was a child. My family's gardener? One day both his wife *and* his girlfriend showed up at our home. They actually fought over him! Physically! I watched it all from my swing set. And all three of them were . . ." She waved her hand in the air, reaching for the word. "Hispanic. Latino. Whatever."

Now Ren was pursing her lips. "Mother, this is insane. The money thing was bad enough. All my life you've stressed — to an extreme — that money is hugely important. Before I found the Lord, I felt the main goal in my life needed to be financial achievement. So I'm never surprised to hear you talking like a wealthy snob."

"Ren!" Clarissa slammed her coffee cup onto the counter, knocking the saucer to the floor.

"But never would I have suspected bigotry on your part, Mother! Where did that come from?"

Clarissa's face was red, and Ren would guess that was as much from anger as embarrassment.

"How dare you call me a bigot!"

"To begin with," Ren said, "yes, Mother, you hit it on the head. Tru's father was unfaithful to his mother. Guess what? Tru's *mother* is from Ecuador. His father, like my ex-husband, was born and raised in America. We don't exactly have the fidelity market all wrapped up here in the U.S., you may have noticed."

"No, but —"

"And you know what? If anyone leans in that direction, between Tru and me, I'd have to say it would be me."

"What?" Clarissa asked, horrified. "You're not saying that you were unfaithful to Greg?"

"No, of course not. But Tru and I had an argument, and what do I do? Within a week I consider taking up with a handsome man at work. Why? Just to convince myself that I'm lovable or desirable or . . . or something. So don't go judging Tru poorly without taking a good look at your weak-willed daughter first."

"But there are other cultural issues inherent with Tru's people, Ren. The lack of ambition —"

Ren screamed. She actually screamed to stop Clarissa from saying another word. "It's as if you're this woman I never knew before! Please don't say any more, Mother!"

They stood there, staring at each other in stark silence, the china saucer broken in two pieces on the floor between them. Ren bent down and picked up the pieces and put them on the counter. Perhaps Clarissa might want to put them back together.

"I have to go."

Clarissa didn't follow her out of the kitchen. They didn't say goodbye, let alone I love you.

Ren was sobbing before she put her car into reverse.

THIRTY-EIGHT

Tru didn't know how blessed he was, having to work that night. Ren was dying to call him, blubber at him, appeal to his sense of outrage over her fight with Clarissa. But she certainly wasn't going to bother him at work. Maybe God blessed her too, by keeping her from overwhelming him with her unintelligible sob fest and way more hurtful information than he ever needed to hear.

Odd, how differently Ren reacted to this conflict with Clarissa compared to the comfort-seeking, junk-food binge she plunged into after her fight with Tru. She cried all the way home from Clarissa's house, shocked at what she had discovered about her mother. And appalled at how horribly she threw honor for her mother out the window, and with such passion. She had screamed at her own mother. Somehow she couldn't quite fit that comfortably within the framework of . . . which commandment was it? The fifth, yes. Some good Christian daughter she was. Why didn't she pray before going over to talk with Clarissa?

Ren still burned with embarrassment over her mother's thoughts about Tru's heritage, as well as how she handled her swift anger at Clarissa's prejudice. Yet she felt no draw toward the kitchen when she got home. Instead, she got into some pajamas, wrapped herself up in her down comforter, curled up in bed, and cried herself to sleep. She wouldn't have been surprised if she woke up sucking her thumb.

But what Ren slowly woke up to was a gentle tapping at her front door. The sun was attempting to pierce through the slats in her blinds, so she could tell it was morning, if not later. The tapping repeated, and this time a gentle, careful voice — a man's — called out to her from beyond the door.

"Rennie? Are you all right, love?"

Jeremy!

Ren jumped out of bed and ran into the bathroom. She found she could barely get her eyes open. She didn't need to look in the mirror to know they had puffed up like a chameleon's. But look in the mirror she did. She almost screamed, but she felt she had done enough screaming for the time being. Along with her toadlike eyes, she had one of those sheet scars across her cheek from sleeping face first, tears flowing, into her pillow. She looked like a refugee from some drunken brawl down on the docks.

That gentle tapping came at her again, more hesitantly now, and Ren sensed Jeremy's concern about whether to keep knocking or not.

"Hang on, Jeremy," she called, throwing on her bathrobe.

"Ah! Ren. Good. No hurry. Sorry. Sorry to bother you."

"I'll be right there. Give me a minute." She splashed water on her face and looked back in the mirror. Yeah, as if she was going to do anything about this mess in a minute. She didn't even have time to put a decent bag over her head. She brushed her teeth, ran a comb through her hair, and gave up. She and Jeremy weren't going to be an item, anyway. What was the point of making him wait outside while she dealt with her vanity?

But what in the world was he doing here, unannounced? She didn't like that.

She opened the door and then her hands, in a resigned "ta dah" gesture, which Jeremy mistook for an invitation to hug.

"Oh!" Ren said, returning a cursory hug before pulling away. She saw the concern on his face. Heaven only knows what he saw on hers, besides splotches, bulges, and sheet crevices.

"Are you all right? I got worried about you. You look as though you've been crying, love."

Ren sighed. "I *look* as though I've been bouncing face first down a few flights of stairs. Come on in. I'll make coffee." She looked at him over her shoulder. "I don't get it. Why were you worried about me?" She knew Jeremy. He was a sweetheart, but insight wasn't one of his strong points.

"You've been so depressed this week, Ren. And I tried not to press. You know, about, um, us. But last night after my racquetball game, I tried to call you. The phone was busy all night, so I gave up once it got late. Figured you were on with Tru."

Ren shook her head while measuring scoops into the coffeemaker. "Tru was working the late shift last night."

"Ah," Jeremy said, nodding and looking down. "So he did finally call."

Ren realized she had lost count of the scoops. She watched Jeremy while he gathered his thoughts. He looked at her and gave her a warm smile. But it was a sad one too.

"Anyway," he said. He walked over to the cupboards, looking away from her. "I'll get some cups down."

Ren honestly loved this guy. Just not the right kind of love. She could see that now. She wasn't enamored with Jeremy. She was powerfully fond of him, whatever that meant. It was all she could do not to give him that hug he thought she offered when he got here.

"Right, then. I'm confused," Jeremy said, taking over the coffee production. "Your phone was busy this morning too. Off the hook, maybe? That's why I came over. Wanted to make sure nothing had happened to you."

Ren picked up the kitchen extension. It was dead. She checked the phone in the living room and found the problem. Apparently she had thrown her purse in the midst of her bawling arrival home last night, knocking the phone askew. She replaced it and returned to Jeremy. "Another consequence of my temper tantrum last night, I'm afraid. Sorry to concern you."

"Did things go poorly with Tru, after all?" He spoke softly. Ren knew there was a measure of hope in that question, but, God bless him, she couldn't hear it.

"No. Actually, things went really well with Tru." She sighed. "I'm sorry, Jeremy."

He smiled that lovely, sad smile at her

again, but this time there was the familiar twinkle in his eyes. "Not to worry, love. I told you that before. I didn't really expect we'd go out together."

Ren didn't say a word about that. He didn't need to know how close she'd come to saying yes.

"Then why the temper tantrum?" he asked, as Ren got out cream and sugar.

She told him about her argument with Clarissa, including its fierce conclusion.

"Blimey. No wonder you were upset. You and your mum are pretty close, eh?"

Ren snorted. "I don't know if that's the right word for it."

"But you're important to each other, aren't you? Otherwise, neither of you would have gotten so emotional."

"I guess that's right." She poured coffee for each of them. "I just don't like to think of my mother as being prejudiced, and I don't know if I can change that in her."

"That's not your job, is it, then?" Jeremy sat down on a bar stool. "There are quite a few things my dad and I don't like about each other, I can promise you that. But I love him, just the same, and I know he loves me."

"What do you think I should do?" she asked him, amazed at how easily they had slipped back into their friendship roles.

"Chuck the whole lot and run off with me, love."

His timing couldn't have been any funnier if he had been able to read her mind. Ren almost spit out her coffee, which made him chuckle.

My, but he was a dear.

"You've got to apologize to her, Ren," he said, more serious now. "Not for how you feel about Tru, but for how cheesed off you were with her."

She took a big breath in and out. "I suppose so. This standing-your-ground thing is hard to get right."

He smiled as he stood and put his nearly full cup in the sink. "You'll catch on soon enough, love. Just remember that you don't have to agree with her. You just have to respect her. She's your mum!"

Ren walked him to the door. "You sound as if you're well versed with the fifth commandment, Jeremy. I'm impressed."

"What?" He put his hand on her shoulder. "You weren't thinking of murdering her, were you?"

Ren cracked up. "That's the sixth commandment, you heathen. I've got to get you to church, Jeremy."

"Maybe some day, love," he said, just as

her phone rang. "You get that." He gave her a kiss on the forehead. "I'll catch you Monday, eh? And call me if you need company."

"Right. Thanks for being such a good friend." She closed the door behind him just as Tru's rich voice beckoned for her on the answering machine. Her heart skipped a beat, and she forgot all about Jeremy, Clarissa, and her puffy, lined face. She was going to live happily ever after. At least for today.

Thirty-Nine

"Our relationship does have a certain *Romeo and Juliet* quality to it, doesn't it?" Tru said the following weekend. He looked wistfully skyward, as if he were reciting poetry.

They had spent every free moment together over the prior week. Tru went to church with Ren again and met her pastor and more of her friends. He was a hit, of course — he already fit in as if he had always been a member. Neither of them got much done outside of their jobs, grabbing spare time together as if it were precious, fleeting. Ren hated saying goodbye to him each night — having to look into those gorgeous, dark eyes — knowing he was leaving her again. More than once she thanked God that she was dating a good Christian man who was avoiding the struggle of temptation right along with her. *Big* struggle.

Right now they were strolling, hand in

hand, on the National Mall between the Washington Monument and the Capitol. The summer humidity hadn't yet set in, so the sunshine was welcome and uplifting.

Twice this week Ren left messages for Clarissa to call her, but she hadn't, yet. Tru's mother had disregarded him too, which was what prompted his comment about their Montague-Capulet romance. Not that their families were warring with one another, like the famous star-crossed lovers.' But neither of their mothers was speaking to them. The silence was both blissful and distressing.

"Hey, let's see if there's a waiting line for the Escher exhibit," Tru said, when they walked as far as the National Gallery. "I love his stuff."

Ren nodded. "You're on."

The air-conditioning refreshed them as they moved among the crowds. They walked past the museum's sculptures and mobiles, following the signs toward the Escher exhibit.

"Wow," Ren said, when they reached the long line. "Guess we needed to plan ahead."

"Ah, well," Tru said, as they turned away from the line. "It was a thought. Maybe next week."

They decided to rest a moment on a bench facing a sculpture by Rodin.

Ren sighed. "I suppose I should call Mother again tonight. Matt told me to just leave it, but Jeremy encouraged me to apologize to her. I'm just . . ."

"Nervous? Certain of another fight? Tired of the whole effort?"

She rested her head against his shoulder. "You too, huh?"

"Mm-hmm. I've apologized several times for hurting my mother. At this point I think she just needs to get through the changes I've asked her to make. I'm going to give her some time for that." He pulled away from Ren enough to look her in the eyes. "I just want to focus on us for now."

Ren looked down. She experienced a strange sensation — and not for the first time — at Tru's talking about them in such a permanent way. Ren had yet to say she loved him, despite his saying it to her. Despite what she thought she felt. She was concerned about letting anything too strong develop before he knew exactly what her situation was.

"Uh, Tru." She looked back at him. "I need to talk with you. Can we go back outside, where our voices echo a little less?"

He chuckled, but she heard concern in his voice. "Sure."

Ren started talking as soon as they stood.

"I don't want to sound presumptuous in telling you this, but you need to know something about me."

He took her hand as they walked. "All right."

"There were a lot of reasons my marriage didn't work out, but I'm not sure if I've been honest enough with you about one of them."

He didn't say anything.

"You remember when we first met? And you overheard me talking with Kara about the problems Greg had caused with the adoption we had been attempting?"

"Yeah."

"Well, we considered that adoption because we hadn't been able to . . . we had tried for four years to get pregnant. We weren't certain what or who the problem was."

He walked a little slower, still saying nothing.

"But not long ago, I ran into Greg with his girlfriend."

"Mm-hmm?"

Ren stopped walking and faced him. "And their baby boy."

He just looked into her eyes for a moment. His were full of sympathy. "That can't have been easy for you."

She didn't say anything. She wasn't sure if he understood the implications of what she had just said.

Finally he said, "So you figure it's you who couldn't conceive."

Ren looked down, nodding. "I already suspected it, anyway. I had endometriosis when I was younger. The doctor warned that scar tissue might interfere."

"But you were willing to adopt, right?"

Could their problem be that easily solved?

"Well, yeah. *I'm* willing to adopt because that may be my only option for having children." This was so difficult to phrase since they hadn't talked marriage. But Ren didn't want to risk his talking marriage without knowing he might never be able to have his own children with her.

He tilted his head, still looking at her. "Whatever happened to the child? The one you planned to adopt. I'm remembering it was a little boy. Am I right?"

At the thought of Casey, her heart lurched. "Right. Casey."

"Oh, Casey. Yeah, you've talked about him. I didn't realize he was the one. One of your students, isn't he?"

Ren sighed. "Yeah. My sweet little guy. Been living with foster parents most of his life. His mother is in prison for grand larceny."

"Whoa."

"It was all related to her drug problems. From what my friend Sandy says — Sandy's the counselor at my school — Casey's mom has done well in drug rehab. Casey's gone to visit her a few times. I think I probably still could have adopted him, but —"

"You didn't want to single parent adopt."

"Right."

They just stood there, not having made it outside. Then Tru wrapped his arms around her, giving her a warm squeeze. He kissed the top of her head before pulling away. "I'd love to meet Casey. Would you be willing to share him with me, or are you going to keep him all to yourself?"

The smile that crinkled around his eyes was infectious. But Ren wasn't absolutely sure what he meant. Was she willing to share Casey as a friend? Was she willing to co-parent him with Tru?

She decided it was too early to worry about that. He wanted to meet Casey, to see how they got along. That could be accomplished harmlessly. And if Tru and Ren did continue on the path they were walking, they'd both have to know that Tru could handle adopting, whether it was Casey or another child.

Before Ren could say anything, though, they heard a woman's wail just around the corner. She sounded as if she were in pain. And frightened. They both ran toward her cries.

She was young, maybe twenty, with long, stringy blond hair hanging down in her face. She was with a gangly young man about the same age, who was trying to support her as she doubled over in pain. She was in khaki shorts and an oversized T-shirt. She was hugely pregnant, and water was running down her legs and all over the museum floor.

Tru ran to her side, adding support. "Rennie, take her other side." To the young man he said, "Call 9-1-1. Tell them her water broke and she's about to deliver."

"I don't want to leave her."

"Here, I've got her," Ren said, pushing her way to the woman's side and handing him her cell phone. "Make the call." She cocked her head toward Tru. "He's a labor-and-delivery nurse. She's going to be fine. Stay here with her. But call!"

"Help me get her to a more private place, Ren," Tru said. "Over there." He nodded toward a corner of the busy museum. Privacy was at a minimum, and they weren't going to be able to move this poor girl much farther than that.

Two older women hurried toward them. "How can we help?" one of them asked.

They lowered the girl to the floor, her legs facing the corner. Her moans of pain were coming close together.

"It feels like it's coming, already!" she cried. "It's coming!"

Tru and Ren were on their knees on either side of her. Without looking at the older women, Tru told them, "Run downstairs to the cafeteria's kitchen. We need a couple clean tablecloths or something like that, and an armful of clean towels. One of you bring those, fast as you can. And one of you get some string, or dental floss, even. Anything I can tie the cord with. It has to be clean."

As they ran off, he added, "And scissors!"

The young man closed Ren's phone. "They're coming, Connie. Hang on to it, babe."

"I *can't* hold on to it, Eddie!" she yelled, grunting her words out. "It's coming out, I'm telling you!" She grimaced and tensed up her whole body, her moan almost a scream.

Tru spoke to her calmly. "You're having another contraction, Connie. I know it hurts, but try to breathe through it. Try to do it with me."

She opened her eyes and watched Tru, struggling to match her strained grunting with the slower, deep breaths he was making. She appeared more relaxed as the pain subsided.

"You the father, Eddie?" Tru asked the young man.

"Yeah, the . . . father." He said the word as if it was the first time he had ever thought about his upcoming role.

"Okay, Ed, get your shirt off. Help us slip it under Connie." Tru yanked off his own shirt at the same time and draped it across Connie's hips.

"Not much coverage, I'm afraid, Connie, but it will help until we have some towels or something better for you." He glanced at Ren. "Ed and I are going to lift Connie a little. As quickly as you can, get her shorts and stuff off, and then slip Eddie's T-shirt underneath her. Just do your best." He looked into Connie's eyes and smiled at her. "Sorry for the cold floor. We're going to get you as comfortable as we can, okay?"

She looked at him, pain and fear in her face, and nodded.

Halfway into their efforts, she had another contraction. They had to lower her and let her work through it. This time Tru sensed the pain coming and focused on communicating with Connie. She followed his breathing and stared into his eyes with childlike trust. But within a minute the next pain had already seized her.

After what seemed like hours, one of the ladies returned, several white cloths and towels bundled in her arms. Two museum guards were with her.

Tru reached up and took one of the towels and handed it to Ren. "You can slip this under her too, Ren. Okay, Eddie, let's lift her just a bit."

Ren managed to get something between Connie and the floor at all points. Tru opened a towel across Connie and threw his shirt aside.

"Connie, your water's broken," he said, standing and taking the linens from the lady. "But it's clear, and that's a good sign." To the guards and the woman, he said, "Hold these sheets up around the area, like a curtain. Keep people away. Give her as much privacy as you can, okay?"

He handed Ren the rest of the towels, and then he dropped back to his knees.

Connie struggled through yet another contraction, this time breathing without Tru's guidance. When the contraction ended, Tru gently examined her. Despite his gentleness, the exam seemed to trigger another contraction.

"I gotta push!" Connie screamed. "I need to push!"

Tru nodded. "You're ready, Connie. Eddie, get down here, over on that side."

The other woman ran back to them. "I have string! And clean scissors."

Tru grabbed the towels from Ren and handed them to her. "Great, thanks. Hold these too until we need them. Ren, get on Connie's other side, opposite Eddie."

Connie yelled out again. "I gotta push!"

Tru said, "Ren, Eddie, hurry and get your arms under her knees, yeah, like that, and your other arms behind her back. Connie, they're going to lift your back and your knees toward each other. Take a deep breath and give us a good solid push for ten seconds. Now!"

Tru counted for her, skipping "four, five," to say, "That's it, that's good."

At ten, they let her back down. She released a weary cry and gasped for breath.

"Okay, Connie, the head's already showing," Tru said. "You're doing great. When you feel another contraction coming —"

"It's coming!" she said.

"All right, big breath, push for ten!" Tru said, shooting a look at Eddie and Ren.

They pulled her together again the way he had told them, not releasing her until Tru told them to.

After the third push, Tru beamed. "Head's out, Connie! Almost done. Now, I'm going to turn the baby's shoulders to help it out, okay? You let me know when the next contraction's coming."

Ren couldn't believe Connie didn't scream ten times worse than she already had while Tru worked on her. She couldn't believe what she was seeing; that helpless, frighteningly quiet little head, waiting for them to help it into the world. How could it breathe? Ren was glad Connie couldn't see from her angle. But when she looked at Eddie, she realized he could see as well as she could. He was gray.

"You okay, Eddie?" Ren asked.

Tru looked up at him and then up at one of the older ladies. "Take his place for a minute, could you?" He looked at Eddie. "Just scoot aside for a minute. Don't try to stand just now. Get some air."

Everyone followed his orders beautifully, although Eddie looked crestfallen.

"Another one's coming," Connie said, her breathing increasing.

While she pushed, Tru supported the baby's head, which was now facing sideways. He gently pressed down with his other hand, and one of the baby's shoulders emerged.

"One more push, Connie, and you're baby's born." He took a towel from the pile the woman held.

"Let me back in there," Eddie said. He had regained some color. He resumed his original spot, next to Connie. "I love you, sweetie. You're almost there."

The moment she began her last push, Tru lifted the baby's head, exactly the opposite of what he had done before. Ren gasped as the baby slipped free, and Tru quickly wrapped it, then held it briefly upside down, patting its back. He laughed. "You've got a baby boy here, Mom and Dad!"

"Max!" Eddie said. He laughed and hugged Connie, who looked exhausted but thrilled. "Honey, it's Max! I love you so much, sweetie."

Connie, weeping, touched her hand to Eddie's cheek. "Max," she whispered. She turned weakly to Tru and the baby. "Is he all right?"

The baby coughed a few times, and Tru cleaned its mouth. Then it let out a miserable little cry.

It made Ren laugh. Then she started to cry.

Emergency workers hurried to join the scene, having arrived when nearly everything was already over, like the police in those silly dramas where ordinary people have to solve murders or land 747s.

Ren looked up at Tru, who was looking at her, tears and love in his eyes. Then he looked away, taking another towel from the lady who stood, crying, next to him. He snuggly wrapped little Max with clean towels and gently placed him on Connie's chest. He said a few things to the emergency workers, and then he let them take over. One of the workers helped him clean himself up with alcohol and antiseptic wash. Warmth spread through Ren as she watched him — still shirtless, as humble a hero as she'd ever seen.

What a man. This is what he talks about, what he sees daily. Yet he had cried too, as if this were his first birth. Ren wasn't sure that her tears — and his — were just from the ecstasy of this moment. She couldn't help but wonder if there wasn't some pain over what they'd never experience together if they wed.

When he looked at her again, no one noticed them. They were alone in that crowd, while everyone else tended, mended, and rejoiced. He walked up to her and took her face in his hands, gently wiping her tears with his thumbs.

Ren touched his cheek with her hand. Regardless of what their tears meant, she would have been made of stone to keep from saying it. She started crying again.

"I love you, Tru."

FORTY

The chaos of the last day of school was in full swing. Ren and her class spent the morning in a raucous awards assembly in the gym. Their ultracreative principal devised the ceremony to enable each child to win a certificate for something.

"Blimey," Jeremy muttered to Ren, forty minutes into the event. Several children had just received Best Hopscotcher awards. "What's next, awards for pencil sharpening?"

Ren smiled as she whispered, "Don't be ridiculous. The Juice Drinking awards come before the Pencil Sharpening awards."

Her heart melted when Casey won the Second Grade Art Student award. While the art teacher placed the medal around his neck, Casey tried to act as if he weren't bursting with pride, but Ren could tell he was.

The remainder of the day was devoted to

cleaning desks, stuffing take-home papers into backpacks, and the all-important end-of-school party. The room mother had arranged everything, so Ren was able to just enjoy the children and their delight with the start of summer vacation.

While she chatted in the hallway with one of the mothers at the party, the woman arched an eyebrow, her eyes focused on something beyond Ren. "*Ay, caramba,* who's the hot tamale?"

Ren turned around to see Tru approaching. He gave her a stunning grin. The woman was right — he was a hot tamale. Ren laughed as she looked back at the mother.

"That's my boyfriend." Ren glanced over her shoulder at him. "It's Tru!"

"Oh! Uh, of course!" The mom turned red. "Yes, I believe it's true. I don't doubt you for a second, Ren. You're a wonderful girl."

Ren laughed again. "No, I mean his name is Tru." Ren introduced them, putting her hand on the woman's shoulder to assure her she wasn't offended by the "hot tamale" comment.

When the woman's daughter called for her, she excused herself quickly and stepped away.

Some time had passed since Tru asked to meet Casey, but this was the first time they'd all been somewhat free at the same time. Ren prayed every night before dropping off to sleep, asking for help with the niggling fear that plagued her about the timing with Tru, Casey, Casey's mother, and herself. Just when Ren gave the fear over to the Lord, she'd grab it right back again.

Ren trusted the Lord, but she also wanted the perfect family. She couldn't help trying to tell God what she thought the perfect family would be. Her mother wasn't the only control freak, apparently.

The decibel level in the classroom rose along with the sugar intake, and the room mother signaled to Ren that she was ready to lead the kids in some outdoor games. Ren flicked the lights on and off a couple of times, and the noise died down to a whisper or two.

One of her more adventurous boys called out to Tru. "Who are you?"

The daughter of the "ay, caramba" mom loudly boasted her knowledge. "That's Ms. Young's boyfriend. My mom said so." Her poor mother blushed again and seemed to shrink before their very eyes. All the other parents laughed along with Tru and Ren.

Once everyone filed outside and the room

mother began the games, Ren was able to talk more privately with Tru.

He nodded toward Casey. "Is that him?" He smiled in Casey's direction.

"Yeah! How'd you know?"

"You described him as if his image were branded onto your brain. Besides, no one else here looks quite like an 'impish angel,' I think you called him."

When the children ran relays, Tru helped, which gave him a chance to interact with the kids, including Casey. When Ren could, she watched them together. Such a stark contrast, between Tru's dark, romantic looks and Casey's blond, cherubic curls and blue eyes. But they looked perfect together.

At one point Casey approached her, and Ren squatted down to talk with him. "I like him," he said, pointing at Tru. "I like your boyfriend."

"I'm so glad, Casey." She put her arm around him. "I like him too."

"Does Mr. Greg like him?"

Oops. Ren thought Sandy had explained to Casey that Greg wasn't in the picture anymore. Now that she thought about it, Sandy had. Ren was certain of it.

"Casey, remember? Mr. Greg . . . moved away." Ren hoped she wasn't traumatizing him.

He looked at her blankly. Then she saw realization light up his expression. "Oh! Yeah. Now I remember." Not a bit of trauma on his honest little face, God bless him. Sandy had done a good job in making his vague future seem like a secure one. Ren marveled at the resiliency of children, and she hoped Casey wouldn't have to bounce back from many more disappointments in his life.

Casey looked at the rest of the kids and smiled. Several children were chasing Tru, who pretended to steal a basketball from them. Casey laughed and ran to join the fun.

That evening Tru and Ren joined Kara and Gabe for dinner at a local seafood restaurant. Now that Maryland blue crabs were in season, they were all ready for a messy, spicy crab feast. The tables were covered with brown paper and set with nothing but rolls of paper towels, knives, small wooden hammers, and small bowls of red spice, melted butter, and vinegar. As all experienced blue crab pickers did, Ren and the others had dressed in T-shirts and jeans. Definitely not a fancy night out.

Kara and Ren were eager for Tru and Gabe to get to know each other better. The two men hadn't talked much beyond the few minutes between services at church.

They ordered sodas and salads to eat while they waited for their crabs.

Tru's face glowed as he told Kara and Gabe about his adventures on the playground that afternoon. He was like a big kid, himself, mentioning several of the children by name.

Kara said, "You're going to have to make new friends next school year, Tru. Think you can handle that?"

"No, actually, he won't," Ren said. "I'm looping next year."

Kara laughed. "What do you mean next year? You're loopy now."

Ren chuckled. "Not loopy, smarty pants. Looping. It's when the teacher moves up to the next grade with the same class. It helps with transition 'cause the students are already in sync with the teacher. Remember? I did it with this class when they went from first to second too. So I'll be teaching third grade next year."

"And you'll have Casey again?" Tru asked.

Ren smiled at him. Who knew what to expect in Casey's case? "As long as he's still at the school, yeah." She looked at Kara and Gabe, tilting her thumb toward Tru. "Tru and Casey bonded today."

"Easy to do," Tru said. "Great kid."

"Yep," Kara said. "He's a sweetie pie, all right. I'm praying for that little fellow big time."

There was a brief silence. Ren didn't want to talk any deeper about Casey. There were so many unspoken factors involved. She tried to think of a new subject, but Gabe came to the rescue.

"I understand you two had a rather unorthodox museum experience recently."

"That was amazing," Ren said. "I loved it! That couple, that baby. And to get to watch how beautifully Tru handled everything."

Tru chuckled. "I'm feeling a little pressure about how I'm going to top that date for excitement."

"No, believe me," Ren said, laughing, "it was probably the most memorable date we've had so far, but we can lower the excitement level a few notches and I'll be just fine."

He looked at her, a twinkle in his eye. "I'm kind of sorry to hear that."

Ren sipped her soda and smiled back at him, but she wasn't sure what that comment meant. Had she really said the wrong thing? They'd seen each other every free moment since that weekend. Was she starting to bore him? Or was he feeling pressed to be constantly exciting? Maybe he actually craved more excitement than they'd had on some of their more casual dates recently.

She self-consciously reached up and pulled her hair back behind her ear, just for something to do. Then, graceful as ever, she hit one of the crab knives with her elbow, causing it to flip into the air and land with a loud, tinny clang under the table.

She didn't know if any other diners turned to look, but in her mind, everyone did. They all laughed. Ren's laugh was the only one salted with embarrassment, but only a little embarrassment.

They were all a bit giddy. Maybe because of the upcoming summer. Maybe because of Kara and Gabe's engagement. Maybe because Tru and Ren were in love. Everything just felt good. They were happy.

"Here, I'll get your knife." Tru bent to look under the table.

"No, leave it, Tru," Ren said, even as he struggled to reach for the knife. "I won't use that one anyway. I'll tell the waitress and she'll bring another. Don't, really."

"But I must!" He spoke in a valiant-knight kind of voice. He got out of his seat to reach the knife, even going down on his hands and knees, which caused all of them to laugh. Not exactly the top drawer of society, their group. Ren was glad they had chosen such a casual environment for dinner.

"Aha!" Tru said.

When he reemerged, he placed the knife on the table.

"My hero," Ren said, chuckling.

He chuckled back and rested his elbow on the table, next to the knife. Tilting his head, he looked at her. "You know, Rennie, our first meeting was unusual. Since then, our dates, our experiences together, even our families have been a bit unusual. I don't know about you, but I'm getting hooked on unusual."

What a marvelous thing to say. How could she ever get embarrassed with such an accepting man? "Me too."

But then she noticed he wasn't returning to his seat, which was a little embarrassing in itself. Heads were starting to turn, especially when a waitress had to maneuver around him.

"Um, Tru —"

"I know we've only dated a few months," he said. "But it seems to me that, if we want to keep life interesting, we're going to need to spend it together."

He was still there on his knees. Then he placed one foot on the floor, as if he were about to push himself up . . . but he didn't push himself up. He opened his hand and looked at Ren. There was a small, gray velvet box in his palm.

For a split second Ren thought he found the box on the floor. But then she knew what he was doing. He had planned to take advantage of a moment like this. Her mouth dropped open in a gasp.

Kara let a small shriek of surprise escape, realizing just after Ren did that Tru was holding a ring box. At her outburst, everyone in the restaurant did look at them. But Ren suddenly felt as if she and Tru were all alone.

He opened the box. "Rennie . . ."

And she started crying.

"Will you marry me?"

Nothing else in her life held the weight of what he offered her. Not her struggle with her mother or with his. Not the uncertainty about whether she'd be a mother to Casey or any other child. The only thing more important to her at this moment was God, and Ren felt with absolute certainty that He was with them now, smiling on the moment.

She smiled at Tru. "Yes," she whispered.

The entire restaurant erupted in shouts and cheering. Ren laughed as she glanced around her. Wasn't it great how people connected with a good love story?

Tru stood and brought her to her feet. That twinkle returned to his eyes, and he gave her a gentle kiss. Then he hugged her with such energy that he lifted her off the ground.

Ren hugged him right back. He was right. They'd had some uncommon experiences together, most of which caused them to be real with each other early on. Although some of the events had been challenging, they had helped Ren and Tru grow closer together. Now they could look forward to the rest of life as an adventure — a journey — because they'd be exploring it together.

Of course, standing there that night, embracing each other and the future, neither of them realized how bumpy that journey would be.

FORTY-ONE

Summer was insane. Both Ren and Tru wanted a simple wedding, but they also wanted it soon, for many reasons. To become a family, to pursue adoption of Casey, to quell the frustration of arrested passion (and not necessarily in that order). If Ren had planned what she (and Tru) actually accomplished over the next few months, her list would have looked something like this:

1. Share terrific news about engagement with families. Jump up and down girlishly with sister-in-law and future sisters-in-law, hugging, laughing, crying. (Okay, that last was all me — Tru didn't take part in that one.)

2. Apologize effusively to respective mothers for: hurting their feelings prior to the engagement, not alerting them to how serious we had

become, not allowing them to take control of all wedding preparations.

3. Meet Sammy, Tru's adorable, golden retriever. Fall in love again. (This love also mutual, but far more slobbery, with Sammy wanting to go home with me the first day we meet.)

4. Enroll in premarital counseling class at church. Nab pastor for a late-August ceremony.

5. Whip through premarital counseling class, suffering the occasional tiffs over things like determining each other's personality type, strengths, weaknesses. Uncover and break down a few walls (none of which really hurt much when they fall).

6. Talk with Sandy and social services about possibility of beginning adoption of Casey again. Lots of red tape. No answers.

7. Engage in several special outings with Casey. At Sandy's strong suggestion, never mention adoption. Outings are simply between three very good friends (who are becoming something mighty close to a family).

8. Take advantage of Kara's wedding research. Order and pay ridiculous amounts for invitations, wedding dress, tuxedo rental, flowers, photographer, music, food, reception, and honeymoon (Bermuda).

9. Start extreme workout program under taskmaster Kara for said trip to Bermuda. Experience love-hate relationship with Kara at each session (love her when it's over, hate her when she doesn't give in to my spoiled whiney-girl complaints).

10. Try to act surprised for wedding shower (courtesy of the fabulous Kara and Sandy, two of the worst secret keepers of all time). Value of meeting between my mother and Tru's mom: priceless. Each subtly trying to gauge the other's worthiness as an in-law from this brief meeting. They might actually like each other if they ever deign to sit on the same side of the room together.

11. Praise God daily for saving Tru for me. Ask for His help in understanding His will regarding Casey, whatever that turns out to be.

12. Love, love, love my fiancé, the dear-

est man ever.

And so it happened. The last Saturday in August, it all came together. Although Ren was clearheaded, she experienced a feeling of breathtaking unbelief as she became Mrs. Ren Sayers. With just a few words, she joyfully gave her heart to a man she would know and love for eternity.

And Tru, while claiming, "I take you, Ren, to be my lawful, wedded wife," gave her a look he had saved for today. For his wife. Ren could only describe it as smoldering, and she just about fainted (which would have been an interesting way of bringing their experiences full circle).

The day was windy but sunny, the church was dazzling, and nothing went wrong. At least, nothing they didn't expect.

Clarissa had never completely thawed after the fight she and Ren had in the spring, despite Ren's apologies. She had backed off the control issues, as Ren requested, but Ren couldn't say she'd ever seen a women hold her lips so tightly for so long.

Tru's mother seemed to have adjusted better. She approached Ren at the reception and gave her a kiss on the cheek. "You're a beautiful bride, Ren. My son, he deserves a beautiful bride."

Ren was about to thank her, when she added, "And he deserves a happy life. You'll give him that, no?"

Ren smiled. Somehow she knew a mere "I'll try!" would prompt Mrs. Sayers' personal version of "Trying doesn't cut it, soldier!" So Ren promised what she would strive for, anyway. "Absolutely. That's the plan!"

And — still no surprise — Clarissa extended her cordial but chilly welcome to Tru. "Well, Tru. It's done. I wish the best for both of you. Welcome to the fam—"

Ren's darling new husband leaned forward and gave his rod-stiff mother-in-law a wonderful hug and a kiss on the cheek. Under his kind embrace, Clarissa's arms hung to her side, and her hands fluttered, as if she wasn't sure where to place them. Despite her looking slightly unraveled and politely shocked, Ren could see it. The tiniest thaw around Clarissa's wrinkled lips. Given time . . .

But the sibs would take no time at all.

You'd think Ren was the fourth sister in Tru's family. Everything that should have been treated lightly, was. From her meeting Tru after fainting like some Victorian, corseted damsel to the nonsense about calling Anna a donut hound to her apparent desire to pluck out all her eyelashes at his mother's party. And everything that should have been given weight, was. Her faith, her aspirations for motherhood, her deep, deep love for their brother.

And Ren's brother, Matt, was just as quick with a warm welcome for Tru. Before Tru and Ren left the reception, Matt had already made plans for Tru and Ren to join him, Sybil, and the girls on their next hiking expedition.

"Ren's quite the hiker," Matt told Tru. "Always looking for a risk. Quite a challenge to keep up with. She's especially wild at ravines. Like a kid on a water slide." He would have continued in this vein if Ren hadn't interrupted.

"Never mind." She looked at Sybil. "We'll hike with you guys if I can follow Tru, instead of Mr. Hey-Let's-Go-Off-the-Path here."

Even their friends mingled well. Kara and Gabe made fast friends with Gray Guy, the OB-GYN, and his wife, Round Rhonda. Sandy and The Marvelous Rick were thrilled when they recognized Tru's coworker, Bill — the Cosby look-alike — as the coach of their son's soccer team.

Most amazing of all was darling Jeremy.

Who would have pictured him with young Braces Brenda, Tru's fellow nurse? But, as Kara pointed out, it looked as if a new romance might actually be blossoming there. Brenda — as cute as a pixie — no longer wore braces but still looked border-line adolescent.

"Nope," Tru said. "She's in her early twenties. She can't be much younger than Jeremy."

The two of them looked as if they were in their own little world. And it hadn't started at a bar! There was hope!

"Ren, look at this," Tru whispered, taking her hand.

They kept doing that all afternoon, pulling each other aside to witness together things they knew they'd cherish for years. Matt and Sybil making Tru's mother laugh. Tru's nineteen-year-old brother, Harris, coaxing Ren's mother onto the dance floor, where he tried to teach her some hip-shaking salsa dance. Guy and Rhonda cracking up over something The Marvelous Rick had said. Braces Brenda looking at Jeremy as if he were the most fascinating man on the planet.

The entire wedding, the entire reception, verified what they already knew. They had struggled a bit with the "leaving" part, they had eagerly begun the "cleaving" part, and if they trusted in God, their two worlds would blend in ways they had never thought possible before.

Ren and her husband left their reception, loved and cheered by many terrific people. They rode to the airport, glowing with the feeling of newness. Of a blessed future together.

At that moment, neither of them considered that blessings aren't always packaged like pretty wedding gifts. Sometimes blessings seem far from perfect.

FORTY-TWO

Ah, Bermuda.

Ren and Tru didn't want to come home. But at the same time they did. Yes, they felt they had tasted a bit of heaven while there as they explored the island on their rented scooters. They loved the delightful weather; the bright, salmon-colored homes next to pale, kelly-green homes; the little zoo with its big-billed toucans and fat-lipped groupers. But what they really loved was what they would be bringing home — each other. Their family. *They* were a family.

Plus, they were both eager to see U.S. prices for food again. Eight dollars for a cup of French onion soup? Please. And driving on the wrong side of the road, British style? Yikes! Ren just couldn't get used to it.

So they arrived home and set up shop in Ren's house. Because her place was bigger, they decided to put Tru's condo on the market. They both wondered how Sammy would adjust to having his doggie dish elsewhere. But talk about heaven! Ren's backyard wasn't much, but it was more than Sammy was used to, unleashed. He always looked as if he were smiling, anyway, but now his smile traveled all the way to the tip of his feathery, wagging tail.

It was difficult to go back to work, though. Ren sighed as she and Tru passed each other in the kitchen. It wasn't like the blissful sighs he'd heard from her over the past ten days of their honeymoon.

He stopped and looked at her. "You all right?"

"Mmm. I feel a little tired. Just not all that eager to get back to the grind, I guess. I'm going to miss you."

There was that smoldering look again, the one he gave her when he vowed to stick with her forever. He set down his coffee cup. Then he gave her a wonderful, slow, warm kiss. "I'll miss you too," he whispered.

That did not make leaving any easier.

The most exciting thing about going back to work, Ren decided, was the idea of coming home to her husband. She couldn't wait.

But as the morning bell neared and the children arrived, their squeals of joy at seeing Ren again were all she needed to remember why she loved her job. It was so nice to see all those familiar faces — some a little tanned, some even surprisingly older looking.

The end-of-summer orientation took place while Ren was honeymooning. The principal had talked to the children and their parents about her new marriage and new name.

"Mrs. Swinson said you got married," one boy said.

Another asked, "Why can't we just call you *Mrs.* Young now? I don't want to call you that other name." He pointed at the name Ren wrote on the blackboard: *Mrs. Sayers.* "It's weird."

Ren had always been Ms. Young to them, even in the beginning, while she and Greg were still married. But she felt a love and allegiance to Tru that flowed into so many areas of her life. So, Mrs. Sayers it was.

"It's hard for me to adjust too, Alan," Ren said. "But we'll get used to it together, okay?"

"I like it," Casey said, grinning. "Sounds like talking. Mrs. *Say*ers."

Of course, Casey had spent time with Tru and Ren over the summer, so Tru's surname was less foreign to him. "Thanks, hon — Casey," Ren said, nearly slipping into the endearment she had used over the summer.

Ren didn't receive the news about Casey until the school day was over. Sandy left a note in her mail slot, asking to see her after school.

"There she is, the happy newlywed," Sandy said, as soon as Ren walked into her office. She came and gave Ren a big hug, and then she held her a moment longer, giving Ren an emphatic squeeze, as if she were trying to transfer some strength to her. Something was wrong.

Ren pulled back and looked into Sandy's eyes, which looked sad. "What is it?"

"Have a seat, Ren."

She had brought a grown-up-sized chair into her office for Ren. This was serious.

"I have some bad news. About Casey. About his adoption status."

Ren sank into the chair, saying nothing.

"Britney — his mother — has filed papers to restore her custody of Casey."

The weariness Ren felt this morning spread, heavy and acidic, down into her chest. Her heart. Her stomach. Could the timing be any more ironic? Ren was finally in a position to adopt Casey, with a husband as eager as she was, and Casey was disappearing from her again.

"But how can that be, while Britney's in prison?"

"She's due for release soon, getting out early for good behavior. She's been clean for a year now."

Ren squeezed her eyes shut and dropped her head into her hand. "I can't believe this, Sandy."

Sandy handed her a tissue, giving her free hand a squeeze as Ren took it. "I know, sweetie." She sighed. "And I'm afraid there's no point in trying to fight this, Ren."

Ren looked up at her. "Oh." She shook her head, frowning. "No. I wasn't thinking of that. I just . . ." Ren started really crying now. "I just started thinking I was going to get it all, you know? Tru, Casey, the works. I'm just being selfish, I guess. He's not just any boy to me. Especially since the engagement, I couldn't help it. I thought of him as our future son."

Ren saw Sandy swallow hard before she grabbed a tissue and dabbed her own eyes. "If it helps at all, Ren, I think she's really come around. I think she'll be a good mother to him."

Ren nodded. She wanted that for Casey. If she were a better person, that'd be all she wanted, she supposed. "So does Casey know about this?"

"Not yet, no. Britney just filed the papers — while you were on your honeymoon — so nothing's finalized yet."

Ren pictured Tru and herself, motoring happily around the island, completely oblivious to what they were losing back home. That was probably for the best. "How do you think Casey will react?"

Sandy sighed again, less mournfully. "Honestly? He might be all right with it. He's been referring to her as 'Mommy' when I meet with him in here, and he seems to look forward to visiting her." She snorted ruefully and opened up the file on her desk. "You've finally been given the okay to come with us on the next visit, by the way."

Ren tsked and sighed, closing her eyes. "Lot of good that's going to do now."

After a moment's silence, Sandy said, "Hey, you know what? I think it would do you some good to come with us for the next one."

"What? That sounds like torture to me," Ren said. "I don't think I can handle meeting her now, Sandy. Seeing Casey with her."

"I'm not saying it will be easy, Ren. But you know about closure and all that."

"Oh, Sandy —"

"It will give you assurance, Ren. I think you need this."

■ ■ ■ ■

And that was how Ren ended up, two weeks later, driving to prison with her good friend and the son she was losing. Tru had wanted to come, but Ren said, "I wish we could do this together, but by the time you get approved for the visit, Casey will be in high school. The system isn't exactly streamlined."

Casey was enthralled that Ren was finally coming with him. And, although he hadn't mentioned his mother much over the summer, she was all he could talk about during their drive.

"She's fun." His husky little voice was full of energy. "She plays games with me and hugs me lots when I'm there. She's pretty good at basketball. And she always has candy bars. And Cheetos. And she laughs all the time."

Every twinkle in his eyes was a beautiful, happy spark that pierced Ren's heart. Sandy was right. Ren needed this assurance that Casey was headed toward a contented life. But the closer they got to the prison, the more lonely Ren felt. She prayed that she would honor God in how she acted toward Casey's mother. That she wouldn't throw any of her pain on Casey or this woman who had fought to come back from a place of darkness.

Once inside the grounds, they pulled up to a gated area surrounded by chain-link fencing. Two guards stood outside the gate, and a group of women in dull, burgundy prison uniforms milled about on the grassy section inside.

They got out of the car and walked toward the women, joined by several other groups of children and guardians arriving for their visits. Ren thought she spotted Britney the moment Casey did. She was young. Small. And had hair exactly like Casey's — blond, curled, cherubic. She was leaning forward, as if her stance would enable her to see better past the fencing. She held both hands at her mouth, as if the anticipation were unbearable. By the time Casey took off running, Ren was close enough to see tears in Britney's eyes.

And Casey? He ran to her so fast, his shirttail flew out behind him, revealing his T-shirt below. In her own, tear-filled state, Ren suddenly recognized his T-shirt as the one she had finally found for him months ago, when she shopped for him at Wal-Mart. When she fainted. When she met Tru.

Ren stopped for a moment and put her

hand on Sandy's arm. "Does she know about me, Sandy? Does she know I wanted to adopt Casey?"

Sandy rested her hand on Ren's. "She knows, Ren. She knows you loved her son when she wasn't able to."

Ren watched him jump into Britney's arms. They hugged each other so closely, their heads — full of soft curls — so near each other, that it was hard to tell where the mother ended and the son began. Despite the pain tearing through Ren's heart, she knew. The Lord made her see. Casey was finally home.

FORTY-THREE

Ren wanted to report a quick bouncing back on her part — a mature, full-acceptance-of-God's-will kind of happiness emanating from her every pore.

She wanted to report that, but she'd have been lying. What a soggy mess she was by the time Tru got home from work that evening. She understood God's will for Casey — He had blessed her with His assurance when she saw Casey and Britney together. So all her tears were just for poor, pitiful Ren. Just as people cry when a loved one dies, even if that loved one knew the Lord and was now having a great time with the angels and Abraham and John the Baptist and such — that's how she was crying. She was in mourning for what she knew would be missing from her future: Casey.

And when Tru tried to comfort her, she could tell her crying was making a phonetic mishmash of her words, because he gently said, "What?" after everything she babbled. He finally gave up on verbal communication and just hugged her until her eyes ran out of water.

The following day was Sunday. Over their morning coffee Tru asked his puffy, dragging wife, "Would you rather stay home from church today?"

Ren shook her head. "If there's one thing I can't afford to miss, it's church. I need the comforting. The teaching. The worship. All that." She looked into his eyes — those warm, accepting eyes that never failed to make her sigh. "Do you mind being seen with such a crybaby?"

He gave her a sad smile. "Comforting you has actually helped me a little. Takes my mind off my own . . ." He shrugged. "I was going to say disappointment, but this feels worse than that."

Ren uttered the tiniest moan of commiseration and took his hand across the table. He was right. As soon as she remembered that he hurt too, she felt more protective of him and less sorry for herself.

Then she stood and took a deep breath in and out. "All right, handsome. If I'm going to get presentable for church, I'm going to need extra time with my cosmetics arsenal." She pressed her palm against her forehead.

"And aspirin. All this crying has given me a killer headache."

Going to church was the best decision Ren could have made that morning. She didn't know why she was always surprised by God, but she was. And she had to admit, she enjoyed it when He surprised her.

Pastor Dan addressed the passage in John where Jesus, from the cross, sees His mother and John and commits them to one another, as mother and son. Dan talked about John's honor at Christ's choosing him. He discussed Mary's sorrow in seeing her Son suffer. Then he said, "Imagine Jesus' emotional pain. He's fully God, yes, but He was fully man too. This was His *mother.* When He looked into her anguished face, He felt the same kind of agony you or I would feel, knowing this was it. This was goodbye."

Ren actually thought about Casey at that moment. Goodness, her "goodbye" to Casey would be nowhere nearly as bad as what Dan was describing.

Dan said, "Once again, Jesus demonstrated obedience to God's will when He entrusted His mother to someone else's care."

Obedience. Entrusting. Tears flooded Ren's eyes, and reliable Tru handed her his handkerchief. She didn't know if he understood why she was crying, but, as usual, he sought to comfort first and ask questions later.

She didn't feel guilty or selfish for being so sad about losing Casey. She just felt as if Jesus were telling her He understood. Of course He understood. Look what kind of loss He endured while He was on earth.

But she also felt Him encouraging her to trust that He knew best about Casey being with Britney. And He knew best about Ren. She should take comfort in that. And she did.

Okay, so all of that was wonderful and cool. But what happened next was what really floored her.

Kara and Gabe had served in the nursery during the service. So when Tru and Ren walked into the fellowship hall afterward, Ren was watching for them to emerge from that end of the church. She almost didn't see Tiffany, who slipped out of the ladies' room, clearly crying. But that auburn mane and hourglass figure were unmistakable.

Ren put her hand on Tru's arm, and he followed her gaze. They watched Tiffany move quickly through the crowd and head for the exit. On impulse Ren started toward her, but then she had second thoughts. She looked at Tru. "Should I —"

He didn't hesitate but nodded agreement. "Yeah. Go."

Ren wove between people, praying for guidance as she went. She wasn't sure if Tiffany would appreciate her stopping her to talk. It had been three or four months since Tiffany had come to church, as far as Ren knew. She'd shied away from the subject of faith the few times Ren tried to engage her at the gym. Kara said she'd had the same experience with her. And Tiffany definitely didn't seek any of them out today, so maybe she wanted them to keep their distance.

But she *was* upset about something. Maybe she was just afraid to seek the comforting she needed. Those certainly didn't look like tears of joy she was crying.

Tiffany got outside before Ren could reach her, so Ren followed her into the parking lot.

"Tiffany!"

She turned briefly, looked at Ren, and scurried away again.

Ren sighed and almost turned to leave, but Tiffany abruptly turned to look at her again and released a sigh so full of exasperation Ren heard it as if Tiffany were right in front of her.

"Well, come on!" Tiffany said, evidently

impatient that Ren hadn't read her obscure body language correctly. It seemed she wanted to get away from the crowd but needed to talk, just more privately.

She had already turned and taken off again, and Ren followed her as if she were Tiffany's little lackey. It was a bit humiliating.

"Only for You, Lord," Ren muttered in prayer. "Help me be like You here, okay? 'Cause I'm already feeling a tiny bit ticked off."

Tiffany stopped at her car and dug another tissue out of her purse when Ren joined her.

"Are you okay?" Ren asked.

"I just . . ." She lowered her head, apparently trying to gain emotional control. She waved the tissue a couple of times, like a little flag of surrender. "I just can't believe He dragged all these people here today, just for me."

Ren looked behind them, at the throng of people milling around the front of the church. She frowned in confusion.

"What people, Tiffany? What do you mean?"

Tiffany looked at Ren as if she were an idiot. She pointed at the church, aiming her shaking finger toward the sanctuary, where Dan had given his sermon.

"That . . . that sermon? That was God. Talking to me. Didn't you hear what that pastor guy talked about? For weeks I've been . . . I don't know what to do about my mom. The cancer's metasti— mestash—"

"Metastasized? Spread?"

Tiffany nodded, then blew her nose. "Yeah. And she won't do the chemo. She refuses." She looked up at Ren, almost rolling her eyes about her situation. "So I . . . I was, you know, praying last night, telling Jesus I don't know what He wants me to do. I told Him, I said, 'Just help me deal with whatever You've got planned for her, you know?'" She abruptly looked down and even looked humble for a moment.

Ren raised her eyebrows and fought back tears. "Tiffany."

Tiffany looked up at her.

Ren swallowed. "Um, you asked Him to . . . does that mean . . ." Ren sighed at her own verbal stumbling. "Tiffany, I think you might have accepted Christ."

A frown touched down for a moment over Tiffany's teary eyes. "I still don't get that term. And what does that have to do with my mom?"

Ooo. Could use Your help here, Lord. Please take my foot far from my mouth, and help me say the right words.

Ren said, "It's just that you sound as if you've given Christ control of your life. And your mom's. And maybe . . . everything?"

Tiffany cocked her head at an angle. "Yeah, so?"

Ren glanced behind herself to see if Tru or any other troops were coming to help her, but she appeared to be the only one God planned on using for this situation. "That's a big deal, surrendering your life to God. And you said you were praying to Jesus, right?"

Tiffany nodded.

Ren nodded once in return. "So, basically, you haven't only surrendered your life to God, you've given your life to Jesus."

Tiffany suddenly looked about five years old. "But I thought Jesus and God were kind of the same person."

Ren felt her heart break open, spilling joy all inside of her. Her throat tightened again. Before she could say anything else, Tiffany spoke again.

"I thought that's why He could take away my sins. And come alive again, and all. You know, after He died for me. Because He's God."

Ren just nodded. Then she pointed at Tiffany and spoke softly. "That. That's accepting Christ, what you just said." A little laugh escaped her before she said, "You're a believer."

Tiffany looked at the ground for a moment, then she lifted a shoulder and looked at Ren. "I guess."

What did Ren expect? Leaping and dancing and praising God? This was Tiffany, after all.

Tiffany said, "So is that why He did this whole church service about me and my mom?"

Ren frowned. "About — ?" And then she realized what Tiffany meant. He spoke to Tiffany that morning, just as He spoke to Ren about Casey. Tiffany just hadn't realized yet that He can speak to everyone at once if He wants to.

"What did He tell *you* today, Tiffany?"

Tiffany lifted her palms quickly. "Well, isn't it obvious? I'm supposed to go home and take care of her. As long as it takes. I'm outta here, soon as I can quit my job."

"What?"

Ren turned at the voice and saw Kara, who had just approached them.

"You're quitting your job at the gym?" she asked Tiffany.

"But, Tiffany," Ren said, "why don't you just take some time off?"

Tiffany shook her head emphatically.

"Nope. I'm supposed to move down there and stay with her until —"

She stopped sharply, drawing a quick breath. She looked into Ren's eyes and then at Kara. "Until it's time to say goodbye."

None of them said anything for a while. Kara looked confused, having missed most of Ren's conversation with Tiffany.

Then Tiffany narrowed her eyes slightly and looked at Ren. "What did you mean when you said, 'What did God tell you today?' Are you saying He told you something in there too?"

Ren couldn't help smiling. She nodded. "Sure. He's God — He can address more than one need at once, don't you think?"

That prompted a smile from Kara.

Then Miss Tiffany LeBoeuf — the most self-centered woman Ren had ever met, the queen of self-indulgence, the gal Ren would vote least likely to look beyond her own desires — blew both Kara and Ren away.

She looked at Ren thoughtfully for a moment before saying, "Hmm. What's *your* need, Ren?"

FORTY-FOUR

"I swear, this headache is going to kill me," Ren complained to Kara at the gym the next day. Despite all the thrilling "God things" at church yesterday, Ren still struggled with waves of depression over Casey. But she kept her workout appointment with Kara after school on Monday, hoping for renewed energy.

"Now, don't start with me, young lady." Kara selected two dumbbells from a rack. "You're doing great. Just shoo those excuses away." She nodded toward Ren's water bottle. "You never drink enough water. You're probably dehydrated."

For three weeks? Ren took the weights from her and rested them beside herself on the workout bench. After a long drink from her water bottle, she said, "You're right. I'm wallowing. Poor, poor me. But I don't know why I can't get out of this funk, Kara. It doesn't make sense. Every time he walks

into the classroom, I just want to cry —"
She stopped, knowing she'd cry right there if she said any more.

Kara dropped her gung-ho attitude and sat next to Ren on the bench. She put her arm around her, and Ren went ahead and cried a bit. "I'm sorry, Ren. You've been hoping to become Casey's mom for over a year now. I don't think it's unusual for you to feel sad for a while."

Ren sighed and tried to pull herself together. "Yeah, I know. But I'm not making the situation any better. And the stress of my moodiness is no bonus at home. Tru's been great — he has to deal with the disappointment too. But I can tell he's feeling helpless about me. This morning he said he was worried that I was making myself sick, you know, with all the crying and brooding."

"Is he right? You have been complaining about those headaches lately."

"Yeah, and backaches. And fatigue. So I guess he's right."

Kara gasped, as if something occurred to her. But she just as quickly dismissed it. "Um . . . never mind."

"What?"

Kara frowned, obviously bothered with herself. "Nothing. You don't need . . . well, you don't need to get your hopes up just to have them dashed again, so —"

"You're thinking pregnancy?"

"You already thought of that?"

Ren snorted softly. She knew her smile was cheerless. "Are you kidding? I've been thinking pregnancy since our wedding night. But I finished my period just before the wedding, and I'm already starting the next." She sighed. "Right on time, as usual."

"But you haven't given up hope on that front, have you? I mean, it's only been a month of trying."

Ren shook her head. "No, I have hope. It's just kind of submerged right now. Eventually, if nothing happens naturally, we can start seeing specialists." Another sigh. "I don't have the heart for any of those thoughts just now."

Kara gave her back a gentle pat and then stood up. "All right. I'm going to leave it up to you today. If you *are* just down, or if stress is lowering your immune system, working out will be just what you need. But if you think we're talking something more serious, I don't want to push you."

"Let's keep at it. I need a good dose of those whatcha-ma-callits, those dolphin thingies."

Kara laughed. "Endorphins."

"That's the stuff. Maybe if I work hard enough, my dolphins will chase away my blues."

"Okay, then. Up you go. Feet shoulder width apart. Give me twenty bicep curls, each arm. Let's go."

But Ren's dolphins were completely useless against her blues, as it turned out. By the time she got home, not only was she still down, she was actually sick to her stomach. That happened if she worked out on a full stomach, but she hadn't eaten for hours. As a matter of fact, she had barely eaten anything today, and the thought of food was pretty unappealing to her right now.

So she probably didn't look as pleasant as she should have when she pulled into the driveway and found Clarissa, sitting in her Mercedes, waiting for her. At once Ren felt snappy about her mother dropping by unannounced, especially after their boundary issue talk last spring. Clarissa was out of her car the moment Ren pulled into the driveway, and Ren didn't have a chance to take a calming breath before she opened her car door for her.

"Ren, I need to talk with you."

"Hello to you too, Mother." Ren could barely mask her annoyance.

Clarissa ignored her sarcasm. "Tru tells me you're not feeling well. Why haven't you told me about this? Am I not entitled to a little notification when you're ill?"

Tru told her? Since when had they been chatty? "What do you mean, Tru told you? When did he call you?"

"I called him. Or, rather, I called you. This morning. But you had gone to work, and he hadn't yet."

"I'm fine, Mother. Just a little tired. I'm not dealing very well with how things worked out with Casey, that's all. I'll buck up and be back on my feet in no time."

Ren stepped out of the car and immediately felt a cramping in her abdomen like she'd never felt before. Everything before her flashed brilliantly white.

The next thing Ren knew, Clarissa was kneeling over her, calling her name. Clarissa looked blurry. Then she looked frightened. A moment later she was up and gone.

Ren squeezed her eyes shut. Amazing pain! What was this? Drastic thoughts crowded her mind. Was it cancer? Was she going to die a slow, withering, painful death, now that she'd finally found the perfect man? Heart attack? No, this pain was too low. Burst appendix? Was her own body poisoning her? Was she slated to die like some pioneer woman, when a simple surgery could have saved her, had she only bought a home closer to the hospital? Greg was the one who chose this house — this was all his fault. And now he and Trixie, or whatever her name was, were able to have a baby. Already had a baby. And what did Tru and Ren get? A tumor?

Ren tried to raise herself up off her back, stopping to rest on her elbows. But the cramping started again, and she couldn't get the pain to subside without lying back down and curling into the fetal position. She shivered with chills, despite the beads of sweat she felt along her hairline. She became aware of Clarissa's voice. Ah. She had run to her car to get her cell phone.

"Yes, she passed out the moment she stood up. Hurry. She's in terrible pain."

Ren heard her give the address, so she figured she had called 9-1-1, not Tru or Matt. Ren heard her scuffle around again, this time closer to her. By the time Ren was able to turn to see her, she had reached Ren's car. It looked as if she were going through Ren's purse! Now? Ren wanted to yell at her. Boundaries, Mother! But nothing came out but a moan.

Clarissa returned to her, moments later. She dropped to her knees next to her.

Ren managed to ask, "What —"

"Shhh. Relax. The ambulance is coming." Clarissa flashed Ren's cell phone at her and began pushing buttons like a pro. "I needed your speed dial," Clarissa said.

Ren remembered Clarissa's prowess with her cell phone that day at the shopping mall — she never considered how handy that would turn out to be today.

"Yes," Clarissa barked into the telephone. "This is Tru Sayers' mother-in-law. I need to speak with him immediately. Something's happened to his wife. This is an emergency."

Despite Ren's pain and disorientation, the thought went through her mind, as it had in the past. Her mother made her crazy, but, when the floodwaters came, she was the one to have in your boat.

Tru was waiting for them when they wheeled Ren into the cold, bright emergency room. The intense pain had subsided, so she felt a little embarrassed about all the hubbub.

"I . . . I think I'm okay now," she said to Tru, the moment he approached. She started to lift herself up, even before they had reached one of the cubicles in the ER.

Tru kissed her quickly, looking into her eyes. He pressed her gently back onto the gurney. "You just stay right where you are. Don't get up until the doctor's had a chance to check you out." He glanced over at Clarissa. "Thanks, Clarissa." He put a hand on her shoulder and gave her a peck on the cheek. "What a blessing that you were there when it happened."

Clarissa nodded, appearing startled by his kindness, as always. Ren never understood that, since Tru had always treated her this way. It was almost as if she felt she didn't deserve his kindheartedness. "Yes, a . . . blessing."

A doctor showed up about half an hour later. "Dr. Nielson," she said to Ren, giving her a professional smile. Petite, tidy, blond, and no-nonsense. She pulled the curtain around them and addressed Tru and Clarissa. "I'd like privacy while I examine Mrs. Sayers, please."

Ren wanted Tru to stay, but she didn't want to make Clarissa leave on her own, so she kept her mouth shut. The doctor asked her questions the entire time she examined her. What were her symptoms? How long had she been having cramping? (*On and off the past week or so.*) Any flu, colds, bronchitis recently? (*No, no, and no.*) Headaches? (*For about three weeks.*) Other body aches? (*Well, yeah.*) On one side or both sides of your body? *(Mercy, who knows?)* Fatigue? *(For a few weeks.)* Nausea? *(New today.)* Could you be pregnant? *(Sigh. No.)* Last period? *(Just started.)* Problems at home? *(None.)* Stress elsewhere? *(Casey. Losing Casey.)*

Ren started to feel the many questions were repeating themselves. Finally the doctor opened the curtain and let Tru and Clarissa come back.

"Okay, Mrs. Sayers," the doctor said to Ren. "We're going to admit you —"

"But I'm feeling much better now."

Tru stepped forward and took her hand. "Ren, honey. I'm so worried about you. Please, let's find out what's wrong."

"I've just been a little depressed lately. That's all this is."

He leaned in to her. Even though he whispered, he showed no concern about anyone hearing what he said. "I've waited my whole life for you. You mean more to me than anything. Anyone." He pulled back and looked at her, his eyes pleading. "Please."

"What I'd like to do," Dr. Nielson said to Ren, "is to run some tests. You're exhibiting symptoms that point to a number of different diagnoses —"

"Like what?" Clarissa and Ren both asked her.

"Well, why don't we wait until we've run the tests? I don't want to alarm you without getting more information."

"Just tell me what you're thinking of or I'll imagine the worst," Ren said. "Please."

"All right. Offhand, some possibilities are cysts, fibromyalgia, chronic myofascial pain, chronic fatigue syndrome, endometriosis —"

"She's had endometriosis," Clarissa said, before Ren had a chance. "When she was sixteen."

Ren looked at Clarissa. She was startled that she not only remembered Ren's problem but even her age when she had it. *Ren* didn't even remember that she was sixteen at the time. She had to admit that she was touched.

Dr. Nielson nodded at Clarissa and then looked at Ren. "We may be seeing a reoccurrence. Now, these are only ideas, mind you. We could be looking at something else altogether. But those are my first thoughts."

"I don't even know what most of those other things are," Ren said.

The doctor patted her hand, finally showing a warmer bedside manner. "We'll fill you in on all of that as we go. I promise."

She looked kindly at Ren.

Ren looked at Tru, who gave her a smile filled with concern. She was suddenly tired again. "Okay. Let's do the tests."

"Good," Dr. Nielson said. "Just stay here and rest a bit. It will take some time to get you admitted." She looked at Tru, still in his scrubs. "You work here, Mr. Sayers?"

"Yes. Labor and delivery."

"Are you on your shift? Do you need to get back?"

He shook his head. "I'm fine. One of the other nurses filled in for me."

The doctor glanced at Clarissa, who immediately said, "I'm staying."

A flicker of amused appreciation lit Dr. Nielson's eyes. "All right." She looked back to Tru. "One of the nurses will come get you, Mr. Sayers, when we're ready for the admittance information." She looked at Ren. "Please try to rest."

And rest Ren did. Eventually, anyway.

The cramps didn't come back, but the nausea remained. And her heart raced whenever she thought about that blinding pain — extreme enough to make her faint. She was afraid it would happen again.

Then she'd get the thought that she was actually fine and just imagining these symptoms. Strictly psychosomatic. She needed to get over Casey or she'd spend the next ten years hooked up to an IV. Or on a therapist's couch.

She didn't want to fall asleep and leave Tru at Clarissa's mercy. She had never fully explained to him her mother's horrible generalization about men of Hispanic descent. But Ren guessed the Lord thought He could handle that situation on His own. Because the moment Ren began to pray about it, she was out cold.

FORTY-FIVE

For hours Ren floated in and out of sleep, sometimes uncomfortably warm, sometimes aching with chills. At times she awoke on her own — at first disoriented and then saddened to remember where she was. Occasionally a twinge in her abdomen would startle her awake. At other times the nurses and doctors woke her to take more blood or to explore some part of her body. She had enough pelvic exams to last until her eightieth birthday.

At one point a doctor had her stand so he could prod her shoulders, neck, arms, knees, and backside. (Sore? *No.* Sore? *No.* Here? *No.* How about here? *No.*) That made her remember childhood days when Matt would pinch her and poke at her repeatedly, asking, "Does this hurt?" "Does *this* hurt?" "How about *this?*" until eventually Ren would whine to Clarissa, who would send them both elsewhere to get off her nerves.

The memory of Matt was a nice diversion from thinking about herself so much. Then the next doctor walked in, suggesting yet another pelvic exam, and it was all about her again. Ren propped herself up to look at yet another new face. Her patience slipped. "Again? Aren't you guys writing any of this stuff down?"

The doctor chuckled. "Of course we are, Mrs. Sayers." He held up the chart at the end of her bed, pointing to the chicken scratch written over the course of the last several hours. "See?" He smiled with condescension.

Ren sighed and plopped back onto her back. She muttered to the ceiling. "Are you all having trouble reading each other's writing, maybe? It's not as if we're growing crystals in there — I can't have changed that much since the last exam."

The silence caused her to look back at the doctor. He was smiling at her. A real smile this time. He gently patted her feet, which were covered by her blanket. "You're right. We can hold off on this one for a bit. I'll come back later."

He walked out, and Ren felt a bit guilty for complaining but relieved at the outcome. Again, she dozed off.

Tru was usually sitting in the room, often

sleeping, whenever she woke up. He awakened if she moved the slightest bit in the bed, so she tried to lie as still as she could. He couldn't just open his eyes and doze back off. He seemed to feel the need to get up and comfort her if he saw that she was awake.

Clarissa had gone home when it got late. Tru told Ren, "She didn't want to leave while you were awake. She wants me to call her back as soon as we hear some results." He stroked Ren's hair back off her face and gave her a loving smile. "She's worried about you."

He said it as if the statement would make her feel good. He was right.

At one point Ren woke up feeling restless. Almost refreshed. She felt as if she'd been sleeping forever. The room was dark, and light from the slightly open door peeked in. The air-conditioning system ran incessantly, reminding her of an overnight stay in a cheap hotel. No one was in the room with her, but she heard voices just outside, in the hallway. Tru's and . . . yes, Clarissa's. Ren raised herself up onto her elbows. Had he called Clarissa back? Had they gotten results? Ren almost called out to him, but she stopped when she heard her mother speak.

"I'd like to say something to you, Tru." She sounded dead serious.

Ren grimaced. *Please don't insult him. He's the perfect husband, a wonderful son-in-law. Who knows how little sleep he got last night?*

Tru waited quietly. Ren pictured him, sitting next to Clarissa out there. Of course, he was beautiful. A little disheveled, no doubt. Needing a shave. Absolutely kind toward Clarissa. Fully prepared to take whatever she felt like dishing at the moment.

Clarissa said, "When Ren brought you to my home that first time — you remember the dinner party? The one with Russell from my husband's law firm?"

Ren heard the subtle amusement in his response. "I seem to remember that, yes."

"Yes. Well, I formed an impression of you almost immediately after meeting you. I've known a number of . . . what's the proper term these days? Latinos?"

Ren nearly cried out to interrupt them, trying to protect him. But she felt the Lord calming her, telling her to let it go. Either that, or she was still too tired to do anything about whatever Clarissa might say. Yet Ren strained to hear, not wanting to miss a word.

485

"Latino works, yes," Tru said.

"Well, I love my daughter, Tru. I know I don't tell her that very often, but I do." She sighed. "I've always been harder on her than I was on Matt. I suppose I thought he could bounce back from failures and heartbreak easier than she could. Matt always shrugged off disappointment, but Ren took everything so much to heart. Whether it was having a best friend move away or getting a B when she expected an A. She just seemed easily devastated. I felt it was my job to either toughen her up or protect her. And she was . . ."

Ren was amazed to hear a tightening in Clarissa's voice. She was trying not to cry.

"She was so hurt by that . . . that . . ."

"Greg?" Tru supplied.

Ren heard her sigh again. "Horrid man. I never liked him. Never trusted him. It was so clear to me that he looked out for himself before he looked out for Ren. I don't know why Ren never saw that in him."

Hmm. Ren didn't know why, either. But Clarissa was absolutely right. Now that Ren could see the contrast between Greg and Tru, she could see that Clarissa was right. Oh, goodness. Could Ren handle this — Clarissa being right? Even worse, could Ren give Clarissa credit for not trying to force her to see Greg as he was? For allowing her to make her own mistakes? This was a side of Clarissa that Ren hadn't thought existed.

She could almost hear the shrug in Tru's response. "I guess she loved him, Clarissa." He said it as if it had nothing to do with him, which, of course, it didn't. But so many men would struggle with the idea of not having been the one and only. Ren wished Tru had been her one and only. How dear of him, how secure of him, to accept the love Ren could give him now, free of judgment about her past.

"Yes, well," Clarissa said. "She's a loving girl, I'll give her that. And now . . ."

There was a silence, during which Ren nearly lost her balance as she craned her body sideways to hear better, causing her elbow to slip off the side of the bed. A fumbling grunt escaped as she grabbed at the bed rail to keep from falling onto the floor. Fortunately, a couple of nurses in the hall spoke to each other at that moment, drowning her out.

Then Tru spoke in a warm, comforting voice. "Don't worry, Clarissa. Don't cry."

Don't cry? She was crying? Maybe they *had* heard some of the results. Was it cancer? Why didn't they tell her? Were they going to hold back on her? Let her go on her merry way, thinking she was all right, just to drop dead in the middle of some awards assembly at school? What about the children? What about —

"Now, don't you start," her mother said. "I didn't mean to make you cry."

That did it. Ren was going to call out to them . . .

"You're such a wonderful man, Tru," Clarissa said. "Such a wonderful man."

What? That *was* Clarissa's voice, wasn't it? Forget about cancer — Ren was going to have a heart attack right there and then.

"That's what I wanted to say to you," Clarissa continued. "I was all wrong about you. I couldn't have found a better husband for my only daughter if I'd picked him out myself. And believe me, I tried."

Yep. That sounded more like Clarissa. But how amazing! Ren felt so happy with the way her mother was talking that she actually laughed a little. So, of course, Tru's radar picked her up, and he stuck his head in to check on her.

"She's awake," he said to Clarissa. They walked in together. Tru's arm was around Clarissa's shoulders, and she looked completely comfortable with it there. If Ren didn't know better, she'd think she'd already died and gone to heaven.

A knock at the door brought her back to earth. One of the doctors was at the door.

"Mr. and Mrs. Sayers," he said, "we need to talk."

FORTY-SIX

At the sound of the doctor's voice, Clarissa turned away from Tru, glanced at the door, and then walked briskly over to Ren. She took Ren's hand in both of hers.

Ren didn't know which of them had colder hands, but they were a chilly duo.

Clarissa's eyes looked tired and were rimmed in red. She spoke more quietly and warmly than Ren could remember her doing in all of her adult years. "Now, Ren, I want to honor your privacy. I want to respect your wishes. And Tru's." She looked at Tru and back at Ren. "But if you two would let me stay to hear these results? Well. I'd just really appreciate it."

Ren looked at her and smiled. It was a huge understatement to say Clarissa had done her share of worrying about Ren through the years. Ren knew most of her control issues had been wrapped around that worry (as well as her firm belief that she knew better than Ren did what was best for her). And now the suspense was killing her, and she needed to know that nothing was killing her daughter.

Ren needed to know that too. And if the news was bad, she couldn't imagine two people she'd rather face it with than her husband and her mother. Of course, as far as Ren could tell, she hadn't yet been tested for anything life threatening. But something in that doctor's expression told her the results were serious.

Ren nodded at Clarissa, giving her hand a squeeze. "Stay, Mom. Please."

Clarissa didn't quite smile — just looked comforted. And Ren saw her lips silently form the word *Mom.* Until then Ren didn't think about it. She had called her "Mom." Ren couldn't remember the last time she had done that. She had been "Mother" to Ren, the ever-formal lady, as long as she could recall, even though her father had always been Dad. Clarissa looked at her now as if Ren had just given her a hug.

Tru reached out to shake hands with the doctor. "I don't think we've met," he said. "I'm Ren's husband, Tru Sayers."

"Dr. Graves. Michael Graves." He shook Tru's hand.

Yikes! Ren had an odd thought about the

descriptive names Charles Dickens gave to characters in his novels. Getting medical news from a Dr. Graves? Not a good sign.

He said to Tru, "I think you were upstairs changing out of your scrubs when I met your wife."

She met him? Looked like a total stranger to her. But, then again, there had been quite a few doctors passing through, and Ren had been groggy for many of the exams.

He smiled at Clarissa and looked about to shake her hand. But rather than following suit, Clarissa blurted, "What? What is it? What does she have?"

For the briefest moment, he froze, his hand midway between them. Then he redirected it to give Clarissa a gentle pat on the arm. He said nothing to her, but he smiled at her kindly. Then he turned to face Ren, gently placing his hand on the bed, near her knees. "You've been very patient with us, Mrs. Sayers."

"Ren," she said.

He nodded. "Ren. Dr. Nielson had requested this first set of tests, and they're exactly the tests I would have prescribed, given your symptoms. Let me tell you what we've found out so far."

Ren didn't like the sound of that "so far," but she kept her mouth shut and shot a quick prayer for peace up to God.

The doctor said, "We can pretty conclusively say you do not have CMP, because —"

"CMP?" they all asked at once.

Dr. Graves chuckled at himself. "I'm sorry. Chronic myofascial pain. A neuromuscular disease. You had a number of the symptoms. However, when I examined you, you showed no pain at any of the characteristic trigger points —"

"Ah! You were the poker!"

Clarissa and Tru looked at her, puzzled.

"I mean, I didn't recognize him when he came in just now. But when he was here before, he made me think of Matt, so I didn't really pay attention —"

"He looks nothing like Matt," Clarissa said. "Why would you —"

"No, but remember how Matt used to poke and pinch me when we —"

A clearing of the throat stopped her. Clarissa and Ren looked at Tru (the throat clearer).

"Sorry," Ren said. "Please go on."

Dr. Graves patted the blankets on Ren's knees. "No problem. If you have questions or comments, interrupt at will."

No one said anything, but in the silence Ren could hear a soft tapping. It was Clarissa's foot. Maybe the doctor wasn't in a hurry, but . . .

"So," Tru said, "you were saying . . ."

"Chronic myofascial pain, yes." The doctor turned to Ren. "We've managed to rule that out. Likewise, you don't appear to have enough symptoms to be diagnosed with either FMS or CFS." To Ren's blank stare, he quickly added, "fibromyalgia or chronic fatigue syndrome. Both of those can reach the pain level you experienced yesterday, and worse. But the pain usually comes on gradually, not acutely, as yours did."

"But I have been having some pains here and there for the past several weeks."

"Yes," Dr. Graves said, "I'm getting to that. I talked extensively with Dr. Nielson before she left early this morning. We both feel strongly that you're experiencing the effects of endometriosis, which I understand you've had in the past. You may remember that endometriosis also comes on gradually. But it's not unusual for the symptoms to sneak up on you as they have here. The worst pains generally accompany menstruation. They're often tied to your monthly cycle and are often confused for regular monthly cramping."

Clarissa, Tru, and Ren all looked silently at him. Then Ren sighed deeply. She couldn't say whether she felt relief or dread. Endometriosis was certainly less frightening than cancer or any of those diseases the doctors had considered. And she didn't have to worry about her appendix — or anything else — exploding anytime soon. Always a plus, she supposed. But the idea of more scar tissue developing around her various baby-producing organs? Well, that made her want to cry. Ren was struggling to accept whatever God's plan was for her regarding children. Conceiving seemed even less likely now, and adoption hadn't exactly been a picnic so far.

Please help me accept Your will, Lord. I know You know best. I'm just so weak willed, and I can't understand why You wouldn't want me to have children. Wouldn't I be a good mom? Do You know something I don't know?

The absurdity of that last thought struck her. She snorted ruefully, prompting Tru to come hold her hand.

"I'm sorry, sweetie." He raised her hand to his lips. Ren saw tears in his eyes, mixed with relief, and she realized that her eyes were wet too.

Dr. Graves said, "Now, there's also the chance that some of your symptoms are being caused by cysts. It's not uncommon to find cysts and endometriosis occurring si-

495

multaneously."

"You mean, you don't know if she has cysts?" Clarissa said. "Isn't there some test for that? You seem to have examined every single inch of her body. Surely there's a way to diagnose a simple cyst."

He nodded, raising his eyebrows at her. "Absolutely. We'll probably do a sonogram later today and see what we can find." He looked back at Ren. "But, of course, we're not going to be able to prescribe an MRI for you, and that would be our most definitive method of detection."

Ren frowned. "Why can't you prescribe it? I think our insurance would cover an MRI —"

"And we'd be willing to have it done, regardless," Tru added. "Don't you think it's worth it?"

"I'll pay for it," Clarissa said to the doctor. "Let's get it done as soon as possible. I don't like the idea of all these unknowns with regard to my daughter's health. Money is not an issue."

The doctor shook his head. "No. You're right. Money isn't the issue here."

At that moment a lively rap at the door drew their attention away from each other. Guy — Tru's OB-GYN friend, Gray Guy — walked briskly into the room. He looked

immediately at Dr. Graves. "You haven't
—"

"No," Dr. Graves said, quickly. "But I
didn't realize you hadn't been down yet.
You cut it close, Dr. Forman."

"What's going on?" Clarissa said, voicing
exactly what Ren was thinking. "Who are
you?" she said to Guy. She clearly didn't
remember him from the wedding.

Tru introduced them, but Guy seemed
intent on getting over to Ren. He stepped
right up to the bed, and leaned forward to
give her a peck on the cheek. "I have a
diagnosis for you, Ren."

"You do?" She felt a little like *Sleeping
Beauty's* Princess Aurora, being granted
medical diagnoses like fairy blessings at her
royal birthday party.

"Yep. EPT. Ever hear of it?"

"Again, with the disease initials?" Ren
sighed. "Go ahead, lay it on me." She
snorted at the irony. "The only EPT I know
—"

But Tru's quick intake of breath shut her
up. He and Guy exchanged looks Ren
couldn't decipher. Then Tru looked at her,
dewy-eyed, and leaned down to hug her.
Hard.

Guy kept on talking. "You might want to
make use of this the next time you experi-

ence these symptoms." When Tru straightened up, Guy handed her a little white box that had EPT emblazoned across the front. It was an early pregnancy test. Suddenly it all sank in. Almost.

Clarissa grabbed the box from her and leaned her head back a bit, squinting, to read it. Then she made a sound as if someone had pinched her from behind. "She's *pregnant?*"

Ren started laughing and crying at the same time. "I . . . I don't understand. I would have used one of those, but I'm having a period right *now.* How can I be pregnant?"

Guy shook his head. "No. You're spotting right now. Very common."

Ren heard Clarissa sniff and looked around to see her dabbing at tears. Her voice shook when she spoke. "So," she said to Dr. Graves, who had stepped back from the group but was watching them with a big smile on his face. "Ren doesn't have endometriosis after all?"

"Oh, yes," Dr. Graves said. "She does. But her symptoms are likely to be alleviated as her pregnancy develops."

As her pregnancy develops. Ren sighed. Were there four more beautiful words in the English language?

Dr. Graves continued. "We'll probably be able to wait until after the baby is born to address the endometriosis."

"I didn't think I could get pregnant," Ren said, "because of the scar tissue from before. And I certainly wouldn't expect this to happen while the disease is coming back."

Guy said, "Actually, endometriosis is a disease of fertile women, Ren."

Ren stared at him, and then she looked at Tru. She whispered, "I'm a fertile woman."

He laughed and they hugged each other, crying.

"Thank You, Jesus," Ren whispered aloud, prompting her dear husband to repeat the words after her.

Her thoughts ricocheted in many different directions. They had to call Kara right away. And Matt and Sybil. And Tru's family. Even Jeremy. And Sandy.

Then Ren thought of Casey. What a blessing that he would be reunited with a mommy who was healed and who loved him. Would he have received the kind of love he deserved if Ren had had her way with the adoption? Would her pregnancy and illness have drained her of the energy she needed to nurture him the way Britney would?

Lord, You knew. Of course You knew. Why

did I doubt You? Thank You, Jesus, for being so patient with me. Oh, but, Lord, we both know I'll doubt You again — please help me to remember this moment the next time. I worried so much about Casey. About Tru's mother. And mine. In Your patience with me, You showed me how to wait. And trust. Here I thought I'd never survive losing Greg's love. And look at the man — at the love — You brought me. Better than ever.

And this time it's true.

This time it's Tru.

ABOUT THE AUTHOR

Trish Perry is an award-winning writer and editor of *Ink and the Spirit,* a quarterly newsletter of the Capital Christian Writers organization in the Washington DC area. She has published numerous short stories, essays, devotionals, and poetry in Christian and general market media, and she is a member of the American Christian Fiction Writers group.

Says Trish:

"I live in Northern Virginia with my ever-patient husband and brilliantly funny son. I have a gorgeous grown daughter who eloped with the perfect son-in-law and eventually blessed me with an amazing grandson. We also have three lovable, goofy dogs and two feral cats who think they're our pets and force us to feed them."

If you would like to contact Trish, you may

do so by mail at:

Trish Perry
c/o Harvest House Publishers
990 Owen Loop North
Eugene, OR 97402

Or via her Web site at:
www.trishperrybooks.com